Howl . . .

Vaughn jerked his head around in time to see something enormous and dark burst from behind Boone's side of the tree.

Boone raised the shotgun. It didn't even get halfway up.

Moving incredibly fast, the animal sidestepped closer to Boone and flung out an enormous left arm. Vaughn heard a *boom*! and thought he saw fur fly up near the shoulder blade.

A hairsplitting scream drowned out the noise of the shot; the massive arm launched Boone backward, and the shotgun cartwheeled through the air.

The animal ran off. . . .

DARK WOODS

Jay C. Kumar

BERKLEY BOOKS, NEW YORK

DARK WOODS

A Berkley Book / published by arrangement with
the author

PRINTING HISTORY
Berkley mass-market edition / July 2004

Copyright © 2004 by Jay C. Kumar.
Cover design by George Long.
Cover art by Cliff Nielsen.

ISBN: 0-425-19707-7

BERKLEY®
Berkley Books are published by The Berkley Publishing Group,
a division of Penguin Group (USA) Inc.,
375 Hudson Street, New York, New York 10014.
BERKLEY and the "B" design
are trademarks belonging to Penguin Group (USA) Inc.

PRINTED IN THE UNITED STATES OF AMERICA

10   9   8   7   6   5   4   3   2   1

For Catherine, for everything.

All scientific greatness must integrate external data with the internal power of a fruitful view of life—the more iconoclastic the better, for Lord only knows that hidebound tradition and stupidity stand as the greatest barriers to enlarged understanding.

STEPHEN JAY GOULD

It is in man's power to content himself with the proofs he has, if they favor the opinion that suits with his inclinations or interest, and so stop from further research.

JOHN LOCKE

What is the most cunning of all animals? That which no man has seen.

TIBETAN PROVERB

Chapter 1

Tuesday, May 7
Early Morning
Skookum County, Washington

THE rifle in his hands felt lighter now.

Deputy Sheriff Frank Vaughn held it across his chest and placed his boots with care, avoiding sticks or anything else that would make a telltale noise. Slowly, so slowly that he barely felt the cold on his face, he kept to the left of the faint tracks that led deeper into the dark woods.

His leg pushed through a clump of sword fern that somehow glowed a vibrant green in the grey, silent morning. The fronds hung on his fleece pants, but made no sound when they flexed back. The only record of their disturbance was the wetness that deepened the random brown, green and black splotches of his camouflage.

Usually, on a normal hunt, he would fall into a routine: three or four slow steps, stop for a few seconds to listen and slowly look around, then move again. It mimicked the way an animal moved through the woods.

But this time was different.

This time something felt wrong.

The feeling came up gradually, the way you suddenly re-alize crickets are chirping at night. And it didn't leave, be-cause his brain was trained to pay attention to it, cultivate it, keep it there so it colored everything.

It felt like a worm crawling under the skin of his neck.

When he realized it was there, he thought it probably started when they hadn't seen any deer on the way in. They always saw a few, but today not even one—though that might be explained by Ed Ricks' truck. Who knew how long Ricks had been poaching this area.

But to spook that many deer, Ricks had to be doing a lot of shooting and that didn't make sense. Why would he be killing deer now? The bucks had long since dropped their antlers, and after the long winter the animals would all be half starved, the meat worthless.

Then Vaughn thought: *Maybe it feels different because I'm hunting a man instead of an animal.* Hunting a man definitely would cause something conscious to kick in.

He stopped walking and looked ahead. Then he glanced behind, to gauge the direction of Ricks' travel. He felt Geek look at him, caught Boone's eye, then turned around and started forward again.

Stems crunched softly under the soles of his boots.

He had to admit that part of the reason for his discomfort might be that this was unfamiliar ground. Boone and Geek got special permission to hunt this tract of forest, where a rapidly growing black bear population needed thinning—for its own health, and for human safety.

Having a new area all to themselves was great, but Vaughn didn't have any intimacy with this place. Not like where they usually hunted, where he knew every rise, deadfall and lava tube as well as he knew the rooms in his own house.

Even so, he loved to explore new areas, especially old-growth rain forest.

These stands were rare now. The huge trees, up to six feet wide and two hundred feet high, rose from the ground like enormous Corinthian columns. Only the first fifty feet of their bare trunks was visible; their tops disappeared into the om-nipresent fog.

They looked like they'd been there forever—as if, during

an ancient cataclysm, they had been thrust out of the Earth's crust to hold up the sky.

Usually the trees, the yawning ferns and the old silence made Vaughn feel hyperaware, as if he was in a different time: A dinosaur could stomp by and not seem out of place.

But now it felt different. As if the forest was alive and watching, holding its breath.

Slowly he followed Ricks' trail deeper into the gloom. The only noises he heard were the slate sounds of breathing; his own, and that of Boone and Geek behind him. Especially Geek's.

Vaughn's breath puffed out in white clouds that hung in the cold, humid air. With each breath in, the smells of vegetation, moss, water and rotten wood swam up his nose. Some part of him detected them all. But none of the smells registered. None were out of the ordinary.

He focused his attention on the scuffs Ricks' boots had made on the skin of the frozen earth, and the occasional bent stem from a sloppy step. Though the trail was faint, he could make it out fine. Still straight and regular.

He realized that was strange, too.

Everyone in the county knew Ricks was a longtime poacher. And as one, Ricks should easily have been able to conceal his tracks by stepping lightly, random direction changes and a few other tricks. Yet he didn't.

He obviously thought no one else would be here, but that didn't explain it. Years of habitually making himself hard to track wouldn't disappear overnight.

Not without a damn good reason.

Vaughn felt it again: the worm, wriggling.

He stepped over a two-foot-high log eaten red and black with rot, and when he came down on the other side the rifle jerked in his gloved hands.

Maybe he was just angry, he thought. This wasn't the hunt he'd anticipated, the one he'd waited the whole long winter for. When he saw Ricks' truck, for a moment, less than a second, he'd considered forgetting about it and just going hunting.

But he couldn't.

At least he'd have the satisfaction of catching the son of a bitch, hopefully before—

Krak-whoom!

Vaughn's head jerked up. *Damn,* he thought.

He felt Boone and Geek stop behind him.

Suddenly, from the direction of the shot, a sound rolled toward them. Loud, louder—the scream crashed through the trees and roared past them like a wall of water—*eeeaaaaaaAAOOOOoooo!*

Then it disappeared, soaked up by the forest.

Vaughn didn't move. His eyes stared in the direction of the shot, the scream reverberating in his skull. His brain automatically cycled through the sounds it knew, trying to figure out what animal made it.

"What the hell was that?" Geek whispered.

It took a second for the question to register. Vaughn blinked his eyes into focus, then turned around.

He looked at Boone first. Boone's lean, bearded face betrayed nothing, but his eyes told Vaughn that he didn't know what it was either.

Geek, round even in full-body camouflage, had that wide-eyed, in-between look Vaughn had seen many times in criminals: You didn't know what they were going to do, run away or give up.

"That wasn't a bear, was it?" Geek said.

"No way," Vaughn said. "Not an elk, either." Bears couldn't scream anywhere near that long and loud, even one that was badly hurt. And this noise was much louder, deeper and longer than a bull elk's bugle. Plus the rut was months away.

"Cougar?"

"Nope." Boone said it without looking at Geek.

Vaughn knew that cougar shrieks were eerie, but they were brief and higher pitched. This was more like a bellow.

That only left a man, he thought. But no way—not unless the guy had a chest twice normal size and was lugging around a small PA system.

"What was it, then?" Geek said.

Vaughn didn't know what it was, but the scream sounded like pain.

And whatever made it was big—and close.

He realized that his camouflage gloves were clamped onto his rifle. He relaxed them enough to flick the .30-06's safety off.

"Let's go find out," he said.

Chapter 2

IT didn't take long to reach the bodies.

From the corner of his eye Vaughn saw Geek fidgeting by one of the massive Douglas fir trunks, shifting his weight from one leg to the other like he needed to pee. The tree stood about twenty feet away, and Geek wouldn't come any closer.

Just as well, Vaughn thought. He didn't want Geek messing up the scene.

Boone poked around the undergrowth looking for some sign of the attacker. Vaughn knew Boone would be careful. And quiet.

He watched Boone for a moment, then turned his attention back to the bodies. He felt the worm wriggle again, and reached back and pulled his collar up around his neck.

A deer and a man lay next to each other on the cold forest floor, a fern clump between them. Both had been killed recently. Both had broken necks.

Ed Ricks lay on his back, arms and legs splayed out everywhere, like a rag doll flung in a corner. His left ear pressed against the wool jacket that covered his chest as if he'd been listening for his own heartbeat when the beating stopped.

For some reason it looked natural: The head just rested there, as if all necks could bend that way.

Vaughn stepped around the body, unshouldered his rifle and squatted by Ricks' shoulders. His fleece camouflage whispered as it tightened around his thighs.

The smells of cigarettes, coffee, bacon and eggs jumped off Ricks' jacket. Vaughn was disgusted. To him, that showed disrespect for the animals. If you didn't prepare to hunt, if you didn't learn how to become part of the forest to fool all of an animal's senses, you were not a hunter. You were just a man with a rifle.

He bent forward, and detected another odor. His nostrils opened wide and he sniffed—then he jerked back.

Whew, he thought. Foul. He wondered how long it had been since Ricks washed that jacket.

He moved up to Ricks' bearded face. The poacher's wide eyes gazed past Vaughn to the fog canopy. A crust of yellow mucus clung to the inside corner of the left eye.

Even dead, the eyes had a hardness to them—the hardness of the conscious lawbreaker. Vaughn had seen it many times.

But in more than a decade of law enforcement, dealing with car wrecks and all sorts of injuries, he'd never seen a neck broken like this. So clean.

He looked for some sign that Ricks had been struck by something—a rifle butt, a log or a rock. But he saw no dirt, no debris, no bleeding, no sign of trauma to the skin. Nor was there a log or a big-enough rock nearby, though he knew the attacker could have taken the murder weapon with him.

He wanted to turn Ricks over to look at the back of his neck, but didn't so he wouldn't contaminate any evidence that might be there.

One more time he peered into the face for some sign, something in the expression. But in true lawbreaker fashion, Ricks would give him nothing, even in death.

Vaughn stood and carefully walked around Ricks' body to examine the deer.

The animal lay on its side with its long-lashed eyes open and its front hooves almost touching Ricks' left shoulder. A buck, Vaughn saw, antlerless, its ribs protruding after the long winter.

Apparently the deer had been killed first: From a foot-long gash in its belly, its viscera spilled out onto the ground. Blood, already coagulating, stained the white belly hair a deep red and ran down to pool on the frozen earth.

Vaughn saw the long cords of intestine, still white, and the slightly bulging stomach. But he noticed that the heart and liver were gone, and that none of the meat had been touched.

It seemed like a man had field-dressed the animal and then, starving, ate the most nutritious organs.

He glanced over at Ricks. A leather sheath hung from the poacher's belt. Vaughn wouldn't check, but he knew the knife was in there. And not just because the tarnished brass snap was still closed. He figured that Ricks, like most poachers, had been fanatical about his equipment. The blade of his knife would be sharp enough to slice a page of newspaper neatly in two, and keen enough to zip through bear hide. The reason was to make the quickest possible work of gutting an animal.

But the opening in the buck's belly was ragged, like someone sawed through the skin and hollow hair with a dull knife.

Vaughn's eyes followed the line of the belly up to the chest and shoulders, and then to the long antelope-like neck. It ran in a soft grey-brown curve until, about eight inches from the head, it snapped downward.

Vertebrae bulged under the skin. One set of bones angled up from the shoulders and the other plunged down into the skull. Between the break the skin was stretched, but not broken.

He leaned in close to the neck. No dirt, no bark, hardly even a misplaced hair. No claw marks either, not on the neck or anywhere else.

It looked like the deer's neck had simply snapped on its own. But someone, something, had done it.

The problem was, who could get close enough, what was quick enough, to kill a deer by catching it and snapping its neck?

Maybe a bear. That seemed like the only possible explanation, but there were no claw marks. And bears weren't this neat.

Plus, a bear couldn't have screamed like that.

He scratched at his neck.

None of it added up. Ricks looked like he'd been thrown off a cliff, but Boone said they were at least a mile from the nearest cliff. The old Douglas firs were tall enough to fall from, but there was no evidence Ricks had attempted to climb any of the nearby trees. Besides, the huge bare trunks were impossible to scale without climbing gear, which Ricks didn't have, and there were no gouges in the ground to indicate a fall from a great height.

They had also heard a shot. And Ricks' rifle, lying nearby, had been fired recently. But neither body had a bullet wound.

So someone, or something, had been shot, had screamed and run off. Something big, something strong and something that made a noise none of them had ever heard before.

Vaughn stood, and his knee cracked with a wet pop that made him glance at Ricks' neck.

"We need to get out of here."

Vaughn looked, saw the vapor of Geek's breath roll out and disappear, but didn't respond.

Geek glanced over his shoulder then took a half step forward. His arms hugged the black Zytel stock and stainless steel barrel of his new .280 like it was a security blanket.

"Frank," he said, "don't you have to call this in or something?"

Vaughn didn't answer.

His left eye caught movement. Boone came around a tree and walked over.

"Found a trail," Boone said, keeping his voice low. His breath felt warm on Vaughn's ear. "Blood," he said. "And tracks."

"Not a bear," Vaughn said.

"Nope."

"How big are his boots?"

"No boots," Boone said.

Vaughn turned and eyed his friend carefully. For a second the skin of Boone's face twitched, like it would explode into a yell. But then the edges of his mouth crept up into a smile, one that Vaughn had never seen before.

Vaughn's neck itched.

"Bare feet," Boone said. "The tracks are of bare feet."

Chapter 3

VAUGHN squatted in the ferns and stared at the footprint. It was much longer and wider than a man's bare foot, but otherwise had the same shape. He'd seen these kinds of tracks before, in the newspaper.

For a second he suspected his friends of an elaborate joke. It wouldn't be the first time. As a transplanted Easterner, he'd been the butt of a few good-natured woodland pranks. But they had ended years ago.

He looked over his shoulder. Geek, usually the first to betray a joke, looked like he hadn't smiled in months.

And then there was the track's depth. Their boot prints barely made an impression on the frozen soil, but this track was an inch deep. Vegetation had been mashed into it with such force that the leaves and stems were compressed into the ground, as if by a pile driver.

He saw spots of blood on the green leaves next to the track.

Blood.

The track.

The blood.

His eyes flitted from one piece of evidence to another. He almost didn't believe what he was seeing.

Almost, but it was there.

He reached out to the track, toward the half-frozen, pressure-cracked wave of earth that was its edge. Something in the track's compacted base caught his eye.

A stone. It protruded.

The foot had curled over it.

His hand stopped in midair, then withdrew.

There, all right. And real.

"Let's get out of here," Geek said.

No one responded.

"Frank—"

"Let me think a minute," Vaughn said.

A second of silence and then Geek said, "I'm all for thinking, and I think we should get the hell out of here. What if it comes back?"

Vaughn stood and looked ahead.

"Frank," Boone said, "I think Geek's right. If that thing comes back we may be in big trouble. I mean, I'm not sure we could kill it even if we wanted to. And I don't want to."

Vaughn turned around.

"Trouble?" Geek said. "We could be in trouble?"

"It's wounded," Vaughn said, his attention on Boone. "We should go after it."

"Jesus," Geek said.

Boone's mouth dipped into a frown. His eyes glanced ahead and then returned to Vaughn. "If you really want to go after it, I'll go with you," he said. "But I really think we need to think this out. Before we go after something that big, I mean."

Vaughn stared at his friend. The Boone he knew would never question the obligation to go after a wounded animal. Somehow this was different for him.

But not for Vaughn.

Geek said: "How about thinking back at the truck?"

"You can go back," Vaughn said, "but I'm going after it. Right now."

"What?" Geek said. "Frank." He looked at Boone. "Boone—"

Still frowning, Boone stared at Vaughn. Then he looked down at the Remington 870 he'd been carrying as a backup for Geek, and checked the 12-gauge's safety. He clicked it off.

Vaughn did the same with his worn .30-06. "Ready?"

Boone nodded.

"Wait!" Geek hissed.

Vaughn looked at him.

Geek said: "I'm not going."

"Okay," Vaughn said. "Wait at the truck." With his rifle he gestured behind them, at the dark, silent trees.

Geek's head swiveled around and then came back to Vaughn. He didn't say anything, but his wide eyes and pudgy face made him look like a kid about to cry.

Boone put a gloved hand on Geek's shoulder. "Just stay behind us," he whispered. Then he pulled his hand away and moved off into the woods.

"Keep your safety on," Vaughn said.

Geek's head jerked up. "What?"

"You're nervous and will be behind us. I'd rather not take the chance."

Geek looked unhappy.

"Do it," Vaughn said. "Or leave the rifle here."

Geek pushed the safety to the "On" position.

Vaughn turned and followed Boone. Though Vaughn was a good tracker, Boone was better so Vaughn let him lead.

Vaughn carried his rifle safely but ready: across his body, his left hand on the rifle's fore-end, the barrel up and slightly forward. The camouflaged nylon sling wound around his right arm like the dappled body of a boa constrictor. The butt rested in the crook of his elbow and his index finger curled around the trigger guard.

If the need arose, he could have the rifle up to his shoulder and ready to fire in less than a second.

Boone stopped and knelt at the side of the next track—six feet away from the first one. Vaughn walked up and watched him examine it.

First Boone stared at the track, cocking his head at different angles. Then he probed the track with his fingers. Vaughn had seen him do this a few times before, and sometimes was amazed what Boone deduced.

For his part, Vaughn noticed five things about the track. The first three were that it was fresh, there was no blood and it was deep.

The depth meant that what they were tracking was far heavier than a man—denser, like a gorilla. He wondered how much the animal weighed. Five hundred pounds? Eight hundred? Big grizzly bears weighed that much. This might be even heavier.

The track also deepened toward the toes, which meant the animal had been running.

The final thing he noted was shape: again the humanlike impression. Similar to a human's, but not the same. It had no arch and was disproportionately wide. Also, the toes were shorter, the big toe less prominent and the heel impact less pronounced than in a human footprint.

It hit him that he was actually tracking an animal that had humanlike feet. Its weight alone meant it couldn't be a man. Part of his brain started to disbelieve what was going on. It told him that he was pursuing a creature that didn't exist, so what he was seeing couldn't be real. It wasn't happening. But it was.

He shook his head to clear it. He couldn't afford to be distracted.

Boone beckoned him down. "It's limping." He whispered just loud enough for Vaughn to hear, but it sounded like a shout.

He pointed to the ground just ahead. Vaughn looked and saw a shallower track. That meant the animal had put more pressure on its left foot, to compensate for the wounded leg.

Boone stood and resumed walking slowly ahead, placing his feet carefully. He passed the shallower track and squatted again.

Vaughn walked up and saw the same pattern: one deeper track, one shallower. He noticed that the distance between the first and second sets of tracks was more than four man-length strides.

Boone rose, stepped forward and then stopped. He reached down and lifted up a curved fern frond.

Against the light-green underside of the serrated leaves Vaughn saw a black-looking smear.

Blood.

A fair amount, too, he thought. Enough that if it were a deer and he'd seen where the shot hit, he might say it was mortally wounded. But this was an animal he didn't know anything about. It limped and bled, but the blood didn't gush as it would have from an artery. So the wound might not be fatal. Or even serious.

Boone pulled off a glove and touched the blood with his fingertips. Then he wiped his fingers on his pants and crept forward.

Temperature, Vaughn realized. *He's feeling how warm the blood is.* If the animal was long gone, the blood would be cold. But if it had hung around, watching, and only recently moved deeper into the forest, the blood might still be warm.

Vaughn glanced back at Geek and then followed Boone.

Again Boone stopped at a fern and used his bare fingers to feel the blood there.

This time he waited for Vaughn to catch up.

"Blood's not cold," Boone whispered.

Vaughn's head didn't move, but his eyes looked past Boone and darted from tree to tree.

Behind him Geek whispered, "What's going on?"

"It was just here."

Geek didn't say anything, and in the silence Vaughn heard his own heart pounding.

"No fern stalks broken," Boone said.

"Yeah," Vaughn whispered. "Moving slow." He took a deep breath that rushed out too quickly. "You ready?"

Boone looked ahead. Vaughn noticed that Boone's face had creased into a squint, like he'd just heard an earsplitting noise. Then the creases relaxed, and Boone took a single, careful step forward.

Instead of following right away, Vaughn stood completely still, looking and listening.

Feeling.

Nothing.

He stepped forward—and that's when it struck him that the silence was odd. Even though it was cold and fewer animals were active, he ought to be hearing *something.*

Boone kneeled again and, keeping his hand low, slowly waved Vaughn up.

As Vaughn got close, he immediately saw something different about this track. The front part of it, from the toes through the ball, was clearly defined, but a scatter of black soil covered the heel. He recognized it as a track showing quick, explosive movement; pressure from the forepart of the foot had scattered the earth backward.

He looked around and didn't see a companion track. The animal had jumped forward somewhere.

Not daring to speak, Vaughn raised an eyebrow at Boone.

Boone pointed at the right side of the print and made a short, slow motion with his hand, diagonal and down to the side.

Vaughn saw what he meant. The right side of the track, by the big toe, was deeper than the other side and slightly undercut, as if the foot rolled slightly to that side before pushing off.

Something grabbed Vaughn's shoulder.

"We have to get out of here," Geek whispered.

Geek's breath smelled sour. "What are you talking about?" Vaughn said.

"Don't you feel it? It's here!"

No shit it's here, Vaughn thought. Somewhere close, probably. The last thing they needed was someone panicking about it. "Calm down," he said.

Vaughn turned to get Boone's reaction, but Boone wasn't paying attention. Instead he stared ahead with that funny half smile on his face.

A prehistoric fear slithered across the bottom of Vaughn's stomach.

He followed Boone's gaze to an old Douglas fir about ten feet ahead and slightly to the right. The enormous trunk stretched wide enough to conceal four men standing shoulder to shoulder.

Vaughn's heart thundered so loud he thought everyone could hear it—just like the adrenaline rush when he had a big buck or bear in his sights, but this time he also felt fear.

Slowly he stood. Boone did the same.

"I'm going back to the road," Geek whispered in Vaughn's ear.

Vaughn barely heard. He focused on the tree.

Boone pushed his hand out, motioning for Vaughn to walk wide to the right of the trunk. Then he pointed the other way, indicating he would do the same to the left. They would try to get a look behind the tree without getting too close.

Vaughn moved off the trail, his rifle halfway up, only taking his eyes off the trunk to look where to place his feet: slowly raise one foot, look down, place it carefully, shift his weight forward.

Again.

And again.

He felt his heart beating in his fingertips.

Twok. A soggy branch snapped behind him.

The sound slammed into Vaughn's hypersensitive nervous system, but he controlled the urge to whirl around. Instead, in the hunter's practiced way, he turned his head excruciatingly slowly.

Only his head moved. He knew from doing it in his living room that turning it ninety degrees took twenty seconds. But in the woods, with his heart pounding, it felt like twenty minutes.

He couldn't turn his head any further. From the corner of his eye he saw Geek frozen, his weight awkwardly forward.

Anger flashed through him.

Then, from his left, a low growl.

Adrenaline sparked like lightning through Vaughn's body. Suddenly: *Roaaaaaaaaaarr!*

The noise exploded through the forest. Vaughn jerked his head around in time to see something enormous and dark burst from behind Boone's side of the tree.

Boone raised the shotgun. It didn't even get halfway up.

Moving incredibly fast, the animal sidestepped closer to Boone and flung out an enormous left arm. Vaughn heard a *boom!* and thought he saw fur fly up near the shoulder blade.

A hairsplitting scream drowned out the noise of the shot; the massive arm launched Boone backward, and the shotgun cartwheeled through the air.

The animal ran off—so fast that Vaughn's mind again began to doubt its own sanity.

In a second it was gone, the forest quiet.

Chapter 4

STUNNED, Vaughn found himself standing with his rifle at his shoulder. He pulled the rifle down and looked to his left. Boone lay on the ground.

Vaughn raced over. Boone's eyes were closed, his skin the color of concrete. His left forearm jutted unnaturally to the side.

"Boone," Vaughn said. "Boone!"

No reaction.

"Holy shit!" Geek said, running up. "You shot it!"

That's when Vaughn realized he, not Boone, had shot the animal.

Geek looked excited until he saw Boone. His face tottered, then fell.

Vaughn said: "Geek."

No response.

"Jimmy!"

Geek looked at him.

"Get the truck and back it in here as far as you can. Don't park against any trees. You hear me?"

Geek didn't say anything. His eyes had returned to Boone. "Go, dammit!"

Geek hesitated, and then ran off through the trees, leaving a trail of bobbing ferns.

Vaughn tore off his gloves and racked his brain for the first-aid information he'd learned years ago. He'd worked on plenty of minor injuries, but this was different.

"What's first, what's first," he said aloud.

He realized he was breathing fast and tried to control it. Okay. Coming back to him.

First make sure the rescuer is safe. Vaughn was the rescuer and he didn't know if he was safe or not. He looked over his shoulder and saw only silent forest. The animal might come back, but he couldn't do anything about that right now.

Next assess the patient's condition. "Patient is unconscious," he said, and had an obvious broken arm. Forget the arm for now. Head and back come first. What were the signs of skull fracture . . . bleeding from the ears and some other stuff he couldn't remember. Bruising? No bleeding or bruising he could see, so he assumed no skull fracture. Probably a concussion.

Carefully get the patient on his back. Already there.

Check to make sure the patient is breathing and has a pulse. Boone's chest rose and fell regularly, but Vaughn went through the procedure anyway. He put his ear to Boone's mouth, heard him exhale and felt warm breath on his ear. Then he pressed two fingers on the carotid artery, near the Adam's apple. Boone's pulse bumped under his fingertips.

Whoa! Vaughn recoiled. What was that stink? He sniffed around and found a localized, powerful odor on the front of Boone's jacket. Smelled like a rotting gut pile. For a half second he thought of the stink on Ricks' coat, but then he focused. He turned his head, took a breath and continued.

Always assume the patient has a broken neck until it's proved otherwise. Brace the patient's head. That way, if Boone regained consciousness he wouldn't injure himself further.

Vaughn wondered what he could use as a brace. He glanced around for rocks but didn't see any big enough to do the job. The pickup had to have something he could use, but it wasn't here yet. *Damn,* he thought.

He looked over his shoulder again to make sure the animal wasn't coming back—and saw Boone's 12-gauge lying on the ground. Quickly he retrieved the shotgun, pushed the safety on and placed the butt by his friend's left ear. On the other side he did the same with his .30-06.

Okay. What was next? The arm? Not yet.

Feel the body from head to feet for any other injuries. Get as close as you can to the skin. Since he'd already checked Boone's head, he began at the chest. He started to unzip the camouflaged wool jacket and then stopped. What if Boone was in shock—would the cold air on his skin make it worse? He concentrated: *Shock usually happens because of major blood loss.* That wouldn't happen with a fracture, but getting attacked by an animal that isn't supposed to exist had to be enough to cause shock. He glanced behind him and decided to make it a brief inspection.

With a soft tug he finished unzipping the jacket, and gently pulled up the two shirts Boone wore underneath: a wool hunting shirt and a tight polypropylene undershirt. He placed his hands on Boone's skin. It was warm, and he didn't like putting his cold hands on it.

He brought his hands to his mouth, breathed into them and rubbed them together. Then he started again. He looked for non-life-threatening injuries: bruises, fractures, bleeding, depressions, distention . . .

The clanking sound of Boone's Dodge diesel pickup came closer, stopped and then the truck whined in reverse. The noise got louder, then quit.

Vaughn didn't look up, but he could tell the truck wasn't close. That meant they would have to carry Boone. But because of the risk of spinal injury, that wasn't a good idea.

He unzipped the bottoms of the wool pants and probed Boone's lower legs. They felt normal. Good enough. He pulled the zippers back down.

He heard Geek slam the door.

Vaughn shouted, "Get the first-aid kit and my radio! The radio's in the yellow watertight bag in my pack—just bring that whole yellow bag."

"Okay!"

Vaughn noticed Boone's clothes weren't ripped, indicating

that the animal didn't have claws. If it had been a bear, parts of Boone's clothes and the skin underneath would have been shredded.

He checked again to make sure his friend was breathing. Okay.

Nothing more out of the ordinary except that arm. "What's the procedure?" Vaughn muttered.

"What, Frank?" Geek said, hurrying up. He held out the yellow bag and the first-aid kit, one in each hand.

"Nothing. Thanks." Vaughn grabbed the soft-sided first-aid kit and zipped it open. He hadn't looked in it in a few years and couldn't remember exactly what it contained. But the folks at the hospital had put it together, so he knew it was well-stocked.

His eyes zeroed in on the bright orange SAM splint, which he removed along with rolls of gauze and tape.

Time to get a look at that arm.

The question was how. The break was in the lower arm. He couldn't roll up the sleeve or take off Boone's coat, so he had to cut the fabric. But Boone had on his expensive King of the Mountain wool hunting jacket. He liked to call it the ultimate hunting coat; Vaughn remembered him showing it off the day he got it.

Vaughn hated to ruin it, but realized he had no choice.

He unsnapped the case on his belt and removed the Buck lockback. His thumb eased the blade open until it clicked into place. He ran it up Boone's arm from wrist to elbow, then sliced through the next two layers.

"Oh man," Geek said.

The lower part of the forearm angled almost ninety degrees away from the upper forearm and elbow. At the break, bones humped under skin that had the blue-green color of pond weed. Vaughn touched the fracture and heard a muffled grating sound.

Geek gagged.

Vaughn looked up. On Geek's face, a slick of sweat glistened like a slug trail.

"I need your help," Vaughn said.

"For what?"

"This isn't a damn negotiation! Boone's hurt, he needs our

help and we need to get the hell out of here in case that thing comes back. Okay?"

Geek looked scared.

Vaughn said: "Hold his arm at the elbow. Gently. With both hands."

Geek blinked, and then laid his hands on Boone's arm.

"Make sure you hold it tight," Vaughn said. "I'm going to pull it to straighten it out."

Geek swallowed.

Vaughn grasped Boone's wrist.

"Wait!" Geek said.

Vaughn looked up.

"I, uh, wasn't ready," Geek said.

"You ready now?"

Geek swallowed again, then tightened his hands on Boone's arm.

Vaughn gripped Boone's wrist and was about to pull it when he remembered: *Check the patient's pulse before straightening, after straightening and after applying the splint.*

"Hold on a sec," he said. "I need to check his pulse."

"Jesus."

Vaughn reached up to Boone's head and put his fingers on the carotid artery. Bump . . . bump. Regular.

Back to the wrist. "Okay. Hold on."

He pulled.

The rough edges of bone grated, then rasped like a saw on bark. The noise made his teeth itch.

Suddenly a moan climbed out of Boone's mouth, a dying animal sound from deep inside that hung in the humid air like a ghost.

Geek let go of the arm. The bones scraped together and fell out of alignment.

Vaughn controlled his anger and quickly rechecked Boone's pulse.

Steady.

He looked over at Geek, who had crawled to the side on his hands and knees. Geek's heavy belly heaved and then sagged.

"Let's try again," Vaughn said.

Geek's head swung around like a cow's.

"C'mon, c'mon," Vaughn said, glancing over his shoulder. "We have to do this now."

Geek hung his head. He hacked, spit and watched it drool to the ground. Then he crawled back and put his hands on the arm. This time he looked away.

"Hold *tight*," Vaughn said. "And whatever you do, don't let go."

He grabbed the wrist and pulled. The bones clicked and sawed; he felt them grind, and then lock.

"Okay," he said.

Geek let go.

Vaughn felt for a pulse, then picked up the orange splint, placed it over Boone's arm and wound the gauze around it. He taped it in place, laid the strips of Boone's jacket over the arm and for the last time checked Boone's pulse. All okay.

But now he faced a critical decision. Should he call for an ambulance or transport Boone in the pickup?

If he waited for the ambulance, he risked staying in an unsafe area and potentially getting everyone killed by a wounded, dangerous animal. If he attempted to transport Boone, he might injure Boone's spine and paralyze him. Though he doubted Boone was injured that severely, he couldn't be sure.

He turned around and looked. The animal wasn't there—or was it? He couldn't see far into the dark forest. And he suddenly realized that every trunk, every shadow, was wide enough to hide it.

Damn.

He would have to take the chance.

Chapter 5

VAUGHN jumped out of Boone's truck and sprinted to the emergency room entrance. He saw that the ambulance was already gone. It had met them at the paved road and the paramedics transferred Boone, still unconscious, from the makeshift backboard of ladder, tarp and duct tape to the real thing. But Boone's old pickup didn't go more than fifty and soon the ambulance had raced out of sight.

Before him, two oversized glass doors hissed open. The red letters spelling EMERGENCY parted in the middle and warm air rushed out, enveloping him in the hospital's antiseptic smell.

He jogged toward the triage room and the nurse looked up. "Where's Boone?" he said to her. At that moment the blue doors leading to the patient area swung out, and the sheriff came through them. As always, the "Old Man," as the deputies privately called him, looked at ease and in charge. And he should: It was his town.

Sheriff of Skookum County no longer was an elected position, but it might as well have been. You still had to play political poker well enough to get appointed. The Old Man had been elected thirty-odd years ago, and his gamesmanship was so astute that he'd been in office ever since. He knew when to bend the law—just enough to make him liked and respected, and to earn a few IOUs, but no more. He was known as being fair, and razor sharp. Everyone respected him.

"Frank," the sheriff said.

"He awake?"

"No, but they think it's just a concussion."

"How about his spine?"

"Can't tell yet," the sheriff said. "Looks like a bad break on that arm, though. What happened, he fall?"

Vaughn hesitated. "Sort of."

The glass doors slid open again and Geek walked in.

"Jimmy," the sheriff said.

"Hey sheriff," Geek said.

Everyone called the Old Man "sheriff" and probably would even after the sheriff retired, as if he were a general or an admiral.

The Old Man put a hand on Vaughn's shoulder and said: "Frank, can we talk outside?"

Geek's eyes shifted between them.

"Boone'll be okay," the sheriff said to him.

Geek still looked worried.

The sheriff held an arm out toward the door. "Shall we?"

Vaughn walked out, down the concrete ramp and followed the sidewalk around the corner. Thirty yards away, a few smokers clustered near the hospital's main entrance. No one was within earshot.

"Okay," the sheriff said.

Vaughn turned around.

"What happened out there?"

"This is going to sound crazy," Vaughn said.

The sheriff's white eyebrows arched above his eyes, but he said nothing. Then his face relaxed, his eyelids closing slightly. Vaughn recognized it as the Old Man's listening mode, as if the sheriff were sweeping away the clutter in his mind, at once becoming open and focused. It always reminded Vaughn of a lizard basking in the sun on a warm rock;

it seemed to be asleep, but if you approached too closely it would bolt away faster than your eye could follow.

Vaughn took a deep breath and recounted the events of earlier that morning. The sheriff listened without interrupting, and at the end asked only two questions: whether Vaughn was certain that what he saw wasn't a bear, and whether he was sure about the depth of the tracks.

Vaughn answered yes to both.

The irises of the sheriff's eyes, fixed on Vaughn, glowed glacier blue. He said: "You're not kidding."

"No sir."

The sheriff stared at him hard for a moment and then looked away. A long breath steamed from his mouth and curled into a cloud that appeared white against the tall, dark firs rimming the parking lot. "I've been called out to look at those kinds of tracks a few times over the years," he said. "Never seen anything more than that. Though there was this one time . . ."

He paused, still gazing off across the lot. Then he brought his eyes back to Vaughn. "An old-timer living at the foot of Long Mountain took me out behind his house to show me some tracks. Said something had been breaking into his shed. It was dusk when I got there, so I looked around quick and then we followed the tracks back into the woods. About a quarter mile in I got a funny feeling, like something was watching us. And then I smelled this god-awful stink."

Vaughn's pulse jumped.

"First I thought the guy was putting me on," the sheriff said. "But when I saw how scared he was . . ."

"You smelled the same stink on Boone's jacket."

"Similar, yeah." The sheriff thought for a moment. "You're certain this wasn't a hoax."

"Absolutely, sheriff. No man's that big, that heavy and that quick. No way."

The sheriff crossed his arms. "The doctor's going to want to know what happened." His thumb rose up and rubbed the grey stubble on his chin. "I'm going to tell him Boone fell into a hole. Old lava tube, maybe."

Vaughn didn't say anything. He would rather tell the doctor exactly what happened because it might help Boone.

His face must have given him away because the sheriff said: "Look, Frank, you think if you told the doctor what you just told me he'd believe you? He'd probably want to x-ray your head too."

Vaughn didn't feel like arguing. "Okay if we go back inside?"

"You bet," the sheriff said.

Chapter 6

VAUGHN walked back into the hospital and almost ran into Jack-O, who was coming out.

Roughly Vaughn's age, Deputy John O'Sullivan Jr. was a decent deputy—when he was around. At the office it had become a standing joke: "Jack-O here today?" "Who?" Jack-O's laziness irked Vaughn, despite the fact that he'd been getting a good chunk of overtime covering for him.

The guy should have been fired, but that would never happen. Everyone pretty much knew that Jack-O had gotten the job—and kept it—because of his father.

As the county executive, John O'Sullivan Sr. occupied the county's highest political office, and had been in the timber business before selling out to Carolina Pacific. He was the richest man in the county and had friends in high places, including the sheriff.

Jack-O acted as if he had the same friends, and as the only other senior deputy besides Vaughn, he liked to brag that he would be sheriff after the Old Man retired. It had gotten so out of hand that Jack-O's father told him to shut up and do something to distinguish himself for the position or he might find himself cleaning up campgrounds instead. That was the rumor, anyway.

Maybe the sheriff had said something about it to Jack-O Senior. But it didn't matter. Vaughn knew the only way Jack-O Junior could distinguish himself was poorly.

"Hey Frank," Jack-O said. As usual, a wry smile climbed up one side of his face.

"Hey."

"Rough morning, I hear."

"Yeah. What're you doing here?"

For a second Jack-O chafed at the question, but he didn't lose the smile. "Thought I'd check on Boone."

"You guys friends now?" Boone had known Jack-O since they were kids, and had never liked him.

The smile faded. Jack-O's eyes narrowed and he hunched his shoulders into his brown duty jacket. It looked new, like he never wore it. "I gotta be going," he said. "I didn't get the day off."

The Old Man understood cabin fever and had given Vaughn today off, even with the county's annual Slugfest coming up this weekend.

Vaughn was going to say something, but just walked away.

"See you tomorrow," Jack-O said.

Vaughn stopped.

Jack-O's lips split open, showing his teeth. "Slugfest planning meeting. Don't miss it." He walked out, and the doors slicked shut behind him.

Vaughn thought that "see you tomorrow" sounded suspicious, but so did everything Jack-O said. Jack-O enjoyed that, making it seem like he knew something everyone else didn't.

Idiot. Vaughn kicked the suspicion from his mind as if it were mud on the tips of his boots.

Inside the waiting room Geek overflowed across one and a half of the blue plastic chairs. His legs stuck straight out, his toes pointed at the ceiling and his arms hung on the chair backs to either side. It looked like he'd eaten too much and was waiting for someone to help him up.

He stared, expressionless, at the television mounted in the upper corner of the room.

"You see Boone?" Vaughn said.

Geek's eyes didn't move. "Yeah. They took him. MRI or something."

"How'd he look?"

"Okay, I guess."

"He awake?"

"Nope."

Vaughn plopped into a chair one away from Geek. He scanned the grimy covers of magazines splayed across a plastic table, but didn't feel like reading.

"You tell the sheriff?" Geek said.

"Yeah."

Geek's face showed no reaction. After a few seconds he said, "I guess he'll keep quiet about it."

"He's telling the doctors Boone fell in an old lava tube."

Geek's blank eyes remained on the television.

Vaughn watched the TV for a few seconds, then leaned forward, rested his head in his hands and stared at the floor.

Boone had been his friend and hunting partner for seven of the eight years Vaughn had lived in Glenwood, and was the finest hunter and woodsman he'd ever met. That partly was because Boone's job as a wildlife specialist for Carolina Pacific meant he spent more time in the woods in a week than most people would in a year. But the main reason Boone had such an uncanny natural sense was because he absolutely lived to scout, explore and hunt. The wilderness was in his blood. In grade school his obsession with the outdoors earned him his nickname, Vaughn had learned, in reference to the explorer.

Some of the out-of-town hunters who met Boone as an adult surmised that the nickname was because he had a bunch of animals in the Boone and Crockett Club big game record book. In fact Boone didn't have any "in the book," though Vaughn knew at least a few of the antler racks and one of the bear skulls in Boone's den would easily qualify.

Despite Boone's modesty, Vaughn knew his friend was proud of his success as a year-round hunter. Boone loved the fact that his family always ate natural protein and never had to buy meat at the store. He also enjoyed introducing others to wild meat, explaining to them that it was healthier—it was leaner and was drug- and hormone-free—and often tastier than meat from domesticated animals. Every year a few new faces would be at his family's summer game barbecue, and the venison chili, grilled marinated elk steaks, oregano roast grouse and other specialties were always the talk of the town for weeks afterward.

Boone also helped feed people he didn't know. A few years before Vaughn arrived in town, Boone and other hunters organized an annual donation of game meat to needy families. That selfless concern for others was something Vaughn immediately liked. They became friends as soon as they met.

Suddenly Vaughn jerked back in his seat, angry with himself. Why was he thinking about this stuff? It wasn't like Boone was dying.

But then he realized that death wasn't what he was worried about. It was the possibility of a spinal injury.

He reviewed what he did in the woods after the attack. The medical procedure was sound, but was removing Boone the right choice? He would be sick to learn that it was his decision that paralyzed his friend and robbed him of the experiences he loved most.

He stood and walked back into the main hallway—not going anywhere in particular, just restless. And impatient. He felt like there was something he should be doing.

"Officer Vaughn?" The triage nurse waved at him.

"Yes?"

"They just called. Boone's going to be fine."

"No paralysis?"

"No."

He looked at the waiting area. Geek stared at him for a second, then sagged into his seat and closed his eyes.

Vaughn felt relieved too, but it was like an icy wind on exposed skin. Invigorating.

"Can we see him?" Vaughn said.

"Not now," the nurse said. "I'm sorry."

He wasn't happy about that, but, dammit, he felt good. Boone was okay. He'd made the right decision.

Now he had to get going. A ride home from Geek and then he would be on his way, back to the woods.

Chapter 7

VAUGHN felt like jogging to Boone's truck, but settled for walking fast. He reached the pickup well before Geek, and just as he put his hand on the door handle he heard brakes squeak and the crackle of loose gravel under tires. He looked over and saw the sheriff's unmarked tan sedan. The window eased down.

"Hop in," the Old Man said. "I'll give you a ride." He leaned across the seat to look at Geek, who was walking up. "You don't mind, do you Jimmy?"

Geek said: "No sheriff."

"Good."

Vaughn grabbed his gear out of Boone's truck, tossed it onto the back seat of the sedan and sat in the front. The sheriff waited for him to close the door, then drove off. He didn't say anything, and Vaughn kept silent.

When they left the parking lot, the sheriff turned down the police radio and said: "Looked like you were in a hurry."

"I'd like to get back out there."

"I think that would be a mistake."

Vaughn was surprised. The Old Man used to be a die-hard hunter and occasionally still took his grandsons into the woods. He definitely knew the hunter's code.

"Sheriff," he said, "I shot the animal. I have to go after it."

"You went after it once already. Three men. And look what it did to Boone. Now you're going to go back by yourself?"

"I have to make sure it's dead or okay."

"You shot in the shoulder and it ran off," the sheriff said. "Sounds like it's okay to me."

"I don't know for sure I hit it in the shoulder. Maybe the bullet went into its back, hit a lung."

Vaughn's street was coming up on the right, but the sheriff didn't slow down. Vaughn started to say something and then realized they were going the long way on purpose.

"Say you're out there and run into a half-dead monster," the sheriff said. "What do you do then? Shoot it? Or do you try to run away from something wounded, angry, and way bigger and faster than you are?"

Vaughn looked over. The sheriff stared straight out the windshield.

"If it's half dead, I guess I shoot it."

"Okay," the Old Man said. "Let's say you shoot it, or you find it dead. Then what do you do?"

"Come back out."

The sheriff flicked on his turn signal and turned right. They passed one, two, three houses and then he spoke again.

"This is a small town, Frank. For that matter, the entire county holds precious few secrets. You know that. If you go back there people will find out about that thing. Some of them will see it as a pot of gold and go looking for it. Might even find it."

His right hand moved from the wheel and turned palm up. The deep lines in the skin looked like fissures cracked into pale rock.

He said, "Say they do find it and bring it out, or maybe just a piece of it. Then what?"

He glanced at Vaughn, who said nothing.

"It'll make the papers, TV, everything," the sheriff said. "*Then* the damn granola-heads will get the feds to declare it an endangered species. And when that happens, and you know it would, the timber industry—and maybe a lot more than that—will be forced to shut down here and every other place these things have been seen."

The sheriff swerved around a parked car. "Right about then hell will seem like a cool place," he said. "Because if all that comes to pass, you, and maybe me, are going to be seriously unpopular around here—that is, if the thing doesn't kill you first."

The Old Man's words spun through Vaughn's mind. The houses passed before his eyes as if they were projected on a screen.

The big sedan turned right again.

The sheriff said, "So, you still going after it?"

Vaughn's mind closed around a rock of conviction. "I have to."

"You have to think about what I said."

Vaughn looked at him. "I—"

"If that animal's dying, you need to leave it there to die. As a hunter you know that. The first time you went after it too soon and spooked it. You need to leave it alone—for a good long time."

The Old Man was right, but Vaughn didn't know if the sheriff meant for a few hours or forever. "You telling me that as a hunter or as my boss?"

The sheriff didn't answer.

They turned right a last time and pulled to the curb in front of Vaughn's house. The sheriff turned off the motor and shifted in his seat so that he faced his deputy.

"What about wanton waste?" Vaughn said.

Washington and most other states had a "wanton waste" law designed to punish people for killing a game animal and simply leaving it to rot. It was something no self-respecting hunter (not a mere killer) would ever do because all hunters eat what they kill. But there were always a few jerks.

"Doesn't apply," the sheriff said. "It isn't a game animal and you weren't hunting it."

Vaughn blew out an abrupt sigh. "Okay, sheriff, you're right. You're right about the letter of the law, but that's not what we're talking about here. I have an ethical obligation to go after this thing and we both know it."

"Did you hear what I said?"

"If this is about the Slugfest—"

"You're damn right it's about the Slugfest. But it's also about everything else I mentioned. You willing to risk all that?"

"The risk is incredibly low, sheriff."

Lines dug deep around the sheriff's mouth. "Don't go."

Vaughn couldn't believe it. The Old Man had never been so rigid before, not with him. "You ordering me?"

"That's right. I don't want to sound patronizing, but I'm doing it for your own good."

Vaughn didn't know what to say.

"Try to forget about that thing limping around out there," the sheriff said. "If you want someone to lay your guilt on, blame it on me."

This is bullshit, Vaughn thought, and almost said so. "Sheriff, I appreciate that, but I have to do this. I couldn't live with myself if I didn't." Something occurred to him. "If you're saying you don't want to give me official permission to go after this thing, I have some vacation days . . ."

The Old Man's eyes flared blue. "You want to take a vacation day? Go ahead. But you'll be making a whale of a mistake."

"Those consequences you talked about will only happen if this somehow gets out," Vaughn said. "It won't."

"You can't guarantee that."

Vaughn said nothing.

The sheriff turned and faced back out the windshield. He let out a long breath that fogged the glass. "I'm telling you not to go," he said. "If you're not at the meeting tomorrow morning I'm putting you on unpaid leave. You get me?"

"I get you loud and clear, sheriff. But with all due respect, I won't be there."

The Old Man slammed the steering wheel. "Dammit, Frank! If there's one thing I've learned in thirty-odd years of doing this job it's that things can get out of control despite your best efforts to prevent it."

"Things won't get out of control."

"I'll have to call Carolina Pacific and let them know."

Vaughn started to protest, but the sheriff cut him off. "Hey—everyone's safety is my business, right? Who knows what CP has planned for the area you'll be in. I don't want you running around with a high-powered rifle, adrenaline pumping, if they have people out there. At the same time, I can't ask them to shut down their operations in that area without giving them a reason."

"What are you going to tell them?"

"The truth. I don't care if they believe it or not. They'll either laugh and then get mad about losing a day of cutting, or they'll ask to send someone with you, a request I can't really refuse."

Vaughn wasn't prepared to take along a stranger.

The sheriff said: "You can see how things begin to get out of control."

"I'm sure whoever they send won't want news of this getting out."

"That person will have to tell other people where he's going, and I'll have to figure out a story for the rest of the deputies. Lord knows what Geek will say."

"He won't say anything."

"How long you figure he'll hold out?"

As a police officer Vaughn knew people talked sooner or later, especially when trying to keep a secret. Geek was a well-known talker, but surely he could keep quiet for a day.

Suddenly he wondered whether Geek had said anything to Jack-O at the hospital.

The Old Man fixed him with a blue stare. "Listen to me on this one, Frank. Don't throw away a promising future." He turned the key, and the big engine growled to life.

Vaughn opened the door and got out.

"Make sure you talk to Katie about this," the sheriff said.

Katie? "I don't see—"

"That's why I want you to talk to her. You don't see. Your idealism's put a tree in front of your face and you're about to walk into it. Now go talk to her."

Chapter 8

VAUGHN'S wife Katie was at her job as an administrative assistant at the G. Loomis plant, all the way down Route 503 in Woodland.

Vaughn didn't want to dump this on her over the phone even if she had the time to listen to it all, think about it and say whatever she had to say. And she definitely did not have the time. The plant was churning out fishing rods at capacity and she was swamped.

And damned if he was going to drive all the way down there just to—what? Ask her permission?

It wasn't that her opinion didn't matter, it's just that this time it didn't apply. None of what happened had anything to do with her. The sheriff was just trying to make him think twice.

Besides, Vaughn knew what his wife would say. She hated the thought of any creature suffering, and so did he. Especially animals wounded by a careless shot. It made him sick.

He'd seen it once and that had been enough. He was thir-

teen, hunting one fall day with a friend's older brother. He remembered the air, so cold and crisp it felt like it could crack.
Their inexperienced footfalls on the dry leaves spooked a
young buck, and as boys will do from time to time, his companion acted rashly. Out of bravado or immaturity, the older
boy threw up his lever-action Winchester .30-30 and fired.

At the crack of the rifle the nearer of the buck's hind legs
swung lazily up, as if suddenly freed of the restrictions of tendon and bone. The black hoof slammed into the deer's rump
and then rocketed back to the ground, jigging crazily as the
buck half-ran, half-hopped away on its three good legs.
Vaughn's companion watched the deer go, but didn't pursue it
to finish it off. In deference to the older boy and despite what
he'd been taught, Vaughn didn't either.

But the image of the maimed deer, its dead leg bouncing
behind it, tormented him for the rest of the day and all night.

Since he'd been old enough to carry a rifle in the woods
his father had schooled him in what he later learned were
called ethics. But when he was young, they were rules. Always point the muzzle in a safe direction. Keep the safety on
until you're ready to shoot. Make sure of your target and beyond. Don't shoot over water. These were rules to prevent
injury to people.

The rules to prevent injury to animals were just as formal
and just as important. He had to practice shooting at different
distances and in different positions to gain enough proficiency
with his rifle so his father would be sure he could make a
clean, killing shot. He could only shoot for the heart-lung
area, behind a deer's front shoulder. And he had to learn how
to track. Because if, by bad luck, the animal moved at the shot
or something else happened that resulted in a nonfatal wound,
he was obligated to go after it.

Not just because it was illegal for a hunter to abandon a
wounded animal without making an earnest effort to find it,
but because he was responsible for the animal, a being that
merited his respect.

So at dawn the next morning he set out alone to find the
deer. First he walked slowly, looking for sign. But the leaves
that covered the forest floor and the wind that scattered them
hid any evidence of blood. He found tracks and followed

some, but deer were all over the forest. The tracks led every-where and nowhere.

As the sun got higher he ran between the trees, branches whipping the skin of his face, frantic because he knew he wouldn't find the deer. Finally exhausted, he dropped onto the cold ground, his eyes blurry with tears and his stomach churning with images of the animal dying a slow and painful death—one he could have prevented.

That morning he vowed to never again let another wounded animal go unpursued, no matter who shot it.

Until now, it hadn't been an issue. From that day he'd learned to choose shots with patience and hunting partners with insight. But now, standing in his kitchen, he felt hot with the same shame and anger behind the promise he'd made to himself so many years ago.

He had to make sure the animal was either fine or dead.

If he didn't, he would be no better than the jerks who, if they wounded an animal with a lazy shot and didn't want to deal with tracking it, said things like, "Coyotes'll eat good tonight." Or like the suburbanites who maimed deer with their cars, watched in their rearview mirrors as the animals dragged their shattered bodies off the road, and drove home trying to forget about it or had ridiculous thoughts about a "wild animal's" ability to heal from a broken leg or back.

Not all wounded animals could be found and put out of their misery, but the effort was what counted. Excuses were bullshit.

The sheriff was right about one thing: he needed to give the animal time to lie down. Just until later this afternoon. Then he was going back.

Chapter 9

Morning
Raleigh, North Carolina

MARK Kingston looked down and pressed the red, call-ending button on the Mercedes-installed car phone.

Braaaaaa!

At the sound of the car horn he jerked the wheel to the left, just missing a blue Chevy Suburban. The Suburban kicked up dust and small rocks from the paved shoulder of the Beltline, and as it pulled back on to the highway the driver flipped Kingston the bird and yelled something lost behind the window glass.

Kingston raised his hand in apology, but before it came back to the wheel he'd already forgotten about the near miss. His mind was occupied with something else: *Should I or shouldn't I?*

On the one hand it was likely nothing would come of what he'd just heard. And as vice president of public and government relations, part of his job was to screen unimportant things from his boss, Bill Gaines, chairman and CEO of Carolina Pacific Timber Corporation.

But Gaines had asked to be informed about anything that could be a potential red flag to BayMun AG, the German conglomerate interested in acquiring Carolina Pacific for $25 billion (two and a half times annual sales), or to FTC regulators who, under pressure from Capitol Hill, were looking for any excuse to scuttle the deal. Though the United States seemed to have few qualms about selling military technology to almost anyone and allowing the Japanese to buy prestigious American real estate, no one—from the Anti-Defamation League down to the unions—wanted the World War II Germans to own a sizeable chunk of the good ole U.S. of A.

The question Kingston wrestled with was: Does this qualify as a red flag?

Not yet. That was the easy answer.

But if all the ifs came to pass, not only would it kill the deal, it might kill the company. Maybe the entire timber industry. Something that serious certainly was worth mentioning. Wasn't it?

The sheriff certainly thought so. "You better get someone out here," he'd said. "You don't want this getting out."

No kidding. Problem was, the whole thing sounded so out of left field, so impossible, that Kingston worried that if he said anything now it would look like panic. Gaines might think the pressure of the sale was getting to him.

But it wasn't. At least he wanted to make sure it wasn't before he . . . *Before I what?*

He turned off the highway at the Saunders/Downtown exit and headed north, into the city.

An e-mail, he thought. An "FYI." That would be easy and would make the whole thing seem less important. But then he remembered that memo from Legal about e-mail messages being recoverable in litigation, so he couldn't.

He had to tell Gaines.

Or not.

He turned the silver Mercedes S500 right onto South Street, and thought about the scenarios.

If he kept his mouth shut and nothing happened, he would neither lose nor gain anything. But if he didn't tell Gaines and the creature was brought out, he was finished.

On the other hand, if he notified Gaines and nothing happened with the creature, he might be praised. And if the worst case occurred, sharing the information with Gaines meant he wouldn't be the only one to carry the blame.

That settled it.

His finger punched the phone's Speaker button and then 2 on the speed dial: Gaines' office number. Gaines had a flight to Munich today and always went to the office before flying anywhere.

It rang once. "Gaines."

"Bill, it's Mark."

"Make it fast. I'm late for my flight."

Sounded like he was outside. "Where are you?"

"Parking garage," Gaines said. Executive parking was underneath the smoked-glass Carolina Pacific building, as was the case with the other corporate towers on the Mall.

"I'm a few blocks away, on Wilmington."

"Mark, I'm late," Gaines said.

Through the phone, Kingston heard the deep roar of Gaines' Lincoln Navigator. "I'll meet you at the entrance," he said. "It's important." He punched the phone off.

A minute later he turned into the dark mouth of the garage where the Navigator waited, its grille gleaming like the oversized fangs of a prehistoric fish.

Gaines, wearing his "I'm busy" frown, looked down at Kingston. "This better be important."

Kingston didn't waste any time. "I just got a call from the Skookum County sheriff."

"Where's Skookum County?"

"Southwestern Washington. He told me something that may turn out to be nothing—it probably will, but if not it could be serious."

"Great," Gaines said. "More spotted owls? Or did they find something else out there?"

"Something else."

"Son of a . . ." Gaines banged the door panel. "Don't those goddamn tree-hugging feds have anything better to do?"

Kingston felt his blood pressure screw up a notch. "Actually the feds aren't involved yet. That's the good news."

"And?"

"The bad news is that it's the Sasquatch."

Gaines' face seized up like someone just hit him in the head with a rock. His eyes glazed over.

"You—are—shitting—me," he said. He spoke the words methodically, like he was reading an eye chart.

"Wish I was."

Gaines' eyes refocused. "Are you sure? I mean, I know they're supposed to be real, but are they sure it wasn't a bear or something?"

"Apparently."

"So they found a dead one," Gaines said.

"Not yet."

"What the hell does that mean?"

Kingston said: "The bigfoot was wounded by hunters and a Skookum County deputy is investigating. According to the sheriff, two of the hunters are CP employees. He also said there's a law in that county that says it's illegal to shoot these things."

Kingston gave him the short version. The law had been enacted as a tourism ploy in November 1969, two years after film alleged to be of a bigfoot was shot in northern California. The county commissioners wanted to capitalize on the film-caused bigfoot hubbub that had consumed the Pacific Northwest, the rest of the nation and parts of the world. To some extent it worked: Articles about the law and its connection to the film appeared in papers all over the United States and abroad. But that fame quickly died, and now everyone thought the law—still on the books—was a quirk of Northwest culture and would never amount to more than that.

"According to the sheriff, killing one is a felony punishable by a fine up to ten thousand dollars and imprisonment in the county jail for up to five years," Kingston said.

"We liable?"

"I don't know. But if they find this thing and bring it out, liability would be the least of our problems."

"No shit," Gaines said. "What else?"

"One of the hunters, a CP guy, was injured by the bigfoot. Broken arm and concussion."

"Jesus," Gaines said. "Any memory loss?"

"I don't know."

"Let's keep our fingers crossed."

"The sheriff said he told the doctors our boy fell down an old lava tube."

"Good man," Gaines said. He turned his arm to look at the blue face of the Rolex Submariner strapped to his wrist. "Please tell me that's it."

"'Fraid not. Looks like the bigfoot killed a man. Not one of ours. A local guy, poacher."

Gaines looked like his head was about to explode, then suddenly became calm. "The sheriff's covering that up too."

"Right," Kingston said. "The only other thing is that the shooting happened in the Gifford Pinchot National Forest, on land we're scheduled to cut."

"I'm not worried about that."

Kingston wasn't either. Like high-level executives in the timber industry, a few high-ranking officials in the U.S. Forest Service and its parent agency, the Department of Agriculture, also knew Sasquatches existed. And like their private-sector counterparts, neither career bureaucrats nor political appointees would want the animal's existence to become public.

"The sheriff said we could send someone with the investigating deputy," Kingston said. "I'm going to ask Chris Mackey to go."

"Mackey? Are you nuts? He's apt to shoot the thing."

"Nah. He's on our side and we definitely want someone out there. Besides, if the bigfoot is already dead, it's not an issue. If it isn't dead, I'm sure they'll just turn around and come back out."

"What if something goes wrong?"

"He isn't an employee. There'll be no ties back to us."

Gaines said: "That it?"

"Yeah."

"Well here's what we're going to do: ignore it."

Kingston sat up. *Ignore it?* "What do you mean?"

"I mean we don't send Mackey, we don't send anyone. We ignore it."

Kingston thought about the consequences.

"Look," Gaines said, leaning out the window. "Assuming it's dead and the deputy can find it, there's no way he's going to decide to bring it out, even if he physically could and I assume he can't. That's logging country out there. Those people have taken a beating from owls, fish and tree-huggers on both coasts. You think a local deputy is going to bring out a Sasquatch because of some old joke of a law? He'd be burned at the stake. And if it's not dead, the whole thing's moot."

"I still think we should send Chris," Kingston said. "That way we—"

"Mark, we are under a fucking microscope right now." Gaines' hand, protruding from the crisp cuff of a custom-tailored Tom James shirt, pressed hard enough against the Navigator's black door panel to make a dent. "The Germans are crawling all over everything, and these people are anal like you can't believe. Yesterday I got a call from one of their auditors asking me about a footnote in a memo written five years ago! Can you believe that? Plus the feds are watching both of us like hawks, and I'm sure them and BayMun have convinced a few of our employees to keep their eyes and ears open. You understand?"

"Of course, but—"

Gaines' voice became more reasonable-sounding. "All this will be over in a week, maybe two. Then we'll be a lot richer, so will our stockholders, and everyone except a few congressmen and bureaucrats will be happy. All we have to do is maintain the status quo."

"That's my point—"

"I'm not going to argue with you, Mark," Gaines said. "This deal won't get killed by something this bizarre. My call. Talk to you Thursday."

He pulled his head back in, and the Navigator zoomed away.

Chapter 10

KINGSTON wound his big Mercedes down the semicircular ramp and parked. On the concrete wall facing him, MR. KINGSTON was stenciled in black paint. He turned off the motor, but didn't get out.

"Shit," he said aloud, and thought: *His call? What the hell is that?* He snorted. *It isn't his call, it's mine, dammit. I was just letting him know.*

Maybe he shouldn't have told Gaines.

But he had. And now that his boss made a decision, Kingston had a problem.

The problem was that Gaines didn't appreciate the stakes. They were *way* higher than just the BayMun deal. How long had Gaines thought about it—a few seconds?

Kingston glared at the wall. He should have expected it. Gaines had been in the timber business all of six years now. Kingston had been in it his whole adult life.

Fresh out of Northwestern Law he'd taken a low-paying job with then Congressman and eventually Senator Michael

Bramhall of Washington. Timber money helped Bramhall become chairman of the Senate Energy and Natural Resources Committee, and Kingston became his chief of staff, a position that gave him more power than many elected congressmen. When, after twenty years, Bramhall wanted to retire, Kingston chose to quit while he was ahead. He left for the far better pay of a lobbyist at the American Forest Products Association, until Gaines' predecessor made him an offer he couldn't refuse.

Over thirty years in and around the timber industry, Kingston mused.

He got out of the car. The soles of his burgundy Johnston & Murphy shoes chuffed on the garage's concrete floor, and his nose filled with the smells of tire rubber and stale exhaust fumes. He shut the door, thumbed the remote and listened to the beep echo through the garage.

The chrome elevator doors beckoned him forward, but he liked to walk and think. He turned and headed down the ramp, his mind already back on the bigfoot and what he should do.

He approached the problem methodically, starting with what he knew about the creatures.

The big thing was that they were real.

The evidence was there. Eyewitness accounts of the animal were easy to discredit because people's powers of observation were notoriously unreliable. But the evidence the creatures left behind: Judging by an article he'd read a few years ago in an obscure scientific journal, the amount of startlingly concrete information that could now be detected from just one real footprint was astounding.

Then there were images. The 1967 film shot in California was the most serious. Although almost everyone assumed it was a hoax, the film was shot in a time when that elaborate a hoax was technologically impossible. *Probably couldn't even get there now with computers,* he thought.

The worldwide interest the film generated broadsided the timber industry. In fact, the film caused enough panic that it reached the upper ranks of the Johnson Administration. On November 17, 1967, less than a month after the footage was shot and two months before the Battle of Khe Sanh and the Tet Offensive in Vietnam, President Johnson signed a Top

Secret directive referred to simply as the "Bigfoot Order." Extremely brief, it instructed the Secretary of Agriculture and
the Chief of the U.S. Forest Service to do "everything possible" to keep the animal's existence a secret because its reve-
lation could "cause a spiritual crisis that would be detrimental
to National Security."

Kingston was told that when it was signed, in the midst of
the controversial war, Johnson said, "I don't need to worry
about goddamn walking monkeys on top of everything else."

So with the government's blessing, timber executives set
up a covert disinformation program. They secretly channeled
cash to people who made outlandish public claims about the
creatures: that Sasquatches were aliens or mystical beings or
overgrown hippies. Paid hoaxers strapped on fake feet and ran
down logging roads, leaving cookie-cutter replicas of giant,
flat, human footprints. Sometimes, when filming obviously
fake home movies, they donned gorilla suits.

Kingston reached the bottom of the ramp, the second level
of the parking garage. The only sound was the clack and
scrape of his shoes.

The disinformation campaign enabled the public to believe
what it wanted to believe: that seven- or eight- or ten-foot-tall
"monsters"—*how big are they?* he wondered—did not roam
the woods. Everything was safe. The creatures really were a
fanciful combination of Native American legends, prankster
jokes, the observations of well-intentioned-but-mistaken people and the hallucinations of outright kooks. As a result, and
despite high-quality research by a few accredited scientists,
the vast majority of people laughed at the film and every other
piece of real evidence. The campaign was a huge, if unher-
alded, success.

And the timber industry prudently continued it, but put
less and less money into it because the existence of the animals was taken less and less seriously by the media and, consequently, the public. One or two hoaxes a year, keeping tabs
on bigfoot research and low-impact techniques like posting
WATERSHED AREA–KEEP OUT signs deep in the woods were
pretty much all that was involved now.

But while media coverage had fallen off, the number of
sightings hadn't. In fact, the industry had a few recent scares,

namely the two videotapes shot by Forest Service field employees. He couldn't remember the exact year when the first one was shot. Sometime in the late '80s, in the Umatilla National Forest in Oregon. The second was shot in 1994 in Montana's Kootenai National Forest. Both tapes were immediately confiscated and disposed of by the Service.

Film, video—as images, they were powerful. But they were nothing compared to actual remains. A body.

Suddenly he stopped walking. He realized what a body would mean. Not only would it be evidence of Sasquatches living in the Pacific Northwest, it would give credence to videotapes and other evidence that had been collected all over the United States. New York, Pennsylvania, Kentucky, Florida, Louisiana, Missouri, Oklahoma, Texas—every state but Hawaii.

He started walking again, down into the darker levels of the garage.

Only once before had the timber industry encountered a problem involving what might have been a body of a real bigfoot. It was back in 1968, at the Minnesota State Fair. The word got out that a few scientists were poking around an exhibit of a dead, hair-covered, humanlike figure, encased in ice. At least one scientist thought the "iceman" was real, in no small part because of the stench of rotting flesh that seeped from the melting ice block. Taking no chances, timber executives quickly anted up enough money to convince the owner to get rid of it—which was easy because the man didn't want to answer the scientists' main question: Where did you get this? Timber executives didn't care, so long as it was gone.

Years later, when the owner again began displaying the corpse at carnival sideshows, the press and scientists weren't interested. Timber executives were amazed, and relieved.

Since then there had been nothing, and hardly anyone took sightings and footprints seriously anymore, despite the better science used to analyze them. Even if Sasquatch DNA was somehow collected and found to be "not entirely human and not entirely ape," Kingston knew most people wouldn't believe it—because they simply could not entertain the possibility of a huge wild ape walking around North America.

Who could blame them? Though Kingston had to accept the existence of these creatures because he was told they were real, the few times he really thought about it made him seriously uncomfortable. Scared, even.

And that's why timber executives undertook the disinformation campaign. Not because they believed the Sasquatch was a matter of national security, but because they were scared. Scared of what this unknown creature could do to their business, their aspirations, their hundreds of millions of uncut dollars standing in the ground. And while the stakes in the late 1960s were large, they were nothing compared to the stakes now.

Because of the Endangered Species Act.

He heard a car vroom into the garage, somewhere above him.

Ever since the U.S. Supreme Court ruled in 1978 that construction of the $100 million Tellico Dam on the Little Tennessee River had to be stopped because of the snail darter (a small fish), the country had been ruled by the Endangered Species Act. Want a housing development stopped? Don't like the paper mill upstream? Find some critter and petition the federal Fish and Wildlife Service to put it on the endangered species list.

The Tellico Dam was an unnecessary project and the court killed it. But in doing so, it doomed the country.

The Endangered Species Act now was routinely used to shut down, hobble and prevent million- and billion-dollar projects. It was one of the most powerful laws in the United States, and the world.

If a dead Sasquatch turned up now, environmentalists would use the body and the act to kill what remained of the timber industry in the Pacific Northwest. Maybe everywhere.

Why didn't Gaines see that? Kingston wondered. Discovery of an endangered, walking primate would make the spotted owl and salmon problems look microscopic in comparison.

It would be disastrous.

And now he, Mark Kingston, had to decide whether to abide by Gaines' order to turn his back on all of that.

Tires shrieked right behind him; a car curled, too fast, down the ramp. He flattened himself against the concrete wall and watched the beams from car's headlights swing across the gloom then slam him in the face.

That's when it hit him. Nothing had changed.

If the shit hit the fan it would be his ass no matter what Gaines told him to do.

And since it was his ass, he wanted some insurance.

He peeled himself off the wall, hiked back to his Mercedes and ducked into the driver's seat, a plan already forming in his mind. He checked his watch. Still time, but he would have to hurry.

Chapter 11

Happy Valley, Washington

ARTHUR Lansing wanted to be alone. He listened to the phone ring and ring, and knew it had to be another nut. For some reason the number of calls about spaceships discharging or picking up Sasquatches had increased lately. He surmised that the long winter had brought out the instability in some people.

The ringing mocked him.

The first few years he'd been enthusiastic, picking up the phone with his heart in his mouth as if every call was the big one. He *knew* it was coming.

But it never had. And after hours of listening to stories about tracks and sightings and paranormal, extraterrestrial bunk, he'd learned that virtually all calls were scientifically useless.

Tired of cooking up excuses to get off the phone, and to avoid being outright rude, he changed his phone number—several times. But that wasn't enough. Finally he got caller ID and swore off answering machines. If he didn't recognize the number, he wouldn't answer.

Even though he knew he wouldn't recognize this one, he

pulled his lanky frame off the couch and walked over to the phone—just in case, though what emergency could happen at the anthropology department at Western Washington University he couldn't imagine. Maybe someone couldn't find a key or a file. Or a skull.

Sure enough, the number on the LCD readout wasn't familiar.

He sighed, then walked back to the couch, lay down and folded his hands over his chest.

The phone started ringing again.

Persistent son of a bitch. *Leave me alone, all of you. Just for one day.*

HE'D stayed home. Took a sick day, but wasn't sick. Not physically.

It was an anniversary of sorts. Ten years. Ten years of studying the Sasquatch. A whole decade without a single shred of new evidence. No *specimen.* That sole want had in some way or another been responsible for everything.

With a specimen, his Sasquatch research would have been called brilliant. Instead it was a collar and leash, chaining his career inside the "could've" yard with a bunch of underachievers.

He was still an associate professor—*associate professor!* Annual reviews were a joke, like going through the motions at a parole hearing. And to rub his nose in it, every year lesser scientists—lesser minds—got promoted to full professor and the better salary that went with it.

Carol thought she'd hitched her wagon to a star academician, but it didn't work out that way. It was hard for her when her friends, the wives of his peers, bragged about the careers of their husbands and she had nothing to say. She would smile, but her eyes leaked pain.

He tried to stay positive, but couldn't do it for both of them. "Why are you so obsessed with this?" she finally said. "Can't you just let it go? No one cares if it's real. Only you."

Only you. That was the turning point.

She blamed the Sasquatch. She blamed him. When she left, he couldn't blame her.

Instead he blamed science. And people.

The majority of his work, on human origins, was highly regarded and published regularly. But he suspected—correctly, as it turned out—that he was better known for his pursuit of the Sasquatch, even within his own field. He knew that some of his colleagues at the university called him "Dr. Bigfoot" behind his back.

It didn't help that his yearly predictions about the imminence of a Sasquatch find never came true. There were more tracks, more dermal ridges in some of them, and more sightings. But nothing new. He himself had spent countless hours scouring remote woods with nothing to show for it.

Yet he knew the Sasquatch was real, had not an iota of doubt. The evidence was real, so whatever left it must be real. Unassailable logic that should have been embraced by science.

Should have.

He was confident it would be when, ten years ago today, he stood on the stage of the university's then-new Douglas Auditorium. It was the twenty-third annual conference of the International Society of Primatology and Physical Anthropology, and his presentation was boldly titled "Measurable Evidence for a North American Nonhuman Bipedal Primate."

The auditorium was jammed. But even then, full of conviction, he wasn't so naïve as to think that his fellow scientists attended purely out of interest in the subject matter. Like laypeople, they didn't think it was possible for such an animal to exist without having been discovered already. As a zoologist friend said at the time: "It's 1994, for crying out loud. What's left to discover besides a few more glow-in-the-dark fish at the bottom of the ocean? Our job is filling in the blanks, not creating new ones."

Lansing knew that despite any private curiosity, no sane, "serious" scientist would stick his neck out in a public forum and claim that a non-human bipedal primate could exist—and that was a major reason why the auditorium was full that day. His topic and growing reputation as a creative and diligent thinker ultimately were less interesting than the possibility of witnessing a promising fellow scientist publicly hang himself, thus beginning his plummet into ridiculed obscurity.

But young and confident in the scientific validity of his information, he'd looked out at the full house of skeptics and knew he could convince them . . .

CLICK. The television screen jumped from blue to an image of a younger-looking Lansing.

"Thank you chairperson Olsen," he said to her back as she walked from the stage. Smiling, he turned to the audience. "This morning I will try to present, in a mere thirty minutes, enough evidence so that those of you sitting here with an open mind should acknowledge that it's at least possible that an undiscovered species of bipedal primate lives here in North America. Very close by, I might add."

The expected ripple of nervous discomfort came from the audience, and he met it with energetic good humor. "I can assure you, despite the fact that it appears all delegates are here, none of us qualify." The rumbling changed to polite laughter, and then abruptly died out.

He knew that sightings and other anecdotal information were always suspect, and that mentioning them would do more harm than good, so his presentation would deal solely with evidence that could be checked and verified. It could be disputed, but was indisputably there.

"Let us start first with the physical evidence," he said. "In the order of least impressive to most, we have alleged feces or scat samples, which are barely worth mentioning because they don't tell us much. 'Human-type digestive tract' is a useless determination, though the presence of fur and wood fiber in thus-identified samples is interesting." The implication was clear: People generally didn't eat wood, nor did they eat meat with the fur still on it.

"We also have hair samples," he said, pacing across the stage. Already the heat from the lights was making him sweat. "Some of these have turned out to be fakes. Synthetic hair. But a few have been identified by biologists and forensic experts—including the FBI—as from the primate family. Similar to humans and African apes, but not matching any known primate.

"That's interesting, but unfortunately, as you know, hair samples can only tell us what we *don't* have rather than what we do. So, failing a DNA test—for which we'd need an authentic, uncontaminated hair, preferably with follicle—hair is of limited value."

He stopped beneath the lower edge of an enormous white square hanging over the stage. His right hand shook out a telescoping pointer while his left felt for the button on the slide remote.

"Then we have these," he said, and rapped the bottom edge of the screen.

A slide popped up, divided into four sections. The upper left photo showed what looked like large, bare footprints in snow. Shaped like human feet, including five distinct toes, the only thing obviously different was that the tracks lacked the heel-to-big-toe curve caused by an arch. Tape measures ran alongside and across one of the tracks.

The upper right photo showed a similar but more distinct track in mud, again with a measuring tape alongside.

At bottom left was a photo of three plaster casts, upright and side by side, obviously made by the same type of feet. Next to them was a regulation-size soccer ball that appeared strangely small, a little bigger than a softball.

The black-and-white photo at the bottom right of the screen looked like a close-up photograph of a dirty fingerprint.

"Footprints." His voice boomed through the huge PA system. "Huge, humanlike footprints in the snow and mud." He gazed up at the screen.

"The ones in the upper left were made in the Mt. Baker-Snoqualmie National Forest in 1985. That's in Washington, east of here near the Canadian border. They're seventeen inches long and a bit over seven inches wide at the ball.

"That print," now waving the pointer toward the upper right, "was found with several others along a logging road in western Oregon two years ago. It is fourteen-and-a-half inches long and nearly six inches at the ball.

"And these casts," he said, slapping under the bottom left photograph, "were made from tracks discovered in northern California in 1969. They're in the same size range as the others.

"Similar tracks, or footprints, have been found all over the Pacific Northwest. In fact," he said, wiggling his pointer at the audience, "reports of these animals have come from all over North America. But as I'm only dealing here with the physical evidence, I've chosen to focus on this region, which has the highest frequency and concentration of reported tracks."

Predictably, the audience was silent. That something or someone had been leaving huge, humanlike footprints all over the Pacific Northwest was no secret.

He said: "Some of these tracks have telling signs, such as push-off mounds, toe-pad expansions, a depth indicating great weight and, of course, a notable absence of claw marks, ruling out bears."

The audience remained mute.

"Possibly you're not impressed," he said. He turned and slapped the bottom of the fingerprint-like picture. "However, *this* should impress you."

His left hand clicked the remote and a full-screen version of the fingerprint appeared. At that scale the skin's loops and whorls stretched a foot across. Imposed on them were baseball-size, opaque black circles that looked like supermagnified specks of dirt.

Murmurs of interest swirled in the audience, just as he'd envisioned. He'd wanted to hit them hard right away.

Despite the scientific detachment he was supposed to have, adrenaline flooded his system. This was his discovery and he knew it was good. He took a deep breath.

"This is a blowup of the last photo, and as you can see it shows dermal ridges. From a toe. A *big* toe."

Brief laughter from the audience.

"Not literally." Lansing smiled. "Although these animals have a prominent big toe, these ridges happen to be from the fourth toe.

"Since fakery is the complaint most often associated with evidence for these creatures, the obvious question is whether someone could have faked these dermal ridges and similar ones found on other freshly cast tracks. My opinion is that the only person who could have has to be sitting in this room, and in addition to having an advanced degree in anthropology or primatology, has one in chemical engineering, forensics and, not least, sculpture."

He didn't get the laugh he expected.

But I'm not an expert on finger- and toe-prints. So I took the plaster originals of the tracks to experts at the FBI, the Seattle Police Department, the New York City Police Department and Scotland Yard. My question was simple: Are the ridges fake?

None of the experts thought the ridges and associated sweat pores, which you can see here and elsewhere," he pointed at one of the black circles, "could have been faked. In fact, one of the experts was concerned that if the ridges were faked, it would represent a significant leap in what criminals are able to do now.

"But," he paused for effect, "another of the experts was more profoundly disturbed. She went a step further, and identified the ridges as being from a nonhuman, higher primate's foot—and was deeply troubled by what that indicates. In other words," he paused again, "that there exists another species of bipedal primate besides ourselves."

More murmuring in the audience. Mindful of his thirty-minute limit, he quickly went on.

"This is the most compelling physical evidence that

exists for these creatures." He paced across the stage. "And it is compelling. Although evidence of dermal ridges doesn't occur in every track—naturally because most are too old by the time they're found—I submit that this evidence is enough for you to consider that these creatures may exist."

He stopped and faced the audience. "Certainly it amounts to at least 'reasonable doubt,' which means the idea should not be simply waved off by the scientific community—including the distinguished members of the audience."

He paused to let the small compliment settle, and to let them think. Someone coughed.

"In the event some of you are still inclined to think that all tracks are hoaxed, let me ask you a question every scientist should be familiar with: What would it cost?"

As he'd intended, chuckles rumbled across the audience in common acknowledgment of the double-edged joke. On the one hand, scientists were irritated that the Holy Grail of "pure science" was constrained by access to money, of which there was never enough. On the other hand they had to constantly grovel for funds to keep their research afloat, a duty virtually all "real" scientists detested.

"A short but important digression," he said. His left hand clicked the remote and the screen showed a series of equations.

$$1,000 \text{ (tracks found)} \times 100 \text{ (probability more)} \times 100$$
$$\text{(probability found)} / 20 \text{ (years)} = 500,000$$

$$50 \text{ (fakes)} \times 5 \text{ (days/week)} \times 50 \text{ (weeks)} = 12,500$$

$$500,000 / 12,500 = 40 \text{ (people needed)}$$

$$40 \text{ (people)} \times \$25,000 \text{ (annual wage)} = \$1,000,000$$

$$\$1,000,000 \times 20 \text{ (years)} = \$20,000,000$$

"Let me explain the values," he said, looking up at the screen. "The first number, one thousand, is seventy-five percent of the number of *reliable* tracks—one per account—measured and/or found in the last two decades. I use a percentage that's less than one hundred merely to be conservative.

"Given the remote and random places in which these tracks are found, I think hundreds of times as many are *not* found nor reported. But to be conservative, I multiply that already conservative one thousand by only one hundred. And again, as nearly all the tracks are found in remote locations, we can easily assign a probability of finding them of one in a hundred.

"Multiply those three numbers and we get ten million—a useable, conservative figure. Ten million divided by a span of twenty-one years yields roughly half a million footprints per year.

"Moving on to the next line, I estimate that the most tracks a talented faker could make per day in remote locations without being seen and without being needlessly redundant is fifty. Working full time that's fifty prints, five days a week for fifty weeks, which equals twelve thousand five hundred.

"If we divide that into half a million, we get forty. Forty people multiplied by a conservative living wage of $25,000 per year gives, conveniently, one million dollars per year," Lansing said, tapping the screen, "or twenty million dollars to date."

He spun on a heel and faced the audience. "This is a cocktail-napkin approach, but it demonstrates the infeasibility of all the tracks being faked. Especially when we factor in human nature, and that such footprints have been made and observed far longer than twenty years. Native Americans have seen them for thousands of years, and sightings by white men date back as far as 986 A.D. when Leif Ericsson and his men encountered man-like creatures they described as 'horribly ugly, hairy, swarthy and with great black eyes.'

"But if you believe they're all fake, here's what

must have happened: Somehow Ericsson and his Native American allies handed down the conspiracy to Spanish missionaries, French trappers and other American settlers, whose descendants established a highly secret international organization. This group has spent millions of dollars training agents to operate in the pitch dark and enhancing them physically so they can leap while carrying at least five hundred pounds on their backs. And after this huge investment, the agents are told to carry out their missions in remote areas of North American wilderness where there's no guarantee the fruits of their efforts will ever be noticed.

"Not only that, this clandestine organization has been steadily carrying this out year-round for at least four hundred years without ever getting caught, and without any of its members cracking under the strain of secrecy and confessing. In the United States, that would make it our best-kept national secret."

That got the biggest laughter yet. He felt like he had them now.

When everyone settled down he said: "That's not to say no tracks are faked. But fakes are easy to discern and were not included in the previous calculation. In any case, I trust your minds are still open. So let's move on."

Chapter 12

BREEEEP!

The goddamn phone again. Lansing's teeth grated at the sound. He thought about stopping the videotape, but he knew it wouldn't be the university.

Go away, he thought.

"The second-best evidence we have that the creatures exist is this."

The auditorium lights dimmed and a home movie began showing on the screen. The film stuttered at first and then showed in faded colors what appeared to be a large, black, ape-like creature walking away from the camera toward a stand of large trees. It walked like a person, on two legs.

As he had so many times, Lansing watched the creature make steady, rapid progress away from the camera, even when the person filming ran closer. At one point the creature looked back for a few steps, but didn't stop. It entered the woods and, after less than a minute, the film ended.

He knew this film also wouldn't be a surprise to the delegates, all of whom must have seen it at least once before. In the late '60s, when it was new, it received worldwide attention and since then had become standard fare on every "strange creatures" television show in the world.

The house lights brightened. "That was the sixteen-millimeter film amateur investigator Roger Patterson shot in October 1967 in Bluff Creek, California," he said, "and I'm sure you have your opinions about it. It has been called a hoax by everyone from zoologists and paleontologists at this very institution to Hollywood special-effects artists. But what the hoax proponents have in common is that none of them have performed a rigorous scientific analysis of the film. Now I'd like to briefly show you what such an analysis tells us."

One frame of the film came on the screen. Superimposed on the picture were red and yellow graphics that showed ruler-like measurements of the Sasquatch and of objects in the background and foreground.

"I won't take you through the entire analysis, but here are the important points." Indicating with his pointer, he began.

"At the right of the screen you can see measurements of the trees. We were able to measure the trees, of course, because they were still at the scene of the filming. From that and the relative distances involved, we were easily able to calculate the dimensions of the animal.

"Its walking height is approximately seventy-nine inches, or a bit over six and a half feet. Given the considerable slouch it has when walking, roughly five inches, its standing height is estimated at seven feet one inch, which allows for a one-inch depression in the ground.

"Looking at height alone, the creature could have

been a man in a monkey suit," he said, "but that's where the possibility ends.

"By various methods too detailed to go into here—but absolutely rigorous, I assure you—its weight is estimated at roughly six hundred pounds; which, naturally, would cause flat feet.

"The width at the shoulders is three feet eight inches. I don't have to point out that that shoulder width and the accompanying arm swing would be impossible for any man to fake, certainly with that degree of accuracy." He knew every scientist in the audience was intimately familiar with the skeletal anatomy and physique of *Homo sapiens sapiens* and its closest relatives, living and extinct.

"Theoretically, it is possible for a tall man weighing approximately two hundred and fifty pounds to have walked along that ground with another six hundred pounds, minimum, strapped to his back—the extra weight needed to overcome the snowshoe effect of the fake flat feet and still obtain the track depth found at the site. But," a calculated pause, "I submit to you that it's impossible that such a disproportionately large and strong man would remain undetected by the NBA or the NFL."

He heard chuckles and a few short laughs, but they quickly died out.

The film restarted from the middle, this time in slow motion.

"You will recognize that no human can walk that way," he said. "Or, I should say that no human of that height can walk that way. The deep knee flexion *could* be seen in a short human moving extremely quickly, but the film is plainly of a large bipedal animal walking at a comfortable pace, with no loss of balance and no unnecessary movements. And even without an extra six hundred pounds, no human could walk as comfortably, as *economically*, while maintaining a left foot-to-left foot stride of seven feet."

At that the audience murmured. "Yes, seven feet," he said. "You see that it becomes less and less likely that the film was a hoax."

He clicked the remote and suddenly the audience noise became louder. People in the first few rows sat forward as if to get a better view.

The frame on the screen was one where the animal glanced back at the camera. Impossible to miss were hair-covered human-looking breasts, sagging toward the bottom of the ribcage.

He knew that at least a few primatologists in the room had written off the Patterson film for the sole reason that the Sasquatch's breasts were hairy. The only other higher primates, including humans, had originated in the tropics so the breasts of the females were completely or partially bare. But an obvious reason existed for the difference.

"You'll also note the hairy breasts," he said, "which you would naturally expect to see in a primate adapted to living in a cold climate." Obvious, yet no other scientist had proposed this explanation.

"Also, I'm sure you noticed how the large lower jaw, extending beneath the level of the shoulders, requires the animal to turn from the torso. I don't have to point out that this is consistent with all the larger apes. We, of course, would merely turn our heads," he said for the benefit of the reporters he knew sat in the audience.

"So we're again at the point where charlatanism becomes much less likely than fact," he said. "Patterson and his partner, Robert Gimlin, didn't have access to large sums of money and knew nothing about primate anatomy. So if they faked the creature and the film, they would have to have gotten lucky about the turn from the torso, the unusually large buttocks, the saggital crest and other details, and also had the creativity to include flexible breasts—without, I might add, simultaneously enlarging the pelvis, as you would of course find in a human female.

"They would have had to find some way to realistically animate the long arms and hands, to mimic anatomically correct muscles tensing at the exact right moments beneath the skin, and to make anatomically correct tracks—each exhibiting different flexion—an inch deep in sand so hard that a horse with a man on its back made imprints less than half that depth."

He walked to the middle of the stage, a spotlight following. With the back of his hand he wiped sweat off his forehead.

"If the men faked it, they told no one at the time, died without admitting it, and did it so well that film experts from around the globe said it couldn't be duplicated. Obviously, that's highly unlikely.

"Even more unlikely is the possibility that someone played a joke on these men. Patterson and Gimlin were in the wilderness, had no known plan of travel and carried loaded high-powered rifles. Who would risk his life to play a joke on someone and never admit to it?"

He stopped walking. "It was impossible to fake all of this in 1967 and it's impossible now. I submit to you, then, that this is actual footage of a heretofore undiscovered primate, the only other bipedal primate besides ourselves."

The audience's murmuring resumed. It indicated interest, but he was a little unnerved by its tone. Instead of a higher-pitched, interested murmur, it was lower, skeptical.

Still, he knew bias about the film would be tough to overcome. That's why he put it in the middle. He would finish strong, with something everyone in the audience valued.

GOD damn it! Lansing thought. The phone had been ringing for what seemed like ten minutes. That SOB just would not give up.

He picked the remote off his chest, pointed it at the VCR

and pushed the Pause button. The video of his presentation stopped; the frame on the screen warped.

The arm holding the remote sagged to the floor.

He didn't want to stop watching, but that damn ringing felt like a drill boring into his skull.

He'd never watched the video before. Never even thought about it. But for some reason, today it was there, in his mind. He had to watch it. Didn't really want to, just had to.

So far it had given him conflicting emotions. He felt sorry for the young man on the screen, but he also enjoyed the presentation. It was better than he remembered.

Breeeep!

Maybe there actually was an emergency.

He pulled himself off the couch and padded over to the phone in his socked feet.

No emergency. Same number on the caller ID.

He dropped his hand to the receiver and thought about ripping the phone off the table and flinging it across the room. As he stood there, debating with himself, the tape started playing again.

"Bones," Lansing said over the buzz of the audience. "We have no bones for this animal. Yet if it's real, it has to have been around for at least as long as we have and therefore you'd expect some fossil evidence.

"Though you're aware that we lack such evidence for chimpanzees and gorillas, we do have it for a potential Sasquatch ancestor," he said. "I'm referring to these."

He clicked and a slide of four sets of lower jaw bones appeared onscreen. The jaws, all of which had most of their teeth, were mounted so they looked like inverted *U*s. The biggest was on the far left; next to it were two slightly smaller jaws, and a vastly smaller one was at the far right.

"You may recognize the first three as *Gigantopithecus blacki* fossil jaws found in Liucheng Cave in Liuzhou, China, near northern Vietnam. They and other fossil jaws and teeth found at the site have been dated at between five hundred thousand and one million years old.

"At the far right," he indicated with his pointer, "is a

human lower jaw. Note the significant size difference."
The human jaw was tiny, not even half the size of the
others. He knew it made for a powerful comparison.

"While some have advocated that *Gigantopithecus*
were knuckle-walkers, I believe the surprisingly wide
spread of the jaw rami and the reduced sectorial complex in the teeth indicate that the necks of these animals
were positioned forward—*between* the rami rather than
behind—signifying an upright posture." As he spoke,
Lansing used his hands to demonstrate the positions of
the neck and skull; first inclined forward, as in apes,
and then upright as found in humans and *Giganto*.

"The jaw spreads also make it impossible for *Giganto* to have had projecting canines, as you would see
in gorillas but not, obviously, in humans. And in fact,
the fossils of mature *Giganto*s don't have them. These
animals had teeth somewhere between ape and
human, more hominid than pongid. So, despite the
large jaws indicating a herbivorous diet, I propose
that the creature was an omnivore."

That was a risky conclusion. Not because the evidence for an omnivorous diet was tenuous, but because
he knew the audience would find the implication—another bipedal, omnivorous ape—disturbing.

If he'd been describing similarities to any other
species but *Homo sapiens sapiens* it would have been
different. But the thought that a nonhuman-ancestor
bipedal ape could ever have lived—let alone was living
now—provoked discomfort in everyone. And like all
people, scientists would find a set of intellectual reasons to explain their emotional discomfort that would
boil down to this: The Sasquatch couldn't exist and
therefore the evidence was ridiculous.

Wanting a result and looking for the evidence to
support it was antiscience. But so powerful was the
feeling of human uniqueness that it fooled even scientists, people trained to ignore it.

Lansing knew this but persevered, confident he was
appealing to the audience's strong scientific curiosity.

"Using the jaw bones, tooth-to-jaw ratios for other primates, an assumed ape-level cognitive capacity, and what we know about primate anatomy, we can make a fairly detailed anatomical reconstruction of the animal's skull. The result you can see in this next slide."

On the screen appeared a mount in near-profile of what looked like a real skull, light brown in color. As with the known great apes, the skull slanted up and back from the upper jaw at a much softer angle than a human's. But the skull was more massive than any known ape's. The lower jaw was much larger than a human's, and atop the skull a ridge of bone ran down the middle, like the crest on a knight's helmet.

He was proud of the skull reconstruction and was surprised no one had attempted it before. Then again, other scientists acted like all that existed were *Giganto* teeth, without the attached jaws—perhaps because they saw *Giganto* as an evolutionary, and professional, dead end.

"As you know, it's possible to estimate the size of an animal using a head-to-body ratio," he said, pacing. "Here, even with a conservative ratio of one to six-point-five, the calculation returns a ten-foot-tall, eight-hundred-pound animal."

He stopped stage right and faced the audience. "I used an adult male *Giganto*'s jaw for the skull reconstruction, so those dimensions presumably apply to a full-grown male. Based then on the smaller sizes of female primates as well as the smaller size of the adult female *Giganto* jaw, a female of the species equates to an animal that is a reasonably good match for the size of the creature that was in the Patterson film—which, at the least, made tracks very similar to the ones collected all over the Pacific Northwest."

That was a good way to end. His audience placed high value on bones, and the *Giganto* jawbones were indisputable. They were from extremely large primates, alive half a million to one million years ago, and contained teeth that were intermediate between ape and human but leaning to the human side. How could they ignore that?

When pressed by the media, a few scientists had speculated that if the Sasquatch were real, it could be descended from something else.

So he said: "Some feel these undiscovered primates could be remnant *Australopithecus* or Neanderthals. For reasons I can't go into here but which I'd be happy to explain later, I believe these hypotheses are incorrect, at least as applied to the North American evidence. For the Sasquatch, *Giganto* appears to be the prime candidate."

Of course, the evidence he'd presented left open another logical hypothesis for the Sasquatch's origin. It was thrilling to think about what it might mean for his field and for the human race, but he'd decided not to mention it in this presentation. It would be too much.

He walked to the edge of the stage and flashed a big smile.

"So, ladies and gentlemen of the scientific jury, that's where I'll end. It's not as specific nor as thorough as you and I would have preferred, but I trust you'll agree that the physical evidence I've presented is intriguing. After all, there's more than enough to get one of these animals convicted of a crime in any court in the United States.

"But I'm not telling you to accept that these creatures are real. I'm merely suggesting that what's known as the North American Sasquatch, or bigfoot, is worthy of study—at least until we can prove conclusively that it does *not* exist.

"However, if the opposite occurred, I'm sure you'll agree that it would be the greatest scientific discovery of our time. Thank you."

HOLY shit, Vaughn thought. He wanted to tell somebody. For a second he glanced around, as if he would jump up from the cubicle, pull someone over, point to the screen and say, "Look! Look at this!"

But he didn't. Earphones on, he'd watched the video on the monitor in the far corner of the Skookum County Library's video room, away from the window and from everyone else because he didn't want people to see what he was researching. He still didn't want anyone to see. But it was amazing.

This Lansing guy was incredible. He knew all that ten years ago—what did he know now? Why wasn't anyone paying attention to him?

The library had a book by Lansing that covered the same information, and the professor was quoted as a Sasquatch expert in every news article that treated the subject seriously.

He'd found other bigfoot books at the library, but most were uninteresting, and the Internet was full of all kinds of stuff. He had spent the rest of the morning and afternoon reading, fascinated by the sheer volume of information, and looking for anything that might give him some insight into the creatures. Something that might save his skin.

From reading about what other people saw, heard and smelled, and how they described their confusion, shock and then terror, he knew they had seen Sasquatches too. But while interesting, the information was largely useless to him. Even the more-detailed and trustworthy observations of hunters and law-enforcement officers only reinforced what he already knew: the animals were reclusive, big, strong, and fast.

He pushed Rewind on the VCR, and checked his watch. Almost five. He'd given the animal enough time.

Judging by how fast it moved, it could have run a few miles before collapsing, even if fatally wounded. So unless his shot had done far more damage than he thought, he figured he would be spending the night out there.

A feather of fear whispered across the back of his neck, but he shook it off. He'd camped in those woods hundreds of times without a problem.

He popped out the tape and stood. Sunset wasn't until 8:15, but in the woods darkness would come earlier. Home to pack and leave Katie a note. Then he'd be back out there.

Chapter 13

"*WHY?*" Katie said. Pools glimmered in the bottoms of her eyes. "You don't have to do this."

She said the sheriff had called her and told her to come home. Didn't say why, just that Vaughn needed to talk to her and that it was important.

Knowing his wife, Vaughn figured she probably got upset as soon as she heard the sheriff's voice on the phone. She had supersensitive radar for any potentially bad news—like a bloodhound, one sniff opened up the whole world to her.

So now, when he'd explained what the sheriff said about the potential consequences of finding the Sasquatch, she immediately forgot about the odds of anything happening. Instead she jumped right to the worst possible outcome, viewed it in terms of their future and became upset.

He knew she would be that way. The only thing he could do was explain things over and over until, hopefully, logic soothed her fears. Sometimes that worked, sometimes it didn't.

"Yes, I do have to do this," he said. "I explained why already." He softened his voice. "I know you know what I'm saying here, honey."

Her hands, little fists, pressed into her lap. "Yes, Francis. I know. I know that your conscience might make us move again."

"My *conscience?*" Then he forced himself to calm down. He didn't want a fight. He just wanted her to realize that she was overreacting. "This isn't only about my conscience, like it's some academic point. You're trying to make it seem less than it is. It's about being a decent human being. A good, responsible human being. I thought that's something you liked about me. Loved, even."

The look in her eyes changed, and he suddenly saw that her face had become like a cedar tribal mask, gouged deep and drawn at sharp angles to represent anger, grief, and something else he couldn't put a finger on, but equally as bad. He hadn't seen her this way in a long time. And for a moment, he felt her pain like a bruise deep in his chest.

She said: "I do like that about you. But you're not being a good, responsible human being right now."

"Really."

"Our *future,* Francis. You're jeopardizing our future." Her hands gripped her elbows and hugged them to her as if she was becoming cold. Red blotches formed on her neck.

He grabbed the top of his forehead and squeezed. "Shit, honey. I *told* you. All that stuff the sheriff said, what you're worried about, I just can't see it happening. It's so remote it's pretty much impossible."

He sighed. "Dammit, Katie, *why* are you getting so upset about things that will never happen? We'll be fine. We'll have a family."

Usually talk of children raised her spirits, but now she wasn't even looking at him. "Are you listening to what I'm saying?"

She met his eyes. He said, "Why can't you just support me and trust me?"

Her eyes darkened. Red streaks shot down her cheeks, like tears running beneath the skin.

She said: "In case you don't remember, those things *have*

happened before and I don't want them to happen again." Her voice trembled. "And as far as *supporting* you and *trusting* you, I can't believe you'd say that. I really can't believe it. Why the fuck do you think I'm so upset?"

Her reference to the past poked a hole through his anger. She had stuck with him the whole way, giving up her life in New Jersey and moving out here where they knew no one, where he loved the forest and she thought it spooky, where she quietly tolerated the lack of sunshine and family and friends just so he could be happy again.

But he was right then, and he was right now. Somewhere, deep down, she knew it.

Suddenly he realized she'd used the F-word. She hated that word. Never said it unless she was really upset.

He took a deep breath: "I can't express how much you standing by me in all that means to me. I really do appreciate it, honey. I hope you know that." He put a hand on her thigh. "You knew what was right then."

She pulled her leg away. "That involved a *person* being an unbelievable shit to other people. This time it's about an *animal*, a big, dangerous one that probably just wants to be left alone."

"It's also different because the consequences in Jersey were definite and unavoidable," he said. "Here they aren't. Not even close."

He stared into her eyes, hoping to see understanding. Hoping she would about-face, say what really worried her was his safety, and throw her arms around his neck and cry into his shoulder.

On her cheeks, the streaks merged into little blood-red lakes. She said: "This time it's different because you're actually looking for trouble."

"Looking?" He threw his hands out to the sides. "Are you nuts? That is absolute bullshit. I'm looking for trouble, looking for something that will make us move again and trash our lives? Is that it? Well I resent that, big time. I'm not *looking* for anything, dammit! I'm just doing what's right. You want me to leave that animal out there to suffer?"

"This isn't about the fucking animal!"

"You just—"

"I don't care what I said. This is about *us*. I . . ." She faltered, but her eyes held his. She rubbed her cheek with a knuckle. "I don't want to start over again, Francis. I won't. We've spent eight years building a life here and I will *not* move again . . . start over again. You hear me?"

"Isn't it important for me to do what's right?"

She didn't respond.

"Well?"

"I take it back," she said, her voice suddenly quiet. "It's not about us. It's about you."

"No it isn't."

"You better be sure about that, Francis. You better be sure you're doing what's right for us, not just you, or . . ."

"Or what?"

"Or I'll do the right thing for me." Her mouth curled into the beginnings of a sob, and she jumped up from the couch and ran into the den.

He watched her go. The television blared on and the volume rose. Here and there through the din he heard crying noises.

Damn. He leaned back on the couch.

He expected her to get upset, but not this upset. And though he was angry, frustrated at her unwillingness to be reached, her crying made him feel awful. The sound pulled at him; he wanted to walk into the den and hug her.

But he knew she was too far gone for that right now.

And damn it, he had a right to be angry. She reacted as if she believed all the sheriff's ifs were certainties, no matter what he said. Plus she was being selfish, treating the sheriff's warning about his job as if it affected only her. *Threatening to leave me? Unbelievable.* She could have been helpful, supportive. But she wasn't.

Same thing went for the sheriff. The Old Man and Katie had both overreacted. It was like this bigfoot thing was making everybody crazy.

He looked up at the ceiling and pictured the woods, the stalk, and then walking up to the bodies. Ricks—Vaughn had forgotten about him. He wondered what the Old Man would do about that.

Then he figured he already knew. He snorted. Crazy, all right. *Get in, track it and get out,* he told himself. That's all it would take. Then he would apologize to the sheriff, the Old Man would forgive him and Katie would see that all of her negative thinking had been a waste of energy.

All he had to do was get through the next twenty-four hours. Then everything would be okay.

Chapter 14

VAUGHN knew he was driving too fast, but he was angry. Angry that he had to waste time picking up this Mackey guy, and angry at the sheriff for calling Carolina Pacific.

He rolled down his window to help clear the fogged windshield, and thought: *Jesus. What the hell is that?*

He didn't have Joe Kelly's shop in sight yet, but he could hear the immense booms of . . . what? Instead of the typical crack of a rifle, it sounded like a small cannon. He was glad Mackey had enough sense to sight-in the weapon, but what he heard concerned him. If it was a rifle, and he assumed it was, it had to be enormous.

It also sounded like this Mackey guy was shooting a heck of a lot more rounds than he needed to sight-in whatever it was. He hoped that meant Mackey was prudent. The alternative was that the guy was a yahoo, the kind who got turned on by massive firepower.

Vaughn came around a bend in the road. Ahead, in the cleared field on his right, a Sikorsky Skycrane crouched on the frozen grass like a huge dragonfly. Used for hauling logs out of remote areas, the Skycrane was one of several heli-copters of different types that Carolina Pacific rotated through Joe's shop.

As he drove closer it became obvious that the Skycrane had seen better days. Black smears marred the white finish and the green CP logos on the doors and belly. One of the tires was nearly flat, giving the machine a list, and the tips of the thick blades sagged.

Even so, the huge helicopter had the athletic look of a real insect, like it could clatter off at any moment.

The cleared field where it rested was about half a mile square. Joe never filled it with helicopters so he'd set up a makeshift firing range at the far end, by the woods. Vaughn and the other deputies used it occasionally.

Vaughn passed Joe's shop, a cinder-block building roofed with sheets of rusting tin, and turned his Toyota Tundra pickup onto the road that ran by it. The truck bucked across the pitted gravel surface; he heard his gear banging around in the bed, but he didn't slow down.

At the end of the road a shiny red Jeep Grand Cherokee sat on the pale, flat grass like a giant ladybug waiting for spring. He parked next to it and jumped out. The pungent smell of gunpowder reached his nostrils.

Boom, boom!

Instinctively he clapped his hands over his ears.

Chris Mackey leaned over Joe's homemade wooden shoot-ing bench. Remington in bright orange stitching glared at Vaughn from above the brim of Mackey's camouflaged cap, turned backward on a round head. The same pattern of cam-ouflage covered the rest of his body so that he looked like a moss- and oak leaf-covered boulder.

Two more shots rang out; Mackey jerked with them. Downrange a paper target twitched against an earth backstop.

"Hey!" Vaughn yelled, his hands still over his ears.

Mackey's head jerked around, his eyes wide. Then he smiled. He turned back, fiddled with the weapon and rested it on a sandbag. He popped the plugs from his ears and walked over with his hand out. "You must be Frank," he said. "Chris Mackey."

"Good to meet you."

Mackey's firm grip reassured Vaughn, but the rest troubled him.

Like his hands, Mackey's face and neck were a deep brown. Pink patches of sunburn glowed on his cheeks and nose. The guy obviously spent a lot of time outdoors, but doing what? The accent told Vaughn that Mackey had to be from Carolina Pacific's headquarters in North Carolina. The fishing was supposed to be great there. Maybe that's how Mackey got his tan. Only problem was, plenty of fishermen with healthy-looking tans also had beer bellies and smoked. And though Vaughn didn't smell the stink of cigarettes, Mackey was pudgy. About five-seven, one-seventy. No creases on his face even though he looked to be in his mid-fifties.

Not fat, but overweight—and that was the problem.

Hiking in the Pacific Northwest was strictly up and down. No flat land to speak of. So unless Mackey was in better shape than he looked, he could be a hindrance.

Despite this concern, Vaughn smiled. "Hope you weren't waiting long."

"Just got here myself," Mackey said. "Stopped in town for a bear license."

Mackey's eyes twinkled, but something made Vaughn think he was serious. "That so?"

"Yeah. Picked up a few recipes, too."

"For bear?"

"Spotted owl," Mackey said. "Pretty good eating."

Vaughn smiled at the joke about eating endangered species. Loggers told it all the time. "Not as good as bald eagle," he said.

Mackey laughed and hit Vaughn on the shoulder. "You're all right, ol' boy."

Vaughn glanced at the sky. It had remained the same shade of grey all day, but he knew the sun was still traveling its course. In a few hours the grey would begin to darken. He said: "You ready to get going?"

"Absolutely." Mackey took a few steps back to the bench. "What you shooting there?"

"ATF agents. Killed 'em, too, I bet." Mackey wasn't smiling now. He picked up black Zeiss binoculars and looked downrange.

"Yep," Mackey said, the binoculars at his face. "Dead. Take a look."

Vaughn took the binoculars, held them up to his eyes and thought about Mackey's comment.

The ATF- and FBI-led Ruby Ridge and Waco screwups under former President Clinton, and the push for gun-control laws and other things smacking of federal overcontrol, had given many people in Skookum County and other rural areas a serious case of Big Brotheritis. They feared what they saw as an out-of-control federal government, and felt they had nothing in common with the urban people running it. Chris Mackey appeared to be one of those types.

Vaughn understood their point of view. It seemed as if everyone these days knew better than you did about what was good for you. And when the city people made the laws, rural folk naturally found some of the laws stupid and offensive, and mistrusted the people making them.

He felt some of that mistrust, but inflammatory talk always made him nervous.

And even though his experience in New Jersey meant he now only half bought that law-enforcement "brotherhood" crap, joking about killing officers of any law-enforcement agency didn't strike him as too funny.

He focused downrange. Through the binoculars he saw that Mackey had pinned up a new target. A large orange-and-white bullseye sat in the center and four smaller ones floated at the corners. A single black hole punctured the center of each bullseye—and Mackey had been firing in groups of two.

Phenomenal shooting.

"Good shooting," Vaughn said. He handed the binoculars back to Mackey. "But what I meant was, what's that Howitzer you have there?"

Mackey cradled the rifle and hefted it off the sandbag. Vaughn immediately saw that it was expensive. And big.

The dark walnut of the stock set off the polished scroll-work and gold inlays on the receiver, and the barrel looked as big as industrial pipe.

"Wow," Vaughn said.

"It's a .375 H&H Mag," Mackey said. He lifted it up and checked the action. "Not just the caliber, a real Holland and Holland. Got it for black bear back home and the occasional grizz out west. Had the barrel chopped to twenty inches and a muzzle brake put on. Shoots 300-grain Nosler Partitions at twenty-five hundred f-p-s. Scope's a one-point-five by four Leupold. Good for close-up on big animals. Punch through anything. Here," he said.

Vaughn took the rifle. His left arm dipped; he corrected it. "Heavy."

"Damn right."

Vaughn pulled the stock up and nestled it under his cheekbone. The wood felt cold on his skin and he caught a whiff of polish: it even smelled expensive. He'd read about these guns in African safari books, but never figured he would get this close to one. It was a legendary rifle, one of the finest pieces of craftsmanship money—lots of money—could buy. A small cannon, with cartridges to match: big as fingers and shaped like ballistic missiles. Enough power to drop a charging grizzly. Maybe even a Sasquatch.

"Seems a little much for black bear," he said, looking down the scope at the target. Heavy, but the rifle balanced well.

"They get over eight hundred pounds back home," Mackey said.

"You're kidding."

"They're like starlings, all over the place. Damn nuisance. Have to carry this with me."

Vaughn looked over. Mackey waved a large revolver. A worn leather holster lay on the bench seat.

"Forty-four," Vaughn said.

"Yep. Ruger Super Blackhawk, .44 Mag, seven-point-five inches. Down east you shoot a deer and a bear'll run to the shot. Gets pretty hairy."

"You're allowed to carry a handgun during rifle season?"

Mackey's smile widened. "Who said that?" He shoved the revolver back into the belt holster.

Vaughn took a last look through the scope, then returned the rifle to Mackey. "Nice," he said.

Mackey popped open a pine-green hard-plastic case

shaped vaguely like a rifle. It had a molded-in carrying handle and the surface was pebbled, like a basketball's. He placed the .375 H&H Mag inside, on some kind of high-tech foam padding. His hands pressed the lid closed and the case locked with a muffled click.

"I need to stop at the office to pick up a sat-phone," Vaughn said. "You can follow me and leave your rental in the parking lot."

"Sounds good to me."

Vaughn watched Mackey walk toward the Grand Cherokee and thought: a government-mistrusting marksman in full camouflage carrying two large firearms? It looked like Carolina Pacific was taking no chances.

On the face of it, that seemed to be prudent. Maybe even good. But a feeling of unease squirmed in the back of his brain.

Chapter 15

VAUGHN stepped out of the pickup's cab and walked quickly toward the main entrance. All he had to do was run in and grab a portable satellite phone—and avoid the Old Man.

Mackey pulled into the next parking space and cut the motor.

"Be out in a sec," Vaughn said loudly.

Mackey held up a hand, then busied himself with something in the front seat.

Vaughn cleared the stairs in one leap. Before him a chrome strip streaked with rust ran across the top of two glass doors. Gold lettering on the glass read:

SKOOKUM COUNTY SHERIFF'S OFFICE

George Hendricks, Sheriff

Your Safety Is Our Business

Every time he read the words it crossed his mind that the Old Man would be retiring soon, and someone else's name would be on the door.

He pulled open the door.

"Hey Frank." As usual, Deputy Billy Treadle wore the grin that punctuated everything he said. It seemed to reach right up to his ears.

"Hey Billy. The Old Man around?"

"Somewhere." Billy reached for the intercom. As the youngest deputy, he usually got stuck with phone duty. "Want me to find him for you?"

"That's okay. Just need to grab a sat-phone and then I'm gone."

Vaughn bumped through the swinging, hip-level wooden divider that separated the waiting area from the office and jogged back to what the Old Man liked to call the "possibles room."

An unlabeled wooden door opened to a steel hatch with a keypad on it. Vaughn punched in the five-digit code, the numbers beeping under his finger, and the door clicked. He pushed it open; odors of grease, rubber and hot plastic wafted out in a puff of warm air.

He stepped through the opening. To his left glowed an irregular line of green and red LEDs. He reached over and grabbed a phone, then backed out of the room and pulled the metal door shut. A few yanks of the handle to make sure it was locked, and he backed into the hallway.

The black phone warmed his palm. He pushed the On button, raised the phone to his ear and heard two beeps, a pause and then a dial tone. Satisfied, he folded the antenna down, turned the phone off, and shoved it into his parka pocket.

On his way back to the lobby he kept an eye out for the sheriff.

Deputy Tricia Burlock walked up to him. "Someone's here for you."

"Short guy, pudgy, tan?"

She looked at him strangely. "Pretty much the opposite of that."

He didn't know who it could be, but he had to get rid of whoever it was, and fast.

A few more strides and he arrived back at the waiting area. Framed in the grey daylight seeping through the glass doors stood a tall, lanky man. A little taller than Vaughn, so about six-three; a little older too, late thirties. Jacket in hand, the man looked expectantly, nervously, at Vaughn, his eyes intense, a little wired.

Vaughn recognized him immediately.

"Deputy Vaughn?"

"Yes."

"Art Lansing."

VAUGHN couldn't believe it.

After a few moments he realized no one had said anything more. He glanced over at the desk. Billy still grinned, but looked plainly curious. Vaughn's mind scrambled to figure out a way to get rid of the professor. Then he heard the sheriff's voice in the back of the office.

Vaughn said: "Dr. Lansing, let's go outside."

He raised his arms to herd Lansing out the door, and followed him down the steps to the sidewalk.

When the door closed, Lansing said: "You know who I am?"

"I watched your video today. Your speech." Vaughn thought Lansing's eyes sparked for a moment, but whatever he saw was gone before he could be sure. "What are you doing here?"

Lansing shoved his pale hands into his jacket pockets. "Deputy Vaughn, I won't waste your time. I realize you weren't expecting me and you probably don't want to take anyone with you, but I won't be a burden. I know how to take care of myself in the woods. As you might imagine I've been out in them, often by myself, many times. I'm also an expert at Sasquatch track analysis, which may be helpful from a safety standpoint."

Vaughn thought about playing dumb, but decided it would be a waste of time. "Who told you?"

"I'm sorry but I can't say."

"Well, I'm sorry but you can't go," Vaughn said, staring straight into Lansing's eyes.

Lansing didn't flinch. He said, "I'll find some other way of getting there. I'll follow you or get directions from someone inside." He gestured at the building with his head.

"I could have you detained."

A slight frown, but Lansing didn't look away. Then he shrugged. "I have no doubt you could, but that would be in no one's best interest."

"How's that?"

"More people would know why I'm here, for one thing. And you'd be wasting more time."

Lansing didn't elaborate. Vaughn couldn't tell whether the professor meant more people in the sheriff's office or persons unknown whom he might call. But it didn't matter. Lansing had correctly deduced that the Sasquatch wounding had to be kept secret, and that time was critical.

Then he wondered whether he was giving Lansing too much credit. All of that might be obvious.

Regardless, the professor was right. So he had two choices.

If he left him here, Lansing would run around the woods on his own and be a mental distraction and potential safety hazard to him and Mackey. And if Lansing found something on his own he might go and get someone: some other expert, the press. Who knew what might happen then.

Or Vaughn could have Lansing where he could see him, control him, and thus be able to focus on the tracking job. If they happened to find the Sasquatch dead or had to shoot it, he would cross that bridge then.

Two shitty options. What was the overriding factor?

Vaughn peered at the sky—still the color of a dirty shower curtain, but he knew that somewhere up there the sun was sinking.

He glanced at his pickup and saw Mackey waiting by the tailgate, his gear piled at his feet. To Lansing he said, "Grab your gear. Leave your car here."

In the first parking space sat a blue Subaru Outback station wagon he didn't recognize. He pointed at it. "That yours?"

"Yes," Lansing said.

Vaughn walked over and looked in the rear windows. The back seat was folded down. Inside rested a few cardboard boxes stuffed with papers, and one backpack.

"Not much gear."

"I'm used to leaving on short notice," Lansing said.

Vaughn grunted. "What's in the pack?"

"Sleeping bag, one-man tent, camera, track-casting materials, snacks, water, that kind of thing. A few emergency items: space blanket, mirror, water purifier."

Lansing popped the wagon's hatch.

"No gun?" Vaughn said.

"No."

Vaughn tried to see the professor's face, but the rising hatch obscured it.

Lansing easily hefted his pack out of the Outback. Vaughn walked to his pickup, but after a few steps realized Lansing wasn't following. He turned around and saw the professor staring at his car.

Vaughn said, "Can't get much safer than right here."

Lansing seemed to come out of it then. He picked up his pack and said, "I think I'll lock it up anyway. We might be gone for a while."

Vaughn said: "Hopefully not."

Chapter 16

AS they drove east out of town on the two-lane highway, Vaughn felt better. His annoyance at Lansing's surprise appearance gradually gave way to anticipation and focus. *Get out there, track it, come back,* he kept saying to himself. That's all he had to do.

Quickly the town of Glenwood fell away, and only power lines and dense second-growth forest lined the road.

A little over a mile out they approached a combination of two signs that signaled a change in road ownership. The top one, mostly green, was a state sign, immediately recognizable by the black lettering inside the white profile of George Washington. It read, END 503 SPUR. Underneath a brown sign read, BEGIN 90, NATIONAL FOREST.

About fifty yards farther down the road squatted another brown sign, a Disney-like trapezoid with rounded corners and fifties lettering that proclaimed: ENTERING GIFFORD PINCHOT NATIONAL FOREST. Just past this a big wooden Smokey the Bear with jeans, hat, and shovel stood next to the words FIRE

DANGER LOW TODAY! PREVENT FOREST FIRES. Excluding Smokey, everything was brown except the Low sign, which, inserted for the day, was green.

He'd seen the signs a million times and usually never paid attention to them, except for a passing glance at the fire danger rating. But now he noticed them all in detail, as if the forest was new to him.

Lansing and Mackey traded information, explaining what they did for a living.

Mackey was a former wildlife biologist and game warden who had become a natural resource consultant. He didn't disguise that he was sent by Carolina Pacific, but made it clear that he wasn't an employee.

Lansing asked no questions of Mackey, and didn't seem surprised that a timber company would send someone out to check on a Sasquatch sighting.

Sasquatch *shooting,* Vaughn reminded himself.

Lansing omitted any mention of how he got there and Mackey didn't ask. Nor did Vaughn. Not the right time.

The professor began to explain his research into the Sasquatch, but stopped when Vaughn slowed the pickup. Vaughn turned off the two-lane highway onto a logging road marked by two small plastic signs nailed to a pressure-treated four-by-four. One read simply, 43, the Forest Service road number. The other sign was slightly larger. Green letters on a white background proclaimed, CAROLINA PACIFIC TIMBER SALE—NO TRESPASSING. Beneath the words sat a prominent letter *A,* and under that a logo: a *C* and *P* stylized to form a Christmas tree-shaped triangle, with the *P*'s stem extending down as the trunk.

Until this morning Vaughn hadn't ever been in area A, but now it seemed a lot more familiar to him.

"Feels just like home," Mackey said.

"How so?"

"Back where I'm from, if you're not hunting on farmland or state land you're hunting on CP land. Carolina Pacific is the largest landowner in North Carolina and one of the biggest in the entire United States."

"Not for long," Lansing said.

"I don't know," Mackey said. "Lot of folks opposed to that German buyout."

To Vaughn it sounded like Mackey was one of them.

He powered down the windows. Air washed over them, cold and damp, like the breath of a stone giant.

"We do that back home, too," Mackey said to Lansing. "Old hunter's trick. If you wait 'til you get where you're going to feel the cold, it shocks your body and makes your brain focus on the cold instead of the hunt."

"I see," Lansing said.

For a while no one spoke. The silence was interrupted only by the humming vibrations from washboard patches of road and the splashes of snow tires plowing through puddles.

"How far in?" Mackey said.

"Few miles. About twenty-five, thirty minutes," said Vaughn.

Their words floated out the windows and were lost in the perpetual gloom of the old-growth forest.

Again it was silent. From habit Vaughn scanned the dark woods for wildlife, particularly the horizontal forms of deer. As his eyes adjusted to the darkness they swept around the un-evenly spaced, immense trunks, between the mossy shells of rotting logs, and above the green carpet of sword ferns.

Most of the trees were Douglas fir. Their furrowed brown bark looked almost blue in the eerie grey-green light that seemed to come from within the forest rather than from above. Here and there among the fir, thriving in the perennial shade, stood western hemlock, a few of which also were gigantic.

Interspersed between the big trees were smaller ones he recognized as young Douglas fir, straining to propel themselves past the shade and fog to the sun. Scraggly and pale, they looked like lost, starving men.

Suddenly he realized he was looking too high for deer.

What the hell's a matter with you?

It was ridiculous to think that giant apes would be peeking out from behind every tree. But dammit he was having trouble shaking that feeling.

Mackey said, "Supposed to snow today?"

Vaughn opened his mouth to answer, but Lansing beat him to it. "That's the way it looks most of the time, because of the wind. The prevailing winds are from the west, the Pacific," he said. "Moisture-laden air blows in and hits the Cascades, which force it to rise. As it rises it cools, and the moisture falls as rain or snow, over twelve feet a year in some places."

"Just shy of that here," Vaughn said. "Annual precip's about a hundred and twenty inches."

He told Mackey that in some places it had snowed a tremendous amount this winter, sixteen feet on the south slope of Mount Saint Helens. But at this elevation, around five hundred feet, far less had accumulated. All traces of it had been melted and washed away by a belated, brief spring that had been booted out by the current cold snap.

"This weather system has been hanging around for three weeks," he said.

Mackey said, "That what delayed the opening of your bear season?"

"Yeah," Vaughn said. "It opened today. It was supposed to open in mid-April, like Oregon's, but the biologists said the extended cold might have caused some of the animals to hibernate longer than usual."

Mackey grunted. "I'm sure they felt like they knew best."

As the truck moved deeper into the forest, Vaughn realized he was seeing less of it. The fog thickened, giving everything but the ferns a blue-grey cast. Overhead it bridged the trees and sagged from one side of the damp gravel road to the other like grey nets heavy with fish.

Mackey looked up.

Lansing stuck a long finger into the air. "That fog is why these trees are so large," he said. "It's a year-round sunscreen. The weather is more consistent, there isn't as much evaporation and the trees thrive. Douglas firs like these can get over two hundred feet tall."

"Trees that big could hide a whole lot of things," Mackey said.

Vaughn glanced over. "Yeah. Lot of planes lost out here. Close to a hundred have never been recovered."

Conversation stopped again. Soon they passed an unmarked dirt road on the right, a parked Cat with its hydraulic arm and bucket bent around like a scorpion's tail, and then another unmarked road on the left. Vaughn noticed that neither side road had fresh tire tracks.

A few minutes later Vaughn turned right onto a smaller logging road. The mud, softer here, showed tire tracks from two vehicles. One was Boone's truck and Vaughn figured the other was from the Old Man coming out to get Ricks' body.

He knew the sheriff's report would list Ricks' death as some sort of accident. Ricks had no relatives and few friends in the county so no one would be asking questions, and the body would be quickly cremated. Although Vaughn understood the complications of the truth in this case, he didn't like the thought of an intentional lie.

The road cut through a valley and along a good-sized meltwater stream running cold and fast. "Not too far now," Vaughn said.

Lansing said, "Deputy Vaughn, I assume Chris has heard the story of what happened, but I wonder if you'd consent to tell me. I'd like to know before we get there. It'll help with the investigation."

"What have you heard?" Vaughn said.

"Only that a Sasquatch was wounded."

Vaughn hesitated for a moment, and then, finding no good reason why he shouldn't tell Lansing, recounted the events of that morning. At the part about discovering the bodies, one of Lansing's eyebrows raised but the professor said nothing.

When Vaughn finished, Lansing asked if he could be more detailed about the creature's description. "Did it have fingernails?"

Vaughn tried to hold the running animal in his mind. "It had hands. Real hands, not feet-hands like apes. It wasn't walking on its knuckles or anything."

"Did you see a penis or breasts?"

"No. I only saw it for a few seconds and it was running away from me."

Lansing stared out the window and said nothing more.

A fork in the road came into view, and Vaughn saw the mashed shoulder vegetation where they had parked this morning. He drove on.

When he got to the fork he slowed and pointed down the left road. "My friends went that way," he said. "It dead-ends about a mile down, but halfway between here and there is a road on the left. They were going to hunt over some jack fir that's bordered by another road at the bottom. That bottom road winds around and leads back up here"—he pointed down the right road—"that way. It comes up around a ridge that looks across to a clear-cut about four hundred yards out. That's where I was headed 'til I saw Ricks' truck." He glanced at Mackey. "Out here poachers sometimes shoot their way out of getting caught, so I went and got the other guys before tracking Ricks."

"Good thing you did, ol' boy," Mackey said.

Vaughn depressed the accelerator and started down the right fork. "I hunted up this road and—"

He stomped on the brakes; everyone lurched forward.

A log that had to be at least eight feet long and more than a foot in diameter stretched across the road, blocking the truck. Pieces of moss and shards of black, half-rotten bark lay scattered around.

For a moment Vaughn was confused. Were they on the wrong road? But he knew they weren't.

He got out, walked to the front of the truck and looked at the ground.

Mackey came up and said, "I was going to say we'd get in trouble for blocking a road back home, but I'm guessing you didn't do it."

Vaughn didn't see any boot prints, and besides, there was no way the sheriff could have moved that log on his own. "It must have fallen," he said. "Or maybe a bear pushed it over."

"Those'd be my guesses."

They walked to the side of the road and right away Vaughn felt uneasy. He didn't see what he expected. No upturned earth, no rotten stump. So it wasn't a rotten snag that fell, nor was it pushed over by a foraging bear.

The log had to come from somewhere else, but there were no drag marks—which meant it must have been carried.

No bear could do that. Nor could a man.

About twenty feet into the woods, Lansing bent over something.

"What you got there, Art?" Mackey said.

Lansing stood up and Vaughn immediately saw what it was. A Sasquatch track. A deep one. And beyond it, an eight-foot-long strip of reddish-brown earth.

Goose bumps prickled up his arms. "You're going to say the Sasquatch put that log there."

"Not exactly," Lansing said. "It threw it there."

"From here."

"Yes." Lansing smiled.

"That log's about eight feet long and has to weigh," Vaughn looked back at the road, "at least six hundred pounds."

"Yes," Lansing said, still smiling. "Amazing, isn't it?"

Mackey stared at the track. "Art," he said, "if you had to kill one of these things—if you had one shot—where would you put it?"

"The head."

"More specific."

"An eye. The skull is extremely thick."

Vaughn said: "Why are you asking?"

"You never know, ol' boy," Mackey said.

Vaughn walked back to the truck. "Let's move that log. If anyone from CP drives by and sees it in the road, he'll stop and take a look."

Thirty minutes of vein-popping effort and a push from the truck were needed to roll the log onto the road's shoulder. Vaughn was still sweating when he parked the pickup, right where Geek had backed into the woods.

Lansing hopped out, walked to the rear of the truck and opened the hatch. Vaughn got there as Lansing pulled a small camera, a plastic bottle filled with water and a handful of large Ziploc bags, some of which contained white powder from his pack.

"I'm going to get started on a few casts," he said. "How far in are the bodies?"

"It's only the deer now," Vaughn said. "Follow the tire tracks and then go another twenty yards or so in the same direction."

Lansing turned and walked into the woods.

Vaughn watched him for a second, then pulled his worn leather rifle case from the back of the truck and zipped it open.

"Pre-'64 Model 70," Mackey said.

"Yeah," Vaughn said. "Got a .357 Mag too." He patted the shoulder holster under his camouflaged parka.

"Ought to be enough for anything we come across."

Mackey laid his plastic rifle case across the tailgate, opened it and lifted out the .375.

Vaughn said: "Hope you don't mind me asking, but what's something like that cost?"

"Got it for a song."

"A song?"

"I'm a pretty good singer," Mackey said.

Vaughn snorted—and then his ears perked up. The police radio in the cab. "Excuse me a sec," he said.

Billy Treadle's voice crackled through the radio. "Frank, come in, Frank. You there?"

Vaughn grabbed the mike. "Vaughn here. You looking for me, Billy?"

"Yeah. Someone's here. A woman, from the U.S. Fish and Wildlife Service. Sheriff told me to call you."

Fish and Wildlife Service? Vaughn thought. He didn't know anyone from the Fish and Wildlife Service. "He say why?"

"Thought you might know something about it."

"She say she knew me?"

"Nope. She said she's supposed to be doing some field work with someone in the sheriff's office about something she doesn't want to talk about."

Oh shit, Vaughn thought. He stared into the woods. "That all?"

"She says it's her or the FBI."

Vaughn released the talk button and swore. Un-fucking-believable. This was turning out to be a circus. He wanted to tell Billy to get rid of the woman, but then what? The FBI shows up, the sheriff blows a gasket, his career is toast.

"Frank?"

He pushed the button. "Bring her up," he said, and gave Billy directions.

Chapter 17

THE cold had preserved the tracks well, and Lansing was pleased to see that all were slightly different. A few looked like they had been punched into the ground by perfectly shaped steel feet. Others smeared the frozen earth as if it were mud at the bottom of a pond. Though he wasn't sure if they would show any evidence of dermal ridges, the tracks were obviously genuine.

As he'd done so many times before, Lansing measured them and wrote down the dimensions. Then, leaving the tape measures in place, he snapped several photographs.

He also took several pictures of the deer. For some shots he moved the intestines out of the way to show the absence of the most nutritious organs, a finding that did not surprise him.

Someone had scuffed up the area, but he scanned the ground around the deer anyway. He was looking for a hand-print: Handprints, further proof that Sasquatches were bipedal apes, were extremely rare. Over the years he'd collected thousands of casts of footprints, but had only two partial prints of alleged Sasquatch hands.

A quick search turned up nothing. He knew he should examine the area more carefully, but he wanted to get back to the blood.

Small drops had splattered and smeared on leaves, and he found three purplish splotches on the ground where blood had leached into the soil. One was big enough to get his heart thumping.

With a sterile knife he cut off a few of the leaves and dropped them into a new Ziploc bag. He also scraped some of the blood from the ground, dirt and all, into another bag. It had been cold, so perhaps bacterial growth hadn't yet ruined the sample. Still an outside chance it could be analyzed by DNA experts.

He tapped the blade with his forefinger, and as the dirt fell into the bag he again felt something stir inside him, something he'd been trying to ignore ever since the phone call. He recognized it because he'd once succumbed to it, many years ago, even though he knew he was foolish to do so. It had no place in science.

Hope.

Hope handed out ifs and maybes like they were crack cocaine. It could kill you if you let it.

And here it was again, knocking. A possibility. Not a lot of blood, but the animal might have been hit badly enough to die. And if so, he, Art Lansing, would find it, the answer he knew was there.

Suddenly the smells of the forest rushed into him: the rich earth, the ferns respiring, the soaked bark, the epiphytes in the trees straining water from the air. He sucked them all in until his lungs were full, and then let them go. He felt giddy.

He almost laughed to think how he'd avoided answering the phone. That would have been the ultimate irony. Ten years of waiting and hoping for the call, and he would have chosen not to take it.

It had been so long that on some level, he almost couldn't believe this was real.

He tried to unscrew the blue top of the Nalgene bottle, but for some reason couldn't do it. He focused, wrapped his long fingers around the top and twisted hard.

This time he succeeded, and poured some of the water into a large Ziploc bag containing dental stone plaster. His thumb and forefinger pulled across the top of the bag, sealing it, and then he shook and kneaded the bag to make sure the mixture was even.

After repeating the process with three more bags, he poured the plaster into four consecutive tracks.

Finished, he stood by the last track and thought about what to do while the casts cured. He considered looking more thoroughly for handprints, but instead decided to go back to get the rest of his gear. He didn't want to make the deputy angry. Not yet.

He walked back to the deer and circled around it the other way, to his right. He'd learned over the years that people often missed Sasquatch evidence because they only looked one way, usually straight ahead and down at the ground.

By looking up he'd found Sasquatch hairs caught in bark, usually above eye level and many times off the straight trail of footprints that people followed. From the positions of these hairs, on a few occasions he'd been convinced that a Sasquatch had laid a fake trail, to misdirect people. Possibly to observe them.

At first he circled wide of the deer, walking from one tree to the next, looking up. Then he moved closer and looked down. But among the ferns and new shoots of trailing blackberry, he saw nothing.

Almost at the deer, he turned to head back to the truck when something caught his eye. He stopped and looked.

Between his feet was a Sasquatch track. From a left foot. He walked ahead, but didn't see another one. So he went back to the first track and then moved to the right.

Yes. The first track had a mirror image, about five feet away.

Each track pointed slightly outward. It looked to Lansing as if the Sasquatch stood here, in place, watching.

The animal must have come back later, but why? he thought. To see if someone had taken the deer?

Wait a moment.

He took the measuring tape from his pocket and ran it alongside one of the tracks. Then he stretched it across the track's widest part.

Was that right?

To make sure, he flipped open the small notebook and read the measurements he'd written down earlier.

He shoved the notebook back into his pocket, mixed up another bag of plaster and poured it into the first track. The milk-white liquid ran across the dark earth, filling even the smallest spaces. Just as it started to spill over the track's edges, he pulled the bag away and pinched it closed.

He eased down onto his hands and knees beside the other track. As he was about to pour in the plaster, he noticed something. He pulled the bag back and then leaned forward so that his nose almost touched the ground. Moisture soaked through his pants and numbed the skin of his knees.

He stared. He blinked and stared some more.

It definitely looked like it.

He quickly poured the plaster into that track and, leaving the casts to cure, walked back to the truck.

VAUGHN felt like putting his fist through the pickup's window. Someone, somewhere, leaked. And the two prime suspects were standing right in front of him.

"Which one of you guys called the Fish and Wildlife Service?" he said.

Mackey's eyes almost popped from his head. "It sure as hell wasn't me," he said. "I wouldn't invite them to my own funeral, and they wouldn't come if I did."

"I certainly didn't," Lansing said.

Vaughn said, "Well someone else—someone I surely didn't tell—must know what we're doing here. A woman from the Fish and Wildlife Service showed up at the sheriff's office and is on her way here. Said it was her or the FBI."

"Well, shit," Mackey said, kicking at a roadside fern.

Either Mackey was a great actor or he was genuinely upset, Vaughn thought. Lansing didn't appear fazed by the news.

Lansing said, "I wonder if I could ask you a question."

"Yeah, sure," Vaughn said.

"Did you measure the Sasquatch tracks?"

"What does that have to do with the Fish and Wildlife Service?" Vaughn said.

"Bear with me."

"No, I didn't."

"In rough terms they're about sixteen inches long and six and a half inches wide," Lansing said.

Vaughn just stared at him.

"Tracks in snow can expand as the snow melts," Lansing said. "But tracks in dirt can't. They will, slightly, if it rains enough. But it hasn't rained here since the tracks were made, and in any case it's been too cold for any expansion to occur."

"What's your point?"

"There's a set of tracks in there that's three inches longer, an inch wider and definitely deeper than the tracks made by the animal you shot. In other words we're dealing with two Sasquatches, not one. And the second one's bigger."

Chapter 18

GREY sky and black trees cycled across the approaching windshield. That's all he could see, but Vaughn stared at the glass anyway, hoping to get a glimpse of the woman from the Fish and Wildlife Service. Would she look grim, ready for a confrontation? Would the eyes above her smile reveal that she knew something he didn't? He hoped for a clue because he had to convince her to leave.

The patrol car rolled to a stop and the glass cleared—and what he saw made him forget about the woman.

Jack-O.

The only way Jack-O could have been the driver was if he had insisted on it, without the sheriff's knowledge. And if he did that, he obviously suspected something. Vaughn wondered again what Geek said to Jack-O at the hospital.

Jack-O exited the car, slammed the door and, heedless of the noise he'd just made, walked over. The woman was left to pull her gear out of the back seat by herself.

From the easy way she hefted her pack and the vein that

popped out on her neck, she seemed to be in decent shape. And attractive, though short, and younger than Vaughn expected, mid- to late twenties.

But that jacket. Fluorescent yellow probably looked good in a city or on a ski slope, but here it stood out like a lone lightbulb in a dark room.

"Hey Frank," Jack-O said, the same lopsided smile on his face. "What's going on?" His eyes shifted to Mackey and then to Lansing who was about ten yards away, walking back into the forest.

"Not much. Helping a few people out."

Jack-O stood near Vaughn's right shoulder and looked over at the gear spilling out onto the pickup's tailgate. "On an overnighter?"

"Gotta be prepared," Vaughn said.

"Hi." The woman walked up to them, smiling. "I'm Alison Lombard with the Fish and Wildlife Service."

Vaughn took her hand. It was small, but it squeezed his hand tightly. "I'm Deputy Sheriff Frank Vaughn. This is Chris Mackey."

Mackey smiled. Alison's eyebrows knotted as she took his hand, but her smile didn't change.

"Nice to meet you, young lady," he said. "Welcome to the fun."

Vaughn was surprised Mackey sounded so friendly.

Jack-O stepped around Vaughn and headed toward the woods.

"Hold on," Vaughn said, grabbing Jack-O's bicep. "You're taking her back."

Jack-O scowled and shook off Vaughn's hand, but he stopped.

Vaughn backed up a step to keep Jack-O in front of him.

"I'm not going back," Alison said. Her smile was gone.

Mackey moved quickly—Vaughn saw a flash of metal and then Mackey's .44 Mag appeared in front of Alison's face. The muzzle pointed into the woods.

"Did you bring one of these?" Mackey said to her.

"No!" Alison looked horrified.

Vaughn suddenly had a bad feeling. He said, "Do you know why you're here?"

"To do some field work."

"Involving what?"

Her lips tightened. "I wasn't told."

Jesus, Vaughn thought.

Mackey stared at her as if he was a cat daring a mouse to move.

"Alison," Vaughn said, "if you don't know why you're here, you should leave."

"I'm not leaving," she said. "I was sent here and was told that if I wasn't allowed to go along, the next people you'd see from the government would be the FBI."

"Who told you that?" Mackey said.

"Someone very high up."

"In Interior or the Service?"

"I can't say."

Mackey said, "Does Brenda Underwood know about this?"

"I can't say."

Vaughn didn't know who Brenda Underwood was, but Alison's body language told him that Brenda Underwood definitely knew.

Jack-O was looking into the forest. Vaughn wondered if Lansing was still visible, but didn't turn to look. He knew that if he did, Jack-O would use it as an opening to start walking.

"Alison," he said, "if you don't know what you're doing, this country can be dangerous. We're trained for . . . certain things. We're familiar with the terrain. If you come along you might be a danger not just to yourself, but to all of us."

She crossed her yellow arms. "Look, if you didn't mind a visit from the FBI I wouldn't have been brought out here, right? So why don't we just get moving."

Vaughn stared at her, thinking, *great.* Another crappy choice: a bunch of FBI agents—and maybe Jack-O as the next sheriff—or a lone woman in a yellow jacket?

Jack-O tried to get around Vaughn again.

Vaughn backed up and held an arm out. "Jack, we really need to get going. And I'm sure the sheriff needs you back right away."

Jack-O stopped. His eyes swept all of them, like a child suspicious of what the adults were up to. He opened his mouth to speak.

Vaughn said, "I'll just give him a call and let him know you're on your way."

Jack-O's mouth stayed open for a second. Then it closed and his eyebrows relaxed. "No problem," he said. For the first time, he looked at Alison. "If you need anything, just let me know."

Without another word, he walked to the patrol car, got in, K-turned and left.

Vaughn expected spinning tires or some other display of temper, but the car just ambled around the bend and was gone.

"That was easy," Mackey said.

"Yeah," Vaughn said.

He knew Jack-O was a slacker and a braggart, and like all such people had built-in juvenile fears, of authority and of disappointing the people he wanted most to impress. In Jack-O's case those people were his father and the sheriff. Push those buttons and Jack-O would react—predictably most of the time, though occasionally he would rebel.

Vaughn ran a hand through his hair and looked at the dull grey mud of the road. *Fucking Jack-O.* Slugfest preparations should keep Jack-O busy until well after the tracking job was over, but he knew Jack-O wouldn't think twice about skirting his duty. Hopefully he'd triggered enough guilt or fear to discourage Jack-O from returning.

He looked at Alison and pointed at her pack. "Any pots or anything else that can make noise in there?"

"Modular cookware."

"Leave it—I have some—and make sure everything's packed so it's quiet. How about a tent? You have one?"

She nodded. "Three-m—, uh, three-person."

"Bring it."

She raised her foot to move to the side of her pack.

"Watch out!" Mackey said.

She froze, her eyes big.

Mackey dipped down like a chubby heron and plucked something off the weedy shoulder of the road.

"Look at the size of this thing!" He held up a six-inch slug the color of milky coffee with dark-brown spots. It contracted toward his fingers and squirmed slowly. He pushed it toward Alison. She leaned back and her nose wrinkled.

"You almost killed it," he said.

"I did not."

Vaughn said: "That's a banana slug. He'll be people food in a couple of days."

Alison looked horrified.

"At the Slugfest," he said. He explained that the Slugfest was an idea Skookum County stole from enterprising towns in northern California. Billed as a celebration of the indigenous banana slug, it really was an excuse for college kids from Portland and Seattle to get off campus and gross each other out, for parents to put their kids on benign rides and feed them various forms of pure sugar, and for the county to pick all of their pockets.

It had turned into a big deal—thousands of people attended last year, making law enforcement critically important. Deputies worked around the clock, handling everything from first aid and lost kids to directing traffic and confiscating beer from teenagers.

The main attraction was the banana slug, a huge land mollusk that lives only in the perennially moist forests that stretch from the spine of the Cascades west to the Pacific Ocean. Named for their color (bright yellow to black) and size (up to ten inches), the slugs were collected by Skookum County children and then worked into all manner of culinary favorites that people paid money—piles of it—to eat.

The Slugfest windfall made Skookum County's police force, schools, and library the envy of rural counties all over Washington and Oregon, whose financial fortunes had been waning for years along with salmon runs and the local timber industry.

"Maybe we should keep him for supper," Mackey said, staring at Alison. "Stuff him in some spotted owl."

Alison grimaced at him and then knelt and fiddled with her pack.

Mackey tossed the slug into the woods.

Vaughn lifted his pack off the tailgate and stuck his arms through the straps. He bounced it until it cinched comfortably, and then locked the sternum strap. To Mackey he said, "I'm going to keep an eye on the professor. Meet us where it happened. You'll see it."

"Sure thing, ol' boy."

Vaughn grabbed his rifle and walked in.

Chapter 19

HE waded through the weeds that crowded the shoulder of the logging road, and entered the woods.

Thirty feet in, it felt like a heavy curtain had closed behind him. The canopy of interwoven branches blocked out the light, and the vegetation covering the forest floor absorbed all sound. It created a prehistoric gloominess that made the air feel dense, like mist.

He caught the soft swish of his fleece camouflage as it rubbed the sprawling fronds of sword fern. An unseen raven croaked overhead and then quit. He heard the faraway *pup, pup-pup-pup* of a foraging woodpecker and once, at his feet, the high-pitched alarm chitter of a surprised chipmunk. Tail up, the tiny rodent dashed away from him and disappeared.

Normal forest sounds. He interpreted them as meaning that the wounded Sasquatch wasn't nearby, and from the speed at which it ran off he didn't expect it to be. Still, even though he moved faster than he had this morning, he was cautious.

He arrived at the deer. It lay in the same position, but he

noticed that its intestines were turning purple, its legs were stiff and its eyes weren't as clear. He was surprised no coyotes or other scavengers had run across the carcass yet.

A breath of movement made him freeze.

Slowly he rotated his body so he could see.

Lansing walked toward him from deeper in the forest, a foot-high stack of white plaster casts in his arms. His eyes were locked on the ground and he apparently had no idea Vaughn was there.

Not a good sign, Vaughn thought. Tracking an animal—especially a dangerous one—required total awareness of everything in the woods.

"Art!" Vaughn said in a loud whisper.

At his name Lansing looked up, but didn't seem startled. He kept walking and, waving his hand, beckoned Vaughn over.

Ten feet from the deer, he stopped.

When Vaughn reached him, Lansing said, "Look." He pointed at two big, white Sasquatch tracks in the ground.

Vaughn noticed that the tracks faced the deer and were about five feet apart. "The bigger one," he said.

"Yes."

"Is this the one that threw that log?"

"I didn't measure that track, but it's probable." Lansing gestured at the deer. "It appears that the larger Sasquatch heard the commotion and came to have a look."

He bent down and placed the casts on the ground. "I want to show you something else," he said.

He headed deeper into the woods, and stopped about eight feet away.

Vaughn walked up to him and saw another track. His first thought was that the bigger Sasquatch jumped from there to the two white tracks, but this wasn't a jumping track.

Lansing glanced at him, then walked another eight feet deeper into the forest.

Vaughn followed. Another track.

For some reason he couldn't tell if the animal had been walking or running: Both tracks were deep and flat. Running strides were longer, and an eight-foot running stride didn't seem so bad. But an eight-foot walking stride was incredible. The animal had to be huge.

He heard a commotion behind him.

He turned and saw Mackey and Alison approach the deer. With them was Jack-O.

Goddamn that guy.

Jack-O was asking questions, but no one was responding. Mackey ignored him and Alison stared at the ground.

Vaughn walked toward them so fast that the pack banged against his back.

Mackey knelt at the side of the deer. Jack-O glanced at the carcass while he talked, but didn't seem interested.

Vaughn walked up and said, "You need to go."

"What's so top secret around here?" Jack-O said.

"None of your business."

"Who says?"

"Just get out of here."

A sneer twisted one corner of Jack-O's mouth. "Only the sheriff can give me an order, Frank, and you're not him. Think you'll ever be?"

What an asshole, Vaughn thought.

Suddenly Jack-O's eyes shot wide open and he pointed. "Holy shit!"

Vaughn turned and saw Lansing holding a plaster cast of one of the big Sasquatch's tracks, freshly pried from the ground. It was the size of a large serving platter, and though streaked with dirt glowed unnaturally white under the dark trees.

Jack-O stood there, frozen—then his finger started wiggling. "Shit, it's Boone, isn't it? He was attacked by a damn bigfoot, you shot it and now you're going after it!"

It seemed Geek didn't tell Jack-O everything, Vaughn thought. And the sheriff apparently hadn't told the other deputies about Ricks.

Jack-O yelled his stupid redneck yell: "Whoooeee!" He pointed at Mackey's big rifle. "You're going to kill a damn bigfoot. I knew it!"

He beamed like a kid who just got his first A in class. He was so proud of himself Vaughn half expected him to pull a brass band out of his pocket.

This time Vaughn had to get rid of Jack-O for good. He held his rifle out to Mackey and said, "Mind holding this?"

He gave Mackey the .30-06, dropped his pack and headed back to the truck.

He wanted to radio the sheriff, tell him what a fool Jack-O was and get him to order Jack-O back to the station. But he knew that would only aggravate the Old Man. And besides, if he couldn't handle an idiot like Jack-O on his own, Jack-O was right: He would never be sheriff.

He strode out of the forest and pushed through the roadside weeds, then yanked open the pickup's door and grabbed the mike off the front seat. "Billy, Frank here. C'mon back."

The radio crackled and then he heard: "Yeah, Frank. Billy here."

"Listen, I don't want to know why Jack-O's here instead of you. I just want you to tell the Old Man that Jack-O came out here and wouldn't leave. Got it?"

"Uh, ten-four. You sure you don't want to tell him yourself?"

Vaughn knew Billy didn't want to get in the middle of something involving the two senior deputies and the sheriff. He felt bad about it, but there was nothing he could do. "Can't do that, Billy, sorry. If you would, I'll owe you one."

"Sure, Frank."

"Appreciate it. Vaughn out." He threw the mike on the seat and pressed the door closed.

Jack-O stomped out of the woods, his face red. "What did you tell him?" he said.

"The truth. You came out here and wouldn't leave."

Jack-O stood close; Vaughn felt the vapor of Jack-O's breath on his face. They were about the same height and weight. The only advantage Vaughn had was psychological.

"Y'know what, Frank? You didn't have to do that. I was leaving."

"*I* didn't have to do that? Did you have to pull rank on Billy and come up here? Did you have to turn around and come back after you left the first time? Gimme a fucking break. Whatever you think I'm doing here, the fact is I have to get it done and get back fast or I'll be in deep shit with the Old Man. And so will you, unless you get out of here A-S-A-P."

Jack-O held Vaughn's gaze for a long moment. He glanced

into the woods, then his eyes returned to Vaughn. "Yeah, well. You still didn't have to do that."

He walked to the door of the patrol car. "I'm going. For now." He got in and slammed the door.

Vaughn thought about telling him not to do anything stupid, but realized it would be a waste of breath. It might even egg Jack-O on, like a schoolyard dare.

Jack-O gunned the motor and the rear tires spun before catching on the gravel embedded in the hard mud. Vaughn watched him speed off. The brake lights glowed red at the fork, and the car turned and was gone.

He stood there for a moment, thinking, *this is crazy.* Four people tracking a Sasquatch and Jack-O hovering around like a raven waiting to scavenge a kill.

He was tempted to pack it in.

But if he did that, chances were good that the Old Man might actually respect him less. And giving in when things got tough instead of sucking it up and doing what was right was bullshit.

Then he realized he was thinking about himself. He should be thinking about the Sasquatch. It might be dying a slow, painful death, dragging its leg along and coughing up blood hemorrhaging into its lung.

That's why he was here.

He hurried back into the woods. When he reached the others, Lansing was stashing his casts with Alison's help. She stared at the stack of giant footprints cradled in her arms as if she were in shock. Mackey watched her with amusement on his face.

"I apologize about Jack," he said.

"Not at all," Mackey said, holding out Vaughn's .30-06.

Vaughn said to Alison, "You okay?"

Her eyes went from the casts to his face, then dropped to his rifle. "Are we going to kill a bigfoot?"

"Only if we get lucky," Mackey said.

Vaughn said, "Chris is joking. We're going to track it. That's all." He thought for a second and said: "Now do you know why you're here?"

She shook her head; the end of her ponytail jumped from one side of her smooth neck to the other.

"Well as soon as you have an idea, I'd like to hear it."

She turned and followed Lansing, who also carried a pile of giant white footprints, their bottoms and sides dirty with mud. The professor walked thirty feet away, bent over a clump of ferns, and gently dropped the casts.

Before proceeding, Vaughn took the opportunity to get an idea of what Mackey knew. He said, "Did you look at the tracks of the wounded animal?"

"Sure did."

"What did you see?"

"The plaster messed them up some, but they're obviously human-shaped and huge. No claw marks, so no bear made those tracks." He cocked his head. "I guess they could be fakes, but I doubt it. Each track is different, and deep. And then there's that blood. Not enough to be from an artery, so unless it's one of those freak wounds that barely bleeds, I don't think our boy's dead." A big smile crossed his face. "But damned if he isn't real."

Vaughn picked up his pack and shrugged into it. Seemed like Mackey knew his stuff.

Lansing and Alison came back and he addressed all of them, keeping his voice low. "We're going to track this thing and that's all, okay? Chris and I will go first, you two will come behind us. Give us at least fifteen yards." He looked at Alison's banana-yellow parka. "Don't suppose you have another jacket?"

She looked at her sleeve. "No."

"Didn't think so. Like I was saying, don't walk right on the animal's trail." He spoke mostly to Alison. "Walk to the sides, and keep quiet. Watch where you're going; don't step on sticks or anything that can make a noise. Also, watch your packs. Try not to hit branches or trees. We want no unnatural noises: We're tracking a live, wounded, dangerous animal. So don't talk unless you absolutely have to, and if you do, get as close to the person as you can and whisper."

He thought for a second. "Oh yeah. We might run into a bear or two. Don't worry. They should run the other way."

With that he pulled his rifle close to his body, and fighting a sudden case of nerves, walked deeper into the woods.

Chapter 20

VAUGHN walked slowly, and tried to free his senses. He wanted to relax, to let go of everything in his brain and will himself toward a state where he would see, hear, and otherwise sense everything only for what it was. No interference from the "higher" brain. No motives, no desires, no worries, none of the everyday distractions that got in the way of raw perception.

The air currents carried scents he would never be able to discern no matter how much he tried: His nose, like the noses of all human beings, was next to useless. But the air, like the earth, also carried sounds, and these he could actually feel once he entered the hunting state. His subconscious would decipher the sounds instantly: a "get out of here" bird call, an odd rhythm of footfalls, a soft snort or grunt—and, when he was in deep, the force of air being moved aside by a wing or a paw, or something he couldn't put a finger on but knew was there.

Submerging into that place in himself that meshed with the

earth, the rocks, the trees, the animals, the air, the sky—it was beautiful, a much more vivid world. Like a plastic sheet lifted from an oil painting. Or like being able to breathe underwater, without an Aqua-Lung.

He couldn't describe exactly how it felt to people who didn't hunt, and for those who did, he didn't need to. This experience was ninety percent of the enjoyment, and the peace, of hunting.

But this time it was different. He couldn't relax, the peace wasn't there. Just the wriggling in his neck.

The tracks, now farther apart, led deeper into the dark woods. Vaughn saw that the Sasquatch still favored its right leg, but because it had been running, the limp wasn't as noticeable.

At regular intervals he examined a track to see if he could discern any change in the animal's movement: whether it had stumbled, slowed or jumped off the trail to hide. He found nothing unusual and all the tracks were similar, which told him that the Sasquatch had maintained a constant pace.

A muffled metallic clank jerked him out of the hunt.

He glared back past Mackey—and saw only Alison. He waited a few seconds, but Lansing didn't appear.

He stalked back down the trail. As he neared Alison she took off her pack and started to unzip it. "Sorry, I—"

"Where's Dr. Lansing?" he said.

"He went back to where the . . . it was shot."

Vaughn left her and eventually found Lansing snooping around the tree the wounded Sasquatch had hidden behind. The professor held a pair of tweezers in one hand and a clear plastic bag in the other.

"Dr. Lansing."

Lansing looked up.

"While we're out here you're my responsibility," Vaughn said. "Everyone is. If you run off, you put all of us at risk. So stay with the group."

Lansing's eyes flitted to Vaughn's rifle. He sealed the bag and pushed it and the tweezers into a jacket pocket. "My apologies."

"Don't let it happen again."

•   •   •

ON the way back something odd registered in the corner of
Vaughn's eye. He stopped and slowly turned his head. There:
a grey rectangle, hanging from a branch about shoulder high.
Reflective tape.

Every ten or fifteen yards Mackey wound the tape around
the scrawny arm of a small Douglas fir or western hemlock or
whatever he could find. It was his idea; in case anyone had to
make it out in the dark, a flashlight would light up the tape
like a highway, just as it did for hunters walking to or from
their stands in the dark.

The tape marked a route Vaughn figured was almost parallel to the road but angling slightly away. The ground over this
route had remained level, but then sloped downhill toward a
narrow valley.

He took the lead again and kept their progress slow, using the
pace to submerge back into the woods. Retrieving Lansing had
sparked his brain into conscious thought and something even
worse: emotion. So he placed his feet with care, and breathed
regularly to hypnotize his higher brain into suspension.

The Sasquatch's trail continued in the same direction for
another few miles, then turned abruptly to the right. Here
Vaughn stopped and waited for Mackey. He didn't see anything out of the ordinary, didn't feel anything odd, but with
that sudden change in the animal's course, he wasn't taking
any chances.

When Mackey saw the change of course, he seemed to understand immediately. Without exchanging any words, they
spread five yards to either side of the track and crept forward.

With each step it became apparent that other than that one
turn, there was no change. The Sasquatch had continued running at the same pace.

Another twenty yards and they came to the top of a steep
slope scattered with ferns, shrub-like salal and flowerless
berry plants of various types. The big trees didn't grow here,
as if it was contaminated ground. Vaughn had seen a similar
slope once before, with Boone. Probably shifted in an ancient
earthquake, Boone had said.

Mackey grunted and Vaughn knew why: The Sasquatch
had walked straight down, unfazed by the steep angle.

As he looked, Vaughn suddenly realized that he couldn't see exactly where the slope bottomed out. All he saw was black. The forest was getting dark already.

They had to descend diagonally, across the slope's face, digging the sides of their boots into the frozen earth. At the bottom, Vaughn waited until he saw Alison's yellow jacket at the top of the slope and then continued on the Sasquatch's trail. After a few hundred yards his ears picked up a sound like faraway applause. He stopped.

When Mackey reached him, Vaughn whispered: "Hear that? Maybe the Sasquatch sat in the stream and died." Game animals sometimes did it. The Sasquatch might have, too.

"You read my mind, ol' boy."

"Give me a sec."

Vaughn walked back to Alison and told her to stay put. Again Lansing lagged behind; Vaughn saw the white blast of a camera flash discharge against the slope, and had to stop and blink a few times to get rid of the yellow afterimage.

He returned to where Mackey waited and then followed the tracks straight toward the stream. The rush of water became louder, and the air on his face felt colder and smelled wet.

Near the edge of the treeline he motioned to Mackey that he would walk upstream, off to the left of the Sasquatch's trail. He took out a small flashlight and without turning it on waved it at Mackey.

Again Mackey seemed to understand. He fished a flashlight from his jacket pocket and they split up.

Holding the flashlight under the fore-end of his rifle, Vaughn crept up to where the trees stopped and the vegetation spilled out onto the smooth, rounded stones of the riverbank. He could barely see the whitish-grey stones, even under the open sky above the river.

He stood just inside the treeline and listened. All he heard was water, and the relatively even, loud sound told him it ran shallow and fast.

He lifted a fern frond with the barrel of his rifle and stepped out onto the stones. He clicked his flashlight on.

Slowly he scanned the rushing water with the beam. The water was black except for where it jumped and sprayed over boulders, white and then gone, plunging into the river and downstream.

No Sasquatch.

Downstream he saw Mackey's light stab into the water and move back and forth, up and down.

Vaughn checked downstream and upstream, then shined the flashlight at the opposite bank. He saw lots of cutting-size Douglas fir, but no old growth. That meant it had been logged sometime within the last twenty or thirty years.

The trees grew from a slope that climbed steeply upward, and he realized that might be a problem. If the Sasquatch's trail went straight up, tomorrow they wouldn't cover as much ground as he'd hoped.

A circle of light bobbed on the stones, coming upstream. Vaughn walked toward it.

"Anything?"

"No," Mackey said.

Vaughn thought for a second. He knew the stream flowed cold and slick over a rocky bottom, so crossing at night wasn't wise. And even if they tried, finding a camp-site in the dark on completely unfamiliar, sloping ground would be unwise.

His stomach gurgled, and he remembered he'd forgotten to eat lunch. He said: "Looks like we're camping here for the night."

Chapter 21

ORANGE flames flickered across the damp wood. Water vapor escaped in bursts that sounded like the claps from cap guns.

Usually a campfire was the time to relax, laugh about the day's mishaps and solve the world's problems. But Vaughn knew that tonight's conversation would be work. Tomorrow was a critical day, and he was determined to use this time to learn as much about the others as he could. Particularly Alison.

After a dinner of rehydrated pasta, some trail mix and a few strips of elk jerky, he told her why they were there. He omitted the part about Ricks' body, figuring it would do no good to mention it.

Any surprise seemed to be past Alison, but as she listened small crow's feet formed in the skin at the outside corners of her eyes.

As soon as he finished, and before she could ask any questions, he asked her what she did at the Fish and Wildlife Service.

She hesitated for a second, then said, "I'm in the Office of Congressional and Legislative Affairs. I write recommendations about what the Service should and shouldn't do. Policy stuff."

"In what areas?" Mackey said.

"Mostly endangered species."

"There's a big surprise."

Vaughn felt like he'd been slammed in the forehead with a brick. Of course. The Fish and Wildlife Service was in charge of endangered species. That's why she was here. Suddenly the sheriff's warning seemed real.

But wait a minute. "You're not a biologist?" he said.

"No."

Mackey said, "That's even better."

Alison's dark eyebrows pulled together, crumpling the skin above her nose. "You have a problem?"

Mackey picked up a stick and poked the fire. "When it comes to the Fish and Wildlife Service? Several."

"Involving endangered species."

"For the Service that's all there is," Mackey said. "And Brenda Underwood has people like you, who haven't spent any time outdoors since they were ten, making recommendations about how it should implement the law."

Alison said, "I've studied endangered species my whole career. Before the Service I worked for the International Wildlife Society and helped protect Bengal tigers in India, orangutans in Borneo, mountain gorillas in Rwanda, all kinds of species in the Amazon rainforest, wolves—"

"Did you actually go to any of those places?"

Alison didn't say anything.

Mackey smiled and poked the fire again. "How old are you, twenty-five? You're not old enough to have a career yet. And a career studying nature from a desk is ridiculous."

Though his words were blunt, Vaughn noticed that Mackey's face was calm, like he was used to confrontation. But Alison's face glowed red, and her expression made it clear it wasn't because of the campfire.

Suddenly she sat up straight—but Vaughn headed off whatever was coming. "Dr. Lansing, I'm sure she's already guessed, but why don't you tell Alison what you do."

"My pleasure," Lansing said. Alternating his eyes between Alison and the fire, he summarized his academic career and his professional interest in Sasquatches. He included a brief recap of evidence for the creatures—the same stuff from the ten-year-old video, Vaughn noticed.

Mackey said, "Don't take this the wrong way, Art, ol' boy, but I'm surprised you'd stick your neck out like that. Advocating the existence of an animal, let alone a bipedal ape, that everyone believes isn't real. It must have affected your career."

"No offense taken," Lansing said. He stared, unblinking, into the fire.

It seemed like he wouldn't say anything more, but then he leaned forward and said, "My career has been affected."

Light flickered across his face.

"The best way I can explain it is that science has become an institution. And like any institution—governments, political parties, large corporations, the big religions—it's a bureaucracy presided over by bureaucrats. These people like order and lack imagination, which used to be a key ingredient for science. Therefore they're terrified of change, especially radical change.

"A change that threatens what's accepted scientifically is difficult enough. But if it also threatens what's accepted culturally, which is what the Sasquatch does, the institution of science ignores the change or pronounces it impossible. So the bureaucracy actually discourages major scientific discoveries."

Lansing threw a branch into the fire. Orange sparks shot up and quickly winked out.

"Perhaps this is because world culture is different now," he said. "In Darwin's era, people discovered new fauna all the time. It was exciting and the lay public was interested, their imaginations fertile. But that's no longer the case. Even when large mammals are discovered, like the new species of Vietnamese deer and antelope found in the 1990s, people don't care. Animals aren't as sexy as a faster microchip or a killer virus or genetically altered frost-tolerant tomatoes.

"People don't live outside anymore. They live inside, literally and metaphorically. And science reflects that. Or perhaps, since science and technology are irrevocably linked, causes it."

His mouth smiled, but his eyes didn't. "The irony is that as we get smaller and smaller in our analyses of life, we appear to comprehend less of it."

"I completely agree," Mackey said. "I've said the same things about environmental groups."

Alison looked up.

"These groups were started by people who understood nature," Mackey said. "Almost all of them were hunters. But they forgot their roots and became money-hungry bureaucracies. Now, instead of being led by people who know the outdoors, they're headed by high-paid fund-raisers whose job it is to get the money that's needed for the large staffs, junk mail and, especially, the attorneys.

"And to keep it flowing, there's always a new cause. If it isn't the whales, it's the pandas or some other cute-looking, big-eyed critter like the spotted owl. If it isn't animals, it's rain forests, acid rain, global warming, you name it. And if it isn't a problem here, it's in the Amazon, Africa or somewhere else exotic. That way they keep their members, the urban and suburban people, whipped up and the money coming in."

Vaughn's leg jerked away from the fire; his shin had suddenly become burning hot. He rubbed it and said, "You're not saying environmental groups haven't done any good, are you? Because I've seen things get done here that wouldn't have if some group didn't stand up for them."

Mackey said, "I'm saying that things have gotten out of hand. I used to be proud to say I was an environmentalist, someone who understood ol' Mother Nature well enough to conserve her. Now, by the current definition, I'm not one. And I don't want to be one, because that word labels people who sit in environmental *institutions* in Washington, D.C., and New York City and issue opinions while knowing next to nothing about the outdoors or the critters in it.

"They worship nature as something apart, like it's a big terrarium sitting on an altar. That's why they've overlapped with the animal-rights nuts. They're all coming from the same lack of understanding. They don't understand that if you have a house, drive a car, take public transportation, buy food, even breathe, you're involved in nature. And the worst irony is that the people *most* involved in nature, hunters and anglers, are somehow viewed as less human. Can you believe that?"

Vaughn knew what Mackey was saying. Every hunter did. That was another thing he liked about the Pacific Northwest; it was still rural, and people understood hunting. Back in suburban New Jersey, talking about hunting was one of the surest ways to end a dinner party conversation.

"Environmental groups know the only way they can keep their urban members on the financial hook is to 'save' things," Mackey said. "And saving means no killing, despite the fact that that's sometimes the only thing that'll keep animals from disappearing. You want to save elephants? Allow limited, legal hunting. Legal ivory will cause the price of ivory to drop and poaching to decrease. And when you start charging rich tourists to hunt, then money and food—the reasons people poach—will flow into local communities. Only then, when there's a monetary value on wildlife that's felt by the locals, will their governments choose to protect elephants."

He looked around the fire.

"The head honchos at environmental groups understand this. I've talked to them about it. But they won't touch it because for them, it's all about the money."

"No it isn't," Alison said.

"What's that, hon?" Mackey said, cupping his left ear. Vaughn recognized it as a telltale sign of someone who had spent a lot of time shooting without hearing protection.

Alison's face clouded at the "hon."

"No, it's not all about money," she said, louder. "I worked with a lot of dedicated people at InWild who got paid peanuts but worked hard because they believed human beings shouldn't ruin the planet."

Mackey smiled at her. "That sounds noble, but it's wrong. What we now call 'the environment' has never been static. Our ancestors altered it for hundreds of thousands of years by setting forest fires to concentrate game. And humans weren't the only animals that did it. Mammoths kept forests down by eating juvenile trees. Beavers alter land and rivers by cutting down trees and building dams. Prairie dogs cause erosion. Ducks and geese overfertilize water by pooping in and around it. So clear-cutting, dams, tree plantations—all of that's no different from what other animals do."

He looked at Vaughn. "Seems obvious, right? These kinds of natural observations should be obvious to environmentalists. But they'd rather blame us for everything and then use that guilt. Give us money and you can feel guilt-free about your garbage, your car, the stuff you use to unclog your drain and your lawn fertilizer. Guilt relief, that's what they're really selling, and it's an easy sell."

Alison held up an index finger and stabbed it at Mackey. "First of all you're way off on scale. Beaver dams in little streams aren't even worth comparing to the gigantic concrete dams on major rivers. Erosion caused by prairie dogs isn't comparable to the amount of damage caused by bulldozers, and waterfowl don't produce nearly as much waste as people do. And unlike fires, clear-cutting doesn't leave standing snags, and natural regrowth wouldn't be monocultural.

"As far as what environmental groups are *selling*," she said, "it's care about the environment. They're reminding people to care, and they're providing a way for ordinary people to fight the effects of greed. If the environmental movement didn't exist here, you think the United States wouldn't look like the Soviet Union or East Germany? Ever see the pollution over there?" Her arm pointed into the forest.

"Environmental groups have done some good," Mackey said, "but that was in the past. Conserving the environment isn't good enough anymore. They have to go beyond that and *preserve*, which is nuts." He snorted and poked the fire. "Preservation, endangered species, ecosystems, biodiversity; it's all the same crazy notion."

A look of incredulity exploded across Alison's face. "Wait a second! Are you actually saying that you don't believe in biodiversity and ecosystems, the fact that everything in nature is connected?"

"I know everything's connected, but not in the steady state that 'biodiversity' and 'ecosystems' would have you believe," Mackey said. "The Earth has all kinds of critters, but diversity rises and falls. Scientists are just cataloguing what's here now. But thanks to the Fish and Wildlife Service blabbing about ecosystems, everyone thinks we have to save everything. Because by calling nature a system, people see it as an elaborate machine. And since a machine has to have all the parts to work, people are led to believe that everything in the system has to be preserved or the machine won't run. Or worse, that it'll stop running."

"It will," she said.

"No, it won't. Not just because species disappear. Extinctions, including mass extinctions, are natural. Dinosaurs died so humans and other mammals could evolve and rule the planet—a fact which by itself completely sinks the ecosystem and biodiversity theories. Problem is, people in their world of pavement and cute TV bunnies don't like to think about that. But things that don't make them think too hard are okay, like an image of a web of life. 'Break one strand and everything begins to unravel.'"

"You can't be saying that's wrong," Alison said.

"Damn right it is! What if we had a global nuclear war? Most species would become extinct, but *life* would persist and new species would evolve. The web would tear, but it would re-form."

Lansing said, "In fact that's what happened after the icc ages."

Mackey held his hands out to his sides. "There you go. Change is the most natural process there is."

"So you don't care that our rush to pave over the world means we'll lose things that could help us? A compound in a rare salamander's skin, alkaloids from an Amazon plant that might cure cancer, AIDS or some future horrible disease?" Alison waved her hand to the side. "Forget about saving them. Let's trample it all. Burn it. Pave it out of existence."

"Now hold on—"

"Commercial fishermen are literally stripping the bottom of the Georges Bank clean," she said. "Did you know that? They drag chains to scare fish into their nets, but the chains scour the bottom. Some species may be gone forever, like what happens with land clearing in the Amazon rainforest. Shark attacks have increased on Hawaiian surfers and scientists think it's because commercial fishermen from the Far East are fishing out the oceans. Fishing out the *polluted* oceans. Can you imagine how much neglect it takes to pollute

330 million cubic miles of water? That isn't 'sustainable development,' it's rape!"

"Whoa," Mackey said. He held up a hand. "Easy now, Alison. I'm not saying people should do whatever they want, however they want. But too much regulation is bad, especially when it comes to private property—if there is such a thing anymore. When the federal government can come to your home and your land and tell you exactly what you can and can't do down to the last blade of grass, that's wrong. And that's what's happened in some places."

"That's crazy," Alison said, flipping her hand at him.

"You're damn right it is."

"No, I mean *you're* crazy."

Sitting halfway cross-legged, Mackey folded his hands and let them rest on his ankle. The flames that waved across the wood were not reflected in his eyes.

He said, "You're coming up with policies for this whole country based on a totally wrong understanding of the natural world. And you know why the government you work for likes it? Not because they want to improve the environment. It's because laws like the Endangered Species Act give them more control, over land and over people."

"Oh really. How?"

"The ecosystem and biodiversity concepts take the randomness out of nature."

"So?"

"So political agendas can't be furthered by something that's random."

Alison stared at him and then her eyes dropped to the fire. She didn't respond.

Mackey poked the fire again. "Try to look at this with your brain instead of your emotions. That way you'll stop being part of the problem."

A spark shot onto Vaughn's parka. He batted it out.

Alison sat up, with her mouth curled into a small smile. "What about the people you work for? Carolina Pacific, right?"

"CP is one of my clients."

The smile turned into a smirk. "Isn't it all about money for them?"

"It's about sanity."

"Oh really?" she said. "Then why did they send you?"

"To make sure you don't do anything stupid."

Alison rolled her eyes and stood. To Lansing, she said, "Give me a few minutes," and stalked over to her tent. Earlier she'd chosen him, not Mackey, to be her tent-mate. Vaughn heard the tent zip open.

Lansing yawned, his teeth orange yellow in the firelight. Vaughn yawned too, blowing the last of it at the fire. The embers pulsed red as if alive, and then returned to a dead grey. He felt the cold seeping into his back.

"Early start tomorrow," he said. "I suggest we get some—"

... *aaawoooooooooooooooo* ...

Vaughn's ears pricked up and his body stiffened. The sound was different than the howl of pain, but deep and powerful. No question, it was the same animal.

Everyone sat stock still, listening to the howl trail off.

To Vaughn it sounded like it came from somewhere upstream. Distant, but he couldn't tell how far. And though he couldn't be sure, it didn't sound like the cry of a dying animal.

Mackey said: "All my years in the woods I never heard anything like that."

Lansing said: "Is that the same sound you heard this morning?"

"No," said Vaughn.

"But the same animal."

"Same type of animal, yes."

A flashlight clicked on, pointed right at Lansing's face. He held up a hand and Alison moved the beam to the ground.

"Where is it?" she said.

"Don't worry," Vaughn said. "He's a long way off."

"For now," Mackey said.

Vaughn glanced at Mackey and then stood. Stiff from sitting so long, he put his thumbs on each side of his lower spine and arched his back. A vertebra cracked. "Let's get some sleep," he said. He hoped he sounded more casual than he felt.

He relieved himself behind a tree, walked over to his tent and crawled inside. As he unrolled the mummy bag he suddenly couldn't wait to lie down, and once horizontal started drifting off immediately.

Before going under he thought about balling up pieces of toilet paper and sticking them in his ears. He always did it when he camped with Boone, who snored like a cement truck. He didn't know if Mackey had the same problem and didn't want to be up all night.

But in the end, with the river lulling him to sleep and the Sasquatch howl playing in his head, he didn't.

Good thing.

Chapter 22

AFTER what seemed like only minutes, Vaughn jerked awake. He didn't know why at first, but then he heard it.

A noise. A branch snapping, distinct over the muted rush of the river.

Another snap, then three harsh *kraak*s in a row.

He tried to place the sounds and two more branches broke. Louder this time.

Closer.

No animal would break that many branches by accident, and there weren't that many branches to step on. Was it a person?

Whatever it was, he knew it had to be *trying* to break those branches.

He yanked down the zipper of his mummy bag and sat up. His eyes were wide open, but he couldn't see a thing. The inside of the tent was as black as a raven's eye, and it would be the same outside. No moonlight or starlight could penetrate the thick forest canopy.

His right hand groped around for the .357 that he'd left on the tent floor, next to his leg. His fingers found the revolver's steel cylinder; the metal was so cold he barely felt it.

He palmed the molded rubber grip and rested his index finger on the trigger guard. With his other hand he shook Mackey.

"Chris," he hissed.

No response.

"Chris!"

He felt Mackey grab his arm and sit up.

Two branches snapped again, then a third.

Whatever was making the sounds had circled around toward the river, away from Alison's tent. Two days ago he would have said it was a bear or a person, but now he wasn't sure.

Suddenly electricity shot up his arms and into his neck. His skin prickled.

Son of a bitch! he thought. "*It's—*"

A soft scratching noise came from Mackey's side of the tent wall.

Vaughn listened: *skritch . . . skritch.*

He released a long breath. It had to be a porcupine pawing at his pack. Probably attracted to their camp by the smell of cooked food.

Crash!

Something smashed into the tent, and Mackey fell across his legs. A sound blasted into his skull—*aaaaooooooooo!*—so loud his teeth hummed.

He shoved Mackey off, wrapped both hands around the grip of the .357, raised it over his head and squeezed the trigger.

Boom!

His hands jerked back; the noise of the big revolver drowned out the howl. Vaughn froze with his hands in the air, straining to hear past the noise of the shot.

As the sound wave receded, he became aware that the howling had stopped.

Light suddenly illuminated sagging purple and green nylon. Vaughn squeezed his eyes shut, but not in time: yellow streaks burst across the black behind his eyelids. He heard the tent zip open and cracked open his eyes. Mackey held a flashlight in his left hand and clutched the .44 in his right. "You ready?"

Vaughn gripped his .357. "Go."

Mackey dove out, rolled and came up on one knee, the light and the big revolver facing toward the caved-in side of the tent.

Vaughn pushed through the flaps and stepped out with his revolver pointed toward the other side.

He saw only black. Nothing came at him so he whipped the .357 back the other way.

Nothing.

Mackey panned the trees with the flashlight, but Vaughn didn't follow the beam. Instead he listened. He expected to hear a heavy animal crashing through the woods like a startled bull elk. But he heard nothing except the ringing in his ears and, underneath, the faint sandpaper-like din of the river.

"Clear." Mackey stood and let the .44 drop to his side. He pointed the flashlight at the tent.

Vaughn saw his pack lying in the folds of nylon, part of it snagged on a tent pole. He walked over and grabbed it—then jerked his head away. "Damn," he said. That stink again. Not as intense as it was on Boone's jacket, but potent.

He turned his head, took a breath, then lifted the pack off and looked it over. A pocket gaped open, but he saw no tears or other damage.

The zipper in the other tent ripped open and Lansing's thin frame emerged. He strode into the light with a grin on his face and something clutched in one hand.

"Did you shoot it?" he said, looking around.

"Don't think so," Vaughn said. "I aimed up in the air." He'd almost forgotten about that. He retrieved a flashlight from his pack and stepped over to have a look at the hole in the tent.

Mackey said: "What you got there, Art?"

"Voice-activated recorder."

Vaughn's flashlight showed that the bullet had punched neat circles through the rainfly and the tent beneath. He bent down to get the roll of duct tape from the main pocket of his pack and said, "You're not saying you knew this was going to happen."

"No," Lansing said. "Just prepared."

Lansing held up the recorder and pushed a button. A click, and then the cassette squealed as it rewound.

With his teeth Vaughn ripped off two ragged squares of duct tape and pressed them over the holes.

A light flared inside Alison's tent, bleaching the tan panels almost white. She stepped out carrying a small battery-powered lantern. The fluorescent bulbs, painfully bright, made her face look like it was drained of all blood.

"Is everyone okay?" she said.

Vaughn looked at Mackey, who rubbed the side of his face. "You okay, Chris?"

"Yep. No permanent damage."

"What happened?"

"The Sasquatch threw my pack into the tent," Vaughn said. "Knocked Chris over."

Alison's eyes widened. She pulled one side of her unzipped jacket across her chest and held it there with a pale fist. Her breath puffed little clouds through the lantern light.

The tape stopped rewinding and Lansing played it. Vaughn heard a few tinny clicks, then the eerie howl. The speaker broke up, crackling. Alison's voice said, "Oh my Go—" and then the gunshot blasted through everything. It sounded like the speaker cone ripped; Lansing quickly dialed the volume down.

"Loud as a damn noon whistle," Mackey said.

Lansing said, "May I borrow your flashlight?"

Mackey handed it to him. Lansing slowly played the beam across the ground near the tent. At the edge of the light, one and then two dark patches formed. Shadows.

He moved the beam and the shadows withdrew to reveal giant bare footprints, each smashed more than an inch deep into the half-frozen earth.

"There we go," Lansing said.

"Which one?"

"Looks like the bigger one."

Alison walked closer. "The bigger one?"

Vaughn said: "What was it doing here?"

"Is anything missing from your pack?"

Vaughn bent down and stuck his hand in the open pocket, wrinkling his nose at the stink. Empty. "Took my granola bars."

Lansing said, "It came to get food. There are many accounts of Sasquatches stealing food out of people's packs. Often oatmeal or, when coolers are along, meat. In fact, that's how you can tell a night visitor isn't a bear or a porcupine. Those animals don't have the dexterity to open a pouch and remove something."

"Then why did it throw the pack?"

"I think it simply tossed the pack aside, not intending to hurt anyone. An animal that size could've injured you severely if it wanted to. But the howl, that's the most interesting part. I believe it was trying to intimidate us. Telling us to get out of its territory, so to speak."

Vaughn said: "We'll be doing that in the morning."

Alison said: "There are two of these things?"

Lansing answered: "Yes."

"What if one comes back?"

"Virtually all accounts involving gunfire have them immediately running off and not returning," Lansing said.

Mackey turned to Vaughn. "You get that weird feeling just before it grabbed the pack?"

"Yeah. Strong."

"I felt that once before, in Africa. Leopard moved at the shot and we had to track him through the tall grass. The light was almost gone, and all of a sudden I got that feeling."

"When you were in mortal danger."

Mackey nodded. "The leopard had hooked back around and was stalking us."

Alison's lantern shook. Vaughn couldn't tell whether the shiver was caused by cold or fear. He said, "Now you understand why I didn't want you to come."

She looked at him, but she didn't respond.

Mackey walked toward Lansing, holding out his .44. "You know how to use one of these?"

"Uh, no," Lansing said. "Rifles, occasionally—"

"This is a single-action revolver. You have to pull the hammer back like this," he pulled it back with his thumb, "before you can fire it. Just like in the old Westerns. Other than that there's no safety. Don't point it at anything you don't intend to shoot, and that goes for you, too," he said to Alison.

"I don't intend to shoot anything," she said, staring at the big revolver.

"You never know," Mackey said, and handed the gun to Lansing.

Lansing held it limp wristed and away from his body. The barrel hung toward the ground.

"Come on, Art," Mackey said. "It ain't a damn rattlesnake." He flashed a smile, but no one else reacted.

Vaughn wasn't happy to see another person in the party with a gun, especially somebody who didn't know how to use one. But it seemed like the prudent thing to do.

He made a mental note to make sure Mackey got it back in the morning.

Chapter 23

Wednesday

ART Lansing woke before anyone else and quietly hurried out of camp. He followed the trail of the big Sasquatch for about half a mile, then left it for the riverbank. He walked just inside the treeline and kept looking up, hoping that the fog stacked into the narrow valley wouldn't interfere too badly with the signal.

When he judged he was far enough away, he stepped out of the cover of the trees and onto the grey rocks. The river rushed by, leaving beads of water on stones that had been rounded and smoothed by thousands of years of being tumbled downstream.

He shook off his pack and removed a Ziploc bag containing a cellular phone and business card. "Tom Sun," the card read, "Staff Writer, *The Seattle Times*." For a moment he stood there fingering the card, going over what he wanted to say. Then he pulled out the phone.

The keypad glowed green. *Damn,* he thought. Something in his pack must have knocked into the phone and turned it on. Wasting no time, he punched in the number.

After two rings, a woman's voice: "(static) desk."

"Yes. Hello? I apologize for the connection. I'm looking for Tom Sun."

"(static) sorry (static) can't (static)."

Lansing jogged upstream, running through clouds of moisture expelled from his lungs. Stones clacked under his boots.

"I'm sorry," he said. He slipped on a rock and his voice got louder. "Is Tom Sun there?"

"He doesn't work (static) anymore."

The signal now clearer, Lansing stopped moving. "Do you know where he's employed now?"

"He's at KR (static)."

"I lost you. Is that a radio station?"

"No. KRAQ. It's TV."

"Do you have a forwarding number?"

"No, but he won't be there now."

"Thank you." Lansing ended the call.

A TV station. Television coverage would of course be better, but would be more difficult to obtain. While a newspaper would send a reporter and photographer almost anywhere to check out a lead, he doubted the same would be true of a television station. Especially for a story about a Sasquatch.

He flipped the business card over. Sun's home number was on the back, with "anytime!" scrawled underneath it and double-underlined. But that was ten years ago. The chances Sun had the same number were infinitesimal.

Lansing dialed information and asked for Tom Sun in Seattle.

"(static) address or first name? (static) many Thompsons."

"No," Lansing said. "Last name S-U-N, first name Tom."

A pause and then: "(static) the number. Would you like (static) automatically?"

He said yes, and seven tones beeped off. It rang three times and then he heard a clatter, like someone knocked the phone off the hook.

"Hello?" A male voice, groggy.

"Tom Sun?"

"Hello?"

Lansing jogged farther down the riverbank. "Tom Sun?"

"Yeah."

"This is Dr. Art Lansing from Western Washington University."

"It's six in the morning."

"I apologize. I'll get right to the point. Do you remember talking to me several years ago? You gave me your card."

A brief pause. "I'm (static), Dr. Lansing. I can't place the name. I meet so many people . . ."

"I understand. Ten years ago you covered a conference at the university, a meeting of the International Society of Primatology and Physical Anthropology. I spoke about Sasquatches. At the end of the meeting you gave me your card and asked me to give you a call, anytime, if I ever came across a real Sasquatch."

"Yeah. I remember you now," Sun said. Lansing heard what sounded like a drawer scraping open. "I'm, uh, trying to find something to write with. Where are you calling from, anyway? Cell phone?"

"Skookum County," Lansing said. "Gifford Pinchot National Forest."

"How do you spell your last (static), professor?"

"L-A-N-S-I-N-G. I'm still at the university. I've been there for the last ten years. But I've never had the occasion to call you until now."

"Uh-huh. What do you have? Video?"

"Not yet. But we're tracking a Sasquatch that was shot."

"With bullets?"

"Yes. We're following tracks and blood. And we were visited by one of the animals last night. It injured one of the party."

"You're kidding! Who are you with?"

"A deputy sheriff, a Carolina Pacific representative and an employee of the federal Fish and Wildlife Service, the endangered-species agency."

"Interesting." He sounded fully awake now, and spoke faster. "Can you tell me where in the forest you are?"

Lansing gave him directions, and then said, "If you get lost, follow the river and look for reflective tape in the trees. We've marked the trail. And be prepared to camp out for a night or two."

Silence.

"Hello?" Lansing said.

"We can't afford to send an expedition out there, Dr. Lansing."

Lansing took a deep breath. "Look, Tom, I'm sure you realize something significant must be going on down here if these other people are with me. So at the least, it won't be a waste of your time. But if it works out the way I think it will, you'll have the scoop of this century—and perhaps all the centuries before and after it."

That was his best shot, an appeal to the newshound's nose. He waited.

Again there was silence.

"Hello?"

Nothing.

"Hello?"

Not even background hiss.

A tone blared in his ear. Lansing tore the phone away from his face and looked at the keypad. It glowed red.

Hurriedly he hit Send twice to redial, but the button didn't beep under his finger. On the display an image of a black battery with a jagged split blinking on and off, then disappeared. The red glow of the LCD faded to a flat grey.

He couldn't believe it. A dead battery and no way to recharge it. He felt like hurling the phone against the rocks. He raised it up—

A stone clacked and skittered across the others. Behind him.

He froze, his arm cocked in midair.

Earlier this morning he'd had a funny feeling, as if he was being followed. Once he looked back, but he didn't see anything so he made himself forget about it. Just nerves, he figured. After all, why would the Sasquatch follow him?

The pack, he thought. The big Sasquatch might have followed him and picked up his pack. It could be standing right there.

His heart kicked at his chest so hard he felt the blood pulse in his wrists.

Slowly, without moving his feet, he turned around.

The green pack lay with its black belly to the sky, just as he'd left it. No Sasquatch.

Over the years he'd collected several reports of Sasquatches throwing rocks, but that rock didn't sound like it had been thrown. And it couldn't have rolled because this side of the river was flat.

Must have been loose.

A loose rock?

He pondered it for a minute, then reined in his mind and picked up his pack. He strapped it on and walked into the woods, headed back to where he left the big Sasquatch's trail. Before meeting up with the others he had to see where it led.

Chapter 24

AGGRAVATION picked at Vaughn. Lansing left before Mackey got up and still wasn't back, and Alison hadn't stirred yet.

It didn't help that it looked like yet another day of cold and dull weather.

He walked over to Alison's tent. "Alison," he said loudly.

"Yeah." Muffled, as if her head was buried in the sleeping bag.

"Time to get a move on. Let's go."

He walked back to the fire, set on drinking his coffee whether it had cooled enough or not. He couldn't wait any longer; coffee smelled a hundred times better in the woods.

His hand gripped the handle of the stainless steel mug. Warmth, then heat, seeped into his cold skin. He blew away the steam that billowed off the top, then tipped the mug and swallowed.

The coffee burned his tongue and felt like molten metal going down.

"Damn," he said, his voice scratchy from the heat. "Good coffee." Camp coffee, especially if made by a stranger, could taste awful.

"Done it a few times," Mackey said.

Vaughn cradled his cup and walked past their packed gear to the tracks Lansing had found last night. He backtracked and found several more. The animal obviously was heavy and had an enormous stride, but because it wasn't the one they were after and he was impatient to get going, he wasn't curious beyond that. He returned to the fire.

Mackey said, "You see those branches?"

"What—" And then Vaughn remembered. The snapping sounds from last night. "No."

"Just go on back, and look up."

Vaughn walked back, thinking, *Look up?* He didn't bother with the huge trees: Most were Douglas firs, though one had the shredded bark of a western red cedar. The lowest branches of these bottle brush–shaped giants could be fifty feet or more off the ground. Right now he could only see their trunks, heavy-barked pillars that climbed into the low-hanging fog.

Instead he concentrated on the smaller trees. At first he didn't see any broken limbs. But then his eyes caught a branch that hung down and across some others, and followed it up.

Holy crap, he thought.

The branch, really a limb, was twisted nearly off at its base. On his tiptoes with one arm outstretched, his fingers stopped a foot away from the break. Since he leaned a little, he figured he reached about eight feet.

Across the Sasquatch's trail and a little farther back stood another small Douglas fir. Now that he knew where to look he saw two dangling limbs, each at least two inches wide at the base, broken at about the same height. They had the same twisting break; curls of whitish, inner wood splintered from the trunk.

Beyond this tree cowered a younger fir, and Vaughn saw that the top four feet of its tip had been snapped off. The amputated section hung down limply, attached by only a thin strip of bark.

He didn't need to see any more.

When he got back to the fire, Mackey laughed. "You look like you just saw a ghost, ol' boy."

"You believe how big that thing is?"

"Damn right I believe it. An Alaskan bull moose is about that big, and a boar grizzly'll be bigger than you if he stands up."

"How big?" Alison said, walking toward them from the woods.

"Eight or nine feet at the shoulders," Vaughn said. He fixed his eyes on her. "Think about that."

She kept walking toward the sputtering flames of the fire. "I'm not leaving."

"No shame in it," Mackey said.

Alison didn't look at Mackey, but her face stiffened. Vaughn wished Mackey had kept his mouth shut.

"I'll be fine," she said.

"Then let's get going," Vaughn said. "Our gear's already packed."

She held her hands toward the fire, then walked to her tent and unhitched the rainfly.

Vaughn said: "Dr. Lansing say anything to you about when he'd be back?"

"No," she said. "I was asleep."

The guy just won't listen, he thought. "We're leaving as soon as you're ready."

When she'd finished and cinched down her pack, she brought over Mackey's .44. Vaughn had forgotten about the revolver, but was relieved when he saw it.

Her thumb and forefinger held it gently by the grip.

"It's more dangerous if you hold it that way," Mackey said. "Here." He shoved the grip into her right palm and wrapped her left hand around both. "Hold it straight out—away from everyone." He pulled it forward so her arms were extended. "There. That's what you'll do if you ever have to use it."

"I won't," she said, shoving the revolver at him. She turned to Vaughn. "What about Art? What if something happened to him?"

Vaughn preferred that they all stay together, but damned if he would be distracted or slowed down by Lansing. He told the professor to stay with the group, and not just for safety reasons. He had to get everyone up the mountain fast so they could make it back to the truck by dark. Today was the last day he would be out here, and that timeline—which he'd given Katie and the sheriff—was cemented into his brain.

"Aah, he's okay," Mackey said.

"We have a long day and Dr. Lansing knows it," Vaughn said. "He'll catch up. He can follow a trail, and he said he's been out in the woods by himself. He'll be fine."

THEY crossed the stream in their socks to avoid having their wet boots give them blisters on the hike uphill. The water was so cold that when they arrived on the other side they had to massage their red feet before pulling on dry socks.

While the others finished tying their boots, Vaughn walked across the stones of the far bank and into the ferns clumped like giant green sea anemones under the trees. He kept his eyes on the ground, looking for a track from the wounded Sasquatch—and there it was. Straight across from where the trail ended on the other side.

He returned to the stream bank. "Found the trail. Looks like it goes straight up."

"Not a problem for me," Alison said. She shot a glance at Mackey and Vaughn knew what she was thinking. Mackey better not slow them down.

Because the Sasquatch had been traveling uphill, its toes had dug in so its tracks were deeper and easier to follow. No blood, but Vaughn didn't know if that was because the wounds had clotted or because the Sasquatch had washed them in the stream. Bears did it, people did it, why not these things?

He moved as quickly as the incline allowed, and not just because he wanted to chew up distance as fast as possible. He wanted to get above the fog. No matter where they were on the slope, visibility was less than ten feet—and that made him nervous. If something came at them, his rifle would be useless. He wouldn't be able to fire it in time.

He tried not to think about it, and focused on the tracks. They went straight up the slope, between the trees, and didn't deviate. He hiked as close to the Sasquatch's course as he could.

Twice he encountered slick mounds of rock-hard snow that

the Sasquatch had walked right over, making deep tracks where Vaughn could barely kick in the toes of his boots. He had to swing around and pick up the trail on the far side.

During a water break Mackey came up and said, "Interesting, isn't it?"

"What's that?"

"Straight up." He indicated with his arm. "Animals look for the easiest route. But this thing just goes straight, like a person."

Vaughn nodded and looked up the mountain, embarrassed not to have noticed. But he'd been distracted by Lansing.

As they'd hiked up the mountain, Vaughn occasionally glanced behind, hoping to see or hear the professor and aggravated that he had to split his attention. Tracking the wounded Sasquatch and having the possibility of the bigger Sasquatch constantly ticking at his brain were more than enough. Having to listen for Lansing too—it was no way to track.

Under his breath he cursed the professor. He hoped Lansing wasn't stumbling around lost in the fog somewhere, or injured, because he would be responsible for finding him and bringing him out.

But the longer Lansing stayed away, the more a part of Vaughn wanted something bad to happen to him.

Chapter 25

LANSING felt uncomfortable. As if a fly kept buzzing his ear. He wanted to swat at it, but there was no fly.

It was his brain telling him to turn around. He'd followed the big Sasquatch's trail too far, farther than he'd intended, and the others had doubtless left without him.

He didn't know why he'd stayed on the trail so long. Perhaps it was that these tracks were fresher than those of the wounded Sasquatch. Fresher than any he'd ever seen.

Perhaps it was something else: the possibility that he would catch up with it, that it could be behind the next big tree or the one after that.

All he knew was that he'd stayed with it too long. But was that the reason for the buzzing? Because it was changing.

He'd tracked the big Sasquatch for hours, first through the trees, then near the riverbank, then crossing the river. Now he walked on the other side, around the bottom of a small mountain. He moved more slowly than he would have liked, because of the white fog that enveloped him and because the ground sloped up to his right. The awkward terrain appeared not to have bothered the big Sasquatch, something he found both unsurprising and amazing. But he was forced to stop occasionally, to rest his body from the uneven gait.

Just as he thought again that he should turn around and try to catch up with the others, the buzzing became stronger. He recognized it this time.

Warning.

And then it became fear.

His feet stopped moving. The primitive part of his brain screamed: *Turn around and run!*

But his rational, higher brain knew what the fear meant. A Sasquatch.

Or a bear. *It could be a bear.*

Suddenly he smelled a rank odor, as if a pile of maggot-infested meat had materialized a few feet away. He tried to analyze it and his mind came up with the things he'd heard and read about: sour sweat, rotting garbage, carrion. Unpleasant.

No doubt about it now. Bears had horrible breath—it was supposed to be the hardest thing about playing dead during a bear attack—but a bear's mouth would have to be right in his face for him to smell it.

Gorillas emitted a powerful fear odor, meaning they did it when they were alarmed but not necessarily scared. Depending on the circumstances they could in fact act aggressively. From people's accounts of strong odors associated with Sasquatches, he'd theorized that at least the males had a similar warning mechanism. Now he knew.

His eyes watered. His sympathetic nervous system beat him over the head, urging him to *run away!* The Sasquatch was there. Close.

He blinked and looked around, but all he saw were tree trunks and ground vegetation. And fog. Mostly fog. Involuntarily, he stepped backward.

Suddenly the smell was overpowering. He fought the urge to gag and swallowed a few times. It was difficult: his mouth was dry.

Was the Sasquatch closer? He hadn't heard it move. Or did the stronger odor mean it was angrier, or that it felt threatened?

Fear banged against the walls of his skull. His breath puffed out before him like locomotive steam—and that's when he realized he was walking away.

BY lunch they still hadn't crested the mountain and Vaughn wasn't happy about it.

At eleven-thirty Alison had asked if they could stop, and though hungry and tired himself, Vaughn said to give it another half an hour. By noon he was famished, thirsty and in need of a rest.

They lunched on a small ledge that softened the grade of the mountain. Over a Spartan meal of elk jerky, cheese, gorp and water, little was said.

Mackey gestured with a strip of meat. "Can't be too badly hurt if it went straight up," he said. "And no blood."

Vaughn figured that was for Alison's benefit, and knew he was right when Mackey looked at her and said: "Not endangered yet, eh?"

Alison didn't respond. She just chewed and stared down the mountain.

Now back on the wounded Sasquatch's trail, the fog long gone, Vaughn looked up and figured they would hit the crest no later than two o'clock. There they would rest again. And if the trail continued the way it had been going—straight and strong with no blood—that's when he'd tell them they were going back.

LANSING'S eyes darted upslope, searching out anything he might trip on as he half walked, half ran up the mountain.

Deadfall ahead. He conserved his strength and went around.

He'd never felt this way, terrified, and nothing he could do about it. The big Sasquatch was chasing him and he was reacting. Instinctively.

Part of his brain watched the whole scene, fascinated. At what level was this instinct encoded. Chromosomal? Was this a generic response to intense fear, or was it specific to an animal the human race had all but forgotten?

When he began his retreat he thought the animal would stay put. But it didn't. It walked a little behind and above him—amazingly quiet, but sometimes he heard a heavy, soft padding.

Maybe he imagined he heard it. But he couldn't mistake his fear, which had driven him into a kind of shock. Fear seemed to be a hidden engine in his body and, now exposed, forced him on, smashing his boots into the ground like pistons, pushing him up the mountain. Heedless to everything except one command: *Go.*

A part of him wondered whether he could stop.

The first time he started uphill he hadn't taken four steps when he heard a grunt: loud, deep and intentional. It came out of the fog from every direction, and scared him as badly as if he'd felt the Sasquatch's hand clamp onto his shoulder.

He quickly corrected his course, but knew he couldn't wait until all his energy was spent before heading uphill toward the others. He had to try again. But when?

He thought about counting seconds and counting steps but did neither.

At some point he regained enough courage to try again. He didn't know how much time had elapsed or how far he'd walked. It was just *now*—though a part of him kept screaming: *No! Don't do it!*

As gradually as he could, he turned up the mountain. The muscles across his back tightened, anticipating the Sasquatch's disapproval. But no grunt came, no snapping branches, nothing. The silence was as instructive as any noise.

He kept going. His legs pounded up the mountainside, and he realized he couldn't feel them anymore. He watched them maneuvering around trees and crushing ground plants as if they were being operated by someone else.

He couldn't really hear, either. His whole body boomed and thrummed with each push and pull of his heart.

But his eyes worked perfectly, and every so often flitted to the trees to his left. He desperately wanted to see it, the animal he'd studied and tracked for ten years and never glimpsed. The animal that had been responsible for everything in his adult life.

Still the Sasquatch eluded him. Yet he could see it, as he'd imagined it so many times: a full-grown male, nine feet tall and of gorilla density, about nine hundred pounds. Hard for people to believe, but its size was merely an adaptive advantage to living in cold weather as greater mass meant better conservation of body heat. It also made life in trees impossible. Bipedal locomotion resulted, another evolutionary advantage in mountainous habitat—longer legs and greater strength made it easier to handle the terrain and walk through snow.

Like the Yeti. Some Tibetans called those animals *Metoh Kangmi*. A Native American name for Sasquatches was *Matah Kagmi*.

Matah Kagmi. He kept repeating it to himself, and it became the rhythm of his legs.

He wanted to see one. But he marched away because he also didn't want to see it. He didn't want to see it and be terrified.

Why should I be?

Go.

He scrambled up the mountainside as fast as he could, his pants and shirt soaked by fog and sweat. Though he breathed heavily, he didn't feel tired. *Adrenaline,* part of him said. Flight instead of fight.

Why am I running away?

Go. It's chasing you.

But he knew the Sasquatch wasn't really chasing him. It was shadowing him. If it wanted to catch him, it could. So it was seeing him off for a reason.

And through the haze of his fear, he was starting to realize what that reason was.

Chapter 26

VAUGHN checked his watch, which for hunting was digital: he learned long ago that animals could easily hear the regular ticking of a quartz watch. The flat face read 2:18, so they'd reached the top pretty much on schedule. Surprisingly, even Mackey had kept the pace, though at times he'd breathed quick and shallow, like an overheated dog.

"Let's take a fifteen-minute break," Vaughn said.

The other two walked past where he knelt by one of the wounded Sasquatch's tracks. Though still deep and holding its shape, the track, like the rest, was no longer fresh. Moisture in the air and the earth, along with other minute forces, had caused the edges to crumble and blur.

All the tracks he'd seen had been made yesterday. That meant he was a solid day behind the animal, which, though wounded, had gone straight up a mountain and hadn't staggered, fallen or wavered in its course. There were no signs that it was dying. Surely Mackey had reached the same conclusion, and Alison could be convinced. Her bravado only proved how scared she was and how much she didn't know.

They wouldn't find it, and Vaughn was relieved. Still, a pang of uncertainty persisted. The Sasquatch hadn't died right away, but it could have died later or might be dying now, even though the lack of blood and the animal's strong course made these slim possibilities.

He walked over to where Mackey and Alison sat. It was a large area cleared of trees—a logging deck, cut fairly recently, where timber would be staged for transport. No road reached it and that meant that it would be used for helicopter logging. The practice had become more common since environmentalists had convinced the federal government to curtail road building in National Forests, something he privately applauded. Enjoying the woods had to be done on foot, he felt. Driving through the wilderness was cheating, and cheapened the experience.

Just past the lip of the deck, one tree caught his eye. Its needles shone brick red in the grey light, and against the green background it seemed like a lone lifeboat on a gloomy sea. The red tree made him remember it was bear season.

When black bears came out of hibernation, some sat at the base of Douglas firs, stripped off the bark and ate the cambium layer between the bark and wood to jump-start their digestive systems. This killed the tree, and the needles turned red.

Boone told him that timber companies used to kill black bears because the animals girdled so many trees. At some point the companies decided to try a new tactic, and trucked in drums of sugar beet pulp, oats, molasses and other tasty items that seemed to work just as well for the bears. Fewer trees were ruined, and the timber companies continued the spring feeding program.

But without any bears being killed and the increased amount of berries and other foods growing in clear-cut areas, the bear population exploded. The animals endangered human users of the forest and spread into residential areas. So with the Forest Service's blessing, Carolina Pacific and other timber companies conducted controlled bear hunts, like the one he'd been on yesterday.

Yesterday. Already it seemed longer than that.

He dropped his pack on the ground between Mackey and Alison who rested six feet apart, not speaking. He sat down on it and, releasing a deep breath, raised his eyes and looked out.

Forested mountains folded steeply away from them, each crowded with the sharp, triangular tips of Douglas firs. Clouds capped the peaks—they looked parasitic, with their wispy tendrils snaking down into the trees.

Farther down the mountains, patches of fog reminded him of spiderwebs clinging to massive green bushes. They barely moved, as if the only force they responded to was the Earth's rotation.

Between the peaks, slate-bottomed clouds rested like battleships at berth. Their presence seemed to make the air colder.

He noticed that a few of the mountainsides, like the one they sat on, hadn't been cut for decades. But on others the older, darker trees suddenly stopped and the lighter green of reprod took over. The sharp color and size contrasts were highlighted by the grey stripes of logging roads that bordered the cuts.

"Clear-cuts," Alison said.

The disgust in her voice made Vaughn remember that he'd also thought clear-cuts were ugly when he first moved out here. Since then he'd come to accept them as part of the landscape, as great places to pick berries, see wildlife and hunt.

"Just like the fires set by Indians," Mackey said.

"Native Americans," Alison said. "It looks disgusting. Like they used a laser beam."

"The forest needs that natural cycle."

"That isn't natural!"

"Sure it is," Mackey said. "In fact, it's a lot tamer than what Mother Nature did just a few miles from here."

"What are you talking about?"

"You might be too young to remember. Frank, isn't Mount Saint Helens around here somewhere?"

"Yeah," Vaughn said. "If the weather was clearer you could see it over there." He pointed northwest.

To Alison, Mackey said, "You know how much timber *Miz*

Nature leveled when that mountain blew? Two hundred and thirty square miles. And it's a hell of a lot less pretty to look at than this."

"So?" she said.

"So are you mad at the volcano now?"

"That's ridiculous. You're comparing a once-in-a-lifetime natural occurrence with decades of taxpayer-subsidized rape."

"Did the mammoths rape it too?"

Alison's pink cheeks filled with blood.

"You know what?" she said, thrusting a finger at him. "You are the most completely irrational—"

"Alison," he said, "look and listen while you're out here. You'll learn things you can't from books and reports."

She drew in a deep breath, as if she would try to blow Mackey off the mountain.

Vaughn held up a hand for her to be quiet. He cocked an ear back toward the slope they had just come up.

Alison made a sound; he waved his hand at her. Her mouth closed into a frown.

". . . ellooo . . ."

Faint, but getting louder.

Lansing.

"Over here!" Vaughn yelled, standing up. He felt like an idiot yelling in the woods, but Lansing had already given away their presence to anything that was out here.

"Hello?"

Closer now. The word sounded choked off.

"Here!" Alison said.

Fresh anger about Lansing's selfishness streamed into Vaughn's brain. But when the professor came into view, Vaughn forgot about it.

Lansing's face had the blanched look of a drowned man. Sweat dripped from his chin, and the hair that poked from underneath his black wool cap was dark and wet. So were his green pants. He breathed so hard he couldn't speak.

When he stopped walking his legs trembled, then gave way. He fell to the ground and lay with his face to the sky, propped up like a turtle by his pack.

After a moment he threw up his hand and pulled off the cap. Steam rose from his matted hair.

"What happened?" Vaughn said.

Lansing held up a finger. He smiled weakly at Alison's worried face. White mucus on his lips stretched like congealed glue.

"Was . . . hurry," Lansing said, breathing hard. "Catch . . . you."

"Are you all right?" Alison said.

Lansing pointed at her water bottle. She unscrewed the cap and gave it to him. Between gasps Lansing drained the bottle.

Vaughn thought: *He didn't stop for water?*

"We're glad you're okay," Alison said.

"Give you some," Lansing said to her, still breathing hard. "Have." He jabbed a thumb at his backpack.

Vaughn waited until the heaving of Lansing's chest subsided and then said: "You look spooked."

An odd, high-pitched laugh jumped from Lansing's mouth. "Caught me, deputy. Spooked myself. Heard noises, got scared."

"What did you hear?"

Lansing worked his shoulders out of the pack straps, reached back and pulled the pack around. He tugged a full water bottle from a webbed side pocket and took a long swig. Suddenly he coughed; water flew from his mouth. He coughed a few more times, then recovered and wiped his mouth with his sleeve.

"Followed the tracks," he said, still breathing heavily. "The big one. Tracks angled toward the road, then back—back to the stream, about a mile from camp. Found the trail on the other side. Followed it another mile—figured I went too far." He smiled. "I apologize for getting carried away."

He leaned back with his legs straight out in front of him. One spasmed. He put the bottle down, then grabbed the leg with both hands and massaged it.

"Weren't you scared of the bigfoot?" Alison said.

"Not really. These animals are nocturnal."

"You made that deduction after last night?" Vaughn said.

"No." Lansing brought his knees up and massaged his hamstrings. "Many Sasquatch sightings are at night, which also is when many footprints appear. Approximately the same number of sightings of these animals occurs at night as during the day. As far fewer people are active at night, and because we can't see as well nor as far at night, we must assume that that's when these animals are much more active." He stopped to breathe. "If not, we'd of course see them much more frequently during the day. In fact, that they're nocturnal may be more responsible than any other factor for their continued undiscovered status—and probably for their very survival, since humans have asserted dominion over every other diurnal animal."

"Can they see in the dark?" Mackey said.

Lansing's breathing was becoming more controlled. "Certainly better than we can, which at the least means their retinas have more cones. There have been reports of their eyes glowing when lights are shined at them. If true that could be the same phenomenon as human red-eye in photographs, where the pupil is open and the camera flash reveals an exposed retina. The second possibility is that the animals have a *tapetum lucidum*, or reflective retina, like cats and dogs. But these don't occur in any primates so I doubt it."

Vaughn wondered what else Lansing knew that he wasn't telling them. But it didn't matter. They were outta here.

Lansing said: "Before I answer any more questions, I'd like to eat some lunch."

Didn't stop to eat either. Vaughn said, "We'll give Dr. Lansing a few minutes to recuperate and then we're going back." He didn't wait for reactions. "The blood's gone and the trail's old. This thing moves way faster than we can, and with its speed and strength could stay far ahead of us forever. Especially in this country."

Mackey said: "Grizzlies can travel twenty miles a night over mountains. I bet our friend can move a lot faster, even winged."

Vaughn said: "It's either recovering, which I believe, or dead in a place we probably won't find. So we're—"

"I'm staying out here," Lansing said.

"Me too," Alison said.

Vaughn focused on Alison. "Why?"

"I haven't been told to leave yet."

"By who?"

"By the person who sent me here."

"Brenda Underwood," Vaughn said.

"I'd rather not say," she said.

"Well, why don't you give this mystery person a call right now and ask her whether you should stay or go back? Tell her that the deputy sheriff in charge says this is a wild goose chase, that he's going back and that if you stay you'll be risking your life for no apparent reason. Got that?"

Alison didn't respond.

"You need a phone?" he said.

"I have one—but it didn't work last night."

"Now that you have a horizon it should work. If it doesn't, you can borrow mine."

She mumbled something and walked off.

When she was out of earshot he turned to Lansing and said, "You know you're never going to catch up with this animal. And by being selfish, you're putting her at risk."

"Deputy," Lansing said, "I think you're right. I won't catch up with the wounded Sasquatch, but I may find more evidence of its existence. And Alison is quite capable of making her own decisions. She's not my responsibility."

Vaughn didn't care about leaving Lansing out here. But Alison—if something happened to her, a young woman, because he left her out in the woods, there would be hell to pay. From everywhere: the sheriff, the federal government, the media.

He hoped whoever she was calling would have enough sense to tell her to leave. But somehow he doubted it.

Chapter 27

MACKEY said, "Frank, can I talk with you a minute?" He turned and walked away from Lansing, toward the edge of the logging deck. Vaughn followed.

Twenty feet into the trees, Mackey stopped. In a low voice he said: "If they stay, I have to stay too."

"Why?" Vaughn said.

"What do you think I'm doing here, ol' boy?"

Vaughn said, "I thought if we said we were both leaving, they'd leave, too." But as soon as the words came out, he realized that wasn't realistic.

"C'mon," Mackey said. "You know Art won't leave, and God knows what Alison will be told to do."

A cold spike of stress pushed through Vaughn's belly. If he wasn't back tonight everything—the sheriff, Katie—would become a genuine problem. A big one.

His face must have betrayed his thoughts because Mackey said: "Sorry, ol' boy. The stakes are too high."

"What if Alison says she's going back?"

"Since Art's staying out here, I'll track this thing one more day to make sure it's not lying dead somewhere close. Don't think it is, but I have to make sure. If the trail's still going strong, I'll leave. Art can poke around all he wants after that. He won't find anything."

"What if you find it and it's dying?"

Mackey smiled. "I'll handle it the same way I handle any so-called endangered species. Shoot, shovel and shut up."

"And if you find it dead?"

The usual twinkle in Mackey's eyes disappeared. "I'm the only one with a gun."

Vaughn thought: *Is everyone crazy?*

He remembered something he wanted to ask Mackey. "Brenda Underwood is the head of the Fish and Wildlife Service."

"That's right," Mackey said.

"Is that who Alison's calling?"

"Hell if I know, but it wouldn't matter who she called."

"Any idea why the Fish and Wildlife Service would send a nonbiologist?"

"That's why it won't matter who she talks to," Mackey said. "The Fish and Wildlife Service is all about philosophy now. Science supports the philosophy, and the philosophy comes from D.C. Just like Alison."

Vaughn started to walk back, then stopped. "What do you think she's doing here?"

Mackey said, "She's just a political placeholder. In case this whole thing blows up in our faces, Underwood or whoever will be able to say she had someone out here."

"Endangered species."

"Gotta be."

"I'M supposed to stay." Alison's jaw clamped shut. Vaughn couldn't tell if that signified fear, regret or just plain stubbornness.

"For what reason?" he said.

"To keep my eyes open."

"That's it?"

"That's it."

Fucking wonderful, Vaughn thought. *Keep her eyes open. What is this, some top secret spy crap? In the woods?* He said, "Aren't you scared of getting attacked by one of these things?"

"I wouldn't worry about it," Lansing said.

Vaughn said, "You seemed pretty worried about it when you came up that hill."

Lansing popped some gorp in his mouth and said nothing.

"Well, I'm worried about it," Vaughn said, looking at Alison. "What about you?"

"I'm staying," she said.

"What the hell for? What could you possibly learn that you don't know already?"

He controlled himself. "Look, if that big one comes back tonight we'll be even farther from the truck. But if we leave now we'll be back in civilization tonight—before it gets dark. Do you really want to spend another night out here?"

For a moment the obstinate hostility faded from her eyes. "I *can't* leave."

Dammit, Vaughn thought. He had to tell the sheriff.

"I have to call in," he said.

"Me too," Mackey said.

Vaughn zipped open his pack and took out the satellite phone. "Wait here," he said, directing it mostly at Lansing. He punched in the number as he walked across the bare ground of the logging deck. Just inside the trees, he stopped.

"Sheriff's office."

"Billy, it's Frank."

"Hey Frank! You on your way back?"

"The Old Man in?"

"Yeah. Hold on."

As he waited, dread twisted the steel spike deeper into his guts. The conversation would be hopelessly one-sided: Even appealing to the sheriff's sense of responsibility, this was exactly what the Old Man warned him about.

Maybe I should just leave them all out here, Vaughn thought. But dammit, he couldn't. It would be one thing to abandon them with a local guide or a direct way out, but leaving them in the wilderness with no truck, no road, no trail and two dangerous animals was wrong. The sheriff would of course see that, but he wouldn't be happy about it.

"Frank."

"Hey sheriff."

"You headed in?" The Old Man's tone was friendly, but re-strained.

"I could be out by tonight, but I don't think that's wise." Vaughn explained what the others had just said. It was the first the sheriff had heard of Lansing.

"Goddammit, Frank. You see how things can get out of control?"

"I can see how the unexpected can happen, sheriff, but things aren't out of control." Lansing's face flitted across Vaughn's mind. "It looks like we won't find this thing, so we'll walk around for a little while tomorrow and then I'll get them all out of here."

"So you might not be back until Friday."

Vaughn winced. Tomorrow they might be too far away to make it back to the road by nightfall. The Old Man never missed a thing.

"I suppose it's possible," Vaughn said.

A short silence, then the sheriff said: "You might as well not show up for duty. We're covered for the Slugfest."

Vaughn knew that was a lie. All hands were needed for the Slugfest.

He didn't know what to say, but it didn't matter. The Sheriff had hung up.

Chapter 28

ENSCONCED in his office on the top floor of the Carolina Pacific building in downtown Raleigh, Mark Kingston was all too aware of the shadows forming on his wall. He was desperately trying to wind up his day so he could make it to his youngest son's soccer game that evening. "From the beginning this time, Dad," Brian had said. Kingston felt rotten every time he thought about it.

The phone beeped and his secretary said, "I know you don't want any calls, but it's Chris Mackey. He says you'll want to talk to him."

"He's right. Put him through."

The phone beeped again. From long experience as a public relations man, Kingston took a moment to steel himself for the worst possible news.

He reached toward the Speaker button, then decided against it. He picked up the receiver. "Chris! You on your way home?"

"Only if you call the top of a mountain home—like I might if I was, say, a bigfoot."

e

"I have a feeling I'm not going to like this."

"Probably not. For starters, there's four people out here: me, the deputy sheriff, a professor in love with Sasquatches and a girl from the Fish and Wildlife Service."

"What? What the hell's she doing there?"

"Can't you guess?" Mackey said. "It's a problem."

"No kidding."

"I mean a bigger problem than you think."

Kingston's hand squeezed the receiver. "I'm listening."

Mackey's voice crackled into his ear. "You hear about that red wolf shooting down east?"

Kingston remembered reading about it in the *News & Observer*. Red wolves were a federally listed endangered species, and in 1987 the Fish and Wildlife Service introduced some onto federal land in eastern North Carolina. But Mackey and many others thought the wolves really were hybrid coyotes—not a distinct species—and therefore shouldn't be bred and introduced.

Animosity toward the animals and the Service boiled over when the wolves moved off federal land and started eating game animals and pets. Local citizens swore revenge, but the Fish and Wildlife Service forbade it—which was in direct contravention to what it said initially, when it needed local support for the wolf introductions. The federally protected wolves were not to be touched, the agency stated. Anyone who shot a wolf for any reason would be prosecuted. No exceptions.

Soon after the agency's threat hit the press, a dead red wolf was found on the eastbound shoulder of Route 64 in the Alligator River National Wildlife Refuge. A single bullet had punched a neat hole behind its right ear, just above the radio collar. The U.S. attorney swore he would find and prosecute the killer.

Kingston said, "Don't tell me."

"I'm one of the people under investigation for it," Mackey said. "My lawyer told me not to set foot on federal land until the investigation's over. It's supposed to be finished this week."

"You can't be serious."

Mackey said, "I think it's bull too, but I'm supposed to

take it seriously. He said if I screw this up I'd be effectively banned from all federal contact, for a long while. That would kill my business."

"Why didn't you tell me this in the first place?"

"Because I wanted to go on a bigfoot hunt and because I didn't think there'd be a chance of seeing anyone from the Fish and Wildlife Service here. Besides, a guy as well-connected as you should be able to pull some strings."

Kingston winced. Though he had favors to trade around most of Washington, D.C., he had absolutely no IOUs from anyone in the Fish and Wildlife Service. He'd met the new Service director, Brenda Underwood, only once, at a joint news conference about establishing refuges for endangered red-cockaded woodpeckers. But that whole thing had been so easy: the refuges were on land Carolina Pacific planned never to cut anyway, the environmentalists went away touting their "victory" and everyone got good press, including Underwood and the President.

No political debts came from it. Calling her out of the blue now would make her suspicious, and she was no pushover— especially when it came to Chris Mackey.

Mackey said, "Just give Brenda Underwood a call. She loves me."

"Oh yeah," Kingston said. He picked up a pen. "What's the girl's name?"

"Alison Lombard, from the Office of Congressional and Legislative Affairs. Showed up at the last minute."

Kingston wrote down the name.

"Said it was her or the FBI."

Kingston felt his arteries constrict. "The FBI?"

Mackey said, "Probably a bluff."

Kingston realized Mackey was right. "Why don't you give me the rest of it."

"The first night we were visited by a Sasquatch."

"Don't you mean *the* Sasquatch?"

"Nope. This was a different one. Bigger."

"Are you sure?"

"Does a Sasquatch shit in the woods?" Mackey said. "It threw a pack at our tent. Gave me a shiner."

"Anything else?"

"This morning the professor left camp early and I followed him. He made a call. Want to guess?"

"The media."

"You got it. Some guy named Tom Sun at a Seattle TV station."

"Thompson?" Kingston wrote it down.

"No. First name Tom, last name S-U-N. Lansing told him about the shooting and who's out here."

"Did he mention Carolina Pacific by name?"

Static drizzled across the signal.

"Chris? Hello?"

Mackey's voice came back. "—orry. Connection."

"Did he mention Carolina Pacific by name?"

"Yep," Mackey said.

"Fabulous." Kingston wrote "CP named" on his pad. "Tell me that's it."

"Almost. The deputy sheriff just tried to get everyone to go back. The professor outright refused, and Alison called her handler and was told to stick around, to keep her eyes open. So we're staying out here."

"How long?"

"At most another day."

Kingston thought for a second. "What are the chances you'll find this thing?"

"Slim. I'm just worried about what the bigger one might do. If it gets any friendlier we might have to kill it."

"What?"

"Hey, I'm not saying I want it that way, but that human survival instinct is pretty strong, ol' boy. So in case it happens, you might want to start working some magic at that end."

Yeah, Kingston thought, *coming right up.* "Okay, Chris. Hang in there. And listen—call me, okay? Let me know what's happening."

"Roger."

Kingston dropped the receiver back in its cradle and thought: *What the hell am I going to do about this?*

Brenda Underwood and most of the Fish and Wildlife Service hated Chris Mackey—for exactly the reasons Carolina Pacific employed him.

As an outspoken critic of the Endangered Species Act,

Mackey had powerful friends in Congress. Most were Republicans. Every chance they got they asked him to testify before their committees about the act and the Fish and Wildlife Service's mismanagement of it. Mackey also wrote op-ed pieces that appeared in the *Washington Times* and the *Wall Street Journal,* and was a favorite guest of conservative radio talk-show hosts.

He kept hammering the Service, and Brenda Underwood appeared to take it personally. They were "her people." And although she came from a New York state hunting and fishing family, and had climbed the political ladder at the New York and Florida state fish and game agencies, she seemed to have acquired an environmentally correct agenda.

At the woodpecker news conference she encouraged North Carolinians to "ignore divisive elements" that "exaggerate government power and contribute nothing positive to the process of conserving endangered species." She might as well have named Mackey, whom she specifically asked not to be invited.

Kingston's teeth clamped on the end of his pen.

Always a live wire, Mackey now was a ticking political bomb. If anyone at the Fish and Wildlife Service found out about his being on federal land and that Kingston had sent him there, it would be politically disastrous—especially if Mackey had killed that wolf.

Even if it didn't kill the BayMun sale, his career could be finished.

His teeth ground the hard plastic. He needed an angle. The logical place to start was figuring out who leaked to the Fish and Wildlife Service.

He doubted it was one of the hunters who shot the Sasquatch. They worked for CP, and most of their friends probably did, too. And in any case, Alison Lombard wasn't from out there. She was sent from the main office in D.C., and the possibility that the hunters knew her was infinitesimal.

No one else made any sense, either. But the more Kingston thought about it, the more it seemed that the only possibility was Scott Walsh.

Walsh was chief of the U.S. Forest Service, and Kingston met with him this morning in Washington, D.C. as part of his "insurance" strategy. Kingston explained the situation and made a suggestion: "We send someone out there we can trust to do the right thing. No names—you and the President know nothing about it. That way we have someone there on the ground, while at the same time insulating you, the Forest Service and the President should anything go wrong."

Of course, by that time Mackey was already there.

Kingston knew Walsh would love "insulation" because, like all career bureaucrats, Walsh was a turtle. A turtle was built for one thing: self-protection. It moved ponderously and tentatively, and when it sensed something threatening, retreated into its shell.

So Walsh would leave the risks to Carolina Pacific and keep his mouth shut, unknowingly ensuring that he, not Carolina Pacific, would be the scapegoat if things went badly.

CP had done its duty. The government had been officially informed and Walsh was high enough to make it look like CP had made an honest effort. Kingston would go no higher on the political ladder because that was the realm of political appointees, who had a tendency to act foolishly, leak and sometimes panic.

Kingston doubted Walsh would figure it out. Not until it was too late, anyway.

But if Walsh hadn't figured it out, why else would he involve the Fish and Wildlife Service? He had to know the risk in telling those endangered-species nuts.

Kingston spat the pen from his mouth—and suddenly remembered the soccer game. He checked his watch. If he left now and traffic wasn't bad, he would hear the whistle screech, the first muffled whump of a leather cleat on a leather ball, and see his son race up and down the field for ninety minutes.

But damn it all, he couldn't leave yet. He had to take care of a few things first.

Chapter 29

VAUGHN wanted to walk them until their legs fell off. Until they were cold, sore and so miserable that they would wake up tomorrow beaten and ready to go back. That way he would get them as far from the top of the mountain as possible, and prove they would never catch up to the wounded Sasquatch.

But getting down was taking too long because the wounded Sasquatch hadn't gone straight over the mountain. Instead it angled down and across the slope, heading roughly south. That took the animal deeper into the wilderness, though Vaughn figured it might have angled across merely to lessen the strain on its injured leg.

Regardless of the reason, Vaughn couldn't compensate by walking faster. Even though he felt the Sasquatch was long gone, he still had to be cautious. He placed his feet carefully, and carried the rifle ready in his hands.

•   •   •

"CASE Associates."

"This is Mark Kingston."

"Yes, Mr. Kingston."

"Brenda Underwood and Alison Lombard." He spelled both names. "Employees of the federal Fish and Wildlife Service."

"Anyone else, Mr. Kingston?"

"No."

"What is your deadline please?"

"ASAP."

"You understand that the ASAP designation will bump up our fee."

"Yes."

"Thank you, Mr. Kingston."

He hung up.

Nice euphemism. "Bump up" meant an exorbitant amount of money, which he would be all too happy to pay. And not just for whatever they dug up—even though Case was a legal operation, whenever Kingston called he felt like he was dealing with the Mafia. So part of the reason he would happily pay was that he was afraid of what they might do if he didn't.

Case Associates was his favorite of the Washington, D.C., area "investigative agencies." Privately he called them grave diggers. If any skeletons hung in anyone's closet, no matter how well concealed, these people would find them. Discreetly.

He wanted—needed—dirt on Brenda Underwood as a safety net. Right now he couldn't approach her about Chris Mackey or the Sasquatch without putting himself at her mercy.

With any luck Mackey would return quickly, the Sasquatch would melt back into the woods and no ripples would be made on the political pond. But just in case, he would have whatever bones the grave diggers found on Underwood and Alison Lombard.

Case had to find something. Because if they didn't and anything went wrong, he was screwed.

VAUGHN glanced back and saw Mackey standing with his head cocked slightly to the left, upslope.

Instinctively Vaughn froze. His ears reached out to the currents of air and fingered them for unusual pulses. His eyes probed the spaces between the trees for odd bumps or bulges, horizontal forms, the wiggle of an ear, a wrong texture. Anything out of the ordinary.

But all he saw were identical rigid trunks. He heard nothing except the background sigh of the woods. The ominous silence, the feeling just before Boone got hurt, wasn't there.

Slowly he walked back to Mackey. "Hear something?"

Mackey kept looking upslope. "Funny feeling," he whispered.

No more needed to be said. A few times in the woods and on the job, Vaughn had felt it; an uncomfortable sensation, what people called "being watched." He knew this ability, to feel a presence watching you, was a wild sense humans retained. For most people it kicked in in places like dark streets, restaurants and bars, and usually wasn't intense. People didn't know why they decided to look in a specific direction to find someone staring at them, or started walking faster because they felt someone behind them. They just did.

But for hunters tuned into the wild, the feeling was almost a physical force, like something tapping you on the shoulder. Sometimes it pushed at you, thick as a wall.

Only fellow predators, including people, triggered it. The last time it happened to him, he was camping alone by a stream in the Indian Heaven Wilderness. One night he had an uncomfortable feeling, but couldn't see anything beyond the firelight. In the morning he scouted for tracks, and directly across from his camp, in the soft earth on the other side of the stream, were the pug marks of a cougar. Who knows how long it stood there watching him.

Many North American hunters told similar stories and he'd read that the great African cats caused the same sensation, though far more intensely—like Mackey's experience with the leopard. It was eerie: Hunting guides swore the big cats had to be stalked without looking at them or they would sense you coming, even from downwind.

He didn't doubt it, nor did he doubt that Sasquatches could

sense just as well and project equal power. But if that's what Mackey was feeling, he should be feeling it too.

Alison and Lansing reached them. Lansing said, "What is it? Did you hear something?" He alternated between looking at Mackey and back up the mountainside. Vaughn noticed that Lansing's hands, held at his sides, were clenched.

"Chris got a funny feeling," Vaughn said, "that's all."

"Like last night?"

Mackey said, "Not exactly."

Vaughn didn't want this to become a conversation. "You ready?"

Mackey blinked, then turned to Vaughn and said, "Yeah."

Vaughn resumed walking, a little bit slower now. Again he tried to relax his brain, to let simple awareness push aside everything conscious so he could merge with the woods.

After a time he succeeded, though his muscles maintained a slight tension. It was a tension of expectation, like hunting.

"ANDERSON."

"Tim, it's Mark," Kingston said.

"Hey Mark. How're things at headquarters?"

"Barely have time to scratch an itch. Listen, I think it'd be good if we sent out a few anonymous faxes. Faxes always worked better than e-mails."

"Been a while. Anything I should know about?"

"Tell you later," Kingston said. "First one should be a couple pages, single-spaced typewritten rambling about bigfeet and alien landings in Washington and Oregon. Maybe other places. The second fax needs to be about a hoax specific to the Pinchot."

"Send to all media?"

Kingston pondered that. Mackey only mentioned one TV station, but he knew that peer pressure across all media was a big factor in whether a story got covered. If it looked too risky, they wouldn't bite. Like politicians.

"Yeah," he said. "Seattle and Portland."

"Anything else?"

"No. Thanks. And if you hear anything strange, let me know."

Kingston hung up. Tim Anderson worked for him out of Carolina Pacific's Portland, Oregon, office and knew the drill. A good man.

He pulled over his overstuffed Rolodex and, starting at A, flipped the first card toward him. It was an old habit, a tactile aid in thinking for which his company-issued Palm Pilot was no use. He hadn't needed the number he was looking for in years, and he knew he'd buried it. The only question was where.

VAUGHN still sensed nothing out of the ordinary. He wondered whether Mackey did, and checked.

Mackey walked toward him with his attention focused on the ground. Beyond Mackey was Alison, but where was . . . Then through the trees he saw Lansing, much farther back.

What the hell's a matter with this guy? he thought.

He walked back to Mackey and pointed uphill. Mackey looked, rolled his eyes and leaned against a tree.

"Keep going," Vaughn said, and stalked up the Sasquatch's trail.

When he approached Alison she looked as if she expected him to say something. But he passed her without a word.

Lansing had actually backtracked up the slope, and Vaughn was surprised how long it took his tired hamstrings and calves to get him there. He expected the professor to notice him, but the whole time he approached, Lansing never turned around. Just kept looking up the mountain.

"What the fuck is going on?" Vaughn said quietly.

Lansing practically jumped out of his skin. "Deputy Vaughn. I didn't hear you coming."

"What's up there?"

"I'm not sure," Lansing said.

"You were chased up the other side by the big Sasquatch and now it's following us. Right?"

Lansing looked at him. "I was . . . pushed. Not chased."

"Did you see it?"

"No."

"Hear it?"

"Yes," Lansing said. "Walking."

"How about now?"

"I thought I heard something."

"So these things aren't nocturnal."

"Not exclusively."

Vaughn sucked air into his lungs and blew it out. The cloud shot past Lansing's face. "I'll say this one more time, Dr. Lansing. Your safety and the safety of the rest of group are my responsibility. That's the only reason I'm still here. When you remove yourself from the group you put our collective safety at risk. So stay with the damn group."

Without waiting for an answer he turned and took a step down the mountain.

Pee-weee.

From habit, Vaughn's brain tried to figure out the species of bird that made that kind of call.

A hand clamped down on his shoulder.

"You hear that?" Lansing hissed. His breath warmed Vaughn's ear.

Vaughn turned around and was amazed to see Lansing's eyes afire. Over a bird call.

Pwee, pwee.

This time the call was farther away. The bird had flown on.

Lansing faced the direction of the calls, a maniacal grin on his face. "That's a Sasquatch."

"Sounded like a bird to me."

"That's what it's supposed to sound like. But have you ever heard a bird like that?"

Vaughn thought for a moment. The calls were different, but not that different. "I've heard birds make stranger sounds." Crows practically talked.

Lansing stared across the slope, still smiling. "I'll catch up."

Vaughn felt like sticking his rifle in Lansing's back and marching him off the mountain. "Didn't you understand what I said?"

Lansing looked at him—almost through him. "I understood all of it, deputy. Please remember that I'm a scientist and a fairly capable woodsman. I'm going to go investigate those sounds and then I'll head straight down the mountain and rendezvous with you."

Vaughn's hands tightened on his rifle, but then he thought,

Hell with it. If the guy was nutty enough to get himself lost over a few bird calls, so be it. He wouldn't waste any more time worrying about it.

He walked back down the trail.

"He's being an idiot," he said to Alison as he went by. "He's going to get himself lost, hurt or worse."

Then it struck him that maybe Lansing wanted to get lost. To *appear* lost. The crazy professor would hide behind a tree so they would waste time waiting around or looking for him, and be forced to stay out here longer. That way they would have more time to run into a Sasquatch.

If that's his game, it won't work, Vaughn decided.

He passed Mackey, looked for the next track—then heard something coming down the mountain, behind him.

He whirled around in time to see a rock twice the size of his fist fly between Mackey and Alison at about knee level. He watched it bounce downhill, ricocheting off tree trunks and kicking up dirt.

His eyes searched upslope for Lansing, but all he saw was trees.

Lansing had to be incredibly careless to do that. Vaughn wondered whether the professor was climbing something. A rock wall, maybe. He craned his neck, but still couldn't see anything.

Idiot. The guy was getting more dangerous by the minute.

MARK Kingston tried to ignore the fact that the orange rays of sun streaming into his office were at an angle below horizontal. But it was difficult. The shadow of his LCD computer monitor stretched up the far wall and bent like an old man at the connection of wall and ceiling.

He piled everything back into the desk drawer, shut it and pulled the handle to make sure it locked. "Shit!" he said aloud. The number wasn't there, either.

He glared at the Rolodex. It had to be there, dammit. Twice he'd flipped through the cards, reading every one as if his life depended on it.

He sighed and for the millionth time checked his watch.

Unless his son's game started late, the first half was already finished.

Last time.

Once again his thumbs worked through the cards. One after another after another, though not as many now because he'd thrown out a bunch of old ones.

His mind drifted to the game, to the sounds of parents yelling from the stands and referees' whistles.

His thumbs stopped at another dead contact—literally, in this guy's case. Lobbyist. Died a few years ago. Cancer.

He snatched out the card and stuck it in the shredder. A metallic whir and it was confetti.

When he passed the halfway point he flipped faster, paying less attention now.

Suddenly his brain tripped.

What was that?

Careful not to skip any, he thumbed backward until he found the card that caught his eye: Dr. Arnie Schwarz, local phone number, no address.

Dr. Arnie Schwarz? If he'd seen a Dr. Schwarz it was so long ago he couldn't remember what it was for. He thought for a second. Maybe it was that godawful constipation. Years ago, but he remembered the pain like it was yesterday. He shifted in his leather chair. A barium enema. That was a special kind of hell, far worse than any prostate exam.

No sense keeping that memory around. He dipped the card toward the shredder, but just as its edge touched the steel teeth he hesitated.

He'd been cured of whatever it was, so Dr. Schwarz knew what he was doing. And since he was only getting older, maybe it would be good to hang on to the number—if the doctor was still practicing. The doctor's answering service should be able to tell him.

He dialed and waited. It rang four times, then he heard a click and the soft hiss of a tape running: "You have reached the Raleigh office of animal control. We're not in right now . . ."

He listened to the message, confused.

Then he slammed his palm on the desktop and roared.

Arnie Schwarz wasn't a doctor. It stood for Arnold

Schwarzenegger because the guy he wanted to reach was supposed to be as big as a house.

He'd listed Arnie as a "doctor" because this person was called only in times of need, and he'd used the animal control number because, in a way, that's what was involved.

Kingston congratulated himself for being so clever.

He flipped the card over. At the bottom, where it couldn't be read unless the card was removed, he'd scribbled a number with a 206 area code: Washington state. It occurred to him that he should call from a pay phone, but he didn't have time. He punched in a one, then ten digits.

After two rings he heard: "Yeah." A deep voice, unfriendly. He imagined the receiver being smothered by a meaty hand.

Kingston said, "Big trouble. Pinchot National Forest, Skookum County. Video, Seattle and Portland."

He was supposed to hang up right away, but he had to make sure the guy hadn't forgotten what all of that meant. "Got it?"

"Yeah." This time the voice sounded surprised.

Kingston slammed the phone down, jumped from his chair and ran out of the office. With a little luck he would get to his son's game before it was over.

THE second rock rolled slower because it was bigger, about the size of a bowling ball.

Vaughn watched it bump across their trail and felt like blasting a warning shot over the trees. How stupid could Lansing be?

No, Vaughn realized. Not stupid and not careless. Loose rocks weren't easy to find out here. Lansing actually had to be looking for them.

Then, directly uphill, came a tremendous crashing, as if something big was tearing through the trees.

Holy shit, Vaughn thought. *Lansing was right. He found it.*

Lansing's lanky body came into view, running at them for all he was worth. "Shoot it!" he yelled. "Shoot!"

Vaughn whipped the .30-06 up to his shoulder, centered

the scope on Lansing and then moved it slightly to the left, then right.

He saw it: between the trees, about ten yards behind Lansing. A big black shape, moving fast but still obscured by the trees and Lansing's body. It came straight downhill, right behind Lansing.

"Down!" he yelled. "Get down!" He flipped off the safety and suddenly Lansing's chest filled his scope.

BOOM!

It felt like a stick of dynamite exploded in his eardrum.

He jerked down and away from the sound, and looked up just in time to see the broad black side of a bear rush past.

The bear galloped downhill, dodging tree trunks and crashing through vegetation like its rump was on fire. Vaughn watched until he couldn't tell the bear's black fur from the shadows.

Since it didn't have cubs he figured it was a male. And big, around four hundred pounds.

"It's safe now," he said, flicking the rifle's safety back on. When he spoke he became aware of the tone ringing in his right ear. His voice sounded like it was coming through a cheap radio smothered by a pillow. Though he knew it wouldn't work, he moved his lower jaw up and down to try to pop his ear back to normal.

He watched as Lansing pulled himself off Alison and, apologizing, helped her up. Then he looked at Mackey, half expecting a joke about his eardrum getting in the way of the shot. But Mackey's expression was serious and his eyes searched uphill.

"See something?" Vaughn said.

Mackey looked at him and then at Lansing and Alison. "No," he said.

"You missed him," Alison said.

"What?"

"You missed him," she said to Mackey. "The bear."

"Aw, shoot," he said. "No bear steaks tonight."

She turned away and said something to Lansing.

Vaughn said, "What was it you didn't see up there?"

Mackey stepped closer to him. "Not so loud, ol' boy." He kept his voice low. "You see the face of that bear?"

"What about it?"

"It wasn't looking at Art."

So it wasn't chasing Lansing. Vaughn sensed there was something more. "And?"

"This might sound crazy, but I'd swear that bear looked scared."

Vaughn was about to say that Lansing probably surprised the bear, but he suddenly realized that was wrong. The bear wasn't scared by Lansing because it ran *after* him—but it wasn't chasing him. So it had to be running away from something, and Mackey's shot hadn't made it change its course.

Lansing sat on the mountainside and fiddled with his pack. In a loud voice Vaughn said, "Did you see the Sasquatch?"

Alison looked over. "It was just a bear."

"That bear could've ripped you open like a plastic bag," Vaughn said. He asked Lansing again.

Lansing stuffed his hand inside one of the pack's pockets. "No," he said quietly.

"But it was up there."

"Yes."

"What was it doing?"

"What do you mean?" Lansing said.

"Was it pushing us?"

Eyes still averted, Lansing shrugged.

The closer I get, the less he says, Vaughn thought.

Lansing zipped closed the pocket he'd been working on.

Vaughn walked past the others and stood over the professor. "Dr. Lansing, give me a fucking answer please."

Lansing looked up at him. "It's possible it was pushing us, yes."

"Why would it do that?"

"Territoriality."

Vaughn felt like decking him. "And what exactly is it being territorial about?"

"You mean you don't know?"

Vaughn waited.

"Food."

Chapter 30

VAUGHN kept them moving until well after dark. They walked slowly, following the big tracks in the utter black that is cloudy night in the wilderness. The flashlights barely helped.

He knew it exhausted everyone, but he figured Lansing and Alison wouldn't dare complain, and Mackey had to know that he was trying to get them as far down the mountain as he could. The river they crossed tumbled past the other side, and if he could circle back to it—if the Sasquatch's trail continued around the slope—he would be that much closer to getting them all out.

Sometime after dark the ground became level and the trail kept to this area, a lip between the slope and another stand of old growth that dipped down into a valley.

Along here Vaughn finally stopped. His pack felt like it was filled with concrete and his legs were numb. His watch read a little after ten-thirty.

He and Mackey pitched the tent in silence, then gathered wood for a fire. Last night they used wood from the riverbank which, while still damp, was the driest wood in the forest. Here everything they found was wet, and even with a heavy dose of lighter fluid the hissing flames barely held off the heavy dark.

Smoke streamed up and spread over them like a veil. It suspended between trees that to Vaughn seemed like the ones in fairy tales: inanimate during the day, but alive and menacing at night.

The fire's warmth carried sleep to every cell in his body. It pulled a soft blanket over his brain, and he had to fight the overwhelming urge to crawl into his mummy bag and conk out. He wanted to stay awake because Lansing obviously knew much more about the Sasquatch than he was letting on, information that could be critical for things that might happen between here and the road. Vaughn told himself he would find out everything . . . even if he had to . . .

A branch tip glowed red. He saw its reflection in Lansing's eye, getting closer . . .

Vaughn blinked his eyes open and shook his head. *Dreaming.*

The smell of meat and potatoes hung in the air. He looked to his left where Mackey dug the last scraps of stew out of a blackened can. To his right Lansing and Alison sat on their packs, their vacant eyes reflecting the flames as they took turns picking gorp out of a Ziploc bag.

Everyone had eaten like pigs. A good sign. It meant they were physically wrecked. He definitely was, and he was in shape for this kind of country. The others weren't. So tonight's fireside conversation would be brief, and this time he would control it, starting with Lansing's comment about food.

Vaughn had thought it over on their walk downhill. It made sense, but he didn't know whether to believe it: After Lansing got that crazy look in his eye about the bird calls, he felt like the professor was coming unglued. Or maybe Lansing was just overly excited. Regardless, the professor obviously had his own agenda and maybe the food comment was part of it.

Vaughn raised a plastic water bottle to his lips, tipped it and felt the cold run down his throat. It woke him up a bit. He swallowed and said, "Care to explain your food theory?"

Lansing's eyes pulled into focus and he looked over. "Certainly," he said.

Across his face firelight and shadows lost and took back territory in a continuous war that whittled the bones of his skull into sharp relief. His skin looked paper thin, like it could crack and peel and . . .

Vaughn shook the vision from his head.

"It's simple, really," Lansing said. "The La Niña winter has been unusually long and hard, and consequently food is scarce and the Sasquatches are hungry. These factors make animals aggressive when protecting their food, as you saw with the Sasquatch defending its deer kill."

Vaughn pictured the deer's neck, neatly snapped alongside Ricks.

"These areas of old growth also may contain food items essential to these animals in times of stress," Lansing said. "Since so little old growth remains, the Sasquatches are concentrated here."

"Like animals at a waterhole," Mackey said. The stitched orange REMINGTON on his cap glowed in the firelight.

"Similar, but I doubt Sasquatches would gather in the densities you'd find at a waterhole. Because of their size they require large amounts of space—and food. They're seen infrequently, which means the population density must be relatively low over a huge area, and when they are seen they're almost always alone. Moreover, when tracks are discovered they're almost always of a lone animal. Thus Sasquatches have huge territories, probably on the order of a few hundred square miles. Each."

"You're guessing," Vaughn said.

"No. I base it on the orangutan model."

"The one I saw didn't look like an orangutan."

"Undoubtedly," Lansing said. "I'm merely saying that the orangutan social model seems to fit the Sasquatch. In the few cases where the tracks of more than one Sasquatch were found together . . . never mind. That isn't pertinent."

Alison said, "You're saying the male has a territory and females and juveniles roam."

Lansing looked at Alison. The bottom half of his face tightened into a smile. It looked painful, as if his paper skin would split apart. "You studied endangered orangutans," he said to her.

She smiled.

"So no chance of us walking out of this one's territory," Vaughn said.

"No," Lansing said.

"How about its aggressiveness?"

"I wouldn't say it's being aggressive."

"They're not normally this way."

Lansing said: "Actually, all primates are curious. And Sasquatches, though reclusive, also appear to exhibit this trait. Occasionally they're seen watching people, sometimes through living room windows."

"Dr. Lansing," Vaughn said, "answer the damn question."

Lansing looked over. "They are being unusually forward, but that must be because of the crowding."

Vaughn said: "When I was at the library I only found one mention of Sasquatch violence directed at humans, and that was secondhand."

"Roosevelt's story."

"Right."

Mackey said: "Teddy?"

Vaughn related the story. During the 1800s, two trappers ventured into a pass near the Salmon River in Idaho's Bitterroot Mountains. The pass had a bad reputation: The prior year an animal, presumably a bear, had killed and partially eaten a hunter. But attracted by the prospect of untouched waters brimming with beaver, they walked up into the pass and made camp.

That night and the next an animal harassed them. It left large tracks of a type they had never seen, and the tracks indicated that it walked on two legs. Finally spooked, the trappers decided to leave before the third night arrived.

That morning they set about collecting their traps. With only a few remaining, one man returned to the camp to pack their gear so they could leave faster. His partner retrieved the rest of the traps and headed back, expecting his friend to be packed and waiting. Instead, he found him dead. His neck had been snapped, and whatever animal did it had rolled over and over the body, seemingly in glee. Mindful of the sun going down, the trapper fled the area with only his rifle and never went back.

Roosevelt received the report firsthand from the dead trapper's partner. In commenting on it he felt compelled to say that "frontiersmen are not, as a rule, apt to be very superstitious. They lead lives too hard and practical, and have too little imagination in things spiritual and supernatural. I have heard but few ghost-stories while living on the frontier, and those few were of a perfectly commonplace and conventional type." Vaughn found it interesting that Roosevelt, himself an outdoorsman, did not scoff at the story.

When he finished, Lansing said, "That's not the only account."

"What's that?" Mackey said, cupping his left ear.

"That's not the only account of Sasquatch violence directed at humans," Lansing said louder. "In fact, the Mount Saint Helens area has the greatest historical frequency of Sasquatch attacks."

"Wait a sec," Alison said. "That's near here, right?" Her eyes shifted from Lansing to Vaughn.

"It *is* here," Lansing said. "Local tribes were extremely leery of this area, certain places in particular. The mountain was one. They refused to go up there. They believed it was Sasquatch territory, and that Sasquatches killed and ate people. Cannibals, they called them."

"People that ate people."

"Correct," Lansing said. "And the animals didn't appear to be any friendlier to Caucasians. In the 1890s, the mutilated and pulverized bodies of three prospectors were found near their camp by Spirit Lake. On open ground."

Vaughn saw Ed Ricks lying next to the deer. "Meaning they couldn't have fallen from anywhere," he said.

Lansing nodded. "Bears were ruled out: The severity of the injuries was said to be horrific, but the men were uneaten. Their deaths went unexplained. Then thirty years later, the famous Ape Canyon incident occurred."

Everyone in Skookum County knew about that. In 1924 miners working to the east of Mount Saint Helens found large footprints in the earth and thought a huge "barefoot Indian" was in the area—until they started seeing Sasquatches. One day they shot one of the animals and it fell into a canyon.

That night the miners' windowless wooden cabin was pummeled by animals that screamed and grunted and shoved giant hands through gaps between the pine shakes of the roof, trying to get at the men. Boulders crashed against the roof and the walls for hours. Terrified, the miners fired and reloaded their rifles as fast as they could, aiming through the holes the

Sasquatches made and shouting at the animals to go away. Eventually the animals did.

When the men went outside the next morning they found the cabin surrounded by enormous bare footprints and huge rocks that had gouged chunks out of the log walls. The miners practically ran back to civilization, never to return.

Vaughn realized he'd missed something. "What was it you said about noises?"

"The miners heard whistles and thumping sounds, like fists pounding on chests or dirt."

"I don't suppose they described the whistles."

Lansing stared at him. "No."

"That was eighty years ago," Alison said.

Lansing looked at her. "In 1957, a skier on Mount Saint Helens vanished. The man, described as a very good skier, descended ahead of the others in his party so he could take photographs of them coming down the mountain. His friends never saw him again.

"The authorities were called and they followed his ski tracks. They saw where he came down the mountain, turned and stopped to wait for his friends, but from there the tracks went straight down. Dangerously straight. The man jumped crevasses and small cliffs at great risk to himself, something an experienced skier like him would never do unless the circumstances were dire. The ski tracks ended at the edge of a seventy-foot cliff. He went right over, without trying to stop. Five days of intensive searching for the body turned up nothing. Not even a ski."

"You're saying he was chased off the mountain," Vaughn said.

"It does appear that way."

"Were any Sasquatch tracks found?"

"Apparently not. But no tracks were found three years ago, either, were they deputy?" Lansing stared at him.

"What the hell are you talking about?"

Shadows dove into the corners of Lansing's mouth; it cracked into a grin. "Surely you remember. Three years ago a woman disappeared here."

Now Vaughn remembered. It hadn't stuck out in his mind because it wasn't dramatic. They found no blood, no dismembered limbs, no knife gashes, no bullet holes. Not even a body.

He'd been one of the investigators. For a thesis project a geology student had gone out alone to map the abundance of minerals in certain areas of the forest. She never came out.

When she was reported missing, Vaughn and another deputy packed in from her car, which was untouched, and found her campsite. Her tent was turned over and equipment was scattered, but nothing was torn. Bears couldn't be that neat, but a murderer could.

For a week he and two other deputies, along with local volunteers and National Guardsmen, combed the woods looking for signs of anything: blood, broken branches, a struggle, a cryptic message scrawled in the dirt. They found nothing. And at the elevation she'd camped, the ground was too rocky for tracks.

After the search was called off, they ran down the list of possibilities. She could have been killed, dragged off and eaten by a bear, but no signs of this were found. It was possible she was kidnapped—her father was somewhat wealthy—but no one ever received a phone call or a ransom note. She may have disappeared on purpose, but no one could come up with a reason and her car was still there.

Or maybe a gutless, criminally insane man blundered into her, raped and killed her, then threw her body off an unnamed cliff. That was the explanation Vaughn and everyone else favored. Everyone except Lansing.

When Lansing finished telling the story, Alison said: "Is that true?"

"Officially the case is still open," Vaughn said. "But I doubt a Sasquatch was involved."

Lansing said: "That explanation is as plausible as any of the others."

"The other possibilities involve people and bears. I have to think they're more likely."

Lansing said: "Chris, every year people disappear in the wilderness without a trace. Correct?"

"Can't argue with that," Mackey said.

"Even hunters with rifles."

"That's right."

"Ever wonder why?"

"Just figured they got careless. Or unlucky."

"Perhaps it was something else," Lansing said.

Vaughn wanted to say something, but his brain came up empty. No one else spoke, and even the fire's snapping and popping was muted. He looked up and saw that the canopy of smoke that hung over them had begun moving lazily off through the woods, coaxed by a hidden breeze.

"Wait a minute," Alison said suddenly. "You said the Mount Saint Helens eruption leveled two hundred and thirty square miles of trees."

"That's right," Mackey said.

"All that forest couldn't have grown back already," she said. "All the vegetation and animals couldn't have come back. So the Sasquatches on the mountain—where did they go?"

No one said anything.

"You don't think they're here, do you?" She looked from one face to another.

A little fear was healthy, but too much wasn't. Vaughn said, "Easy, Alison. Those were just stories from a long time ago. These things aren't supposed to be violent."

"Not violent? One puts your friend in the hospital and you have to shoot it. Another one throws a pack at your tent and chases Art. Now we find out that a woman might've been abducted and eaten by one of these things *right here,* and it's been a hard winter, they're hungry and we're in their territory."

Vaughn was glad he hadn't told her about Ricks.

"That's why we brought the big boys," Mackey said, patting his rifle.

"You can't shoot them," Alison said.

"Why the hell not?"

"They're endangered!"

"Hooo boy. I can't wait to hear why you think that."

Alison said, "They're rare, their habitat is declining—"

Mackey leaned toward Vaughn and said, "Now you know why they didn't send a biologist."

Alison said: "I'm sure biologists can prove—"

"I'm sure too," Mackey said. "Biologists can prove anything they want, to further any political agenda they or anyone else wants."

"This has nothing to do with politics."

"Doesn't it? Tell me. In your vast book learning, did you ever run across the story of the Tellico Dam?"

"Of course," she said. "The first major project stopped by the Endangered Species Act, to protect the endangered snail darter."

"Was the snail darter endangered?"

"They thought so at the time."

"Wrong," Mackey said. "Only the biologist who found it thought it was endangered. But everyone else knew it wasn't, even the Supreme Court. But the court used the fish as an excuse to stop an obvious pork-barrel project."

Alison shook her head at Mackey, a small smile on her face.

"I see I'm wasting my breath," he said. "The Fish and Wildlife Service has its own agenda, and to hell with common sense."

Alison said: "So the whole Fish and Wildlife Service is against you, is that it?"

"I didn't say that. A few good people are left, but—"

"Wait a minute!" Alison's finger flew out over the fire. "I know who you are. Chris Mackey—you're the guy who killed the red wolf!"

Vaughn had been prodding his brain to come up with some way of stopping the conversation. Now he sat up and listened.

Mackey said: "That's under investigation, but I can't say I'm sorry it's dead."

"You're not sorry an entire species is that much closer to being gone forever?"

"Wrong again. It's not a species. The red wolf is nothing more than a damn coyote–grey wolf hybrid. Geneticists told your agency that, but were ignored."

"Yeah right," Alison said.

"Look it up."

Her mouth closed into the same smile, and she shook her head at the fire. A log popped; a spark snaked up as if propelled by a miniature rocket, then winked out.

"Alison," Lansing said, "an animal that doesn't exist can't be endangered."

Vaughn saw where Lansing was going. "Can't be killed either."

"Not with what you're carrying," Lansing said.

"It's a .30-06. I've taken elk with it."

"A Sasquatch has a much denser skeletomuscular structure. An underpowered rifle will have little or no effect. I believe that's why people who shoot at Sasquatches with deer rifles think the animals are immune to gunfire."

"Any of the stuff we're carrying now, including Frank's ought-six, can punch a fatal hole in any land animal on the planet," Mackey said.

"Why can't we just tranquilize it?" Alison said.

Mackey snorted. "Why not use a butterfly net? For crying out loud—haven't you at least talked to people who've spent time in the field?"

"I've seen tranquilizer darts used all the time," she said.

"On TV?"

Alison didn't say anything.

Mackey said, "They only show you the times it works. Tranquilizer darts aren't as accurate as bullets and don't have near the same range. So for a good shot on a Sasquatch you'd have to be close, and you'd have to know the right dose. Otherwise you might kill the animal, or it might die trying to get away, or it wouldn't stay unconscious long enough, putting the handlers at risk. And then how would you restrain that big boy when he wakes up? You'd never know exactly when that would be, and what kind of cage or chains would hold him. Only thing you could do—"

"You'd have to shoot it," Lansing said.

Alison's head swiveled toward him.

Lansing's hands rubbed each other for a moment, then he stood. "Excuse me," he said, and walked out of the firelight.

The flames sputtered. Vaughn hunched closer to the fire and thought he, too, should pee before hitting the sack. *Might as well turn in.* There was nothing else to learn. Lansing admitted the Sasquatches had been acting aggressively—because of food, which made sense. It seemed like Ricks had been killed by a Sasquatch protecting its kill, and last night the big Sasquatch had taken his granola bars. Lansing could have been pushed up the mountain because the big Sasquatch wanted him away from another kill or its hunting territory.

Definitely made sense—though something bothered him about it. He searched his brain for a moment, but was too tired to think.

A yawn grew from the back of his throat; his jaw stretched wide then shut. He looked up. Half of the smoke canopy was gone. The thin remains streamed horizontally past the towering trunks and into the black. It occurred to him that the odor of fire and cooked food would be carried for miles downwind.

Slowly he stood—and glimpsed movement. Something flying through the air.

His eyes followed it into the darkness past Mackey. A thump and the sound of something rolling.

He looked to his right, where the object came from, and saw another one zipping toward him. It crashed into the fire.

Mackey yelled. Burning branches cartwheeled outward and orange sparks sprayed in all directions.

Vaughn dove back and heard Alison cry out. He rolled and jumped to his feet. Embers smoldered on his pack—he grabbed it and shook them off.

He heard Mackey's gloved hands making patting noises as he batted fire debris off something, but Vaughn couldn't see him anymore. The campfire was gone. A few flames clung to bits of wood scattered around the camp, but other than that, the forest was nearly black.

He looked toward Alison's tent. Gradually he made out her yellow jacket and the whitish puffs of quick breaths.

A few sparks hung in the air, then died.

Vaughn had only one thought: *Lansing*.

He saw the professor's lean form appear by Alison's tent, and ran up to him. "What the hell was that?"

In the dark, Lansing's face was a dingy oval with black smudges where his eyes and mouth were.

"A rock?" Lansing said.

"How about two."

Lansing paused for a second and then said: "Primate researchers have repeatedly documented the fact chimpanzees and other apes throw rocks, sometimes with great accuracy. They do this to release tension, to intimidate other apes—"

"Are you fucking kidding me? You're seriously saying you didn't throw them?"

"Why would I do that?"

"How about to scare the shit out of us. Make us think there's a Sasquatch here."

"For what purpose?" Lansing said.

"Maybe you want to keep us scared, so we'll put a bullet into anything that moves. Like you tried to get us to do on the mountain."

A pause. "No, deputy. I didn't throw the stones."

"You were out there," Vaughn jabbed a finger over Lansing's shoulder, "where the rocks came from."

Lansing said nothing.

"Did you hear anything? See anything?"

"I was urinating. It was dark."

"How did you know what happened?"

"I heard Chris and Alison yell, and saw the fire go out."

BOOM!

The blast of the .375 H&H Mag seemed to fill up all the space in the forest.

BOOM!

Vaughn whirled around. His eyes barely made out Mackey lowering the big rifle.

"Just in case Art's right," Mackey said. "Any animal that smart ought to get the message."

Vaughn watched Mackey's squat form bend down, then heard the clink of heavy brass casings being picked up or dropped into a pocket. He couldn't tell which. Mackey walked away, the black of his shape merging with the black of their tent.

The zipper of Alison's tent ripped open. With his grainy vision Vaughn saw her yellow jacket duck into the opening and disappear.

Lansing stepped toward the tent door.

"Hold it," Vaughn said.

Lansing stopped.

"When you went after those bird calls today did you do any climbing?"

Lansing said, "I went uphill a bit, yes."

"No. I mean climbing on rocks. Did you dislodge any rocks?"

"I doubt it," Lansing said. "Why do you ask?"

It was too dark to see his face. "Forget it," Vaughn said.

Chapter 31

THEY'RE here, Lansing thought, staring into the darkness that filled the tent. *More than one. More than two!* He almost couldn't believe it. Two was more than he could hope for in a lifetime. Statistically, in several lifetimes.

Perhaps this was destiny. He'd merely had to be patient, superhumanly patient, and it came. They came.

They were here, and so was he.

The pieces were slotting together. Big pieces, rumbling toward something, moved by an inevitability that wasn't frightening because it was manageable. Like riding a private earthquake, a wave of earth no one else could feel.

All coming together.

Couldn't merely be luck. Not the greatest discovery since . . . what? Antibiotics? Lucy? The atom? But this would be different, something people could see and touch. Perhaps the most important discovery since man became self-aware.

He wondered if the other greats felt this way when it was

happening to them. Invincible. As if wielded by some greater power.

They had to.

He expanded his chest until his ribs hurt, held it and then controlled the escaping breath. The air rushed out between his lips.

He knew this didn't mean destiny would come to him. It hadn't up until now, and it wouldn't. He wasn't being served his future in a silver teacup. He would have to take the right risks to stay on top of the wave.

"You asleep yet?" Alison whispered.

Ah. He wanted to laugh because some part of him had anticipated this and planned for the conversation ahead. It was as if he straddled two awarenesses; he was at once the marionette and the puppeteer.

"No."

"Did you throw that rock?"

"No." Hands folded on the back of his skull, he felt the dark leak in around his eyes. And waited.

"What's going on?" she said.

He eased into it. "What you said tonight, you're right. Sasquatches are endangered. Some of it is because of clearcutting, but that's just reflective of the general trend."

"Habitat loss."

Yes. "These temperate-zone mountains are sinks for toxic and carcinogenic pollutants, brought here by rain and snow. That pollution and habitat loss from logging have led to declines in food sources. Freshwater clams, salmon, native plants. We must assume Sasquatch populations have also declined because such large animals require diverse food sources to stay alive. And fewer footprints are being found."

Silence. But he knew there would be more.

"The gene pool," she said.

Hah! He sat up and pushed down his sleeping bag. The heavy air washed over his thermals, chilling the skin beneath. His thumb and forefinger found the door zipper and quickly drew a buzzing arc.

"Art?"

"Need something from my pack."

With his knees on the tent floor and his left arm supporting his weight, he pushed through the flap and reached as far as he could to the right. His fingers crawled along the ground and over moist stems, but found nothing. Strangely, he did not feel cold.

He leaned into the taut nylon and, straining, extended his arm further.

His fingertip brushed something. Definitely man-made. He felt around for a handhold and then tugged. For an instant he expected resistance: a Sasquatch pulling back. But it passed, and the pack slid easily over on the damp ground.

In the main pocket he found what he needed. The only one he'd brought with him.

He rezipped the pack and shoved it away from the opening, then zipped the tent door closed. He felt for the flashlight that lay near the door and picked it up. Holding it close to the floor, between his sleeping bag and Alison's, he pushed the switch with his thumb and a circle of light appeared.

Jiggling slightly, the bright circle shone almost dead in the middle of a white plaster cast of the big Sasquatch's right footprint.

Alison jerked her head away from the light.

He raised the flashlight higher. "What do you see?"

Her hand, lost in dark waves of hair, propped up her head. She blinked a few times, then held her eyes open. "A footprint."

"More closely. The details."

She curled closer. "Lines." She referred to what Lansing knew were skin creases. "Five toes."

He pointed near the little toe. "Look here."

Alison craned forward.

"Closer."

She curled her upper body closer, leaned over and put her nose almost on the track. Her dangling hair brushed the plaster and Lansing felt a stab of excitement in his crotch.

"This," she said, touching the cast.

He felt like giggling.

"A sixth toe?"

"Correct," he said.

Alison looked up. "Inbreeding."

"Correct again."

She smiled.

He said, "As with many endangered species, habitat loss is making it difficult for Sasquatches to maintain a genetically diverse breeding population." He waved the flashlight. "From this you see they're already on the path to extinction."

Far away a part of him squeaked a protest, but he slapped it silent. *It's possible. Inevitable.*

He said: "If they were to become extinct before we officially discover them, that would be a terrible loss. Imagine— the only bipedal ape besides ourselves, one of our closest living relatives, and we'd never learn anything about it."

"And you think one has to die for that to happen," she said. *There it is. Power.* "Unfortunate," he said. "But necessary."

"I don't believe that."

"It would be more cruel to catch one alive. Think about it. A Sasquatch would be history's most intensely studied guinea pig. And if it survived that, no one would want to let it go. Everyone would literally want a piece of it."

"They might let it go."

"Even if it didn't die from the stress of captivity, it couldn't be released. The risk of disease transference would be too great."

Alison frowned.

He said, "The choices are to capture one and condemn it to a miserable death, or to kill one and save the species."

"You sound like Chris Mackey."

"He represents the industries and the politicians that can't allow Sasquatches to be discovered. So does Deputy Vaughn. This is logging country. Timber operations, mills, entire towns would be decimated if the truth about the Sasquatches' existence was revealed." *A quest for truth. Good.* "They'll never allow the truth to get out."

"I mean killing something to save it," she said. "He's wrong. You're both wrong. In the Amazon scientists, don't have to go around shooting one of everything that's there to save them all. That's crazy."

Her voice had risen, so he spoke softly. "Biologists there are cataloging species as fast as they can, to save them. But Sasquatches can't be cataloged. People will accept a written description and perhaps a photograph of a new insect or bird, but a bipedal ape? Eight feet tall? In the United States? In this circumstance, Chris is right."

Alison stared at the cast. "On the mountain this morning they said the Sasquatch went straight up. Like a person, not an animal."

He said, "A logger in northern California once told me a story. Bigfoot, he said, repeatedly smashed a three-hundred-pound boulder into the sides of road-building machinery. The animals also have knocked over trailers of culverts, tossed mining gear off cliffs and blocked newly cut logging roads with trees."

She smiled. "Sounds like they're environmentalists." Her face changed. "Oh my God. They are human."

"No," he said. "They're thinking animals—physically strong ones—being territorial. That's the extent of what they can do. The rest is up to us."

Her eyebrows scrunched together.

He paused for a calculated second and said, "What do you think about developers?"

Her face became sour. "The scourge of the planet."

"The Sasquatch can stop them. Do you understand that power? That's why Chris is here. That's why Deputy Vaughn is here. The only question is—"

"Why you're here," she said. "For yourself, or for the Sasquatches and their habitat?"

He didn't see that coming. *Wait. Not too fast.*

He looked down at the plaster cast, as if he was thinking. But he didn't have to.

He said, "You talked last night about saving things that could help us. Cures for diseases that could be found in endangered plants and animals. That's important, but saving more individuals of an overabundant species is insignificant next to the Sasquatch discovery. If another two-legged primate was found, all of a sudden we as a species wouldn't be alone anymore. We'd have to reexamine ourselves and the things we do. Suddenly people who think nothing of bulldozing the habitats of rabbits and salamanders would have to reconsider. We'd all have a different perspective. A healthier one. You see?"

"I still don't think—"

He sighed. "Alison, every day these animals die in ways that are much more painful than a well-placed bullet. The death of an individual Sasquatch is inevitable. The death of an entire species isn't. We can prevent it."

She said, "Do you have a gun?"

He waited a second and then said, "Why are you here?"

She blinked. "To keep my eyes open."

"Were you instructed to make sure Sasquatches weren't discovered?"

"No."

"Then if you're not representing that part of government, I ask you again: why are you here? You must have been sent for a reason, because of who you are, what you believe. You can't merely be a reporter."

"You want one dead, don't you," she said.

"Don't you?"

The skin around her eyes and nose wrinkled. "You should be sleeping in the other tent. You're no different than them."

She rolled over, zipped up her sleeping bag and jerked onto her side, her back to him.

He clicked off the flashlight and lay down. He locked his hands behind his skull, and he let the dark settle back over his eyes. For a time Alison's breathing intruded on his thoughts. But eventually he slipped away from it.

Trying to convince Alison had been a mistake, he realized. A trick played on himself. A dead end. But at least he'd eliminated that alleyway. Now he would be more focused.

Surely the other greats ran into such diversions, perhaps more tempting ones, the closer they got to their goals. But they found their way and so would he. Alone, as it had always been. Just him. And the Sasquatches.

Chapter 32

RAIN.

Vaughn's mostly asleep brain arrived at that as the answer. The sound on the rainfly was rain.

No problem, he thought. *Under these old trees we'll barely get wet. Back to sleep.*

Wait a minute.

Sleep . . .

Wait a minute.

His inner voice was persistent.

What is it?

Rain. The trees.

The trees.

He dragged his eyelids open. Black. Everything black. He blinked and swiveled his eyes around, looking for a hint of grey.

All black. Must be the middle of the night. What was it again?

Rain, and the trees.

Then he realized: It couldn't rain through the trees. Not in old growth. When the firs got that big and that old, their pointy tops flattened out, caught the rain and channeled it down the wide, interwoven boughs that were covered with all manner of living things that used the water.

But some rain did trickle down.

Had he heard a trickle?

He listened.

No thunder. No trickle.

He closed his eyes.

Brrrrrrrrump.

His eyes shot open. Was that rain? It sounded like a bunch of raindrops hitting at once. But not exactly. It was more like . . . pebbles.

Dropped on the tent.

He held his breath. His ears probed the darkness, but all he heard was his heart beating.

Pwee.

Just like the call he'd heard with Lansing, but softer and shorter. What kind of bird called during the day and also at night?

No kind.

His heart beat faster. The back of his neck itched.

Inside the sleeping bag his hand found the zipper and slowly pulled it down. One by one he felt the teeth release.

After a few seconds he freed his right arm, reached over and touched the hard metal of the .357.

Thumping.

Jesus, was that his heart? It felt like it was coming through the ground.

Then he realized it was. Heavy footsteps. Someone walking.

Some*thing* walking. Coming closer.

The footsteps stopped near the front of the tent. Something brushed the rainfly.

Adrenaline exploded into his head and cold air rushed up his nose. He squeezed the revolver's grip, but didn't move. Didn't dare.

A muffled *huh.*

Breathing? Wheezing?

A faint *zzzzt.*

A pack.

The Sasquatch was standing right there.

He drew the .357 close to his chest and began wriggling out of the sleeping bag.

Kra-pow!

Gunshot—he froze. A rifle. Not close, but not real far, either.

The pack hit the ground with a hush of nylon. He thought he felt the pounding of feet running off, but then there was nothing and he wondered if he'd imagined it. Maybe it was his heart.

He sat up, his mind racing.

Is it running after whoever took that shot?

Is someone actually poaching out here—in the dark?

Is someone lost?

He listened.

No more shots, so the person probably wasn't lost. But it didn't matter. He couldn't place where the shot came from.

Hunting at night was illegal, and wasn't a real possibility anyway. Too dark out here, and no poacher would be this far from a main road.

That left only one reason why that shot was fired: self-defense. But he hoped that wasn't the case. Because the terrain, the darkness and the unknown location of the shooter meant there was nothing he could do about it.

Chapter 33

THE big Sasquatch ran up the mountain, toward the gun sound. With every step it leaped eight feet up, past the trees, over the ferns. Once a massive lower leg brushed the fingers of a high fern frond, but the plant simply bent and then flexed back without a sound.

The Sasquatch saw everything clearly, in shades of grey, and made no unnecessary noise. Other than the soft huffing of its breath, only its feet disturbed the thick hush of the dark woods, like a drum beating far under the ground.

Calloused soles smacked the earth, and strong toes levered the huge body up and forward. Toward the man.

In a minute it climbed halfway up the mountainside.

Suddenly it stopped and listened.

A faint beating.

Running.

Two-footed running, down the mountain, to its right. Not a man, it knew. *Another.*

Something stirred inside the big Sasquatch, and its muscles stiffened with the impulse to follow. But then it realized the running wasn't normal.

Fear run.

It jumped forward, now pushing up the mountain at an angle so it would cross the other's path.

It sucked gallons of the humid air into its nose and mouth, breathing heavily. Not because it was tired. It forced the air in to scrub away the strong human smells of the camp.

Gradually trees, emerging buds, moss, fungi, birds and other animals, food and not food, all came in. It sifted them, but nothing.

And then all at once—

The big Sasquatch's brain slammed into a scent wall. Mixed with the sweet musk, almost overpowering it, was the sour tang of fear and the warm scent of new blood.

The smells swirled in the Sasquatch's head, pushing it into a frenzy. Rage poured from its body and its hands squeezed into fists. A knuckle popped.

It turned straight uphill and followed the scent trail.

The forest rushed by, a blur of grey shapes and vivid smells, and then something made the Sasquatch stop again.

Movement.

It listened, and immediately recognized the pattern of footsteps. Too regular.

Man.

The Sasquatch abandoned the scent trail and walked up and to the left, straight at the man. It cushioned each step by allowing its legs to bend deeper.

Quickly it closed the gap, then slowed down. It didn't want the man to feel it coming.

One more step and suddenly: *Human smell. Gun smell.* The disgusting odors made the Sasquatch angry. And excited.

But with a predator's patience, it waited. Motionless, obscured by a tree, it kept its eyes in one direction—and saw the man: walking, waving the gun back and forth. The man was outlined in the Sasquatch's eyes by an almost silver glow, as if the moon shone directly on the man from a clear sky.

Hunched over, the man walked slowly, gently raising and lowering each foot. The Sasquatch saw that the man was being too careful.

As if he couldn't see.

And then, filtering through the boughs: *Fear smell.*

Aroused by the smell, the big Sasquatch circled around the man, then followed ten yards behind. Quietly, controlling its breathing. One step for every three or four of the man's. Using the trees for cover.

And then the man stepped into an area that had no trees. The man walked faster, toward the peaked shape of a tent. The tip of the rifle jerked from side to side.

The Sasquatch didn't hurry. It walked up behind a tree at the edge of the cleared area and peered around. It didn't put a hand on the trunk, as it usually did, to feel the rough bark under the skin of its palm. But it felt every plant under its feet, every stone.

Fear smell.

The Sasquatch's nostrils opened wider. Its mind fed on the smell, which flowed from the man like a glittering stream.

It began its stalk.

Leaving the trees, it walked straight at the man's back. One long step, then another. Its mind burned with the fear smells, the blood smell.

Rage.

Half a step more and it stood behind the man. Its eyes looked down, at the top of the man's head.

The man stopped. His shoulders pulled up and in.

Fear smell.

The big Sasquatch raised a fist.

The man swung the rifle around.

The Sasquatch slammed its fist down on the man's skull. Bones cracked with the soggy crunch of a rotten branch.

The man fell to the ground.

The Sasquatch raised a leg and stomped on the man's chest. *Crack-snap.* It stomped again, and felt something pop then release inside the man.

It bent down and picked up the man with one hand and threw him into the forest.

Silence.

Branches snapped.

A soft crumpling sound.

It ran over to the man and threw him again.

And again.

Chapter 34

Thursday

GET up and get them out.

Vaughn hadn't even opened his eyes yet, but his brain somehow knew it was morning and was already dashing out the tent and down the trail of the wounded Sasquatch.

He felt as if he'd barely slept. Since the gunshot his mind hadn't stopped twisting, mixing images of Boone's disfigured arm, the shot and the running Sasquatch with phantoms of gnarled Douglas firs and the faces of Lansing, Katie and the sheriff.

A few times he'd jerked awake, eyes wide and heart kicking, listening for something he couldn't name yet swore was there. But after a time he realized nothing was there and eventually drifted back under.

Now, lying on his back and looking at the grey light soaking through the tent, he knew he hadn't gotten any rest. He recognized the flu-like ache in his muscles as a symptom of having been awake for too long.

Next to him Mackey breathed with regular noise. Last

night he woke up briefly, after the shot. "How many shots?" he said.

"One."

"Then he's on his own," Mackey said, and promptly fell back asleep.

Vaughn unzipped his mummy bag and pulled it down. The cold air swarmed over him like carnivorous termites and burrowed straight into his bones. He shivered. It felt colder this morning.

He pulled on his boots and without tying them quickly unzipped an opening in the tent. He poked his head through the hole and almost slammed into someone's leg.

He looked up. Lansing dragged a booted foot across the ground in front of the tent. A folding camp shovel, its spade dirty, dangled from one of the professor's hands.

"What are you doing?" Vaughn said.

"Alison didn't wake up last night. I didn't want her to get alarmed by the tracks." Lansing gestured at the forest floor.

Vaughn glanced around and saw several areas of disturbed earth. "So you're suddenly feeling responsible for her?"

Lansing smiled. "Having her overly frightened would be a hindrance to us."

Vaughn crawled out of the tent thinking, *What about those stories last night?* He stood and said, "How big were the tracks?"

"It was the larger one again."

Vaughn heard Mackey stirring, and kept his voice low. "I heard one of those funny bird calls last night."

Lansing didn't say anything.

"Why would a single Sasquatch whistle?"

"Maybe it was having fun," Lansing said. "All apes have a sense of humor."

Vaughn took a step toward his pack.

Lansing said, "You might want to see if any food is missing."

Who cares as long as the coffee's there, Vaughn thought.

The pack lay between the tent, where he'd left it, and the center of the destroyed fire. The scattered black branches made him want to ask Lansing again about last night's rock throwing. He was thinking about how to phrase the question when Lansing walked up.

"Earlier this morning I found these." His palms held two large rocks, each bigger than a softball.

"For the first time or the second?"

Lansing half smiled. "I was urinating last night, deputy. I can show you the spot."

"The Sasquatch seems to have a pretty accurate arm."

"All apes can throw accurately."

The tent door flopped open and Mackey stepped out. "Mornin'," he said.

He looked as if he'd been in a fight with someone who'd tried to glue his eyelids shut. And for the first time, not a trace of smile lifted his face. Vaughn knew that both were signs of exhaustion.

The .44 hanging from Mackey's hand reminded Vaughn about last night's gunshot. He had an idea who it was, but maybe he was wrong. Maybe the others knew something about it.

Mackey looked at the foil packets in Vaughn's hand. "How 'bout I take the coffee and you take the tent."

"Deal," Vaughn said, and tossed Mackey the packets.

The coffee was hot, but breakfast was cold. Lansing ate quickly and then fidgeted, glancing at the trail. Vaughn wondered why he didn't just get up and leave.

Alison was in good spirits, and Vaughn thought he knew why.

"So you didn't hear our visitor last night," he said to her.

Her smile wrinkled. "Yeah, right."

"The big one came back. Tell her, Dr. Lansing."

Lansing stared at him. "That's right."

"Why?" Alison said.

"We'll never know," Vaughn said. "It ran off at the gunshot."

Her eyes opened wide. "Who—"

"That's what I'd like to know," Vaughn said. "Any ideas?"

"No," she said.

He looked around the fire. "Anyone else?"

No one said anything.

THE wounded Sasquatch's tracks, now in worse condition than they were yesterday, kept to the lip between the mountain and valley and continued on around the mountain's base. Because the tracks were old, Vaughn no longer hunted; he walked fast enough to feel the cold air streaming past his face.

At one point he lost the trail, but after a quick search Mackey found a track off to the right, heading down. Vaughn examined the track, then said, "Back in a sec," and returned to where he'd lost the trail. He was curious about what could make the Sasquatch change direction that radically.

Deer and other animals often wandered without apparent intent, but the wounded Sasquatch acted nothing like that—which left two possible reasons: terrain or threat.

He met Lansing coming the other way.

"Just a big cliff back there," Lansing said.

Vaughn kept walking. Suddenly the trees dropped off and gave way to a view. He looked at the sky and sucked in a deep breath.

Three feet in front of where he stood, the ground dropped away. He peered over a fifteen-foot cliff and saw an old, eroded cut, thorny with weather-bleached deadfalls and exposed grey-brown rocks. It ran at a steep angle for about two hundred yards, then disappeared into white fog. The fog's surface roiled, as if whatever was beneath it was angry.

He knew that meant water. Somewhere down there was the river.

He listened for a faraway rushing sound, but all he heard was a steady whisper. He looked up: Flat-bottomed clouds, the same hue as the grey sky, steamed steadily west. That meant he was looking at the leading edge of a front. Maybe warm, but the way the weather had been, he figured it was more likely to be cold.

Across the fog was the mountainside where he'd parked his truck. He thought he could make out the stony ridge he'd been headed to when he found Ed Ricks' truck. Didn't look too far as the crow flew, but the terrain and the Sasquatch's trail made walking in a straight line impossible.

He went back and found the others waiting for him.

"We have a lot of ground to cover," he said, and started walking down.

Chapter 35

FOR Vaughn, the descent into the valley brought on an instinctive sense of foreboding. Everything seemed heavier. The sagging branches, the Sasquatch tracks sunken into the ground—as if gravity was somehow stronger here.

And the old-growth forest no longer was beautiful to him. He was sick of it. After seeing the sky, he wanted to be out on a road, walk without a pack and go someplace where a hot meal was served on a plate instead of in a can.

But the corroded tracks led him on. They seemed farther apart now, probably because of the downhill angle, and appeared to be paralleling the river.

He plodded along after them, occasionally looking at his watch.

As the morning wore on and the terrain eased flat, his body told him it needed nourishment. But he wanted to wait until he was really hungry—until everyone was, so no one would do anything except follow him to the river for lunch.

At eleven-thirty, after nearly five hours on the trail, he decided that at noon he would make a hard left and lead them all to the water. The river couldn't be that far, and if they spent any more time heading away from the truck they risked getting caught in the woods after dark. He'd never been scared of being in the woods at night before. But something told him that the way things had been going, tonight it was something he wanted to avoid.

He glanced over his shoulder and saw everyone following, even Lansing. *Amazing,* he thought.

He turned his head forward again, then stopped: something to the right caught his eye. He looked and saw a rotten stump, or what was left of it.

It had been torn apart, its reddish-brown innards scattered all over the place. Some pieces lay twenty feet away.

He supposed a bear could have shredded a stump like that. And then he thought, *Probably not.*

The others walked up and Lansing said the obvious: It looked as if the Sasquatch had been searching for food—grubs or small rodents, like mice or chipmunks.

Some so-called scientists claimed there wasn't enough food in the forest for Sasquatches to survive, he said, even though carnivores like bears, cougars and Native Americans had survived fine here for hundreds of thousands of years. Sasquatches had been seen eating berries, leaves, the roots of ferns and aquatic plants, and domestic crops like apples and corn. They had been observed devouring live rodents, carrying trout and stealing dead deer, dried salmon and chickens.

Vaughn said: "Speaking of food—"

"Frank, come look at this." Mackey stood five yards away, partially hidden behind a small rise. From Vaughn's angle, Mackey's torso looked like it sprouted right from the ground.

Vaughn walked over—and almost stepped in what Mackey was looking at. It was a place where an animal had slept, what hunters call a bed.

Vaughn had seen plenty of deer, bear and elk beds, but never one this big. Ground plants were smashed flat over a huge area. Had to be about seven by four: twenty-eight square feet.

Enormous.

He squatted for a closer look. "Looks like our boy had a snack and a nap."

"A long nap," Mackey said. "Look at these tracks."

Vaughn sidestepped over to Mackey and saw an obviously fresher track. *Shit,* he thought.

"That was made last night," Lansing said, behind them.

"Yep," Mackey said.

Vaughn kept quiet.

Lansing walked back to the bed. Mackey whispered to Vaughn, "We're a lot closer to this thing than we were a few minutes ago."

Vaughn knelt and examined the track. Something about it bothered him. "This look right to you?"

Mackey stooped for a closer look. "Looks a little small, probably because it's recent. We've been on old tracks."

"Maybe," Vaughn said. But it didn't matter. He was getting them out of here.

He looked at his watch; his stomach rumbled. Not quite noon, but sooner was better.

He walked back to the bed and saw Lansing on his hands and knees, leaning way over one side of the flattened vegetation. Lansing's nose almost touched the ground.

"I'm going to the river for lunch and some fresh air," Vaughn said.

"How far is it?" Alison said.

"I figure it's about a quarter mile that way." Vaughn pointed across the trail they had been following.

"That sounds good to me, deputy," Lansing said. "I have a few samples to collect and then I'll catch up."

Mackey raised his eyebrows at Vaughn and inclined his head toward the river as if to say, *Forget him. Let's go.*

Good, Vaughn thought. "Don't be long," he said to Lansing, not really caring whether the professor showed up or not.

He walked away.

"I could use some assistance," Lansing said in a loud voice.

Vaughn turned around.

Lansing said, "Alison, would you mind?"

She didn't respond.

"I thought some hands-on field experience would be useful for you."

Good line, Vaughn thought. "I don't think Alison—"

Her face darkened. "I can make my own decisions, thanks." She turned to Lansing. "Just for a few minutes."

Lansing smiled at her.

Vaughn bent toward her and whispered, "Don't do anything stupid. You don't want to be stuck out here another night."

"Don't worry about me," she said.

"We'll catch up," Lansing said.

Chapter 36

AT the end of a wide hallway on the third floor of the Interior Building in Washington, D.C., Mark Kingston rocked on his heels before the assistant's desk.

Even though he'd been in government buildings thousands of times, he always noticed the smell—as if the old concrete walls sucked whatever vitality remained in bureaucrats and politicos and sweated it into the stale air.

But in this particular place he also felt another sensation well known to him: power. The people radiated it with religious zeal.

"I'm sorry to disturb you, director," the assistant said into the phone, "but a Mark Kingston from Carolina Pacific is here. He doesn't have an appointment, but he says you're expecting him."

She listened, staring down at her desk. Then she replaced the receiver and looked up. "She'll be with you in a moment."

"Thanks."

He'd been here before. Not at this location, but he'd occasionally had the sometimes unpleasant, sometimes pleasant job of revealing to a person that he and possibly others knew certain compromising information about that person.

Usually it went smoothly, because everyone accepted it as part of Washington culture. One day you were the fox, the next you might be the hare. All that mattered was to survive.

He faced the oak double doors and tried not to smile. The information Case Associates dug up was dynamite. Never in a million years would he have guessed. It was perfect for Mackey's red wolf problem, the Sasquatch, everything. And it definitely explained the bad blood between Mackey and Brenda Underwood.

One of the doors swung open. He'd forgotten how tall she was.

"Hello, Mark," Brenda Underwood said, walking up. She gripped his hand so tightly he had to make sure he squeezed hard enough.

"Morning, Brenda."

She smiled but her dark eyes revealed nothing. "Please come in."

He walked across the floor to one of the two maroon leather chairs waiting in front of her desk. His fingers unbuttoned his suit jacket and he eased down, resting his briefcase on the carpet. As always, he made sure he leaned slightly forward and sat up so he wouldn't be too low: shortening the legs of guest chairs was a common power tactic in Washington.

His eyes were drawn to a framed needlepoint on the wall facing him. Surrounded by ducks and a jumping trout were the words, "Go get 'em Sweetie!" Hanging in anyone else's office it would seem ridiculous, but here, even with the information he had, he found it oddly intimidating.

Brenda Underwood's short black hair bounced as she walked around the desk. She sat down and swiveled to face him. Her hand reached across the desk, palm up, and she gave him a big smile. "Please, go ahead."

THOUGH he and Mackey walked in a straight line to the river, every ten yards Vaughn broke a few fern stalks or left a scuff mark with his boot. He marked the trail because he knew from experience that it was easy to get lost in the woods on cloudy days, especially if the country was unfamiliar. He also did it because he suspected Alison might be coming on her own.

Their only detour was around the huge base of a fallen tree and the fern-covered pit it had left. The roots that snaked out from the rim of the rotted-out, hollow trunk made it look like the mouth of a giant sea worm.

Soon it brightened ahead, and a rushing sound climbed out of Vaughn's subconscious. Then the crisp smell of water hit him; he drank it in through his nose. Thirty yards more and he pushed through the last of the ferns and out onto the stones of the riverbank.

He dropped his pack and, kneeling next to it, unzipped the main pocket. He lifted out two bags: one with two Gala apples and another containing black strips of elk jerky.

Mackey worked his shoulders out of his pack and laid it at his feet.

"Jerky?" Vaughn said, holding out a piece.

"Thanks." Mackey took it and tore off a chunk with his teeth.

Vaughn chewed, watching the water rush by.

"Think they'll go after it?" Mackey said.

Vaughn swallowed. "Alison's too scared."

Mackey sliced off a hunk of the cheddar cheese he carried. The cheese stuck to the knife blade, and he held it out.

Vaughn peeled it off and nodded his thanks. "If she's not here by the time we're done eating, we'll—"

Aieeeee!

A woman's scream.

Alison.

"OBVIOUSLY you're aware of what's going on," Kingston said. He would be as vague as he could. He didn't know who else might be listening.

Brenda Underwood's head and hair bobbed forward.

"I want to emphasize the stakes here. If things were to go the wrong way, we could have a national disaster of unprecedented proportions."

"It's possible," she said.

He wished she'd reacted more strongly. "I'd say it's likely, and I'm confident the President would agree."

No reaction.

He said: "We simply can't have enormous parts of the United States locked up. The economy would fall apart."

"I understand," she said. "Why are you here?"

"You're aware that one of the people out there—"

She waved him off. "Yes. I know his problem and I know how you propose to solve it."

He wasn't surprised. Most times the skeletons never made it out of the closet. It was enough to know they were there.

"But I'm not buying," she said.

Again Kingston wasn't surprised. Often the initial reaction was anger, but eventually it subsided. He said: "Please reconsider."

She leaned forward and smiled. "Good try, Mark, but here's what happens if you let that information out. First," she ticked it off on one finger, "you screw the guy you're trying to help and in the process tee off all his powerful congressional friends, thereby becoming less effective at your job. Second," another finger, "I'll take every tree-hugging biologist I've got and send them all over the country with a microscope and tweezers to look for endangered species on Carolina Pacific land." A third finger: "And last but not least, I'll let it be known that Mark Kingston is the reason they're there."

Silently he watched the scales rise and fall. "It appears we have a stalemate."

"Yes."

"But we don't. If this goes badly it'll look like you were trying to make sure it was discovered. You knew about it, you sent your own niece out there, and to top it all off because of your affair you didn't—"

"That was a long time ago, and technically it wasn't an affair."

"That's not the point."

She sat back. "No, it isn't." She swiveled to her left and looked up at the framed needlepoint. Her finger tapped the chair's burnished wooden arm.

Kingston waited. After a few seconds she faced him and said, "Let me ask you this, Mark. Are you sure you've thought this out?"

"I'm sure."

"Let me rephrase. Could you be missing something in all of this?"

She was getting desperate. He grabbed the handle of his briefcase and began to stand. "I'll give you a few hours to think—"

"What if I told you you were flat-out wrong?"

"About what?"

"Everything," she said.

"I wouldn't believe you."

"You'd need proof," she said, almost to herself.

He had no idea what she was talking about. She seemed to be using a sophomoric countermove: confusion. "Unless you'd care to enlighten me with specifics," he said, "I'm leaving."

"Do you expect a phone call today?"

"Yes."

"Give him my number. Tell him to call me."

"Why?"

"Maybe I can solve all of our problems."

Chapter 37

"HE pushed me!"

Alison rocked back and forth on the ground, both hands clamped around her right ankle. Streaks of pale skin showed where tears had scrubbed clean paths down her cheeks, but she wasn't crying now. Behind her, her pack lay belly-up on the ground. Lansing stood a few steps away.

Vaughn knelt by her feet. "Let me take a look at that."

She looked at him with anger on her face, but slowly unclasped one hand and then the other.

"I'll need to take off your boots and socks."

"I only hurt this ankle," she said.

"I have to compare one to the other. To judge swelling."

He gently pulled out the knot and loosened the laces of her right boot. "You hear a crack?"

She shook her head.

"You, Dr. Lansing?" Vaughn didn't look at him.

"No," Lansing said. "I should explain—"

"In a minute." To Alison, Vaughn said: "How about a pop or a snap? Feel one?"

"I think so."

He pulled the tongue forward, cupped his hand around her Achilles tendon and eased the boot off.

"Ow!"

"Sorry."

His fingers found the top of her blue thermal sock and pulled it down. She stiffened, then brushed his hand away and said, "Let me do it." Gingerly she peeled down the sock, making a face as she did, then leaned back and rested her palms on the ground behind her.

Vaughn picked up her foot and eyeballed the ankle. "No bruising. That's good."

A relief. Bruising would have indicated a serious injury, probably requiring a splint. And with a splint, she wouldn't have been able to wear her boot, requiring her to be carried out.

"Let's see the other ankle," he said, and removed the other boot and sock.

The ankles looked similar, but it was early yet.

Holding the injured ankle again, he gently rolled her foot to the side. Her leg jerked back.

"Pain?"

Her teeth grabbed her lip and she nodded.

Color looked okay. He pressed one of her toenails. Underneath it went white, and then the pink quickly returned. He asked her to wiggle her toes and then he rubbed each toe lightly on both sides. "Feel that?"

"Yes," she said.

No neural or circulation problems. "Looks like a strain," he said. "I'm going to wrap it." He was about to reach for his pack when he remembered it was out by the river. "You have a first-aid kit?"

"Yeah," she said. "Left side pocket."

Mackey started toward the pack, but Lansing held up a hand and said, "I'll get it." He spun the pack around and from the side pocket removed a blue plastic box with a red cross on the top. He handed it to Vaughn.

Alison frowned.

Vaughn took out an ACE bandage. He wound it onto the foot, then moved to the ankle, wrapping figure eights until the putty-colored bandage was completely used up. Then he taped it.

"How's that feel?"

"Okay."

"Not too tight?"

Her ponytail swung from side to side.

"Put your socks and shoes back on, and we'll get going," Vaughn said.

He waited until she finished, and then said: "Think you can walk?"

"I don't know."

"That's the only way you'll be able to get out of here, unless we carry you."

"No thanks," she said, and struggled to stand. He stepped behind her; one hand gripped her hip and the other supported her under the armpit. He lifted her to her feet.

She took a tentative footstep. A small cry came from her throat and she limped forward, putting almost all her weight on her left foot.

Mackey said: "You look like the Sasquatch now."

"What the hell's that supposed to mean?" she said.

"Easy now," Mackey said. "I meant—"

"Your limp," Vaughn said, glancing at Mackey. "The Sasquatch favors its right leg too."

She glared at Mackey and then dropped back down on the ground, her bad foot out in front of her.

Vaughn rooted through her first-aid kit, found two packs of Motrin and tore them open. "Take these," he said. He dropped the four brown pills onto her palm and handed her a water bottle. Then he turned his attention to Lansing.

"Okay, professor, what's your story?"

Lansing's hands flexed. "I'm afraid I did push her. But I intended to do the opposite."

Vaughn waited.

"She didn't see the hole," Lansing said, indicating the fern-choked pit left by the upturned tree.

"I would have if you didn't push me into it," Alison said.

"Let Dr. Lansing tell his side of it," Vaughn said.

"You didn't even ask me!"

Vaughn faced her. "You said you were pushed, right? Anything else I need to know?"

She looked away.

Lansing said: "Alison, I'm truly sorry. I certainly didn't mean it."

She wouldn't look at him.

Vaughn said: "You were saying."

"I was behind Alison," Lansing said. "I saw the tree, assumed there was a hole there and ran up to her. She was about to step into the hole and I tried to grab her. But as you can see," he gestured at his pants, "I fell, and in the process pushed her in."

Damp dirt stained his knees and shins, but that didn't prove anything. Vaughn said: "You ever think about yelling?"

Lansing's hands flexed again. "I didn't want to scare her and cause her to fall into the hole."

Vaughn examined Lansing's face. The professor didn't seem too upset, but then again it was only a sprain. A mighty convenient one.

"You look skeptical, deputy," Lansing said. "If you doubt it was an accident you must think I have a motive for injuring Alison. Allow me to pose it: You suspect I purposely injured her in order to hinder our travel and force us to remain out here longer."

Vaughn started to speak but Lansing held up a hand. "Please. Let me refute your hypothesis. It has two major flaws. One is that it would hardly make sense for me to slow us down when we just found recently made tracks."

"Unless you wanted more time to run around on your own," Vaughn said.

"That's rendered moot by the second flaw in your theory: I'll take Alison out."

"We're all getting out of here," Vaughn said.

Lansing sighed. "Deputy, I doubt the Sasquatch slept in that bed, not in the conventional sense. Meaning it didn't choose to go to sleep. It fainted."

Vaughn didn't know what he was getting at.

Lansing smiled. "The bed's size indicates that the animal lay in a sprawled position, even though it's been cold. From the age of the recent tracks it appears the Sasquatch stayed there for two entire days. And I discovered a significant amount of blood soaked into the dirt where the right shoulder was. Ergo, the Sasquatch fainted."

"So?"

"So it could be dying. From the wound you gave it."

Chapter 38

RESPONSIBILITY sat on Vaughn's back like a mountain. He was obligated to go after the wounded Sasquatch, but he didn't want to. And not just because he was suspicious of Lansing. His heart wasn't in it anymore.

He watched Lansing and Alison walk down the riverbank. The fern fronds that bowed over the forest side of the stones obscured Alison. She kept her distance from Lansing, who walked near the water. She hadn't wanted to go with him, but Vaughn could tell that part of her was relieved to be heading back.

To make sure she would go, and despite his misgivings about the professor, he reminded her that leaving with Lansing was the only way she would make it out by dark. He knew that wasn't a possibility anymore, but it was a necessary white lie. Having both of them gone was the only way he and Mackey could quickly track the wounded Sasquatch.

He watched: Lansing tall and spidery, Alison short, limping and supporting herself with a walking stick. They reminded him of an illustration from a book he read in high school. Don Quixote with Sancho Panza carrying a broken lance.

Vaughn realized he was getting sleepy and shook his head to clear it. Again he thought about abandoning the wounded Sasquatch.

No, he thought. *That's bullshit.* Anyone could find excuses: I'm too tired, it's probably fine, *X, Y* or *Z* is more important. All of that was rationalization to avoid responsibility. He wounded the Sasquatch so he had to make sure it was dead or fine. If he didn't feel like it, too damn bad.

He looked up at the sky. All he saw was a grey strip, hemmed in by the evergreen walls of trees that bordered the river. The clouds still chugged steadily west.

A soft snapping noise made him look into the forest. Mackey pushed through the ferns and onto the stones, a roll of white toilet paper in his hand. He held it up. "Need to use the outhouse?"

"No thanks," Vaughn said. "Took care of that this morning."

Mackey stuffed the roll into his pack.

Vaughn didn't get up. He should have, but a thought kept intruding on his mind. Ever since he held Alison's small foot and stroked her toes, ever since he felt the jut of her hip bone, he'd wanted to call Katie. He knew his wife would still be angry, but she would also be worried.

And he was worried too, about her feelings and what she might do.

He argued with himself about calling her—it would help/no it wouldn't, it would be a distraction/no it wouldn't—and ended up telling himself that taking that long to make a simple decision argued in favor of not doing it.

But now he reconsidered. *Maybe you're procrastinating.* Heck with it.

"I'm going to call my wife," he said. "Just be a minute." Mackey held up a hand.

Vaughn flipped his pack around and unzipped the pocket where he kept the sat-phone. He stuck his hand in to grab it— but it wasn't there.

He was confused. Had he stashed it somewhere else?

He rooted through all the pockets. No phone.

What the hell?

The Sasquatch had the dexterity to remove the phone, but why would it? Crows, squirrels and even bears took things that were shiny or smelled interesting, but the Sasquatch wasn't a typical animal. And the first night it took his Granola bars and nothing else.

Last night the gunshot interrupted its rummaging and all of his remaining food was there in the morning. He hadn't checked the rest of the pockets because they were all zipped shut.

Then he knew. It had to be Lansing.

The professor could have taken it this morning. And dammit, maybe some of the tracks Lansing had been scratching out at the campsite were his own.

"Sasquatch take your phone, ol' boy?" Mackey said.

"Looks like it. Can I borrow yours?"

Mackey bent over, unzipped his pack and tossed him a Ziploc bag. "Extra battery's in there if the other one goes out on you."

Vaughn said thanks and walked twenty yards upstream. From the bag he took out what he recognized was a satellite phone, though fancier than the ones at the sheriff's office. He laid the bag with the extra battery on a flat rock, then pressed the power button until the phone beeped. His finger punched in his home number, and as he waited for the connection, he realized he didn't know what he would say.

It rang once. "Hello?"

A man's voice. For a moment Vaughn was surprised. Then he said, "Sheriff? What are you doing there?"

Suddenly worry hit him. "What's—"

"Your house was broken into this morning," the sheriff said. "Katie's fine, but she's upset. Scared her pretty bad."

"She was there?"

"Yeah. She took the day off. They locked her in the garage."

"She hurt?"

"No, and nothing was taken," the sheriff said. "But they did leave something. A message on your living room wall, in red spray paint. 'Leave it alone.'"

Vaughn cursed. "Let me talk to her."

"Hold on."

Vaughn heard voices in the background and recognized a few as belonging to other deputies. The sound of a door closing, then quiet.

"Francis?"

"Hi, honey. You okay?"

"No." Her voice started to break up. "Last night I got two scary phone calls and this morning—"

"The sheriff told me. They didn't hurt you?"

"No."

"You sure?"

"They scared me," she said. "They were rough."

"Did you recognize any of them?"

"They wore masks," she said. "Camouflage masks, like the one you wear hunting."

"How about their voices?"

"I didn't recognize them."

"Did they say anything?"

"One of them said something about you interfering with a man's right to make a living. Maybe something else, I don't know. I told the sheriff."

He recognized her imperfect recall as a symptom of psychological trauma, so he abandoned that line of questioning. "How about the callers. What did they say?"

"That we were dead if you didn't leave 'it' well enough alone."

Rage swelled through his body. "Listen, honey. When I get back I'll find them and make sure—"

"By then it might be too late."

"For what?"

"For everything, Francis. Don't you see that yet?"

His hand squeezed the phone. "Katie, if I don't do what's right I'll be just like every other schmuck in the world. Spineless. No honor."

"Honor? Dammit, Francis, what good is that when it makes our lives miserable?"

"Now wait a sec—"

She said, "Listen to me. I love the way you always want to do the right thing. But you're not a kid anymore. What you do or don't do has major consequences, for us and for other people."

"I know that—"

"If what you're doing out there isn't right for us and for our future, who's it right for?"

Vaughn looked at the sky and choked down his anger. All he'd wanted to say was *I love you* and *See you soon.* Having the same old argument was pointless. "Put the sheriff back on."

A pause, and then she said, "If I'm not here when you get back, I'll be at my mom's."

Her mother lived in New Jersey. "That's your choice," he said.

"No, it's yours."

Vaughn heard voices and the sheriff came back on the line.

"Figure out who did it yet?" Vaughn said.

"No, but it shouldn't be too hard. I'd guess loggers, CP guys."

Geek, Vaughn thought.

The sheriff said: "I'm not excusing what they did, but you can't really blame them. They're just looking out for themselves and their families."

Vaughn said: "I'll have everyone out tonight and then come right in."

"No you won't," the sheriff said. "Go home, take a shower, talk to your wife, and think long and hard about your future."

Vaughn didn't know what to say. The phone crackled and then the sheriff said: "If things go badly out there, I won't be able to do anything for you."

Vaughn squeezed his eyes shut. "Yeah."

"That reminds me," the sheriff said. "That woman from the Fish and Wildlife Service mentioned the FBI so I called a friend at the FBI's Seattle office. Asked about her and the rest of your party. Turns out she was bluffing: The feebs have no idea what she's doing there."

Vaughn wasn't surprised.

"The young lady—what's her name?" the sheriff said.

"Alison."

"Yeah, Alison. Just a kid. Only got in trouble once, in college. Vandalized earth-moving equipment as part of some

Earth First! thing. Current member of Sierra Club, International Wildlife Society, few other green groups. Interesting note: Her aunt, Brenda Underwood, is the head of the Fish and Wildlife Service."

Whoa, Vaughn thought. How did that figure in?

"Chris Mackey, NRA member, was a biologist at the North Carolina and New York fish and game agencies before becoming an independent consultant. His specialty is endangered species. Apparently he doesn't like them much: He's being investigated by the U.S. Attorney General's Office in connection with the killing of a red wolf, whatever that is."

Vaughn didn't bother to say anything.

"Only other thing about Mackey is that he's a hell of a shot," the sheriff said. "Won a bunch of rifle and handgun competitions.

"The last guy, Arthur Lansing, is an associate professor of physical anthropology at Western Washington University. Nothing interesting except he was once issued a summons for carrying a rifle out of season. A big one."

Vaughn got a funny feeling. "Let me guess," he said. "A .375 H&H Magnum."

"That's right." The Old Man sounded surprised. "A Ruger."

"He doesn't have it with him."

"I know," the sheriff said. "I searched his car. The rifle was in a gun sock under the folded back seat. Also found a case for a .357."

"Just the case?"

"Just the case."

Vaughn looked downstream at the receding forms of Lansing and Alison. "Thanks, sheriff."

"Watch yourself," the Old Man said.

Chapter 39

VAUGHN stood on the smooth stones of the riverbank but didn't hear the water rushing by. He didn't see the giant firs towering unmoved before him, and he'd forgotten the cell phone clenched in his cold hand.

What the fuck is going on? he thought.

His house had been broken into and his wife terrorized, maybe by people he knew and certainly by people who knew he was a deputy sheriff.

He pictured "Leave it alone" spray painted on the living room wall, the red paint running like blood.

How stupid did people have to be to break into the home of a deputy sheriff? he wondered.

Didn't matter how much they feared for their jobs. When he got back he would show them a new kind of fear. The helpless kind, like Katie felt. Maybe the long barrel of a .357 shoved into the back of their throats.

The first face that came to mind was Geek's, but gagging on a steel tube would be too good for him. Vaughn saw his hands wrapping around Geek's neck and squeezing until Geek's face turned purple and his eyes bulged out like a frog getting squeezed by a snake. Vaughn's thumbs would pop through the fat and hit the hard trachea . . .

Some fucking friend. Really Boone's friend, still a scared little kid who couldn't keep his mouth shut. And because of that, Vaughn's wife had been assaulted in her own home, she was even more ready to leave him and the sheriff had more cause to turn his back on him.

Geek was a dead man.

Then Vaughn's conflict training kicked in. He took a few deep breaths to steady himself. A few more.

Okay, he thought. It had to be loggers who broke into his house, but Geek didn't necessarily have to be involved. The people at Carolina Pacific headquarters knew about the wounded Sasquatch. The phone calls and red paint could be part of an organized effort. A plan.

If so, Mackey had to be part of that plan. Did he know about the break-in? What else did he know? He hadn't said anything about last night's gunshot, so maybe CP had someone else in the woods. If so, Vaughn figured it was to make sure they got the outcome they wanted.

He also assumed Carolina Pacific had to be worried about the other two in his party, particularly Alison, the Sierra Clubber. But she likely was off-limits because CP couldn't risk directly offending her aunt, who had to be interested in Sasquatches as an endangered species. Whether Brenda Underwood's interest stemmed from a desire for more government control, animal rights–driven environmentalism or some other political agenda didn't matter. Not to him. All that mattered was that Alison and her aunt felt Sasquatches were endangered—and that Alison obviously was sent out here because her aunt could control her.

But to what end? And when, out here or after Alison returned to Washington, D.C.? Seemed like a dead end because from the uncertain way Alison had been acting since she arrived, it appeared only Brenda Underwood had those answers.

Vaughn wondered whether Mackey knew about the Alison-Underwood connection. Apparently not, otherwise Alison would have already been bound, gagged and left somewhere.

That left Lansing, who had to be the least of CP's worries.

He wasn't an environmentalist, but he was a scientist, and empirical evidence of Sasquatches could be damaging. Then again, a lone scientist who studied a mythical animal had to be easy to discredit. Probably had a reputation as a nut.

But Vaughn saw that in Carolina Pacific's tunnel-vision thinking about the stakes for itself, it neglected to think about the stakes for Lansing.

Lansing had bet his entire life on the crazy idea that another ape walked this planet, right under everyone's noses. Amazingly, he'd been right. But ten years of enduring other people's doubt and ridicule had to manifest itself somehow. And it had.

Lansing was obsessed. Vaughn now realized that the professor must see this as his one and only chance to prove to the world that Sasquatches exist. To prove that he hadn't wasted his life.

Vaughn should have seen it coming. He knew Lansing wanted evidence that Sasquatches were real, but he'd been fooled by the harmless professor act. Like the first night, when Lansing dangled Mackey's .44 as if he'd never held a revolver in his life. And then leaving it in camp the next morning.

That reminded him that, like Mackey, Lansing hadn't speculated on last night's gunshot. Did he also have an accomplice in the woods?

How many more people were out here?

Vaughn felt himself getting angry again. Everyone was only in it for themselves. Lansing, Mackey, Alison, the loggers, the sheriff, the people back in North Carolina and Washington, D.C. Even Katie. *Or I'll do the right thing for me,* she'd said.

She was being selfish and wanted him to be the same way. But he couldn't be. He'd made that decision long ago. Not consciously, not at a specific time. Just at some point, very early on, it became clear. Selfishness was behind everything bad in life: greed, crime, politics, war.

Obvious, yet most people, the gutless majority, were selfish. Usually they banded together and brought down those who weren't, probably just to relieve their guilt.

So why did he feel guilty?

It's hard to do the right thing, he thought, *that's why.* No doubt selfishness was easier. What if he'd been that way back in New Jersey? He would still be there right now, corrupt like the rest of them because looking the other way was just as bad . . .

HE'D been on foot patrol in Newark's Central Ward, where it looked as if no one had bothered to clean up since the 1967 riots. Everything always had a film of grime, even after a spring rain.

On street corners, crack vials crunched underfoot. Drugs and other crimes were accepted parts of everyday life, which was why the Central Ward was one of the two sink-or-swim areas of the city where young officers were assigned.

He walked along the sidewalk and watched the clusters of dealers and hangers-on dissolve before him as if they were mirages. He knew they would reappear as soon as he left.

Suddenly the graffiti-covered security doors of an apartment building burst open and an enormous black woman pounded up to him, screaming and waving her arms.

"My boy's dying! He's dying!" Tears streamed across her cheeks.

"Where?" he said.

"The hall! He's in the hall!" she said, shoving him toward the doors.

"What floor?"

"Two two three!"

Second floor. He radioed it in and dashed into the building, up littered stairs humid with the stink of urine. At the second floor landing he heard screaming and crying, and when he ran into the hallway he saw people crowded around something on the floor.

He sprinted over, yelling at everyone to stand back. The bodies parted and revealed a boy about five years old lying on the chipped and peeling linoleum. The boy's long-lashed eyes were open, but were glassy like the color of veins, and he wasn't moving. His lips had faded to the color of veins, and the spittle that ran from one corner of his mouth had already dried white.

Vaughn started CPR, but he knew the boy was dead. It ended up being heart failure from a huge overdose of crack cocaine. Either the boy found it and ate it, or juveniles fed it to him in candy. No one would say.

He stopped CPR when the EMTs arrived—and suddenly it felt like he was being crushed by a Coke machine. Brown fists came around and pummeled his chest and stomach.

"You killed him! You killed my boy!"

People hoisted her off.

She shouted at everyone in a uniform—"You all killed him!"—then broke down.

He could still hear her wailing.

He thought she'd been hysterical. But later he found out what she meant.

A cousin of the police chief owned that apartment building and a few other slums in the city. Everyone who lived in them knew it, and assumed it was yet another example of "the man" having it both ways.

Drugs were rampant in all of the buildings, and that bothered Vaughn because the chief had to know about it. But what sent him over the edge was the all-too-obvious reason the drugs were there: Toilets covered with so much mold they looked black. Walls and ceilings that dripped stinking liquid. Roach- and rat-infested kitchens and hallways. He couldn't believe people in America lived that way. It was squalor. Inhuman. Hopeless.

The chief he knew by reputation only, a third-generation Newark policeman with friends and relatives all over town. A few held high positions in the fire department and the city government, and the chief's uncle had just retired after sixteen years as president of the city council. Vaughn figured all of them knew about the cousin, but he didn't want to scandalize the whole family. So he did the honorable thing. He caught the chief alone in the parking garage and suggested that he get his cousin to do something about the buildings.

The chief said, "Forget about it, patrolman," and started walking away.

"You're not reading between the lines," Vaughn said.

The chief stopped and turned around. "What's your name again?"

"Vaughn, sir. Frank Vaughn."

"Vaughn, I haven't heard anything about you yet, which

probably means you're a good cop with a promising future. Don't blow it."

Vaughn had talked it over beforehand with Katie and they figured the chief would say something like that. Vaughn knew his job would be threatened, but he just couldn't get that dead boy and the way those people lived out of his mind.

"Sir, I became a cop because I have a strong sense of right and wrong. I'm guessing you did for the same reason. So I appreciate the warning, but the way those people are living is flat-out wrong. And if you don't do something about it, I will."

Color surged up from the chief's collar. Red, then purple. Vaughn wondered if the blood would burst out of the capillaries and onto the concrete.

"Listen to me, Vaughn," the chief said, jabbing a fat finger at Vaughn's uniform. "I'll tell my cousin what you said. But I'm giving you one month from today to find another job, far away from here. Believe me, you don't want to stay."

The chief was true to his word, and then some. Turned out no police department in the entire state would hire Vaughn. He and Katie went through a terrible period, and things got worse when he had to start looking for work outside of New Jersey. Both their families lived in-state, and hers was big. If he couldn't find work anywhere close that meant she couldn't be around her siblings, parents, cousins and friends as often. And that was a huge issue, especially when they talked about having children.

It took him a year and a half to find a job, and it was all the way out in Washington state. When he told her, she cried.

Would it have been better if he hadn't confronted the chief?

No. He read in the *Star-Ledger* that the buildings were fixed up. Not all of them and not entirely, but the people lived better. Even though kids there probably still died from drugs, hopefully there weren't as many. Hopefully no more five-year-olds.

With all the publicity, the chief's cousin actually ended up looking good. Bastard got a plaque from the mayor.

Suddenly it felt like his mind slammed into the corner of a door.

He realized that in a way, confronting the chief had been selfish. He'd indulged his own sense of right and wrong. And even though he was right, he lost his job and the ability to be employed as a policeman anywhere in New Jersey. As a consequence, both he and Katie gave up regular contact with friends and family.

He did the right thing, but lost everything. Everything but Katie. And this time he risked losing even more: his job, his friends' jobs and Katie, too. Their life. That's what she meant.

All of it was important, but no way was he losing her.

Suddenly he felt better. Not at peace, but unburdened, like he'd climbed over the crest of a mountain and now just had to get down.

He knew what he had to do. He had to control Lansing.

None of them could be trusted, but there was no way Mackey wanted the Sasquatches discovered. And Alison the tree-hugger wouldn't kill a rat, let alone a Sasquatch. But Lansing definitely wanted one dead.

So if Lansing thought the wounded Sasquatch might be dying, why would he leave? Easy. It wasn't dying. Or he had something else up his sleeve. Maybe something to do with that bed he examined so closely.

Either way, the professor wanted everyone but Alison out of the picture while he went downstream.

Vaughn's eyes hardened back into focus. Past Mackey's reclining form he saw that Lansing and Alison had walked out of sight, around a bend in the river.

He remembered the phone in his hand. Still on. He held down the power button until it beeped and the green light faded from the display. Then he strode back to Mackey and handed him the phone and the Ziploc bag.

"Ready to get tracking?" Mackey said.

"I want to check that bed," Vaughn said. "Then we're going after Lansing."

Chapter 40

JUST inside the trees, concealed from where Alison rested on the riverbank, Lansing waited on hold. He hoped for voice mail because that would mean Tom Sun was now in the woods.

"Sun."

Lansing's hand squeezed into a fist. "Tom," he said, "this is Dr. Art Lansing."

"Yes, Dr. Lansing. How are you?"

"Did you come down here?"

He heard Sun sigh like he was standing next to him. The deputy's phone reception was remarkable.

"I couldn't convince the producer," Sun said. "We get so many of these calls."

"How many damn calls do you get from scientists?"

Sun didn't say anything.

Lansing said, "This is an incredible opportunity to get visual proof of this species' existence. Do you realize what that means? Irrefutable evidence that another walking primate is alive right here in the United States? Even if you don't care about the contribution to the human race, it's a guaranteed Emmy. Isn't that possibility worth a camera crew for one day?"

"I thought it was a few days."

"Not anymore."

Sun was silent again.

"Tom, something is going to happen down here."

"I don't know," Sun said. "It'd be like looking for a needle in a haystack."

"Normally," Lansing said. "But there's more than one needle, and I have a magnet."

VAUGHN hurried back along their trail. Now unconcerned with making noise, his boots crunched the vegetation and things clanked in his pack. The straps dug into his shoulders; he'd split most of Alison's load with Mackey and Lansing, and though the additional weight wasn't much, at this speed he felt it.

He saw the stump and, past it, the rise. He ran up on top.

Below him lay the bed. And beyond it, the recent tracks.

They still looked too small.

"He was right about the blood," Mackey said. He bent over the right side of the flattened vegetation. On all fours and completely camouflaged, even his pack, he looked like a giant bullfrog. "But he was lying about the amount. There's not near enough to be fatal."

Suddenly Vaughn realized what was wrong. He walked to where he originally left the wounded Sasquatch's trail and jogged ahead. A few yards ahead he found a track, and then another and another. He cursed his tired brain for being so slow, and ran back to where Mackey waited.

"Lansing said that blood was from the right shoulder," he said.

"He got that much right."

"I shot the Sasquatch in the *left* shoulder," Vaughn said. "I knew those prints looked different." That meant whoever shot last night wounded a different Sasquatch. A third one.

If Mackey realized that, he didn't show it. His eyes flicked toward the river. "He's got a gun, doesn't he."

"Yeah," Vaughn said. "Let's go."

They walked quickly to the water at an angle that would get them well downstream of where they had lunch. Vaughn wanted to jog, but knew he would get too tired.

After about a hundred yards, he felt the pack's weight in his legs. He thought he was tiring easily because of his lack of sleep, but then he realized the terrain was rising. He'd forgotten. "We're going uphill," he said over his shoulder. "Let's head straight to the river."

"Right behind you."

Vaughn adjusted his course, and after another hundred yards saw more light between the trees and a line of scrub ahead. Then he heard the water. A low roar.

He jogged closer and the roar became louder. He figured the river would be running faster and deeper here because of the steeper terrain, and when he got to the edge he saw he was right.

From where he stood the ground dropped ten feet straight down, forming the beginning of a small cliff that rose up to his left. Below him black water squeezed around a midstream boulder, through a narrow chute and surged into a short pool covered with white froth. The churning water stair-stepped downstream in a similar manner for as far as he could see.

The other bank was level with the river, and only a few feet downstream the old growth along the bank's edge changed abruptly to younger, uniformly sized Douglas fir. His eyes followed the tips of the trees as they pointed up toward the dirt and stone scar of the ridge, partially blocked by slow-moving fog. Somewhere to the left on that ridge road was his truck.

He pulled his eyes down and looked upstream. On the stones of the opposite bank stood Lansing.

Water stained Lansing's pants dark from mid-thigh down. He seemed to be yelling to someone, but Vaughn couldn't hear over the roar of the water.

Vaughn looked farther upstream then downstream, but didn't see Alison. "You see her?"

"Sure don't," Mackey said, breathing hard.

Lansing paced back and forth with his head thrown back and his hands cupping either side of his mouth. Vaughn listened, but still couldn't make out what Lansing was yelling. "Looks like he's yelling," he said.

Mackey said, "He couldn't have lost her."

Vaughn stepped back into the treeline and jogged upstream. Soon he could hear Lansing's voice, but no distinct words.

Aided by the decline and the heavy pack pushing him downhill, he moved faster.

When he got close to Lansing's position, his view was blocked by a seven-foot-tall salmonberry thicket that sprung up and ran for several yards along the river's edge. But he finally could hear well enough to know what Lansing was doing.

The professor wasn't yelling. He was howling.

Vaughn ran toward the end of the thicket—the howling stopped. He skidded around the last bush and looked.

Lansing's hands gripped a bleached limb that protruded from a five-foot heap of interlocked driftwood near the forest's edge. It was one of several such piles along the river's course that accumulated during spring floods.

Lansing tugged and strained, pushing with his boot against the pile, but the branch wouldn't come. Then he leaned over the limb and pumped it up and down several times. He heaved again and it came out.

He staggered backward, then ran to the nearest tree. He raised the limb like a baseball bat and slammed it against the trunk. Again and again. Though the tree was alive, the pounding made a hollow *chok* sound.

Lansing hit the trunk three times—*chok, chok, chok*—then howled. Then he did it again.

It looked like he'd gone completely insane, but Vaughn knew the madness had a purpose.

He had to stop him.

From Vaughn's feet a six-foot almost vertical bank of loose rock and dirt dropped down into the river. Unless he felt like going for a swim in near-freezing water, he would have to cross farther upstream where it was shallower. But getting there would take time.

He stood up and shouted. "Hey!" He waved his rifle. "Dr. Lansing!"

If Lansing heard, he gave no sign of it.

Cursing, Vaughn dropped his pack and, with only his rifle, ran upstream.

He'd taken only three steps when a woman's shriek knifed into his skull.

His first thought was to stop and look, but instead he kept running. Only twenty yards ahead the ground dipped and then flattened. He would be on the bank in a few seconds.

He sprinted the last five yards, burst through the ferns, and slipped and almost fell on the slick stones of the riverbank.

He looked to his left and saw Lansing running upstream, howling like a maniac. A shiny silver revolver bobbed in the professor's right hand.

Vaughn looked to his right—and that's when he saw it, on the opposite bank.

It had to be the big Sasquatch because the one he shot was nowhere near this size.

It ran toward Lansing so fluidly, so gracefully, Vaughn almost couldn't believe how fast it moved.

Its arms extended nearly straight and swung in long arcs, as if it were walking underwater. Long dark-brown hair streamed from the backs of its arms and from the area where its shoulder blades met.

It made no noise he could hear over the river, and without pausing seemed to glide over an old deadfall lying on the bank.

He felt like he was watching something moving in slow motion. But it was traveling so damn fast.

In a few seconds it cut the distance to Lansing from a quarter mile to thirty yards.

Lansing raised the .357.

Vaughn brought up his rifle, but hesitated: He didn't know whether to point it at the Sasquatch or at Lansing.

BOOM!

Thwack! A section of tree next to the Sasquatch's head disintegrated in a shower of brown splinters.

The Sasquatch ducked into the forest and, in the blink of an eye, disappeared.

Chapter 41

LANSING continued running up the bank and plunged into the woods where the Sasquatch had gone in.

Vaughn watched for a second, then looked downstream to see where Mackey had shot from. That was a hell of a shot, he thought. A giant, unfamiliar animal moving incredibly fast, and Mackey hit close enough to its head to scare it. To *turn* it.

He didn't see Mackey, but didn't look carefully; visions of the Sasquatch kept getting in the way.

It was much bigger than he'd imagined. Nowhere near as tall as the trees, but big enough to make them look smaller. About nine feet, he figured. That meant he would come up to the bottom of its chest. At most.

And it was unbelievably thick. From the side it looked as deep as a fifty-gallon drum, and when it turned into the woods the muscles in its back flared: They were so massive that even at that distance he could see them though the hair. Or fur.

He couldn't fathom how wide the Sasquatch must be. Four feet at the shoulders? Five?

For a moment he felt as if he'd seen some kind of mythological forest god, and he realized a full-grown man would be like a child—a sickly child—around it. He became conscious of the .30-06 in his hands. It felt light and small, like a toy.

Upstream a stone clattered. He whirled to his right, his rifle up and ready.

Alison limped toward him, taking giant steps with her left leg and swinging her injured foot forward. Her eyes popped from a face so leached of color that it looked frozen.

He dropped the rifle from his shoulder and walked toward her. The closer he got, the more her lips quivered.

When he'd almost reached her she fell toward him. He caught her, and hugged her head to his chest.

She shook and then her stomach jerked with sobs. "It's—so—big," she said. "So—big."

He patted her back and looked across the river. Lansing hadn't returned.

"Frank."

He released Alison and turned around.

Mackey stood at the edge of the forest. He glanced across the river and then looked at Vaughn. Vaughn noticed that Mackey's lips had pulled back, baring the edges of his teeth.

"Nice shooting," Vaughn said.

Mackey didn't even nod a thanks. "You'll want to see this," he said. To Alison: "You might want to stay here. It's pretty far back."

"I'm not staying here alone." She wiped her eyes with her knuckles.

To Mackey, Vaughn said: "It's not—"

"No," Mackey said. He turned and walked into the trees.

Mackey headed downstream and Vaughn followed, slowly so Alison could keep up.

The roar of the water became louder. Vaughn found his pack and retrieved it, and then they passed the salmonberry bushes.

Almost at the point where they had first hit the river, Mackey veered into the forest. Ten yards, then he angled up-slope.

"How much farther?" Vaughn said.

"Just a bit."

Vaughn stopped to let Alison catch up. When he looked ahead, Mackey was gone.

"Chris?"

"Over here." Mackey stepped out from behind a seven-foot-wide Douglas fir about eight yards ahead. Compared to the massive trunk, he looked like a forest gnome.

As Vaughn walked toward him, he saw that Mackey's attention was riveted on something on the ground, behind the tree.

When Vaughn got there he thought, *Shit.*

He'd seen people mangled in car accidents and, once, a timber faller crushed by an old fir. But this was worse.

The body, still fully clothed, was pulverized—as if it was beaten with logs, though he saw only a few abrasions. Everything was curiously flat. Deflated.

The chest looked like it had been stomped on by an elephant—smashed, but also bloated. It sagged out toward the sides as if the ribs and peritoneum were simply gone, allowing the viscera to float free.

Limbs splayed at goofy angles, and one of the shin bones pushed out like a tent pole against a leg of the camouflage pants. A bone of the right forearm had become a spear, puncturing skin, shirt and jacket to stick out ragged and dirty, pointing in the opposite direction from the wrist. One boot was missing, and blood and dirt stained the white sweat sock.

The left arm was gone. Ripped off. Bone and yellowish cartilage peeked out of the dark socket that was surrounded by frayed cloth and tattered skin.

The neck was broken so badly that the head lay parallel to the shoulder. It reminded Vaughn of the poacher Ed Ricks. Same break, but this time the kill hadn't been nearly as clean.

The face was the worst part. It looked like it had been used to hammer in fence posts. The right side of the skull was completely crushed, and folded inward. The eyeball on that side was either gone or pushed so far into the caved-in skull that he couldn't see it. Protruding from folds of skin and gore were spiky eyebrow hairs—where the ear should have been.

The broken socket bones on the other side of the face pulled the skin back so that the eye stared asymmetrically wide. Vaughn could see where the eyeball curved back into the skull. A leaf tip poked out from the back of the socket.

Dark dirt stuck to a jagged piece of ivory-colored skull that punctured the skin of the forehead. Below that, the nose was smashed flat. A trail of dried blood led to lips twisted into a smile, lopsided because the jaws were so badly broken.

Sticky black blood and flecks of earth covered most of the exposed skin.

He was almost unidentifiable. But the crooked smile helped.

"Your buddy," Mackey said.

Jack-O.

For some reason Vaughn didn't feel sad. Maybe because he was exhausted, or because the body barely looked like Jack-O. Or maybe it was because Jack-O's idiocy had caused his own death.

Vaughn scanned the ground around the body. "Any tracks?"

"Nope," Mackey said. "Figure he was thrown here, from upslope."

Vaughn heard a gasp, coughing and then a retch. He turned to see Alison fall to her knees and throw up watery bits of half-digested lunch. He knelt next to her and put a hand on her back, feeling it lift with each heave.

He thought about saying *it's okay,* but decided that would sound ludicrous with Jack-O's mangled body lying right there. He stared at the corpse. Part of him did feel sorry for Jack-O. But his mind kept looking at the body and saying, *You poor, stupid jerk.*

Alison stopped retching. She coughed twice, then spat, and took a few deep breaths. "Okay," she said.

Vaughn helped her up. She was shivering.

She wiped her mouth with her yellow sleeve and looked at Jack-O's body. She said: "We're not going to make it."

"Yes we are," Vaughn said. "Jack-O probably did something stupid."

"Like shot it," Mackey said.

Seemed like it, but something must have been different, Vaughn thought. He shot the first Sasquatch and it ran away. Then, when he fired through the top of his tent the first night, the big Sasquatch ran away. And just now, when Mackey shot at it, it ran away again.

Jack-O only shot once last night—but maybe it wasn't Jack-O. "Why didn't you mention the gunshot this morning?" Vaughn said to Mackey.

"I wanted to see if Art mentioned it."

"Why?"

"The first morning, I followed him. He made a call to a guy at a television station and gave him directions down here. I thought maybe it was them."

"Does Carolina Pacific have anyone else out here?"

"No—not that I know of. But I doubt they'd do that. It'd be too risky."

That sounded right. CP wanted this to go away. It didn't want a Sasquatch shot. And the more people in the woods with guns, the more likely a fatal shooting would happen. But Vaughn couldn't be sure.

"Had to be him," Mackey said, gesturing at Jack-O.

"Yeah." But something was different.

"No bites, no scratches. At least it didn't eat any of him," Mackey said.

"It took his arm," Alison said.

Then it hit Vaughn, what bothered him about Lansing's food explanation: the deer.

"Maybe it's like grizzly attacks," Mackey said. "They don't mean to kill us, they just treat us like another—"

"Why are animals aggressive?" Vaughn said.

Mackey gave him a funny look.

"C'mon, why?"

Mackey thought for a second and then said: "Competition, over food or territory. Or mates."

That's it, Vaughn thought.

He said, "This isn't about food. Remember when we drove up, that log across the road? The big Sasquatch was trying to keep people out. But why? Then we find its tracks by Ricks' body and the deer, like it was checking things out, and the first night it tries to scare us off with that howl. Yesterday morning it pushes Lansing up the mountain and then pushes all of us down. It was pushing us *away* from something."

"So it's being territorial," Mackey said.

"But about what? The wounded Sasquatch and the big Sasquatch are both males, right? On Tuesday the wounded

Sasquatch's tracks suddenly turned toward the river, and this morning its tracks deviated away from that cliff—it was too steep for us, but a Sasquatch could've handled it easily. Maybe the wounded Sasquatch knew to stay away. Maybe it was pushed away. And all that calling Lansing was doing—I bet he was trying to make the big Sasquatch think he was a rival male."

Mackey raised an eyebrow. "That's a little thin, ol' boy."

"Well here's the key part: The deer killed by the wounded Sasquatch was still there. The big Sasquatch went and looked at it, but didn't carry it off. The other one had eaten the heart and liver, but the meat was fine; in this weather it couldn't have rotted. And physical strength sure wasn't an issue. The big Sasquatch just had no interest in the meat."

Mackey seemed to be thinking it over.

Vaughn asked Alison, "What did you say last night, about the orangutans?"

"The male has a territory and females and juveniles roam."

"Right," he said, pointing a finger at her. "Okay. It could be that the big Sasquatch's territory is constricted because of the long winter and that's why he's patrolling it so diligently. But maybe he's sticking to this particular part of his territory because somewhere around here is a female in heat."

"The bed," Mackey said.

"Right," Vaughn said. "Maybe Jack-O ran into her."

Alison burped, then spat to the side.

Vaughn thought of something. "When you were by the bed, did you notice a smell? A really nasty stink, like a dumpster or something dead?"

Mackey thought for a second. "No," he said.

"The males have a stink."

Mackey pulled his rifle across his chest and looked down at Jack-O. "Animals get crazy when they're mating."

Alison looked back the way they came and said, "We're not going to make it to the road before tonight, are we?"

Vaughn didn't say anything. She was right. He would get them out as quickly as he could, but come nightfall they would be in the middle of the big Sasquatch's territory.

In the woods, in the dark.

Chapter 42

MARK Kingston stalked out of Terminal A, headed toward the hourly parking lot at Raleigh-Durham International Airport.

Stupid, stupid, stupid! he told himself.

It seemed like Brenda Underwood was actually telling the truth, but he left her office with a splinter of doubt lodged in his skull. And the more he scratched at it, the more it bothered him.

First he thought it was there because he had to wait to find out about her upcoming conversation with Mackey. That's what he tried to tell himself. But gradually he admitted there had to be more to it than that.

When he stepped off the plane in Raleigh, he remembered something Mackey said before he left: *It's supposed to be done this week.*

The red wolf investigation. Brenda Underwood knew something.

But if she had evidence Mackey killed the wolf she would

have brought it up right then. Maybe she heard something and wanted it confirmed, or maybe the investigation was ending today and she didn't know what she would learn. Either way, she wanted time.

And he gave it to her.

Stupid.

He bumped into someone.

"Excuse me," the woman said.

"Sorry," he said, stepping to the side. He didn't even see her.

He walked past the rows of cars to his Mercedes, thumbing the remote until he heard the beep and the locks click open. He opened the door, tossed his briefcase on the passenger seat and slid inside.

He raised the key to the ignition and suddenly felt ill: "Stupid" was too mild a word.

Brenda Underwood wanted time all right. Time enough to see how everything in the woods played out.

If Mackey and company found a dead Sasquatch out there, Brenda Underwood's environmentalist niece would lead federal do-gooders right to the body. And as Underwood's niece, the young woman was untouchable. Intimidation, marginalization, threats—none of them could be used.

The only thing that would be worse was if Mackey had to "shoot and shovel" a Sasquatch. If that happened there would be no shutting up the young woman, the unimpeachable witness, whom Brenda Underwood would use to put a noose around all their necks.

Mackey would be convicted for killing an endangered species. Maybe two, if he'd also killed the wolf. Kingston would go down as Mackey's handler, and take Carolina Pacific and the whole timber industry with him—unless Brenda Underwood kept the whole mess under wraps. But even if she did, she stayed in the driver's seat. Mackey's in-Congress diatribes on the Endangered Species Act and the Fish and Wildlife Service would be muzzled. And Underwood would reap Carolina Pacific IOUs until the end of time.

So Kingston would still lose his job, and would limp out of the timber industry, and out of Washington, a loser.

It was fucking masterful. He had to admire Underwood's trap, though he hated her for setting it—and himself for stepping into it.

The only certainty he had was that, above all, Mackey must not kill a Sasquatch. No matter what.

VAUGHN and Alison walked upstream, looking for a shallow spot where she could cross. Mackey hung back.

Vaughn figured Mackey was calling his handlers at Carolina Pacific, maybe telling them about Jack-O. But Vaughn didn't care anymore. Figuring out everyone else's motives was a waste of energy now. The only thing that mattered was getting Alison and Mackey back to the road. Tonight.

Lansing, the mad scientist, was on his own.

Vaughn looked ahead for a place where the water ran swifter, indicating a shallow stretch. Once on the other side he planned to take them downstream, keeping to the riverbank. It would be trickier for Alison to walk on the stones, but that was outweighed by the advantages: The terrain was flat, and out of the forest they would have more daylight and feel safer.

Eventually, when they reached the point where they crossed the river yesterday morning, they would follow the trail of reflective tape—the trail Jack-O had to have followed in—to get out. That way they would spend as little time in the woods as possible, and wouldn't get lost; which was important because they would be going through there in the dark. And under the trees it would be as black as a mine shaft.

An eel of fear wriggled in Vaughn's guts. He filled his lungs with cold air and blew it out, willing the fear to go too.

By rough triangulation, using the ridge he saw from the mountain, he figured they were about five miles from his truck. Under other circumstances that wouldn't be too bad a walk. But with Alison hurt, and all of them exhausted, and traveling at least half the way in pitch black, he knew it would be the slowest and longest five miles he'd ever walked.

Upstream he spied a place where the water looked like an ice sheet flowing over the dark bottom. "There," he said, pointing.

Alison's eyes narrowed. "It looks fast."

"That's because it's shallow."

When they reached the spot he stepped into the stream. The water flowed around his boot, but the Gore-Tex kept it out. He took another step and this time the icy water rushed in over the boot top and down to his foot, numbing it.

"I'll go first," he said, and held out his hand. "Come behind me."

Her glove gripped his and they crossed slowly. As soon as they were on the other side, Alison plopped down onto the stones. Pain tightened her face.

"How's the ankle?"

"Hurts." She shivered.

He knew that the more she walked on it, the worse it would get. But she had to handle the pain until they made it out.

"Keep taking that Motrin," he said.

"Art has my first-aid kit."

Vaughn wondered whether Lansing had planned that too. "I've got some," he said. He dropped his pack, took out his kit and gave her four packs of tablets.

She took two pills and stuffed the rest into a pocket of her yellow jacket. She looked up at him and said: "He pushed me."

"I believe you," Vaughn said.

On the far bank, Mackey approached the stream and stepped in. He walked through it confidently, sliding his feet to find purchase, and made it across without a problem.

Vaughn recognized it as a technique used by experienced river fishermen, and said, "Lots of streams where you're from?"

"Lots of stingrays," Mackey said. His normal smile was gone, and the tan skin beneath his eyes was dark. "Let's get a move on."

Alison held out a hand and Vaughn pulled her up. She pointed. "What's that?"

Vaughn looked. At the edge of the stones loomed an old, wide Douglas fir. About five feet up a spray-painted blue band circled the immense trunk.

Mackey said: "That's lumber."

"The blue paint means it's a cutting boundary," Vaughn said. "The whole area's marked for cutting."

"Clear-cutting?" Alison said.

"Yeah. The other side of this stand's already been cut."

"This is old growth," Alison said.

Mackey said, "It'll grow back. Forget about it." He walked off.

Vaughn expected another argument but Alison was silent. She looked at the tree for a moment, then turned away. Staring down at the stones, strands of hair hanging in her face, she limped after Mackey.

Before following, Vaughn took a slow, careful look upriver. All he saw was stony riverbank and a huge deadfall he could barely see over.

He was about to turn around when it sank in.

Barely see over.

That was the deadfall the Sasquatch practically stepped across.

Quickly he turned and walked after the other two, then stopped short.

Twenty yards downstream, at the side of the stones, Mackey stood under a tree with his rifle straight up in the air. Above the end of the barrel, blond wood shone from a gash in the trunk. From Mackey's bullet.

Vaughn couldn't believe it. The big Sasquatch had to be ten feet tall.

Jesus, he thought.

Chapter 43

MARK Kingston's phone beeped. "Yeah," he said, walking around his desk.

"The way you blew past me without even saying hello, I'm guessing you don't want to be disturbed," his secretary said.

"You're right."

"Then you don't want this message from Chris Mackey?"

"What did he say?"

"To call as soon as you got back. It's urgent. He's leaving his sat-phone on."

"Thanks, Gina."

Kingston looked up the number and punched it in. He heard dead air, then it rang three times and Mackey answered. Mackey sounded like he was on the opposite side of the planet.

"Chris, it's Mark."

"Hold on a sec."

He heard Mackey talking to some people and then he was back.

"Things have taken a (static) for the worse, ol' boy."

A claw scritch-scratched at Kingston's heart. "I'm listening."

"Today we found a dead man. A deputy sheriff, not (static) one I'm with. Sasquatch killed him."

The claw caught and began to squeeze. "You sure it was a Sasquatch?"

"Mark, this guy was smashed into Jello. I don't think (static) an unbroken bone left in his body. No human being did that."

"What happened? Did he shoot it?"

"Appears that way," Mackey said.

"It's not dead, is it?"

"Doubtful."

The claw stopped squeezing. "Then I'm sure the sheriff will explain away the injuries. Another fall, maybe."

"Forgive me, ol' boy, but right now I don't give a good goddamn. We're in the big Sasquatch's territory and we'll be walking through the woods in the dark trying to get out."

Kingston said, "Be careful, but whatever you do, don't kill one."

"If it's them or me I'm shooting 'til we hit the road."

"Just don't kill one."

"What the hell are you talking about?" Mackey said.

"Brenda Underwood has us over a barrel." Kingston explained his theory and then said, "So you can't shoot one."

"I may have to."

"Well then do it someplace Underwood's niece can't see it."

"What if that can't be helped? Am I supposed to shoot and shovel her, too?"

"I didn't say that."

"Neither did I," Mackey said.

Kingston rubbed a knuckle into his forehead. "Listen, Underwood wants you to call her."

"What for?"

"Probably about the red wolf."

"She going to have good news?"

"We'll find out," Kingston said.

Mackey didn't say anything.

"Hello?"

"I'm still here," Mackey said.

"Did you kill that wolf?"

"I don't think you want to know. Give me her number."

Kingston did, and hung up.

He leaned back in his chair and thought about the possibilities swirling in his head. After a time he realized that he couldn't focus on anything because one thought kept popping up and pounding the front of his skull: *What am I missing?*

WHEN Mackey caught up, Vaughn noticed that he seemed oddly euphoric.

"Your aunt wants you to call her," Mackey said to Alison, a big smile on his face.

Alison's face flushed. "What?"

"Brenda Underwood," Mackey said, holding out his cell phone. "Here. Just hit this button twice to redial." He pointed at a big button under the display.

She frowned. "I don't believe you."

Mackey kept smiling. The hand with phone didn't move.

She grabbed the phone and limped a short distance off.

"What the hell's going on?" Vaughn said.

Mackey held up his index finger. "Wait a sec." He watched Alison.

With her back to them, Alison held the small black phone to her ear.

Suddenly her head jerked away from it. Without saying anything, she pulled the phone away, walked back, handed it to Mackey and limped downstream.

"Well?" Vaughn said.

"Brenda Underwood and I have an understanding," Mackey said. He smiled at Alison's back.

"You knew Underwood was her aunt."

"Not until five minutes ago."

Vaughn looked for a sign Mackey was lying. He didn't see anything, but he was so tired he wondered if he could. "So what does this mean?"

"It means we caught a break, ol' boy."

IT was the wolf. *The goddamn wolf!* Kingston thought. That was it.

Mackey killed the wolf and Brenda Underwood knew it, so she would say to him, "I'll make that go away if you do this for me."

But what would that be? Kingston wondered. She couldn't ask Mackey to leave the forest because he was doing that anyway. And she wouldn't ask him to let the Sasquatches live because that would do nothing for her. Besides, that's exactly what Mackey wanted.

Instead she would ask him to kill one, Kingston realized.

And once Mackey and his party got out of the woods, her niece would take the other Fish and Wildlife Service tree-huggers right to the body, the Sasquatch would be listed as an endangered species, and by virtue of the Endangered Species Act Brenda Underwood would control millions of acres of land and billions of dollars. She would be one of the most powerful people in the United States.

Mackey would hate to do it, but with the resulting chaos in the conservative ranks he certainly would have no shortage of consulting work. He'd probably become a millionaire.

His heart rabbiting, Kingston jumped up, grabbed the phone on his desk and raised it over his head. He felt everything inside him course into his fingers, urging him to smash the phone on the desktop or throw it against the wall, anything to let out the panic.

How could he be so damn stupid?

He knew how. The ninnies at the Fish and Wildlife Service wouldn't hurt a fly—they were too busy saving them. His mistake was that he'd lumped Brenda Underwood in with that crowd. But she was different. She came from a rural hunting and fishing family, so she wouldn't buy into the emotional antideath crap subscribed to by the urbanites who worked for her. What was the death of one animal to her? Only the results mattered. The political results.

He dropped the phone onto the desk. It clattered, and the receiver bounced off and hit the Speaker button. The dial tone blared.

His fingertip punched Redial and the seven-digit number beeped loudly. After two rings there was a pause and then he heard, "The Iridium customer you're trying to reach—"

He hit Redial again. Same thing.

Then he punched in the number digit by digit, slowly. Same goddamn message. *Fuck!* Mackey's phone was off.

He bashed the Speaker button. The phone jumped and was silent. Then it beeped.

"Hello?" Gina, his secretary.

"Yeah?" he said.

"Brenda Underwood's holding for you."

Chapter 44

VAUGHN didn't know when the knocking began, but it had been regular ever since.

Chok-chok. Chok chok chok.

He didn't say anything about it as he walked down the riverbank, and the others didn't either. The most anyone did was cast a worried look into the trees, but even that stopped after they all realized the sounds weren't going away.

In fact, the knocking had come steadily closer.

Chok, chok-chok-chok. The pattern wasn't consistent.

At the library he'd read on the Internet about noises people heard, ones that sounded like Sasquatches pounding trees. Maybe the big Sasquatch was knocking to try to scare them from its territory, because it realized that direct confrontation could get it shot.

But he knew that was BS. It had to be Lansing.

At first he thought Lansing was beating the trees just to scare them, but that didn't fit with what the professor wanted. Lansing wanted a Sasquatch dead, so he had to be doing it to

attract or anger the big Sasquatch, and was moving steadily
closer to them so the animal would end up near as many
firearms as possible.

Vaughn thought back to when Lansing showed up at the
sheriff's office. He knew he should have locked him up. The
guy was nuts.

Chok, chok, chok.

More than once he'd been tempted to charge into the
woods, find Lansing, beat him senseless and drag him out.
But he squelched that emotion and tried to keep his mind on
the task at hand: getting everyone out.

They had made decent progress. Not great, because of Alison's ankle, but not as bad as he'd feared. He judged their
progress not by elapsed time, since he'd never walked so
slowly, but by the opposite bank. From where they started it
rose fast, climbing from an eroded earth slope to rock and
dense brush, and then into a steep mountainside stacked with
trees.

For a time the river became narrower. White water forced
its way between wet boulders and jumped into foamy pools,
where it became dark again. Then the river widened.

Vaughn approached a long, deep hole. A great spot to
fish; that's all that would have crossed his mind before.
But as he walked past he didn't picture salmon and trout
finning on the bottom with their heads facing upstream. Instead he kept seeing the big Sasquatch rise dripping and terrible from the water. It bothered the back of his neck, and he
was angry at himself for not being able to control his imagination.

"Let's get out the flashlights," he said.

"Don't think we're there yet," Mackey said.

"I know." The slope of the far bank had begun to ease, and
although it wasn't dark yet, Vaughn wanted the lights ready.
That was the only way to see the reflective tape.

He laid his rifle on the stones and shrugged off his pack.
He found his flashlight, thumbed it on and swung it at the
trees on their side of the river, looking for the unmistakable
unnatural glint of the tape.

He saw nothing and didn't expect to. His thumb clicked
the light off and he shoved it into a pocket of his parka.

Chok, chok-chok, chok.
Still coming closer.

BILL Gaines' face filled with blood. "You really, really fucked this one up, Mark."

What a jerk, Kingston thought. *He couldn't see the problem and now he can't see the solution.*

Some of it was ego: Gaines didn't like that Kingston disobeyed his orders. Kingston knew that, but he didn't care. After doing all the worrying for the entire damn timber industry, after enduring the disappointed look in his son's eyes and the silent treatment from his wife, he wanted to tell the boss to go fuck himself—with a fat, raw log. Either that or smash his fist through Gaines' face. The guy deserved it.

Yet he knew that as the BayMun deal got closer to being done, the stress swelled in Gaines' skull like a tumor. It didn't help that Gaines said the Germans had given him a hard time in Munich. So Kingston held himself back.

"Bill, I don't think you understand—"

"No, goddammit," Gaines said, pounding a fist on his cherry desk. "*You* don't understand. She's using you. She's using us."

Could that be right? The panic that had clutched Kingston's heart drowned in the relief that washed through him after Brenda Underwood's phone call. But now he felt that relief evaporate into uncertainty.

Had he actually missed something? He thought her plan was ingenious—he hadn't figured it out because he was thinking too small. It was risky, but when the stakes were this high, the risks had to be too.

Yet Gaines was implying that Kingston had made a bush-league mistake, that he'd somehow been hoodwinked by logic or victimized by her charm. He didn't think so; it was pretty straightforward. But he'd already underestimated her at least once.

Gaines said, "Think about it. If the public goes nuts and everyone chickens out, we'll have admitted to the President and the whole fucking world that we knew what was going on. Get it? *We* will be the scapegoat. And the brilliance of her plan is that even if the whole thing never sees the light of day, you can bet they'll use this to scuttle the BayMun deal."

He pounded the desk again. "God, she's good," he said. "I can't believe you'd be so stupid."

Kingston's hands curled into fists. Tendons popped out white against his knuckles. "You're wrong," he said.

"Am I? Are you ab-so-lute-ly, one hundred percent sure? Because that's important," Gaines said. "If there's even a one percent chance I might be right, then what? What would you do in my position?"

"Trust my judgment."

"I told you to ignore this whole thing," Gaines said.

"That was too risky."

"And this isn't? C'mon, Mark. Get your head, your pride or whatever it is out of your ass and let's stop this."

"We can't. They're out there and we're here."

"I'm going to call the President," Gaines said.

"What will you ask him to do? Drop in a bunch of paratroopers?"

"I don't know, dammit." Gaines slapped the desk and sank back into his plush leather chair. "We can't just do nothing. At least we'll be the first to warn him. He'll be pissed, and Brenda Underwood will be history."

Kingston still thought his boss was wrong, but he knew Gaines would never see it that way. Yet Gaines said something that interested him: *If the public goes nuts and everyone chickens out* . . .

"Hello?" Gaines said. "Anybody home?"

"Yeah. Hold on a sec."

Really, they *wanted* the public to go nuts, Kingston thought, and the keys to the public were the media. Unfortunately he'd already manipulated the media one way: The faxes had been sent and the hoax videotape would arrive tomorrow. Too late to stop that, but not too late to do more.

What was that name Mackey gave him? A funny one. Asian-sounding.

Tom Sun. That was it. Tom Sun would be the key. Sun would make sure that the public went nuts and that no one chickened out.

Kingston stood. "I have to go," he said.

"Where?"

"Need to make a few calls." Kingston walked across the Persian rug toward Gaines' big office doors.

Gaines jumped out of his chair. "Mark! Get back here, goddammit! If you're trying to get me to fire you, I'm not going to do it. You hear me? I won't be the scapegoat for your sorry decisions. If things go to shit I want you personally to tell the board about your 'plan.'"

Kingston stopped, turned around and stalked back to Gaines' desk. Gaines was six inches shorter than him.

He wanted to put his boss' head through the rich walnut paneling and leave him stuck there like a horse's ass protruding from a stall. He leaned over and said, "I'm going to cut our risk down to zero. You got a problem with that, asshole?"

Gaines' face became so red it looked almost black. But he didn't say anything.

Without wasting anymore time, Kingston walked out.

VAUGHN couldn't believe it. It looked right, but it wasn't dark yet.

"That can't be right," he said.

"Hell if it ain't," Mackey said.

From the branch of a small western red cedar two small rectangles of metallic tape glared out at them like the eyes of a raccoon.

"Couldn't be anything else," Mackey said, waving his flashlight at the tape. "Let's go."

"I need to rest," Alison said.

Vaughn had almost forgotten she was hurt. She'd walked the whole afternoon without a complaint or a rest. "Okay," he said. "Quick break."

He unshouldered his pack and laid his rifle atop it, and Mackey did the same. Alison slid down her walking stick onto the rocks. They all sat with their backs to the river, facing the woods.

Vaughn dug out the last of his trail mix and elk jerky, and passed it around. Alison grabbed a handful of nuts, raisins and M&Ms, but waved off the meat.

Vaughn held out the jerky. "This'll be the last chance we get."

"No thanks," she said.

"Alison, you'll need the energy."

She glared at him, then grabbed a strip of jerky and tossed it over her shoulder, into the water.

"Why the hell did you do that?" he said.

She stared into the woods and didn't answer.

Vaughn turned away and tore off a chunk of the salty meat with his teeth. As he chewed, he realized that the good feeling he had about reaching the tape trail before dark was already gone.

One reason was Alison's antimeat gesture. He felt that someone who couldn't put aside some half-baked "principle" for her own good surely was an idiot, and could be a bigger liability than he first thought. Exhaustion wasn't an excuse; they were all tired.

He also realized that now was the hard part. Even with the tape showing them the way, the uneven terrain and the dark would conspire to make them move that much slower.

Chok chok chok chok.

The constant din of the river made it difficult to tell exactly where the sound was coming from.

Suddenly Mackey grabbed his rifle, put it up to his shoulder and—*BOOM! BOOM!*—fired two shots high into the trees.

Alison put her hands over her ears and shrank from the sound. She cast a wild eye at the woods and then at Mackey.

Vaughn yelled, "What are you doing?"

Mackey lowered the rifle. "Trying to scare that idiot."

"How do you know it's him?"

"You think some Sasquatch is playing mind games with us? That thing wants us out, it'll come run us off."

"You're doing what he wants."

Mackey grunted. "Least it stopped."

Vaughn listened. The thumping had stopped.

Mackey remained standing, the rifle across his chest, and for the first time Vaughn saw creases marring the skin of Mackey's plump face. Around the eyes.

Klak, klak-klak-klak-klak.

Vaughn froze.

A rock bounced across the stones, toward the trees in front of them.

His eyes followed it. When it stopped, he saw that it wasn't rounded and smooth like the stones on the bank.

He turned and saw something black against the darkening sky, arcing toward them, getting bigger.

Mackey dove out of the way.

CRACK! KLAK-KLAK, klak-klak.

This one was larger. It landed only a few feet from Mackey, and came from the same place, across the river.

Vaughn jumped up, pulled on his pack and picked up his rifle. "Let's go," he said.

Mackey turned on his flashlight and shined it at the trees that lined the opposite bank.

Alison limped toward the forest.

Vaughn didn't wait to see if Mackey found anything. "I'll take point," he said, and strode past Alison, into the woods.

Chapter 45

THE crisp rush of the river faded quickly to nothing and only a few hints of daylight remained. The greens of the forest became grey, and then black, slowly coated everything. The air felt gloomy and disconcertingly still. It was as if they had been swallowed whole by the forest and were on their way down to its belly.

Every twenty yards Vaughn flicked on his flashlight to outline the trail; to conserve the batteries, he didn't want to leave the beam on until he had to. The highway of little rectangles beckoned him onward, showing him that the distance and time remaining were finite. *Get to the end and it's over,* they winked, like the ambivalent magic of a fairy tale.

But it was more than just the tape. Everything urged him forward: Jack-O's broken body, Alison's injury, Mackey's increased willingness to fire his rifle, Katie, the sheriff, the big Sasquatch. Even Lansing. All of it screamed, *Get out as fast as you can.*

Ahead a wall of darkness rose from the forest floor. As

Vaughn walked closer he saw that he correctly guessed it to be the slope down which they had tracked the wounded Sasquatch two days ago. The steep incline, bare of trees, supported nothing that would help with climbing. The salal, ferns, berries and other plants scattered across it were too small.

He waited for Alison, and when she came up said, "You're going to need some help here."

She only nodded.

He ducked under her arm and carried her up the slope, cutting across at a soft angle that took them well off the tape trail. He had no doubt he could find the trail again, but when they got to the top Mackey was already there and flashed his light to guide them over.

The light seemed unusually bright. Vaughn blinked his eyes a few times to get rid of the neon-green afterimage—and then he realized it was there because the woods were almost completely dark.

If the big Sasquatch was coming, it would come soon.

The trunk beating hadn't resumed, and Vaughn didn't know what to make of it. Maybe Lansing was scared too.

He turned on his flashlight and took the lead. Thirty yards ahead he saw where the tape trail turned abruptly to the left, where it began to parallel the road. He walked toward the turn and was tempted to keep going straight, to get to the road faster. But he knew that's how people got lost. And besides, the road would be just as dark.

He kept his flashlight pointed at the tape. He squinted; to his eyes the beam had a yellowish tinge. *C'mon,* he thought. *Don't fade.* For backup he carried a battery-powered camp lantern in his pack, but it wasn't as maneuverable.

The flashlight batteries only had to last a few more miles. Just a couple of miles. That's all.

SOMETHING told him he'd gotten too far ahead so he stopped and turned around. Mackey lagged, and Vaughn saw why: Alison limped along just in front of him, the arm of her yellow jacket glowing in the beam from his flashlight. Her upper body bent to her left, and with each step her left leg flexed as if she was putting all her weight on it.

When she reached Vaughn she sank down against a tree. The nylon of her jacket made an unnatural *zing* against the bark.

He had to keep her going. "How about some more Motrin?"

She nodded, the skin of her face crinkled in pain.

He reached back for the water bottle lashed to his pack and bent to give it to her. She took out two packs of pills and drank them down.

Chok chok.

Faint and behind them. He looked over; Mackey stared out of the circle of light and into the black woods.

Time to go.

Vaughn reached around Alison's back and lifted her to her feet. She held onto his arm. He thought she was using it for balance, but when she didn't let go he turned around.

Every muscle in her face pulled backward and her eyes stretched unnaturally wide, as if something had a foot against her head and was trying to wrench out her ponytail. In the half light, one of her cheekbones cut a harsh shadow so that it appeared caved-in, like Jack-O's skull. The fear radiated off her like a smell, and it occurred to him that if he could sense it, an animal could too. From much farther away.

Chok chok chok.

Closer.

His eyes shifted toward the sound, then back to Alison. She still stared at him.

He had an impulse to say something reassuring, but instead he peeled her gloved fingers off his arm and said: "We have to go."

"Don't leave m—"

Peee-weee.

That damn whistle. He felt the telltale warning itch in the back of his neck.

The whistle's high pitch made it easier to place and he could tell it came from the direction of the river, roughly parallel to their position. Was it Lansing or . . .

Pweee.

Same place.

Krak. Krrak.

Something breaking tree limbs. Big ones. A wild impulse to run clawed its way out of the primitive part of his brain.

"Let's get the hell out of here," he said, and pulled Alison forward.

Krrak, krrak.

Coming toward them, fast.

KRAAK, KRAK.

Suddenly it stopped.

Vaughn stopped, too, and listened. He heard nothing but the stampeding of his own blood.

Too quiet.

He released Alison and brought his left hand up to cradle the flashlight and the .30-06's fore-end. It felt awkward, like the rifle might slip off the light, and he thought about carrying the .357 instead. But the revolver was buried in the shoulder holster under his jacket and the pack strap.

He started forward again. His right forefinger rested on the rifle's trigger guard. The safety was off.

Thump . . . thump . . . thump . . . thump . . . thump . . . thump.

Something stomped by on two legs, outside the light. It circled in front of them, then quit.

He pointed the rifle and flashlight straight ahead, thinking: *That prick Lansing could be doing all of this.*

The heavy dark seemed to compress the beam. The light revealed only black trunks and the line of shiny tape going back into the forest.

Suddenly, at the outer range of the beam, two pieces of tape winked out.

He waved the light up and down to make sure the beam hadn't simply swung off the tape.

Nothing. They were gone, and he'd heard no movement.

"See anything, ol' boy?" Mackey whispered.

Vaughn didn't answer.

He heard something slap against nylon, and Alison screamed.

Vaughn whirled around. Alison lay face down on the ground. Her hands covered her head.

He bent down and put a hand on her back.

She screamed louder.

"Hey!" he yelled. "Quiet!"

She stopped. Almost immediately a similar scream—more like a screech—sounded somewhere behind them. When it ended there was a deep sound, like the last of a breath released from large lungs.

Vaughn grabbed a fistful of Alison's jacket and hauled her to her feet.

"Something hit me," she said. "In the back."

He panned his flashlight around and found a freshly broken branch. Spikes of white wood poked from the broken end.

"We need to go," Mackey said. "Now, ol' boy."

The beam of Vaughn's flashlight faded. He shook the light and the beam turned whiter, then faded again.

Shit, he thought.

He dropped the dying flashlight, set his rifle on the ground and shrugged off his pack.

"What the hell are you doing?" Mackey said.

"Leaving it."

Quickly Vaughn opened the main pocket of his pack, took out the lantern and switched it on. Then he zipped down his camouflaged parka, reached across his chest and snatched the .357 from its holster. The rifle he slung diagonally across his back.

"Ready," he said, picking up the lantern.

"Hold on a sec," Mackey said. He was doing the same thing.

"We're sticking with the trail," Vaughn said.

"Damn right."

Heavy footsteps thumped by, this time on the other side of the tape trail. The gap between each step seemed like seconds.

"Asshole," Mackey said.

"It may not be him," Vaughn said.

Mackey stood and heaved the big rifle onto his shoulder; the nylon sling made a soft noise as it cinched into his fleece jacket. "You think Art's doing nothing out there?" he said. "That all of a sudden he got scared?" The vapor of his breath curled and drifted out of the light. "Boy's crazy. Going to get himself killed."

Suddenly shooting blasted out of the woods behind them. Vaughn dove to the ground, instinctively counting the shots.

Then the forest erupted. Ungodly Sasquatch scream-howls, shrieking and crashing—it sounded like huge pieces of metal were being thrown around. The noise was so loud it seemed to be all around them.

Vaughn leaped to his feet, yanked Alison up and yelled: "Come on!"

He wanted to run, but instead he thrust the lantern into Alison's hand, hooked his left arm around the small of her back and jerked her forward.

The light bounced crazily, alternating harshly lit green with utter black. Vaughn kept his eyes on the reflective tape and moved as fast as he could, dragging Alison along.

Abruptly, the crashing and screaming stopped.

Behind them, closer this time, two more shots cracked.

Then something running, coming closer.

He whirled around and saw Mackey already on one knee with both hands wrapped around the grip of the .44. Mackey pointed the revolver straight back, into the dark.

The footsteps came closer, straight for them. Then they stopped.

Vaughn heard a soft thump.

Mackey's thumb pulled back the hammer.

"Don't shoot!" Lansing burst into the light.

His chest heaved. Dirt smeared his face and clothes, and his eyes practically spun. A big smile split his face.

Mackey let the hammer down, but kept his revolver up. He said, "What in the hell are you doing?"

A short, high-pitched laugh. "Trying to catch butterflies," Lansing said.

Lansing raised his .357 and pointed it at Vaughn. His left hand, hanging at his side, flexed.

Vaughn looked at the stainless steel barrel. It gleamed silver in the lantern's harsh light.

"Give me your ammunition," Lansing said.

Mackey pulled the hammer back. "Drop that damn gun."

"Give it to me," Lansing said to Vaughn. The revolver trembled.

"If you don't drop it I will shoot you," Mackey said.

Vaughn was about to tell Mackey to put his gun down when he felt something. A presence, like a giant hand pushing at his chest.

Without dropping the revolver, Lansing turned around and stepped backward, toward them. Mackey also backed up so that he was even with Vaughn. His .44 now pointed past Lansing, into the forest.

Vaughn stared, but didn't see anything. The Sasquatch kept just out of the light.

Then he noticed Lansing's head titled back, and he looked up. Five feet above the reflective tape hovered two glowing circles about six inches apart.

He realized the Sasquatch wasn't beyond the light. The animal's coat was so dark it sucked the light into it, like a black dog at night.

As he stared, he thought he made out the Sasquatch's towering silhouette. Enormous head, wide shoulders, long arms. Rectangular, like a giant robot.

He had the distinct feeling that it was angry.

Click. Click.

The hammer of Lansing's revolver smacked on spent cases. That's what Vaughn was going to tell Mackey. Four shots, then two. Lansing was out.

Ruuuuuuuuuuuuuuuhhhh.

It sounded like thunder rising from the bottom of a canyon, a guttural roll that pushed just enough air to flap a thick piece of flesh at the base of the Sasquatch's throat. Deep and powerful and subtly menacing. Vaughn had never heard anything like it.

"Lord," Mackey whispered.

"Shoot it!" Lansing screamed, waving his revolver. "Shoot the goddamn thing!"

No one moved.

The Sasquatch took a step forward.

Vaughn didn't really see it move, didn't know how he knew. Maybe the Sasquatch's eyes coming closer. Maybe he heard something.

No, he realized. He felt it, through the ground.

He saw its outline better now. The Sasquatch had looked enormous from across the river, but here it was out of proportion with reality.

"Did you shoot it?" he said to Lansing.

Vaughn sensed the Sasquatch's attention on him.

Lansing didn't respond and that was enough for Vaughn. Lansing had tried to shoot it, and if he'd actually hit it, all he could do to something that big was make it mad.

Blam, blam, blam!

Vaughn jumped at the shots. Mackey fired almost straight up.

The Sasquatch roared and took another step into the light.

The stink reached Vaughn then, and only adrenaline kept him from throwing up.

Lansing turned to the side and ran off into the dark.

Vaughn saw a giant black arm and then leg swing toward them, then Mackey yelled, "Run!"

In one motion Vaughn turned, stepped in front of Alison and squatted down.

He felt the Sasquatch coming.

"Get on!" he said.

She grabbed his neck and hit his chin with the lantern. Her legs came around his sides; her weight jammed the rifle into his back.

He thrust up, yelled "Hold on!" and lurched down the trail.

Chapter 46

MACKEY wasn't in front of them, and if he was covering the rear Vaughn didn't hear him because the Sasquatch's footfalls shook the ground. The animal kept pace with him off to the right, taking one step for every three or four of his.

Then he heard it pass them.

Suddenly it stepped onto the trail, blotting out the shimmering rectangles of tape.

Alison held the lantern against his chest so that the light almost blinded him, but he could see the hair covering the Sasquatch's body. Darkness still shrouded its head.

Alison screamed, and behind them something else screamed.

He dropped Alison's right leg and raised the revolver.

The Sasquatch growled and stepped towards them.

Vaughn picked up Alison's leg and cut off into the woods to the right, toward the road.

The Sasquatch roared and circled toward them.

Shit! Vaughn thought. *It doesn't want us to go that way.*

He didn't want to go back, and the Sasquatch didn't want him to go forward nor to the road. It was trying to push them out of its territory, and the only direction it wanted them to go—

The Sasquatch roared again, closer.

"Get out of here!" Alison screamed. She pounded his shoulder. "Go the other way!"

Vaughn turned, stumbled back across the trail and kept going.

Toward the river.

THE Sasquatch kept roaring, herding them on, but stayed a consistent distance away; slightly behind and to the right.

Vaughn's mind raced. Sooner or later he would have to drop Alison and then they would move even slower. That might further anger the Sasquatch, which probably didn't understand that walking through the woods at night wasn't easy for people.

That's when he realized that the Sasquatch's objective wasn't the river. It wanted to push them up and over the mountain.

An easy walk for a Sasquatch, but in daylight that hike had taken them the better part of a day. At night, exhausted and with Alison hurt, it would take a lot longer than that. He wondered at what point the Sasquatch would lose what remained of its animal patience.

He stepped into air.

Panicked, he tried to shift backward, but Alison's weight on his back carried him down.

She screamed.

Suspended in midair, Vaughn's only thought was: *I hope she holds on to the lantern.*

His knees hit and then his face slammed into the cold earth. Pain stabbed through his lip. He tumbled through vegetation, getting kicked by Alison and rolling over and under the hard metal and wood of his rifle.

Something cracked him in the head; white streaks rocketed across his eyes.

He rolled a few more times and then stopped, face down.

Quickly he pushed up to his knees and concentrated on the pain. His head hurt and felt a little woozy. His lip stung; he tasted warm blood. But his arms and legs felt fine.

The plastic lantern rested on its side, still intact, and its harsh light revealed the shadowed forms of plants stretching up the slope to his right. Alison lay curled up on the ground and held her ankle. She was tense, but not moving. Silent pain locked the skin of her face, which shone as if damp.

He jumped up and right away his head throbbed. A few sparks shot across his peripheral vision. He shook his head. It hurt worse for a second, but then the Sasquatch screamed and he forgot about it.

Raaaaaaaaaaaarhhh! From the top of the hill.

He grabbed the lantern, thrust it into Alison's hands and bent to help her up. Suddenly he remembered his .357.

"Give me the light," he said.

She stared up at him. Her hands didn't move.

"Give me the light!" He wrenched it from her and held it toward the slope.

Another roar, louder this time.

"What are you doing?" Alison said.

He didn't answer. His eyes scanned the dirt and smashed plants, looking for the glint of metal.

He took a step up the slope. Was it here or had it flown out of his hand near the top?

Roaaaaaaaaaaaaaarhhh!

"Are you crazy?" Alison said. Panic sharpened her voice. "What are you doing?"

"Looking for the gun!" he said.

"Where is it?"

Brilliant fucking question. He took another step up. Bits of earth rolled into the light, and he knew the Sasquatch was coming down the slope.

There. Under a crushed fern, something shiny. He scrambled over, snatched up the revolver and ran back down.

Out in front of him, Alison hobbled directly away from the Sasquatch. He ran up, grabbed her and hauled her forward again.

He felt the Sasquatch coming behind them and thought, *What now?* He had to figure out what to do about the river.

They could jump in and try to ride it down, but he didn't know if the Sasquatch's territory extended downstream, too. If so, the Sasquatch could see them in the dark and could easily keep pace—or pluck them out.

If it didn't kill them, hypothermia would. Quickly.

But what other choice did they have? If by some miracle they were able to cross the river exactly where they hit it, they definitely would not make it up the mountain. To try would be unfair to Alison, and he couldn't leave her behind.

So he would have to challenge the Sasquatch, and that meant he and Alison would die. The animal was so quick and so big that he figured he would only get one shot before it was on them. And he wouldn't have time to aim.

Even if he got lucky and killed it, its momentum might kill them. A thousand dead pounds would crush them like . . . Jack-O.

But he knew a more likely scenario was that the Sasquatch would finally lose its patience and, in a mating hormone-fueled rage, kill them both as easily as a person snapping the neck of a quail.

He tried to keep it together, but panic darted through his bloodstream like frightened minnows. His eyes dodged ahead to the edge of the light, looking for something, anything, he didn't know what.

Raaaaaaaaaaaah!

The goddamn Sasquatch would not shut up! And between the roars Alison whimpered constantly. He didn't know when she'd started and whether it was caused by pain or terror, but it didn't matter. She was useless.

Again he wondered how long they had and when he would have to face the Sasquatch. Maybe he could fire the rifle and the revolver at the same time.

At the outer edge of the beam he caught a glimpse of something big and black. They got closer; it loomed larger and wider, and he saw that it barred their path: a fallen tree. Slippery with moss and fungus, it rose about chest high. They couldn't scale it, but the Sasquatch could step over it.

Son of a bitch, he thought. *This is not good.*

He pulled Alison to the left, toward the top of the tree and the river, hoping the Sasquatch wouldn't think they were altering course.

But after a few steps he turned around and walked the other way, toward the base of the tree—and the Sasquatch.

A roar, different this time, and louder.

Alison pulled back. "What are you doing?" she yelled.

"Walk as fast as you can."

The Sasquatch roared again. He tried to ignore it and instead focused on getting to the end. *How long is this goddamn tree?*

The next roar slammed into his abdomen like a sandbag.

Alison spun away. He snatched her to him and gripped her tighter.

"You're crazy!" she said.

She kept resisting and he kept pulling. The light swung wildly, giving Vaughn glimpses of the tree.

Finally he saw a slight flare in the wood.

She pulled free. He lunged and grabbed the arm holding the lantern.

"Let go of me!" she screamed.

"Goddammit I'm trying to save you!"

He wasn't sure if she heard. The Sasquatch sounded like a hurricane, roaring and ripping limbs off trees and hurling them to the ground.

Then the roars changed to shrieks. Again and again. Each earsplitting screech drove a nail of pain into his skull.

Alison beat on his arm with her free hand. He dragged her along, willing the light to finally show the end of the tree.

Suddenly he tripped. Alison screamed. He righted himself, then yanked her arm forward.

The light showed a thick root twisting from the trunk. Where it touched the forest floor it became red-brown rot.

He stepped over it and wrenched Alison across. She came across it backwards, kicking and still screaming. The root collapsed beneath her, and she fell to the ground and dropped the lantern.

He pulled her up and yelled, "Get in!"

A branch crashed so close he felt the wind kick up from the ground.

He threw her into the black maw of the hollow trunk. "Crawl!" he said. "Fast!"

Chapter 47

VAUGHN backed in and felt his boot hit Alison. "Hurry!" he yelled, kicking at her.

"I can't—" A bellow from the Sasquatch drowned her out.

"Just go!" he said.

He crawled backwards, his right hand pulling the .357 across the damp wood and his left dragging the lantern. The side of his head slammed into something and he ducked under it. The light revealed an ear-shaped clump of fungus perched on a curved wall of crumbling wood.

He heard Alison sobbing as she clawed her way down the tree's rotten throat, but he ignored it. He was more concerned with what was coming.

Roaaaaaaaaaaaaaarr!

The tree shook and debris rained over him. He looked down so it wouldn't get in his eyes.

The Sasquatch screamed again. The tree trembled.

His foot hit Alison again. "Keep going!" he shouted.

"It's blocked!"

Suddenly the dark body of the Sasquatch filled the opening. The eyes in the enormous head stared straight at him, and the animal roared so loudly he was momentarily deaf. The animal's breath rolled toward him in a moist cloud that smelled like rotten compost. In the gaping mouth big teeth flashed.

He raised the revolver and the Sasquatch roared again.

God, the stink! He felt like he was surrounded by a truckload of dead skunks.

His eyes watered, and he blinked his eyes until he saw the .357's barrel clearly.

Because he couldn't kneel, to brace himself he jammed his body against the inside of the tree. Then he wrapped his left hand around his right and, arms extended, lined up the revolver's sights.

The Sasquatch started coming.

And then stopped. It couldn't fit its shoulders into the opening. It was too big!

It shifted and thrust a massive arm at him. He watched the thick fingers crawl forward; yellow fingernails clawed at the wood. He looked for a shot under the armpit and into the chest.

The hand stopped, only a foot from him. The Sasquatch screamed and jammed its body into the opening. It slapped its hand and wood flew up, hitting Vaughn. Its fingers grabbed at air.

It screamed again and withdrew its arm.

Then it stood up and its body disappeared from the opening. A few seconds of quiet. Vaughn breathed.

KRAAAAAAK.

The tree shook and Vaughn fell onto his back. The lantern dropped from his grasp and rolled forward.

BAM BAM BAM BAM BAM. Pounding on the tree.

Rotten chunks of wood fell all over him. The light shook.

The tree moved, almost lifted. *Kraaaak-snap!* At the mouth of the trunk a slice of black appeared.

He realized it was ripping up the trunk to get at them.

The Sasquatch roared and pounded again. The blows vibrated in Vaughn's knees.

Suddenly a huge brown hand smashed through the top of the trunk. Wood crashed onto the rotted floor.

RAAAAAAAR!

Vaughn jammed his back into Alison and pointed the .357 at the wood above.

He heard laughter. Alison. She'd finally lost it.

All of a sudden he felt like laughing too. Because he had no shot.

The Sasquatch was outside, he was inside and there was no shot. They were dead. Killed by a Sasquatch, an animal everyone thought didn't exist. The sheriff would probably say they fell down a hole.

He chuckled as his skull shook with the pounding.

Why can't you just go away? he thought. And then he realized he'd said it aloud.

"Hey!" Bits of wood rained on him so that he had to yell downward.

Alison stopped laughing, but the Sasquatch kept pounding.

"Hey!" he said. "Leave! Get out of here!"

The Sasquatch stopped.

Silence. Then the tree rocked with a blow so powerful that it knocked Vaughn into Alison. Another and then another. The tree thrummed. He felt like he was rolling down a mountain in a barrel.

The Sasquatch pounded right over their heads, and in an instant of clarity Vaughn realized that the only thing he'd done by yelling was give the Sasquatch an exact fix on their position.

He wondered what would be worse, eating a bullet or getting pulverized.

He would have to shoot Alison first.

The wood above him cracked.

The Sasquatch bellowed and pounded more furiously.

Another crack.

He pointed the .357 straight up and tightened his finger on the trigger.

The pounding stopped.

Another crack, and then a muffled howl. A Sasquatch, but not the big one, farther off.

Vaughn heard two more quick cracks. Not wood, he realized. Gunshots.

A long, loud howl reverberated through the tree and made

his teeth hum. Then he felt heavy footfalls slowly pounding away.

He sat there for a long minute with the .357 in the air, waiting for the blows to start again—waiting for the wood above him to be ripped away so he could be plucked from the rotten log like a grub and smashed on the ground.

But nothing happened.

Gunshots meant Mackey was in trouble. He should go out there. But what could he do?

Alison sobbed quietly.

What could he do.

After a while Alison jabbed him with her boot, and he crawled a few feet forward. He shut off the lantern and sat with his back to the curved inside of the tree, listening. He heard two more brief howls, but no more shots.

At some point his head began to throb. His bones ached.

He tried to stay awake, but Alison's regular breathing and the warm and slightly sour smell of decay, rich with earth in the making, pulled him down.

Chapter 48

Friday

VAUGHN jerked awake. Pain knifed through his hamstring so badly that he checked to see if a shard of wood had pierced the muscle.

Just a cramp.

He dove flat to stretch out the leg—and couldn't believe what he saw.

Sun.

Yellow light—not grey—shined into the ragged mouth of the dead tree. And though no beams reached him, he felt better just seeing them.

He shivered and the cramp ratcheted tighter. He knew his muscles needed food. Keeping his legs straight, he flipped onto his back and dug out the dregs of the trail mix he'd stashed in his pocket.

He raised up on an elbow and pushed some of the mix into his mouth. His lip felt clumsy and then stung, and he remembered the fall down the hill and the blow to the side of his head. His fingers probed the area above his right ear: sensitive to the touch and a nice bump, but his hair wasn't sticky so no blood.

Nuts crunched between his teeth and he felt an M&M dissolve. He chewed fast because he knew he needed to get going right away. Lying there, staring at the pitted wood, he thought about his options. Really, he had only two: take Alison out and come back later for Mackey, or try to find Mackey now.

As he weighed each one, he realized that either way he first had to go out alone.

He popped the last of the trail mix into his mouth. Only when he'd swallowed it did he think he should have saved some for Alison.

He sat up and gently shook her leg. "Alison," he said. "Hey. Alison."

Her eyes shot open and her leg tensed. He had his left hand ready to clamp over her mouth, but she didn't make a sound.

She looked past him, down the hollow trunk, and then relaxed a little.

"It's morning," he said. "I'm going to check things out. I want you to stay here."

Vaughn watched a struggle fight itself out on her face: She didn't want to be alone, but she didn't want to leave the safety of the tree.

"I'm leaving this with you," he said, showing her his .357. "It's a double-action, which means you don't have to cock the hammer to fire it. But if you don't it'll take a big squeeze to move the trigger. Okay?"

"Okay," she said. Almost a whisper.

"Use two hands. Right hand around the grip, left hand around the right and extend your arms. Sight down the barrel."

The instructions seemed to increase her fear, but when she took the big revolver she calmed down, like she was accepting the fact that she could use it if she had to.

He said, "Try not to fall asleep else I might scare you when I come back. I'll start talking as I get close, so don't be too trigger-happy."

This was deadly serious. The last thing he wanted was to be one step from walking out of this and then get shot.

"If I'm being chased, I'll be yelling," he said. "Whatever you do, don't shoot. And don't leave here. You have a watch?"

Her voice creaked and she cleared her throat. "Yes."

He looked at his watch, estimated and then added thirty minutes. "It's ten minutes to seven. If I'm not back by nine-thirty and you feel like you can get out of here on your own, go."

"Okay."

He blew out a long breath. "See you later."

He turned around and faced the opening. He checked to make sure the rifle's muzzle was clear and a cartridge was in the chamber. Then he listened.

Birds chirped and called to one another, excited by the sunlight. He heard nothing else, but the Sasquatch could be sleeping right outside and he wouldn't know until he stuck his head out. With the force used to pummel the tree last night, the Sasquatch could put its fist through his skull like a cannonball rocketing through a melon.

Only one way to find out.

He crawled forward, carrying the rifle in his left hand, making as little noise as possible.

When he neared the opening he stopped. His heart pounded.

He looked at every leaf, every stem, every tree trunk; examined everything he could see. The remains of last night lay everywhere: crushed plants, chunks of wood and branches on the ground. But nothing suggested to him that the Sasquatch had come back.

Carefully, he eased the rifle up and forward—and then pulled back. He looked around the inside of the tree for a hefty piece of wood.

There. He reached over, picked it up and threw it out of the opening.

One end hit the ground with a low thump; brown bits of rot flew off. It hopped into the air, spun forward, hit the ground again and jumped into a patch of ferns. The fronds waved, then became still.

He sat as quiet as death, and listened. Not for screaming and crashing, but for anything out of the ordinary—a scuff, a tentative footfall, a rustle, a subtle disturbance of the air.

His hands clenched the rifle.

He crouched there for what felt like minutes. The cramp came back and he squeezed his muscles against the pain.

All he heard were birds and buzzing insects—and something else.

Gradually he realized the background noise was the river. Last night they had traveled farther than he thought.

Here we go.

He tensed and then dove out. His shoulder slammed into the ground and he rolled, flattening a clump of ferns and banging his upper arm on something hard. He jumped to his feet, pulled the rifle up and glanced around wildly.

Nothing.

No Sasquatch lying in wait.

His eyes carefully examined his surroundings, but it was pointless. Though the sun had burned off the fog, all the trees were big. He couldn't even see down both sides of the tree he'd been in without stepping forward and back. A Sasquatch could be anywhere.

He looked behind him, at the sunlight glimmering on the river. Then he shook out his cramped leg and walked toward the rise they had fallen down last night.

Chapter 49

AN hour later he found Mackey.

He'd located the tape trail and headed toward the road in case Mackey made it to the truck last night and now was coming to find them. He looked for signs of recent disturbance on the trail, but found no evidence that anyone or anything had lately passed. He decided it didn't feel right and reversed course.

Fifteen minutes later he found their packs—what was left of them. Only a few ragged strips of green, black and camouflaged nylon remained.

A sharp knife could puncture the heavy-duty material, and he figured bear claws could rip it, but as he inspected the strips he saw that they'd been torn. By strong hands.

Suddenly he remembered the deer's belly. What he thought was a ragged cut from a dull knife had actually been a tear.

He almost couldn't believe the strength of the Sasquatches. Just awesome.

Off the trail he found the rest of their gear. Green, purple and tan scraps of tent littered the ground. A few pieces hung from branches twelve feet up. One tree clutched half his sleeping bag; white synthetic stuffing oozed out of it like the innards of a caterpillar.

Scattered here and there were cooking utensils, a plastic water bottle, cooking pots, the cover of a first aid kit and other debris he didn't bother to examine.

Interspersed among these lay Douglas fir branches. Their flat needles still shone with blue-green life, but jagged strips of raw wood curled outward where the branches had been twisted off. A few were jammed into the cold ground by the stumps; their tips sagged so that they resembled sad children.

Fresh Sasquatch tracks of at least two distinct sizes ran all over the place. When he bent down to examine them, the warming air carried the fertile damp of the earth and vegetation up his nose and into his brain. The warm air also made him remember the time. His watch showed that he'd been away from Alison for almost an hour, and he still hadn't seen any human sign.

Taking care to be quiet, he walked back to the tape trail, intending to follow it to the river. Once on the bank, if he didn't find Mackey, he would walk down to the hollow tree and retrieve Alison.

He'd only gone a few yards when he spied something silver lying on the ground, just off the trail. A revolver. He expected it to be Mackey's .44, but it wasn't. From the smaller frame and barrel he recognized it as a .357.

Lansing's gun.

He scooped it up and checked to make sure no dirt blocked the muzzle. Then he released the cylinder and shook out the spent cases. They clinked into his palm and he put them in his pants pocket. From his parka he removed an HKS speedloader, inserted the tips of the six cartridges in their chambers, twisted the knob and the shells dropped in. He snapped the cylinder closed.

He unzipped his parka and shoved the revolver into the shoulder holster he still wore. Leaving the zipper open, he walked on.

Forty yards down something registered as out of place.

Not threatening, just not right. He stopped and scanned the ground around him.

His eyes dissected the myriad shades of green, but came up with nothing. He took two steps backward, and looked again.

Still nothing. *Damn,* he thought. *What was it?*

He remembered that his head was turned to the left when he stopped, and walked to that side. Almost immediately he saw something brown and black poking from a cluster of fern fronds. He walked closer and it resolved into the sole of a boot. Clumps of dark earth were stuck in the treads.

Gradually the rest of Mackey's camouflaged form became visible. He lay on his stomach, facing to the side. His arms were bent at the elbows and his legs stuck straight out. He looked for all the world like he was asleep—except for the blood.

Had Mackey's hair not been greying, the blood wouldn't have been as noticeable. Dark and sticky, it clotted the hair just above where the neck joined the skull.

Vaughn bent down to check for a pulse and saw coagulated maroon streams running down the side of Mackey's neck to the ground. That meant that when he was assaulted he'd immediately fallen here, unconscious.

He pressed two fingers to Mackey's carotid artery. A regular bump. Skin pallor looked normal.

Technically, he should go through the procedure he'd used with Boone, but this time there were mitigating factors: Mackey seemed okay, Vaughn couldn't carry him out on his own, and from the injury, Vaughn knew he had other things to worry about. Namely that Mackey had been assaulted by a two-legged creature, and despite the events of last night, the evidence indicated that a Sasquatch was the more remote possibility.

For one thing, though Jack-O had been nearly liquefied by repeated blows, Mackey appeared to have been struck only once. And someone had taken Mackey's guns.

Vaughn knew he'd been lucky to find Mackey in the daytime. The chances of Lansing merely stumbling across an unconscious Mackey in the pitch dark of the woods and taking his guns were astronomically low, even with a flashlight.

So Lansing had to be responsible.

Still, Vaughn couldn't be sure. Not without more evidence.

He stepped back from Mackey and walked a slow, tight circle. His eyes took apart the ground, looking for what he suspected was there.

After ten minutes he'd covered almost all of the area within a ten-yard circle of Mackey with nothing to show for it. No Sasquatch tracks, and though the vegetation in a few places had been crushed by a boot, there was no way to tell for certain whose boots they were.

He checked his watch. About an hour until Alison could leave on her own. He decided to circle out to fifteen yards and then quit.

At twelve yards and about two o'clock from Mackey's head he found it: a thick branch—thick for human hands. And not a dark branch from the forest. It was stripped of bark from being tumbled downstream, and weather had bleached the wood to the color of bone. A reddish-black smear stained one end.

Now he was sure.

He stepped away from the evidence and walked straight back to Mackey. His fingers checked the carotid artery again. A regular pulse, and Mackey breathed evenly. The first-aid instructor's voice played in his head: *The caregiver should not leave a patient alone to search for others unless the patient is obviously dead.*

He banished the voice. Then, just in case, he took out Lansing's .357 and put it under Mackey's right hand.

Mackey's hand twitched, then went limp. Vaughn looked: Mackey's eyes weren't open, and he didn't move again.

He patted Mackey's hand. "Back for you later," he said, and walked on.

FOR some reason he had a feeling Lansing was still alive— and he wasn't happy about it.

After all the professor had done, it would be ironic justice if a Sasquatch killed him. But years of police work had taught Vaughn that in real life, things never worked out that neatly.

When he was a kid he used to watch what was called "The 4:30 movie" on TV. Usually it was a "creature feature," a monster flick, and at some point he'd figured out that the role of the scientists in these movies was to get killed. With their white coats and black-rimmed eyeglasses, they sneaked past the sandbag walls and the warnings of generals in an attempt to communicate or do something equally stupid with the monsters or aliens. As soon as they were far enough from the sandbags and the tanks, they were quickly gutted, ray-gunned or otherwise killed by whatever creature happened to be featured that week. Happened every time.

But this time was different. Unlike the movie scientists, Lansing had dumb luck on his side. Or maybe it was that he was actually trying to get killed, that he had some kind of death wish, and that's what was keeping him alive.

The movie scientists also approached the monsters empty-handed. But Lansing wanted to kill a Sasquatch, had weapons and knew how to use them.

Vaughn kept that in mind as he circled back to the river. He traveled in a wide arc that took him well off the tape trail, and walked faster to cover more ground. Even if he didn't run into Lansing he would end up checking out most of the area.

When he hit the rise he walked along it for a while, looking down toward the river. Without the fog, the elevation afforded him a longer view, but all he saw against the green and brown was the occasional darting blur of a bird or buzzing insect, and the lazy flap of a butterfly.

The day was getting warm.

The forest changed abruptly from old growth to replanted Douglas fir, and Vaughn decided to leave the slope. He walked down, still circling upstream.

Soon he heard water and slowed down. He approached the bank cautiously.

For some reason he felt nervous, maybe because he was about to leave the cover of the forest.

He stayed inside the treeline and looked carefully up and down both sides of the riverbank. Then he did it again, slower this time.

He saw nothing.

He stepped out onto the smooth, oval stones. The sunlight warmed his face, and in the distance he heard helicopter blades chopping through the air. The sound comforted him. Men were logging. Things were getting back to normal.

He walked out to the edge of the river, laid his rifle on the stones and plunged his hands into the icy water. He brought the water up and splashed it onto his face. The cold jolted him.

Man it felt good.

He dried his palms on the thighs of his camouflaged fleece pants, and then used his forefingers to pry the crumbs from his eyes.

Krak-owww!

Chapter 50

THE big Sasquatch's head raised off its knees and its eyes cracked open.

Sunlight streamed in. And ache.

It blinked away the pain, then squinted in the direction of the shot. Its thick, hair-covered arms unfolded from around its shins; its knuckles hit the ground with a soft thump, dragged backward, then stopped.

For a moment, warming in the sunlight, the Sasquatch hesitated. But then it rose from its stump-mimicking position and stretched toward the sky. It expanded its chest, sucked in the warm air and felt it curl around inside its lungs.

It glanced at the sky one more time, then stepped forward and ran to the river, where it would be able to see.

It knew it ran toward the man energy. The man energy and man-smell had been in the woods for days. In that time the Sasquatch had barely slept and hadn't eaten.

Now stress churned its hollow stomach. Each step smashed dull pain into its knees.

But it kept running.

Its long arms pulled up and down like pumps, tracing arcs through the air. Gradually the Sasquatch noticed a burning in its shoulder. The pain reminded it of the other.

Gone.

No more gone.

Blood-smell, man-smell. The unnatural stink of men and memories of the last two days spurred the big Sasquatch to run faster. Its wide nose dissected every molecule of air for the wet of the river.

It ran between the trees and leaped over a fallen log. The only sound was the thump of its feet on the warming earth.

The gun smells and blood smells of last night burned through its brain. The harsh noise of shooting.

Again it felt the fear of the other, and it knew what the men were shooting at now.

No more.

It knew it had to stop them.

No more gun.

It ran.

Chapter 51

VAUGHN froze and listened to the reverberation of the shot roll through the valley. He could tell that the initial crack of the rifle came from behind him, up on the mountainside.

Lansing, he figured. And the best chance of shooting a Sasquatch would be in an open area, where there wouldn't be any trees for the animal to use as cover. That meant the road.

Vaughn jumped to his feet, brought his rifle up and looked through the scope at the ridge.

The jack fir were low enough to see over, but because of his poor angle relative to the ridge, he couldn't see much. He let down his rifle and walked quickly upstream to a pile of driftwood. He lifted his leg up onto it to steady himself, and looked through the scope again.

His right eye followed the crowded fir tips up to a cluster of boulders and then to the ridge. He saw a section of open area—the ridge road—bounded on the right by trees. He slowly moved the scope to the left.

Suddenly something big and black bolted across the open-

ing from the left. A Sasquatch—but something about the way
it moved didn't look right.

As he watched, a second shot rang out and a third and then
the Sasquatch went down.

A yell snaked down from the ridge: "Whoooeeee!"

What the . . . Vaughn moved the scope to the left again,
looking for . . .

Then, over the rush of the river, he heard water splash.

AAAAAOOOOOOOOOOOOOOOOOOO!

The howl was so loud that he ducked away from the sound.
Slowly, he turned.

Only ten yards away the big Sasquatch stood in the rushing river. Huge, immovable, like a slab of mountain.

Jesus, Vaughn thought. Every time he saw it it seemed bigger. It was huge, twice as wide as a man. And massive, like a
gorilla with long, human-proportioned legs.

It looked like it could snap him in half without a thought.

It had arms the size of his legs, and legs the size of his
torso. Raw power bulged from under the straggly, dark brown
hair covering its body. It struck Vaughn that the muscles
looked like knots of wood, as if the creature was formed by
the same hands that made the enormous fir trees.

Long arms hung at its sides, slightly tense, and the well-
defined pectoral muscles of its chest heaved with each deep
breath. As he watched, the shorter hair on its thick neck and
broad shoulders stood up like a mane.

Vaughn's eyes took it all in, but fixed on the creature's
face. Mostly hair-covered, the face looked black—like a gorilla's, but not exactly. Atop thin lips sat a wide nose that
looked flat. But the nostrils faced down, like a man's.

Above its eyes jutted a heavy ridge of bone, which merged
into a forehead that sloped back into a massive skull. The
skull continued slanting up and back, giving it an odd, peaked
appearance. Though not round, the head was easily bigger
than a basketball.

But more than anything else, its eyes held him. They
looked completely black. Only when they shifted did he see
the whites on the sides.

The eyes appeared sinister because of their dark color and
the thick brow, yet he felt that the awareness behind them was

more human than animal. He had the impression that the creature was thinking. Evaluating, not merely weighing an animal's two instinctive reactions, run away or attack. Different from last night.

Water slammed into the Sasquatch's lower leg and curled around, creating an eddy. Spray shot upward, and in the sunlight the water droplets hung like glass beads on the stringy brown hair.

For a moment Vaughn was awed by the animal's beauty—until he noticed that its shadow blotted out a huge chunk of the opposite bank.

The massive head turned from the ridge to look at him. Then the Sasquatch roared.

It lifted a leg out of the water and fixed it three feet onto the bank. With a soggy slap, the gigantic, hair-covered foot smothered the stones beneath it. The other foot followed.

It stood there, dripping from its shins down. Vaughn saw that the animal had grey hair on the top of its head and shoulders, and in the middle of its chest.

The hair on its left chest, near the shoulder, looked darker. Wet. But it didn't reflect the sunlight like the water did.

Vaughn realized that Lansing must have gotten lucky last night. He figured that to an animal that big, the bullet probably felt like a hornet's sting, nothing more.

Suddenly he felt something hard and cold jab into the base of his skull.

In that instant he knew what it was.

And who was behind it.

Chapter 52

"SHOOT it, deputy," Lansing said.

"I can't do that," Vaughn said. He cursed himself for not thinking more thoroughly: Besides the road, the riverbank was the only other place where the Sasquatch couldn't dodge a bullet.

Lansing giggled.

Vaughn watched the huge hands of the Sasquatch flex and then release. It glanced up at the ridge again, then turned its eyes back to them.

Son of a bitch, Vaughn thought, his mind racing. He wished he hadn't left that revolver with Mackey.

"Shoot it," Lansing said.

"No."

"Shoot it!"

"I said no."

"Then drop your rifle."

"Can't do that, professor," Vaughn said.

"If you don't, I will have to shoot you with a very large

bullet, deputy. One man's death is a small price to pay for this discovery."

Vaughn heard the chunky clack of metal and felt the muzzle jerk as Lansing worked the bolt of Mackey's .375 H&H Mag.

"Last warning, deputy." The professor's voice had become high-pitched.

Vaughn knew Lansing was crazy enough to do it. So he made a decision.

He figured that Lansing was focused more on the Sasquatch, so he tossed his rifle onto the stones making sure that it angled ahead and to the right.

Ten yards away the Sasquatch stepped toward them, the movement fluid, athletic. Deep lines creased its thigh muscles.

With that one step it was a lot closer.

"Walk," Lansing said.

"Which way?"

"Toward the Sasquatch!" Lansing jabbed him in the skull.

Vaughn took a small step toward the animal.

Lansing poked him again. "Keep going!"

The Sasquatch took another two-yard step, then showed its teeth and growled.

Vaughn knew that Lansing's attention had to be focused on the Sasquatch.

Now or never.

He took another step, then dove to the right, out of the line of fire and toward his rifle. He slammed into the stones, grabbed his rifle, turned over and: *Boom!*

All of Vaughn's muscles tensed—but he didn't feel anything. He opened his eyes and quickly looked himself over. No blood.

He sat up and saw Lansing lying on the stones. Bits of bloody skin clung to a ragged exit wound in the professor's chest. And standing over Lansing, with his hands on his knees and Lansing's .357 clutched in his right hand, was Mackey.

Mackey's stomach convulsed and drool leaked from his mouth. Then he straightened up—and nearly fell over. Vaughn knew Mackey was fighting a concussion. And he knew it was a bad one.

"Never shot . . . anything in the back before," Mackey said. His face was screwed up like he had a migraine headache. "He was going to kill you, ol' boy."

RAAAAAAAAAA!

Vaughn didn't know if it was seeing Lansing killed, the gunshot or the smell of fresh blood, but the Sasquatch was coming faster now—right at them, its muscles bulging with each step.

He jumped to his feet.

Boom!

Vaughn ducked. To the right of the Sasquatch, stones jumped backward and white dust puffed into the air.

He looked over. Mackey knelt on one knee and held the revolver in front of him, but his whole body swayed—which is why he missed.

But what the hell was Mackey shooting at? Vaughn knew it couldn't be the Sasquatch, so it had to be—

Suddenly the animal towered over him and blocked his view of the river. The stink! It surrounded him, almost overwhelmed him. His instincts screamed *run!*, but he stood his ground.

He hunched his shoulders against the blow he expected at any moment and concentrated on the trees to the right, at the edge of the forest. At the second one he saw what he was looking for: the ends of two yellow arms.

Alison's hands held his .357, and it was pointed at the Sasquatch.

Jesus, he thought. *Mackey's going to shoot her.*

"Alison," he yelled. "Get back!"

The Sasquatch turned from the waist, looked and saw the arms. It took a step toward Alison, and then another.

Almost there.

Alison's arms didn't move.

Vaughn knew what he had to do. He aimed for the revolver in Alison's hands and pulled the trigger.

There was a deafening bang.

Alison screamed and her yellow arms disappeared.

Vaughn dropped his rifle and looked.

The Sasquatch teetered and then fell forward, like an old

Douglas fir; in slow motion and without a sound. It crashed into the stones, bounced and didn't move.

HE stared, dumbfounded.

The long hair on the Sasquatch's back jumped and swayed as if alive.

He watched it for seconds, maybe for hours, he didn't know.

The hair danced in different directions, pulling and tugging like it was trying to lift the Sasquatch from the ground.

Suddenly he thought: *Where is that wind coming from?*

He looked at the sky.

A passenger helicopter hovered above the river. Painted on its gleaming white nose was a green Christmas tree-shaped CP.

For some reason he didn't hear the slap of the blades. Didn't feel the wind.

He just stared, at the bank of lenses pointing right at him.

Chapter 53

Friday
Washington, D.C.

OUTLINED against the heavy blue curtain, Carolina Pacific chairman and CEO Bill Gaines strode to the podium as if he would tear it to pieces and walk away without saying a word.

Talking in the press ranks abruptly ceased, but it was a false calm. The air sparked with electricity.

Gaines stopped behind the podium, grabbed its sides with both hands and leaned over the tangle of microphones. The entire room drew toward him.

He glared at the audience and said, "The footage you have all seen is real."

The room erupted. Reporters shouted questions and hands waved in the air. People ran out. All pretense at civility disappeared.

Gaines waited, his face taut with anger.

At the side of the stage Mark Kingston let out a breath he didn't know he'd been holding in. He imagined Brenda Un-

derwood's face spreading into a wide smile as she watched
this on television.

· Half an hour ago Gaines was so steamed no one was sure
what he would say. He and Kingston met at the White House
with Brenda Underwood, Forest Service Chief Scott Walsh
and their bosses in Interior and Agriculture, along with the
majority and minority leaders of both Houses and the President and his chief of staff. The agenda was for Underwood to
brief everyone on the plan. Her plan. Really Chris Mackey's
plan, but no one but Kingston, Mackey and Underwood
would ever know that.

She started the briefing by pointing to recent history. In the
1990s the Clinton-Gore Administration's strategy for dealing
with endangered species was "a joke," she said. It was based on
warm-fuzzy feelings rather than reality. Clinton's environmental
evangelists had to "save" everything, so they twisted the Endangered Species Act into a lance and used it and a shield of
guilt to force their preservationist doctrine on America.

But it was inevitable that a preservationist agenda would
collapse. It simply didn't mesh with the rest of life—notably
economic growth. Citizen aggravation had been steadily
building to that point, and only a catalyst was needed. "The
Sasquatch is it," she said.

Clinton-Gore's condescending "we know what's good for
you" approach was out. Instead the new plan would take into
account the costly train-wreck strategy used by Clinton's predecessor, George Bush. But whereas Bush and his advisors
had seen the collision coming—between environmentalists
and loggers in the Pacific Northwest—and simply let it happen, this time it would be different. Because this time they
had two advantages.

One was that the train-wreck strategy had already been
used. It wouldn't "work" again.

The second advantage was that in this case, a wreck would
be more like a nuclear explosion and therefore wasn't an option. And for the same reason, the courts had to be bypassed.
Letting them use nearly a decade of largely Democratic prece-
dent to rule on the Sasquatch would be economic, and therefore political, suicide.

The only option was to avoid the wreck, by rerouting the

train, she said. Congress had to change the existing law or, better yet, enact a new one.

"Keep the Endangered Species Act for the last-resort law it's supposed to be," she told the Congressmen, "but start talking about a new law that would preserve big chunks of land. We've been doing it, but see if the American people really want it."

Even though Kingston had talked to Underwood beforehand, her vehement language surprised him. He couldn't make up his mind whether she'd been a good actress at the woodpecker press conference or was being one now. Either way, she was a damn good politician.

The President told the legislators they would never get a better chance to demonstrate how the Endangered Species Act was being misused than the Sasquatch. When the ranking House Democrat equivocated, the President said: "There's no way I'm going to be known as the guy who doomed the whole damn country. How about you?"

In the end the Democrats went along. They really had no choice. The Republicans told them in no uncertain terms that if they didn't support it, they and their party would be vilified as the people who wanted to ruin the economy of the United States. And as everyone knew, if the money didn't flow, no one in America would give a damn about anything else.

What in the past would have been seen as so much talk about the oppressiveness of the Endangered Species Act was now true, and Kingston could see that the Democrats knew it. They said they would oppose it in the media, but in the end would go along with "some form" of the new legislation.

On the other side of the coin, he knew that the Republicans rarely acted without extreme circumstances that favored their views, and this was about as extreme as it got.

So everyone was in agreement. Everyone except Gaines.

During the exchanges his face boiled, but he never moved. Not even his hands.

When everyone else finished, they waited for him to say something. He stared down at the polished wooden table for a few long seconds, then looked at the President.

"Carolina Pacific's primary objective in all of this is to make sure the sale to BayMun AG goes through," he said. "To that end I want your assurance that regardless of how this plan shakes out in the public domain, the sale and Carolina Pacific's operations will not be compromised."

"I can't promise you that, Bill," the President said. "I wish I could, but I can't."

"You can," Gaines said.

"I don't think—" the chief of staff began, but the President waved him off.

"Okay, I can," the President said. "But not everything I *can* do is the smartest thing *to* do. How about I get the FTC off your back?"

"No deal. We have that under control."

"We could change that," the chief of staff said.

The President shot him a look that plainly said, *shut up*.

"It would be unfortunate if it came out that the government knew about these animals all along," Gaines said.

The President said: "It would be bad if any of the history of this came out, including the most recent history."

Gaines' ears turned red.

"Look, Bill, it seems we have each other by the," the President glanced at Brenda Underwood, "the short and curlies."

"That's bull, Mr. President. Everyone makes out here but Carolina Pacific."

"I don't know about that," the President said. He looked down at a piece of paper. "Says here your endangered species-related expenses have gone up every year."

"They won't go away."

The President raised his eyebrows and nodded. "Probably not." He glanced at his chief of staff, who tapped his watch. "Listen Bill, time's running short. I hate to tell any man how to do business, and I'm not going to tell you what to do here. I understand why you're angry. The timing's unfortunate. But this is history and some things are going to happen whether you're on board or not. Of course, we'd rather have you aboard. That would make things a lot smoother."

Gaines fumed silently and then looked at his watch. "Give me thirty minutes to think about it."

"Your press conference is in thirty minutes," the chief of staff said.

Gaines looked at the President. "That's right."

He didn't say a word during the short limousine ride to the Watergate Hotel, and neither did Kingston. Outside the hotel's main entrance utility-looking trucks of all colors lined Virginia Avenue. Painted numbers and letters adorned the sides of the trucks, and their roofs were topped with satellite dishes of every conceivable shape. The limousine driver avoided the throng and drove into the parking garage.

It was critical for the government to maintain distance from Carolina Pacific to prevent any suspicion of collusion. So at the press conference, Gaines would be on his own to confirm the existence of Sasquatches and take the first questions.

He was angry about that, and Kingston didn't blame him. But Gaines had done the right thing. The ax had fallen.

Congress would immediately begin hearings on new legislation. The Fish and Wildlife Service's expanding endangered species bureaucracy would be stopped and redirected. And it and the rest of the federal government would stop being used by environmental groups, which had forced increasing amounts of money to be spent on what really was a cultural problem: Endangered species, like all modern environmental problems, were the results of contemporary life, notably the exploding human population.

The environmentalists would wail about "the demise of the Endangered Species Act," but that was okay. They loved bad news. Kingston was sure they would spin everything negatively, make it sound like all kinds of extinctions were imminent, blah, blah, blah. They would make hay from it. For sure.

Everyone would make out all right.

From the side of the stage Kingston watched Gaines field the first question. He'd just started to relax when the cell phone in his suit pocket vibrated.

"Kingston."

"Mark, it's Brenda."

"He did it."

"Yeah," she said. "But we forgot one thing."

Chapter 54

Monday, May 13

FIRST degree assault.

The words perched on Vaughn's shoulder like grinning demons. They had been there since Saturday morning, when he realized what kind of trouble he was in.

Dressed in street clothes, he sat on a wooden bench in the lobby outside the county executive's office and stared at the floor. He was supposed to be suspended without pay for two weeks, but the sheriff called him in early. Called him in here, to Jack-O's father's office. Not a good sign.

He'd thought about wearing his uniform, but didn't want to seem aggressive. Or pathetic.

Lisa, Jack-O's father's secretary, said four people were in there. The sheriff, Jack-O's father and two people she didn't know. She sat at her desk chewing the end of a pen, absorbed in the television. He couldn't hear what was on, and when he looked up all he could see was the reflection of the images flickering across her skin.

That was good, because he hated television.

His face, staring up at the helicopter, had been all over the screen. Four days of beard and three of grime made him look like an outlaw, an impression given life by his swollen, blood-caked lip and the purple bags that sagged under his eyes.

His eyes were the worst part. They stared half wild at the camera and made him look feral, like he'd been possessed by a primeval spirit and cursed to wander the forest, gradually losing his mind.

Maybe that wasn't far off. He didn't know how sane he'd been. He still felt numb.

The media had buzzed into town like killer bees, cluster-stinging everything until it was dead. News trucks jammed his street, and cars and people clogged every campground, motel and restaurant in Skookum, Cowlitz and Lewis counties. They overwhelmed the Slugfest so badly that the sheriff tried to close it down after just one day. He succeeded after two.

The media and the gawkers. Even now they waited out-side.

At home Vaughn refused to answer the door or the phone, and though he avoided the TV he did skim the papers. From them he learned that things were happening all over the place.

The state legislature rushed through a Sasquatch Conser-vation Act which banned the killing, transport or sale of any Sasquatch, dead or alive. When signing it, the governor as-sured people it was not in any way an endangered species law. It was needed to protect Sasquatches from exploitation, she said, largely in response to rumors that wealthy Japanese, Chinese and Koreans were offering huge sums for Sasquatch parts, especially gall bladders and testicles. By virtue of the law, the federal Lacey Act—which prohibits interstate or for-eign transport of any protected species—now applied to Sasquatches.

China accused the governor of prejudice and ignorance, and at the same time announced a large-scale effort to find its version of the Sasquatch, the Yeren. Environmental and ani-mal rights groups condemned the expedition as "barbaric."

A few articles contained speculation that the governor pushed through the law to protect an impending tourism windfall. That theory made sense in light of the joint federal-state plan to create a new Sasquatch Park adjacent to the

Mount Saint Helens National Volcanic Monument. The combination eco-tour and educational complex was to have a
building named after Professor Arthur Lansing.

To make the park possible, the state, the feds and private
endowments anted up $100 million to buy out existing log-
ging contracts and "future timber profits" from the area. A
group of environmentalists calling itself the Sasquatch Preservation Coalition promptly sued all the parties, claiming that
the buyout violated the Endangered Species Act, the National
Environmental Policy Act and a few other laws.

Simultaneously, the group announced that it had petitioned
the U.S. Fish and Wildlife Service to list Sasquatches as endangered species, and that it was undertaking an effort to get
the requisite governments to establish an international U.S.-
Canada Sasquatch Preserve extending from northern California to Alaska, "to protect the fragile habitat on which
Sasquatches depend." The Coalition also said it received
money from several funds named after millionaires' widows
to determine "Sasquatch critical habitat areas across the
United States."

What a crock, Vaughn thought when he read it. He felt the
same way about reports of the Pentagon conducting secret ex-
periments with man-apes, and of religious leaders furiously
looking for some kind of scriptural rationale for the
Sasquatch.

The only thing about which he hadn't read but was curious
was the autopsy of the big Sasquatch. Or was it a dissection?

He knew someone had done one. At least one. And he
wanted to know: Just how similar to man were these things?

Lansing thought he knew. A reporter got a hold of notes for
a paper the professor was working on, the gist of which was
that Sasquatches and humans evolved from a common ancestor. Humans developed a bigger brain at the expense of
physique. Sasquatches evolved more the other way, but were
still very smart.

It seemed logical to Vaughn, but from the subsequent re-
porting apparently no one except environmentalists, a few scientists and the lunatic fringe were willing to believe it.

Even with all of this going on, he was amazed that many
of the news reports focused on him. Maybe because he

wouldn't talk, or because in the photographs and the footage it was him standing alone on the riverbank with the Sasquatch. Regardless of the reason, suddenly total strangers questioned his character. He tried to block it all out, but one headline stuck with him: "Frank Vaughn, Hero or Zero?"

His mind kept returning to it because somehow it captured what he faced. What happened now had nothing to do with his own opinion of himself. Rather, he realized that what others thought, what the four people in the office to his left thought, was all that mattered.

That's why he couldn't talk to Katie. They hugged when he got back, but that was the most physical they had been. She of course wanted to talk about their future and what he could do to make sure he survived the fallout. But he wanted none of it. He knew talking helped her work things out, but what could he say? "Honey, I shot someone. That's first degree assault, a felony, one step below attempted murder. I'll be going to jail. That's our future."

So he said nothing. And after the umpteenth "I don't want to talk about it," she gave him the silent treatment—pretty much what he'd been giving her.

The vertebrae in his lower back began to hurt from pushing against the hard wood of the bench. He sat up straighter and glanced at the big double doors of the county executive's office. *Let's go,* he thought. *Let's get this over with.* What was taking them so long?

Maybe they wanted him to sweat. Then he wondered whether the delay was caused by the sheriff fighting for him.

Probably not, he thought. After all, he had shot her. Really, he'd shot at the .357 and hit it. But Billy told him bullet fragments injured Alison's hands. She lost the tip of one finger and had nerve damage in two more.

Somehow that hadn't come out in the media yet, but it was only a matter of time. Once it did, he would be fingered as the shooter.

And what was his defense? That she was going to kill a mere animal in cold blood? His attorney would be laughed out of the courtroom.

At least he didn't have to worry about Lansing being a hostile witness. Officially the professor had been killed by a stray bullet.

Before all of this happened, that lie would've bothered Vaughn. Now it didn't. Lansing brought it upon himself: He tried to kill Mackey and failed. Mackey tried and succeeded.

Mackey had also succeeded in manipulating the whole situation from the get-go. Vaughn realized that yesterday afternoon. The realization arrived in a rush, as if his subconscious had been working through it without him being aware of it.

Mackey must have called the Fish and Wildlife Service about the Sasquatch. He, Brenda Underwood and maybe Carolina Pacific hatched a plan to use a Sasquatch—a dead one—to rein in the Endangered Species Act and get this new legislation passed that all the loggers were talking about. When Vaughn visited Boone at home, Boone said the new law would be a good thing. He held up his bandaged arm. "Worth it," he said. Vaughn wasn't so sure.

Of course the press hadn't connected the dots to Mackey, and never would. He certainly wouldn't help them. And although he got the short end, he had to admire the plan. Mackey even got the CP sale scuttled.

Hell of a mind Mackey had. Hard skull, too. Even with a concussion, he made it down to the river and shot Lansing. Woozy from the effort, he missed the Sasquatch badly the first time, but then he corrected and put the .357's big bullet into the Sasquatch's right eye socket, killing it instantly. An incredible shot, considering.

Vaughn figured Mackey would agree to be a witness for him, but Mackey's head injury and hospital stay would make his testimony worthless. The prosecutor would tear it to shreds.

That only left Alison, Brenda Underwood's diversion. Whom he shot. At.

He knew Alison the environmentalist would never help him.

Her fellow tree-huggers wanted Mackey burned at the stake, for killing a so-called endangered species and for murdering a "human being," meaning the Sasquatch. They would never know that Alison wanted to shoot it, and wouldn't believe it anyway.

On the one and only day he watched the TV, he saw an angry-eyed young woman interviewed in front of a group of chanting protesters. Her head protruded from a headless gorilla costume. She said that excluding the only other bipedal primate from our laws was "speciesism," and that Washington's criminal code defined murder as the killing of another human being. It was not specific to *homo sapiens,* and therefore Mackey should be tried for murder, she said.

A reporter with a functioning brain pointed out that a murder charge would void the Endangered Species Act applying to Sasquatches since humans are anything but endangered. But she said no, Sasquatches weren't the same species.

"What about things like welfare and food stamps?" the reporter asked. "Do Sasquatches get them too?"

"Don't be ridiculous," the young woman said.

A day later the county prosecutor said he wouldn't use the 1969 bigfoot law or murder statutes to pursue a case against Mackey. The state attorney general's office concurred, and added that Mackey violated no wildlife laws. The environmentalists and animal rightists—Vaughn found it hard to tell the difference—went ballistic.

The remaining outstanding case, aside from his own, was the shooting of a huge man from Centralia who happened to be running on the ridge road in a gorilla costume. Vaughn knew something about that Sasquatch had looked funny. When he read that the man had been shot once in the rump and needed surgery to remove the slug, he almost laughed. The man refused to say what he was doing there, and his companion, who videotaped the incident, pleaded ignorance.

The sheriff's office had no suspects, but Vaughn did. He remembered that "whoooooee!" Jack-O's redneck yell must have been inherited. He didn't know whether Jack-O Senior had been out on the road looking for Jack-O Junior or, as seemed more likely, looking for the next big thing for the county's economy. Either way, he'd been there. Vaughn briefly thought about using that information as blackmail in the upcoming meeting, but jettisoned the idea as cowardly.

The doors bumped, then the brass handle turned and one door swung open. The sheriff stood there, dwarfed by the Sasquatch-size opening. "C'mon in, Frank."

Vaughn took a deep breath and stood. He walked to the door, and looked at the sheriff as he entered. The Old Man caught his eye, but didn't pat him on the back, didn't smile, didn't do anything reassuring. He merely closed the door, then walked past Vaughn and sat in a chair to the right of Jack-O's father.

John O'Sullivan Sr. pointed at a lone chair in front of his desk. "Have a seat."

Vaughn sat, his back rigid.

O'Sullivan gestured to a man and woman sitting to his left. "This is Mark Kingston from Carolina Pacific and Brenda Underwood of the Fish and Wildlife Service."

So that was Brenda Underwood. She made no attempt to conceal the fact that she was looking at him, and smiled when his eyes met hers. He wondered if Kingston was the guy Mackey talked to from the woods.

Vaughn looked at Jack-O's father. "I'm sorry about Jack," he said.

For a moment it looked like water pooled in the elder O'Sullivan's eyes, but he controlled it and said, "So am I." He rested his elbows on the desk and leaned forward. "Do you know why you're here?"

Loaded question, Vaughn thought. "I have an idea."

O'Sullivan's eyebrows arched. "The sheriff tells us you're an idealist."

Vaughn didn't know how to answer that. He didn't see the angle yet.

"Is that right?" O'Sullivan said.

"Yes, sir. I suppose it is."

"But you shot the girl. Why?"

"I didn't shoot her."

"At her, then," O'Sullivan said.

Vaughn looked at the sheriff and glanced at the others. Was this it?

The sheriff said, "Anything you say won't go beyond this room."

"I appreciate that, sheriff, but I don't know these people."

"You have our word, deputy," Brenda Underwood said.

Kingston said: "That's right."

Vaughn looked at them and then back at Jack-O's father. "It seemed like the right thing to do at the time."

"What have you thought about it since then?"

Vaughn had thought about it. His initial impression was that he shot the gun from Alison's hands because that was the only way to stop anyone from killing anything. But he gradually admitted to himself that his motivation wasn't that selfless.

He said, "I thought it would be bad for everyone if the Sasquatch was discovered."

O'Sullivan glanced at the sheriff, and out of the corner of Vaughn's eye he saw Brenda Underwood and Mark Kingston exchange looks.

"Your call, George," O'Sullivan said to the sheriff.

The Old Man stared at Vaughn. His blue eyes revealed nothing. Vaughn got a bad feeling.

"Frank, it would be good if we had a bright spot in all this," the Old Man said.

Vaughn wondered what the hell he was talking about.

His confusion must have showed because Brenda Underwood said: "May I, sheriff?"

"By all means," the sheriff said.

Underwood turned to Vaughn and flashed him a smile. "I'm going to go out on a limb here, deputy. Will you also hold what I say in confidence?"

"Yes," he said.

"Good. Right now there's a lot of excitement about the Sasquatch. But out of five people who went into the woods, two were injured and two were killed. And a Sasquatch was killed too. At some point that will sink in."

Vaughn saw where she was going. They wanted something to counteract that negativity.

But he knew there was more. He said, "Is that it?"

Brenda Underwood's eyes didn't flinch and she didn't hesitate. "No. It also can't seem like we preferred the bigfoot dead."

Preferred, he thought. *Nice way to phrase it.*

He could see that trumping up the "local hero defends Sasquatch" angle probably would drown out the cynics and their troublesome questions. It would be easy to do, too. Already the dead Sasquatch was being portrayed as the martyr and Mackey and Jack-O as the villains. By becoming the martyr's defender, he would get the glory.

But did he deserve it?

He thought about whether he'd made the right decisions, starting from when he, Boone and Geek found the bodies. Then there was everything he'd been through, his job, his marriage, his life.

Last he thought about the big Sasquatch, trying to protect its own.

Damn right I deserve it.

But there was one detail. "What about Alison?"

Brenda Underwood smiled and said: "It was an accident. A ricochet. Maybe not even from your gun."

He looked at the sheriff, who nodded.

"Okay," Vaughn said. "Okay."

Much of the material about Sasquatches presented in this novel is factual. And by that I mean that it's more than just "written down." For example, the story of the frozen "wild-man" exhibited at the Minnesota State Fair in 1968 is true, down to the reports of the smell of rotting flesh. But more importantly, the Sasquatch track or "footprint" evidence presented herein is real. That alone should be enough to say that Sasquatches exist. If you don't think so, just think about the physics of snowshoes.

Why, then, doesn't some scientific institution make it its duty to investigate? Simple: fear. Fear of being ridiculed. The ridicule would start with the announcement of intentions to find a Sasquatch, and progress from there. The few scientists and others who have risked much to talk publicly about the Sasquatch have experienced this in spades. I commend them, and anyone who has come forward to state what they've seen. But it's also a fear of what the Sasquatch could mean. In an era of never-before-seen levels of paranoia about every-thing, fear predominates—including fear about the "dark woods," which many people now view as alien. Would ac-ceptance of Sasquatches mean children wouldn't be allowed in the woods without being tethered to a heavily armed guardian? (Would firearms still be "bad" then?) Or, worse, could another two-legged "higher ape" force us to ask tough questions of ourselves? Absolutely. No one likes that.

As you've just read, the issue of Sasquatches goes beyond science to the most powerful force in the universe: money. Maybe the Endangered Species Act would make the discov-ery of a Sasquatch a disaster for many companies. Or, if they had a plan, maybe not.

Afterword

*One is forced to conclude that a man-like form of gigantic pro-
portions is living at the present time in the wild areas of the
northwestern United States and British Columbia. If I have given
the impression that this conclusion is—to me—profoundly disturbing, then I have made my point. That such a creature should
be alive and kicking in our midst, unrecognized and unclassifi-
able, is a profound blow to the credibility of modern anthropology.*

—JOHN NAPIER, FORMER HEAD OF THE
SMITHSONIAN'S PRIMATE PROGRAM

Are Sasquatches really living in North America? Are there
remnant populations of *Gigantopithecus,* Neanderthal man
and possibly *Australopithecus* roaming other parts of the
world? And perhaps other "macro-fauna" about which we
have no inkling? It's certainly possible, and—depending upon
how open-minded you are—even likely.

The most impenetrable substance in the universe is the human brain; specifically, its ability to believe what it wants to believe. Many times that's an enormous hindrance. But it's also an asset. Do your own research, think long and hard about it, and only then make up your mind.

To help with that, read Grover Krantz's *Big Footprints,* the best factual book ever written about Sasquatches. And to read stories of Sasquatch encounters that will make your hair stand on end, check out the Bigfoot Field Researchers Organization's website at www.bfro.net. Enjoy.

—JAY C. KUMAR

Acknowledgments

A big thank you to the following people. Names are not in any order of importance.

For efforts above and beyond: Greg Tobin, Chris Frisina, Tom Colgan, Robert Montgomery, Don Hamingson, Scot Laney, Terry Brown and all my friends and family, especially my parents and the Joyces. Also the late Grover Krantz, to whom this novel is partly dedicated: You were right.

For technical and background information: Jonathan Silver, Tim Kelly and friends for taking me up Saint Helens, various Sasquatch writers and researchers, and anyone I ever asked a question of over the years.

For teaching me about hunting, and how to hunt: Greg Hise, Fred Bonner and the Terry family. This novel is also partly dedicated to the hunter in all of us. May it live long.

For inspiration: Michael Crichton, Ernest Hemingway, James Fenimore Cooper, Herman Melville, Thomas Harris, William Gibson, Tom Clancy, Stephen King, Stephen Hunter,

Scott Smith, Peter Benchley, Vivian Connell and every author published and unpublished (so far).

Also: Admiral Isaac Campbell Kidd, Jr., and the Kidd family (WHYDFTFT?). And: George Lynch and the Lynch Mob (a huge thanks); Gene, Paul, Ace and Peter; Edward, Alex, Mike, Dave and Sammy; Lynyrd Skynyrd; Ozzy, Bob, Lee, Randy, Jake and Zakk; Dream Theater; King's X; Jimi Hendrix; Michael Hedges; Stevie Salas; Greg Howe; Doyle Bramhall II; Steve Morse and the Steve Morse Band; Wynton Marsalis and musicians; Ludwig van Beethoven; and everyone else pushing the musical envelope to get the adrenaline going. Finally, thanks to everyone who chucked it all to the wind to do what they wanted to do, and succeeded.

Thanks also to: Ray Scott, Bob Cobb, Matt Vincent, Dave Precht, Helen Sevier and B.A.S.S.; Irwin Jacobs and FLW Outdoors; Jamie Heller, Ron Norman and Fieldston; Tom Canavan; Drs. Shulman, Bhandari and McConville; and everyone at Berkley Books.

This novel is also dedicated to Anjali and Neal, who were there, too.

Notes

MUCH of the factual information presented by Dr. Arthur Lansing is based on the writings of, and an interview with, Dr. Grover Krantz, former professor of anthropology at Washington State University. My apologies to the now-deceased Dr. Krantz for making Lansing the apparent villain—though was he really?

Some of the opinions of Chris Mackey are based on the writings of Alston Chase, whose book *In a Dark Wood* should be required reading for everyone who cares about the environment and how people use it for their own ends.

The title of this novel has nothing to do with Chase's book. It is from a haiku hanging in my bathroom.

About the Author

JAY C. KUMAR has fished, hunted and otherwise explored many of the wild places of North America: everything from fishing for bass in the sweltering heat of Florida's Lake Okeechobee, to sea-kayaking in Maine, to hunting turkeys in Virginia's Appalachian forests, to bottom-fishing the rough waters off Alaska, to climbing the Mount Saint Helens volcano in Washington state. He's the founder of BassFan.com, and is a grandson of the Irish writer Vivian Connell. Learn more about him at www.jayckumar.com.